LESBIAN
Bedtime
Stories
2

Gathered by Terry Woodrow

Cover design by Koelle & Gillette, Willits, CA
Computerized composition by Green Mac, Ukiah, CA
Illustrations by Rainbow, 2854 Coastal Hwy., St. Augustine, Florida 32084
Typesetting by Moonyean Grosch
Cover photo by C. Frainé
Cover models: Sossity Oessa Chiricuzio and Deborah Lea Wright

Copyright Nov., 1990 by Terry Woodrow for the collection
Copyright 1990 by each author or artist for their individual work.

All rights reserved.
Second Printing

Almost all of these stories were previously unpublished.

ISBN 0-9615129-2-X

This book, as well as *Lesbian Bedtime Stories I*, is available at all women's bookstores; any bookstore can order it for you. To make it accessible to all lesbians, this book is also available directly from the publisher on an honor system of more if you can, *less* if you can't, and free to lesbian prisoners. Retail price is $10.95 + $1.50 shipping.

Your comments are welcome. We are not now soliciting stories, thanks though.

This book was printed in the U.S.A. on recycled paper (70%).
Save the Trees! Don't just recycle, buy only recycled products.

Tough Dove Books
P.O. Box 1152
Laytonville, CA 95454

Table of Contents

Epiphany by Ruthann Robson 2
Mariposa by Terri de la Peña..............7
Checkpoint: A Lovers' Game by Kathleen Fleming............20
The Wind Between the Stars by Cris Newport...............27
Heat by Caroline Halliday................45
A Second Time by Candis J. Graham...............53
Carpentry by Lida Dowlearn.........................58
An Improbable Parable by Chris Sitka 71
Weaver Loses Her*Wa* by G. D. Rose................78
Fair Play by Rae Wheeler.............................. 89
Unlikely Places by Ann Tabachnikov 94
Summer Thunder by L. A. Patterson 109
Santa Claus at the Right Moment by Elaine J. Auerbach...113
In the Woods by Barbara Harwood.............................122
The Chant of the Women of Magdalena—SDiane Bogus .131
Inside Your Heart by Jackie Manthorne.........................147
The Thing That Would Not Hide! by Julie Blackwomon..155
HOWL by Penelope Pratt...............................163
La Llorona Loca: The Other Side by Monica Palacios.......174
Connexions by Joell Smith...............................178
you've got to be kidding by tova................................184
"One of Them" by La Verne Gagehabib. 195
The Gift by Amanda Hayman. 201
Angel Toes by Heidi K. Pfeuffer................................212
Badwater by Sharon Gilligan.......... 218
Best Things Happen While You're Dancing by Su Stout.229
The Wait by Patty Hennessey........................ 237
Margo by Diana Rivers 247
True Love by Jan Hardy..................................256
Jennifer by Wendy Caster....... 266

Introduction

Despite computer traumas, some interpersonal jousting, more U.S. military posturing and severe climatic changes, we lesbians are alive and kicking and we are deeply pleased and proud to present to you the second volume of *Lesbian Bedtime Stories*. Although this volume of course has its own character and flavor, we aren't inclined to compare it to its predecessor. If 600 page books were affordable (and could easily be read while laying on one's back, in bed) we'd have been glad to make it one book.

These stories were again chosen to sustain, to nourish and to inspire. They were chosen because they have happy endings and truly reflect the nature of our lives. We hope you enjoy reading every one of them!

We heartily thank all the many, many lesbians who worked on this book, especially the 260 authors who shared their stories. We received so *many* fine stories that by the end the selection process began to seem nearly arbitrary... but at least the odds were better than in winning a state lottery. Thank you, everyone!

The most striking lesson we've learned in this project is that lesbians *are* everywhere. And as evidenced by the Lesbian and Gay March on Washington we do not just number in the hundreds of thousands... there are *millions* of us. No matter how shy, isolated or fearful any one of us might feel at some given time we are *not* alone.

Lesbians are always just a hike or a phone call away and we should call on each other, in help or in need and with love because that's what we all want, us women-loving-women. That's what communities are for.

Peace and strength to you in the coming challenging times.
The sweetest of dreams to you!

                                                                                   The Tough Doves

Insight

Epiphany

by Ruthann Robson

Ruthann Robson is a white woman who recently relocated from hurricane country to earthquake land. She is the author of two books of short stories: EYE OF A HURRICANE, *and* CECILE *scheduled for Fall, 1991 publication. She's presently interested not only in lesbian literature (writing and reading) but also in the development of theory that is relentlessly lesbian and also honoring of all diversities among us. We must first dream our dreams before we can realize them.*

Epiphany

I'm spitting out toothpaste into the bathroom sink when I experience an epiphany. Not one of those once-in-a-lifetime epiphanies that changes one's life; not even one of those once-a-year religious epiphanies that come on January sixth; but a daily comfortable epiphany. An epiphany that doesn't embarrass me as I brush my teeth. A comfortable epiphany.

I'm not surprised to find this epiphany in the bathroom with me. For hours, it has been hinting itself. When I looked at my work desk at the end of the day, it was clean: phone calls returned; memos circulated. I could smell the sweet progress of work, sweet even if the work was government administration. When I got to the roller skating rink to pick up Colby, I saw how two older boys smashed their skates into his. He kept going, around and around the rink, intent on his own wheels. I wanted to run across the rink and kiss him, but I stood still until he saw me. Then I waved back.

When Colby and I got home, Cecile was humming a song I don't mind, making dinner. The noodles were al dente, the nuts were sweet, the red peppers were crunchy and the mushrooms were large. Colby added a basil leaf to each plate, picked from the plant that seemed to be recovering from either under- or over- watering. Cecile talked about a new art show while we ate. She kissed my neck afterwards, and even did the dishes without complaint.

Hoping that the pine nuts are out of my gums (even if I didn't floss), I know I can bring this epiphany out of the bathroom and into the bedroom. In bed with Cecile, she and I will make love. Or we will not. It doesn't matter. My breath is minty and it will be minty tomorrow night. If we don't make love, there is tomorrow and tomorrow and tomorrow. Passion is not the compressed beauty of a bud about to burst, but a languid flower, a patch of dirt, the sky.

In the bathroom, I realize I am happy. That I want nothing different; not to be anywhere different. In this rare interstice, I am content.

I am so happy and content I can deflect the anxiety about being happy and content. I refuse the sweat of guilt. I can deny my heritage. Almost.

Like all girls of my culture, class and climate, I was raised on tragedy. My mother's job at night did not prevent her from following what she called "the stories" and what others called "soap operas" or "daytime dramas." I stayed home from school, sick with a cold, or well with the luxury of a snow day, watching my mother iron while she watched TV. I knew Lisa from THE WORLD TURNS and Vanessa from LOVE OF LIFE better than I knew my neighbors. Neighbors got evicted, Lisa and Vanessa were eternal. Only their children grew up and moved away, coming back with their secrets and amnesias. The sons returned haunted by shady business deals. The daughters returned pregnant and not knowing who the father could be. The absent father was my favorite theme. I just loved all those parthenogenic pregnancies.

But there was another theme: happiness is disallowed. Happiness is not natural. Happiness is illusory. Even for people with driveways, new cars, nice clothes, and gardens. Even for people who know only doctors and lawyers. Even for people who live in places called Oakwood. Happiness is fraudulent.

I knew that if there were two people kissing on the TV screen (perversely, it was always a man and a woman), it wasn't real. It wasn't real not because TV shows aren't real, but because their pretend happiness wasn't even real within their pretend world. It was always as if one of them, however passionate a kisser, had her (or his) fingers crossed behind her (or his) back. My mother knew who was a betrayer and as she sprayed water on a blouse she was ironing, she would let me know by hissing out "bitch" or "bastard" as appropriate. If I hadn't been home from school lately, I'd ask for the details. She would tell me which of the two kissers was cheating on the other; or which one wanted the other only for the money; or which one really wanted to be kissing someone else.

But even if both kissers *thought* themselves happy, clutching each other instead of crossing their fingers, loyal viewers knew it wasn't true. One had amnesia. One was pregnant. Or the kissers' parents were arch enemies. Or the kissers were siblings, separated at birth. Whoever they were, as they kissed, the phone would ring with its bad news ring.

One time the kissers were married. To each other. I was home all week from school with a winter flu and watched them kiss at breakfast on Monday. It was an ordinary kiss, in front of their ordinary children. The introduction of these ordinary characters did not seem particularly promising. I noticed they ate bacon. On Tuesday, they kissed their ordinary kiss at dinner. They talked about their ordinary children, who were someplace else. I couldn't tell what they were eating. By Wednesday, their plot hadn't thickened. They kissed and said they loved each other. On Thursday, they got their longest segment; they're kissing in bed, with their hair and the sheets disheveled so that us sophisticated viewers will realize they've been having sex. They say how happy they are. How they've never been happier. How much they love each other. After all these years. They marvel at themselves.

I watched them transfixed. Not because I'd never seen happiness like this before, even though I hadn't. But because even at nine, I was waiting for the ax to fall. I was waiting for the phone to ring. I didn't know their secret, but knew there must be one.

The last segment on Friday was always a cliff hanger. This week, the viewers got treated like passengers in a car: we hear the tires squeal, see the glass crash into our windowed screen. Then it is dark. We hear sirens. We hear the telephone. "There's been an accident."

One of the happy kissers is dead.

Next week, there will be operations and doctors and doubts, but I knew the kisser was dead. Dead from too much happiness. I knew this, even though I'd be back at school next week when one of the doctors that everyone knew made the final pronouncement. I'd be sitting in a desk torn between wanting to study and go to college and wanting to get up and walk out of that place and never come back.

When I got to college, I took a course in the classics. Greek drama wasn't much different from the daytime variety. Instead of names like Lisa and Vanessa, the characters had names like Clytemnestra and Oedipus, but the basic plot was the same. Humans are not meant to be happy. To be happy is to commit *hubris,* to piss off the gods, to bring down their jealous wrath.

It took me three years to walk out of that college, but when I walked out, I never went back.

I wanted happiness that wasn't innocence. I wanted romance that wasn't tragedy.

I found Cecile. But even tonight, in bed with her and epiphany, there's still a large piece of me that is afraid to be happy. I kiss Cecile and whisper that I love her. I hide my epiphany under the sheets, telling it to be quiet.

Maybe if we're silent, those jealous gods won't notice.

If the phone rings, I won't answer it.

It could be a bitch calling to tell me Cecile is my sister; or it could be someone calling to tell me I'm a bitch for being happy while my mother still has to work all night. Or it could be someone to take Colby away. Or reveal my amnesia.

The phone doesn't ring. Not even once, during the night. Or the next night. Or the next...

Romance

Mariposa

by Terri de la Peña

Terri de la Peña is a Chicana lesbian feminist fiction writer and a contributor to the first volume of Lesbian Bedtime Stories *and other anthologies. She has discovered her natural shyness fades whenever she reads her work to lesbian audiences. Whether the setting is a bookstore, a writers' conference, a music festival, or the local lesbian archives, Terri enjoys meeting the women she writes for and believes in encouraging an abundance of lesbian creativity especially among mujeres de color. She has several novels and short stories blossoming within and hopes the universe will answer her wish for enough time and energy to write them.*

Mariposa

Flecked with silver, Jen Avila's sleek hair shone in the dappled Yosemite sunlight. She strode briskly from the public showers, past performers' and child care cabins, to her solitary campsite near the river. Her hurried footsteps snapped twigs and scattered dry pine needles, and with each quick movement her brown hair rose and fell rhythmically, resembling a sparrow's fluttering wings.

Jen had arrived at the West Coast Women's Music Festival the previous evening, pitching her tent far away from the other members of "Chispas," the Latina trio she had co-founded three years earlier. Since then, the trio's dynamics had changed drastically. Cindi Carbajal, the singer and guitarist, had recently left Jen for Rita Solís, the percussionist. They had been booked for the Festival months in advance, and—out of group loyalty—Jen had agreed to continue as flutist. But she dreaded the next day's performance, anticipating the sultry on-stage glances between Cindi and Rita, the whispered comments within the lesbian audience. Jen wished for the long Labor Day weekend to be over; she wanted to escape, back to Los Angeles—or anywhere.

Sighing, she bent to unzip her tent. Her slightly built body leaned forward as she reached inside for her flute case. With the shiny instrument in her hands, she headed towards the river. She needed to rehearse and, for the moment, she preferred to do that alone.

•

Perched on a boulder, Jen closed her eyes, immersed in her music, the river's cadence a soothing accompaniment. She swayed to her mellifluous melodies, transporting herself to the Mexican past, imitating full, conch-like sounds with a contemporary rhythm. She played for a long time before a sudden splashing drew her attention.

She squinted in the morning sunlight. Through an uneven row of pines, she spied a nude brown woman hunched over the edge of the river bank, her face and lengthy black hair streaming into the water. Jen put down the flute and stared. Could the woman be in trouble? Was she attempting suicide? Remembering her own despair, Jen leaped off the boulder and craned her neck for a clearer view.

"Hey! Are you okay?" she shouted.

When the woman did not answer, Jen wasted no time. She scrambled down the ravine's loose dirt walls and almost lost her footing. Slipping and sliding, she stumbled breathlessly to the woman's side.

At Jen's headlong approach, the woman leisurely raised herself, wringing her wet hair. She was a couple of inches shorter than Jen, with naturally burnished skin, a supple body. Releasing her hair, she let it cascade to her waist. Her ebony eyes gazed at Jen disarmingly.

"Buenas dias."

At once, Jen felt like a clumsy interloper. The Latina had been washing her hair, not drowning. Jen allowed herself a sheepish grin. "Hi."

"Why did you stop playing your flute?" The Latina spoke with what Jen guessed was a Mexican accent. Grabbing a comb from a nylon bag beside her, she unselfconsciously watched Jen while beginning to groom herself.

Lesbians from América Latina intrigued Jen, but she tried to behave casually—which was difficult because of the Latina's allure. She could not help herself from staring, and even caught a fleeting glimpse of a purple butterfly tattoo near the dark tangle of the Latina's mound. In black shorts and magenta tank top, Jen felt overdressed.

Remembering the Latina's question, she shrugged. "I thought you were in trouble. Didn't you hear me yell?"

"No. My head was in the water."

"Exactly." Jen laughed, and the Latina joined in.

Jen liked her at once, and tried to convince herself that the woman's ethnic beauty was not a contributing factor. Besides, she reminded herself, she still carried a torch for Cindi and dealt regularly with resentful feelings towards Rita. At this point, Jen reasoned, she lacked the time and motivation to be attracted to anyone—but her somersaulting heart insisted otherwise.

The Latina's remarks interrupted her thoughts. "Esta mañana, I continued combing her hair. "The line was too long, and I got tired of waiting. Tu música lured me to the river. When are you performing?"

Jen took that question as a subtle compliment. "Tomorrow—I'm with Chispas from L.A."

"Ya lo se." The Latina tossed the comb into her bag and drew nearer. "Como te llamas?"

"Jen Avila."

"Jen?" she repeated, her ojos de india widening.

The flutist spread her hands in exasperation. "My mother's all for assimilation. She thinks 'Jennifer' is an all-American name."

"It is. Pero, somos Americanas tambien, verdad?" The Latina flipped silken strands over her shoulders. "Unless they heard you and me speak, los gringos wouldn't even know we're from different sides of the border. They'd see us only as brown women—foreigners. They don't realize Latinas from Central and South America are Americans, too."

Jen found her intensity appealing. "Sounds like Yankee insensitivity is one of your pet peeves."

The Latina smiled slowly. "Muy obvious, eh?" She offered her hand. "Me llamo Mariposa Morada."

Jen squeezed those warm fingers and wanted to laugh again. Translated, the Latina's name meant "purple butterfly."

"Mariposa? Like the county we're in?" She continued to be amused and heard herself impulsively add, "Beautiful name, beautiful land—beautiful woman!"

Mariposa offered another smile before pulling an embroidered dress from her bag and slipping it over her head. Its cotton folds reached her knees, and she presented a striking picture, rearranging her black hair over the dress' scoop neck. At the tantalizing sight, Jen caught her breath.

Mariposa picked up the bag. "Pues, tengo que ir porque soy one of the craftswomen. Visítame, eh?"

Suddenly tongue-tied, Jen nodded. She stood immobile for several moments, frowning against the sun's increasing radiance, watching Mariposa disappear among the pines. She wanted to follow her. But then she remembered her flute lying on the nearby boulder—and the trio's scheduled rehearsal. With reluctance, she turned and trudged up the ravine.

•

Hours later, she lay face down in her tent, sobbing into the sleeping bag's flannel lining. She had never felt so alone. During rehearsal, Cindi had snapped at her, chiding her for missing a cue. Rita had grinned in satisfaction, adding that Jen's playing seemed off-tempo. The flutist had listened to and accepted their criticisms, but she could not stop humiliated tears from stinging her eyes. As soon as they had rehearsed their last number, she had darted away, longing for solitude.

Sighing, Jen wiped her eyes with the back of her hand. Her fingers moved upwards, smoothing her hair, and then they stopped abruptly. She touched the top of her right ear and discovered her turquoise and silver cuff was gone. Quickly, she sat up and searched the tent, frantically pawing the sleeping bag and the surrounding area. The ear cuff was nowhere to be found.

Fresh tears sprang into her eyes. Cindi had given her that delicate piece of jewelry as a birthday gift. How appropriate to lose it now. But maybe it was for the best—one less reminder of their life together.

Calming herself, Jen took several deep breaths. She did not want to cry anymore, especially over a piece of sentimental jewelry. She would get through this emotional turmoil—and the performance—and be stronger for it. She did not care what Cindi and Rita thought; she believed in herself and in her talent. She would not let their disparaging attitudes influence her self-esteem.

Jen exhaled slowly and glanced at her watch. She had the whole afternoon to explore the Festival's arts and crafts area. She rubbed the top of her ear reflexively, missing the familiar cuff. It had been a part of her, the silver and turquoise design blending with her hair's greying strands. But, no matter, she thought. In retrospect, the ear cuff had been an ornament—nothing else.

With an air of determination, Jen crawled out of the tent and stretched, reaching her brown arms to the sky. Once more, she touched the spot on her ear where the cuff had rested. The space felt empty, desolate—but it did not have to remain so. She headed towards the craftswomen's display booths.

•

Terri de la Peña

She admired tie-dyed apparel and goddess-oriented pottery, giggled while testing the latest in vibrator technology, paged through lesbian fiction, and lingered over jewelry counters. She deliberated over each prospective purchase and eventually found herself near the edge of the craftswomen's area. A cluster of rapt women congregated nearby. With curiosity, she approached, peering over their shoulders.

"Michi—oh my," Jen gasped on glimpsing her Japanese-American friend's topless torso. Seated before her, Mariposa intently wielded a fine brush, painting a fanciful dragon between Michi's small breasts.

Raising her crew cut head, Michi grinned. "Pretty nifty, huh? Just the right ethnic touch. You ought to get one, too, Jen." At her friend's skeptical look, Michi added, "Hey, it'll fade off in a few days."

A couple of women opened ranks to allow the flutist a better view. They seemed mesmerized by Mariposa's intricate artistry. The Latina worked expertly, undistracted by her audience.

Jen shook her head, laughing at Michi's smug expression. Her friend was always ready for novel experiences. When Michi wriggled her eyebrows flirtatiously, Mariposa placed a cautioning hand on her shoulder.

"Por favor, chiquita—don't move."

"Sorry." Undaunted, Michi stuck out her tongue at Jen. "You're next, Avila. And I'm buying."

Shrugging, Jen leaned against a pine trunk and watched. She marvelled at Mariposa's skill in creating impromptu artwork, and though she had never liked tattoos of any sort, Jen knew she would not refuse Michi's offer. She wanted Mariposa to focus on *her*.

Before long, Michi sported a full-length dragon, its verdigris tail surrounding one of her nipples. She gazed down at herself, admiring the colorful creation.

"You don't think it'll scare my lover?" Michi asked suddenly.

Mariposa leaned near again. "No. She will want to outline these pointed ridges, to lick your dragon's tail—like this." And her pink tongue flicked lightly across Michi's right nipple.

Several women laughed. Michi blushed scarlet, slid off the stool and tossed a ten-dollar bill on Mariposa's worktable. Too embarrassed to say "thank you," she seemed eager to leave.

Jen had never seen her friend so flustered. As for herself, she was grateful for the pine tree's support. Otherwise, in her surprise at Mariposa's impulsiveness, she would have toppled over.

Michi started to brush past Jen. "See you later."

"Hey, Mich—wait a minute."

"I can't. I have to find Beth." Michi had not stopped blushing. "She's at one of the workshops."

Jen nudged her. "You're not going to hang around?"

Michi rolled her eyes. "No way. I'm not single any more—but you are. This could be just what you need." She handed Jen two five-dollar bills. "I meant what I said. My treat."

"What is this—a bribe?" Jen teased.

"See you later, Avila." Michi soon vanished amidst the throngs of strolling women.

Meanwhile, Mariposa had begun to paint a double women's symbol on a grey-haired dyke's muscular biceps. Two other women besides Jen waited for the artist's attention. After Michi left with her spectacular dragon, the crowd had dwindled.

The Latina painted deftly, swiftly. She did not speak much, but each woman seemed enchanted by her quiet intensity. Jen leaned against the pine's rough bark and remembered the morning's encounter by the river. The filtering sunlight had shone hazily on Mariposa's skin, creating a coppery glow. Beneath her lavender dress, Jen knew Mariposa's breasts were tipped with chocolate buds; Jen could almost taste them. She imagined herself parting Mariposa's black curtain of hair, bending to lick each brown nipple, her mouth longing to venture lower, to that entrancing purple butterfly—and beyond.

Abruptly, Mariposa glanced at her and smiled. Jen blushed and looked away, wondering if the Latina had read her mind. She considered leaving, yet did not want to lose her place in line. But the next woman only wanted a tiny rose on her wrist—and the woman after her asked for a simple heart with "Tania" inscribed inside. Mariposa handled these requests with ease, then eyed Jen speculatively.

"Y para ti—un colibrí."

Embarrassed by her lack of Spanish fluency, Jen approached.

"I'm sorry, Mariposa. What's that?"

The artist lifted a dark brow, no doubt classifying Jen in the "hopeless pocha" category; but she did not comment on this. Instead she answered her. "Un colibrí is a hummingbird—a Mexican symbol of love."

Jen tried to smile, but her lips trembled. "Why does that suit me?"

"Because, chulita, you're unhappy. You need some hope—un colibrí with tiny wings will cause your heart to flutter again."

"But it already flutters for you," Jen thought, wishing she could say that aloud. Gazing into the dark depths of Mariposa's eyes, she tried to forget Cindi's treachery, Rita's ridicule. She wanted to see and hear only Mariposa.

The artist gestured for Jen to be seated. Turning, she reached for another brush and began to mix her paints. "Esta mañana you thought I was trying to drown myself, verdad? You called to me because you sensed I shared your pain."

Jen said nothing, her eyes riveted to Mariposa's. The artist dipped her brush into a vial of magenta paint. Before beginning, she addressed two newcomers.

"Por favor, come back mañana. I promise I will do you first."

Hand in hand, the women smiled and departed.

Mariposa dropped one flap of the canopy, but late afternoon sunlight continued to illuminate the tent. She dipped the brush into the paint again and slowly began to outline a hummingbird directly above Jen's collarbone.

The paint felt cool against her skin, and Jen closed her eyes at the touch of that soft brush, the sensual slide of its fine hairs. She remembered Mariposa's morning nudity and wanted to feel her even closer.

"Asi, Jen," Mariposa whispered. "No te mueves. This takes concentration."

Jen was silent, enjoying the unique sensation. But she wanted to know this Latina, to hear her story. "Mariposa—"

"Let *me* talk. You listen."

Jen did not argue.

Mariposa's voice was nostalgic. "When I was ten years old, I came from Aguascalientes to Delano con mi familia. We worked in the fields, sabes? Y cuando I was—oh, maybe fourteen—I began cleaning house por la familia del patrón. He had a daughter—una rubia con ojos verdes. She was a wild one—her name was Jennifer." Jen opened her eyes briefly, but Mariposa did not look up. She kept talking, working skillfully.

"She used to tease me. At first I thought she hated me, but soon I discovered her feelings were just the opposite. One day when I was cleaning the bathroom, she followed me inside and closed the door. Very slowly, she unbuttoned mi camisa and took una de mis chichis into her mouth. She excited me, Jen. Me hizo loca."

Mariposa paused to dip the brush again. "After that, we made love every chance we got—all through the house, in the storage sheds, even in the fields. One day her father caught us. Que mitote sucedio!" She sighed deeply. "My family was disgraced. We were all fired. Jennifer was sent to boarding school, and I ran away—to Merced and eventually to la comunidad lesbiana. I renamed myself Mariposa."

"And became an artist," Jen murmured. "How did that happen?"

"I've always been good with my hands," Mariposa answered evasively. Jen opened her eyes again, and this time the Latina met her gaze. She smiled, her mouth seductive. "Tu sabes. A lover encouraged me."

"Where is she now?"

"Gone—like all the others."

"Like mine," Jen whispered, her shoulders sagging.

"Ten cuidado, eh? If you move, I lose momentum." Mariposa edged nearer and her glossy hair tickled Jen's arms. She gently touched Jen's shoulder, and soon her wandering fingertips played with the new pewter ear cuff, tracing the labrys carved on its band.

"This isn't the one you wore this morning."

"No. I lost it. Do you like this?"

"Si," Mariposa whispered. "Y ti tambien."

"Mariposa —"

"Shhh, chulita." She pressed her brown hand against Jen's shoulder again. "Déjame trabajar, eh? There will be time later."

•

Alone in that evening's dinner line, Jen wondered about Mariposa's whereabouts. The Latina had agreed to eat with her, but she had yet to appear. Dismally, Jen pondered whether Mariposa came on to every woman who sported her artistry. She remembered the artist's boldness with Michi, her arousing nearness that afternoon. She also recalled Mariposa's morning comments about the shower lines being long—Jen knew that craftswomen had priority for the showers. Mariposa could have gone to the front of the line easily. Had she drifted to the river specfically to meet Jen?

Spotting Michi and Beth further ahead, she decided to join them, grateful for their high spirits, their ready laughter. Annoyed with herself for trusting someone so soon after the breakup with Cindi, Jen hid her disappointment and suspicions by joking with her friends, but she could not help herself from occasionally scanning the wooded grounds for the elusive Mariposa.

She did not see her at that evening's concert either. Jen sat with Michi, Beth and other friends, huddled together for warmth after the sun's torrid rays melted into Yosemite chill. Enjoying Cris Williamson's and Teresa Trull's electrifying performances, she tried not to think about being on stage with Chispas the following day. She already felt depressed enough—missing Mariposa.

•

"Sure you don't want to come to the dance, Jen?"

At midnight, Michi walked beside her, holding Beth's hand, her beaconing flashlight in the other. With hundreds of other women, they had left the main stage and hiked through the encompassing darkness to the campgrounds.

"Positive." Jen hunched her shoulders against the cold night air and tightened her fists within her parka's quilted pockets. "Have to get some sleep. I'm not looking forward to tomorrow."

"You'll be dynamite, as usual," Michi assured her.

"There'd be no 'Chispas' without you," Beth added.

Jen offered her friends a tired grin. "Thanks for the upbeat company. Hope I haven't been too much of a downer."

"You? Not any more than usual." Michi's eyebrows wriggled while she squeezed Jen playfully. "See you tomorrow."

"Good night." Waving, Jen watched them head for the dance, envying their carefree attitudes. Then, she aimed her flashlight towards the ravine. The ground was uneven and she did not want to fall.

Mariposa

Nearing the campsite, she heard a rustling sound within the tent. Jen stood stock still, imagining a sudden encounter with a snoopy racoon or squirrel—worse yet, a curious bear cub or snake. Stealthily, she crept closer, directing the flashlight's beam to the front of the tent.

"Jen?" A soft voice came from inside.

"Mariposa?" Jen was startled. "What are you doing here?"

"I found your ear cuff."

The flashlight's narrow beam illuminated the Latina's features. She knelt at the tent's entry, smiling invitingly, her black hair loose.

"Where?" Jen frowned, trying to ignore Mariposa's attractiveness.

"Near the river." She beckoned. "Come inside. It's warmer."

Jen hesitated, still frowning. "Where were you at dinner? I waited for you."

"Lo siento mucho." Mariposa did not lose her smile. "Remember the couple who stopped by before I painted your colibrí? They came back, and asked for—tu sabes—very personal tattoos. They didn't want an audience en la mañana."

Jen stared at her, wanting to believe her, but leery.

Mariposa brushed aside her hair. "I went to the river with them. The sunlight on the water gave me enough light, and them enough privacy. They were very generous," she added quietly, eyes downcast. "And then I found your cuff, shining beside una piedra. I brought it back to you—see?" In her outstretched hand, she held the silver and turquoise band.

Slowly, Jen lowered the flashlight's beam and crawled inside the tent. Without speaking, she took the ear cuff and slipped it into her jeans' pocket; it felt cold and harsh against her hipbone. Her heart beat rapidly as she knelt beside Mariposa. The flashlight's dimmed beacon cast mysterious shadows across the Latina's face.

"I waited for you, Mariposa."

She answered in a whisper. "I was—afraid."

Jen gazed at her skeptically.

Mariposa lowered her gaze again. "When the women came back, I—" She shrugged. "They gave me the excuse I needed."

"All I wanted was to have dinner with you."

"You want more." Mariposa at last raised her eyes. "I kept

thinking about the other Jennifer—"

"I'm not her." Jen sighed, unzipping her parka. She saw Mariposa's eyes glint at viewing the magenta hummingbird with its whirring wings in the crevice of her open collar.

"Pero eres Chicana. It means more, sabes?" Jen nodded, recalling the pride she had felt in loving Cindi, a Chicana lesbian like herself. Yet she heard the sarcasm in her voice. "If you're so scared, why are you here?"

"Ay, Jen." Mariposa sighed and looked askance. "The women— they apologized for interrupting us earlier. They thought we were lovers. They said they could tell by the way we looked at each other." She stared at Jen's hummingbird. "After they left and I found your ear cuff, I stood there, listening to the river, holding the cuff in my hand. I thought of you waiting for me—and I remembered how homesick your music made me feel, how soft your skin is, how gentle your eyes are. And I wondered how I could be scared of you." Mariposa tilted forward, hands reaching for Jen's shoulders.

Not moving, Jen closed her eyes when their lips met. "Mariposa," she said again. "I've waited for you."

"I'm here now, chulita." Teasingly, her tongue outlined Jen's mouth, much like her paintbrush had glided across her skin earlier. "And I'm not scared anymore."

At those affirming words, Jen did not hesitate. She erased her uncertainty, longing to believe again. She wrapped eager arms around Mariposa, kissing her deeply, and they sank to the rumpled folds of the sleeping bag.

Jen's mouth became lost in the silken veil of Mariposa's hair, and she did not care if she ever resurfaced. Each time Mariposa stroked her, deftly unbuttoning her shirt, longingly reaching inside, Jen felt whatever lingering doubts she had fade. Repeatedly, the Latina's hands performed their incomparable artistry and Jen tingled from their tactile enchantment.

When Jen at last bent over her, her mouth discovering that purple butterfly, she paused, her fingers tracing its indelible pattern. The butterfly seemed alive, ready to flit away, but Jen tenderly held it still with one hand. Then, leisurely, her lips moved upwards, parting Mariposa's velvety labial wings. And las Chicanas soared and flew together into that Yosemite night.

Mariposa

Sexual Healing

Checkpoint: A Lovers' Game

by Kathleen Fleming

Kathleen Fleming writes to explore her experiences and those of the people she's known best. She leads workshops and teaches. She's delighted with the abundance of fine lesbian writing that continues to break into print and particularly happy that most young lesbians now write in their own voices without any muting or disguise.

Her last novel, Lovers in the Present Afternoon, *was published in 1984. A collection of her short stories is forthcoming. Near retirement, she's eager to write full time and to participate in the political and social activities of the lesbian community in which she lives. She hopes everyone will become increasingly involved in healing the planet and in working for peace and enlightenment.*

Checkpoint: A Lovers' Game

If my arm pulls you closer just as my lips meet yours and I find the touching of our tongues exquisite, light and fine...

If my arm pulls you closer just as my lips meet yours and you find the touching of our tongues the first barely heard quiver of the siren's warning wail...

if you hold up your fingers, two, side by side, the way a girl scout salutes, that will mean CHECKPOINT...

and we will separate and sit side by side, only holding hands...

and you will have earned ten points already for identifying the hazard just as it hovered into sight.

•

If you are lying with me in your arms, and we're watching the way the curtains above your bed curl in waves against the wall and catch the moonlight just the way desire rises and falls, rises higher, higher...

If you are lying with me in your arms, and we're watching the way the curtains above your bed curl in waves against the wall and catch the moonlight just the way his profile sometimes hit the wall when he lay with me...

if I lift two fingers the way a priest gives a blessing then we will separate and lie, watching the moonlight, with only our hands touching

and I will have ten points already for identifying the hazard just as it came in sight.

•

If I come into your room before you are awake and lean to kiss your lips, saying, "I love you," and start to lie beside you, thinking how beautiful you are, just waking in the early morning light, and how wonderful it will be to feel you waking fully in my arms, to have you kiss me back, still half asleep...

If I come into your room before you are awake and lean to kiss your lips, saying, "I love you," and I start to lie beside you, and you start to wake, not knowing it is me whose lips grazed yours; if you want to go back into the dark of sleep so you will never wake to his early morning presence, to the stench of his treacherous voice like stale incense rising from beneath your bed...

if you lift two fingers I will stand and go into the kitchen to make tea. I'll bring you toast and tea, fresh berries, with flowers on the tray and I'll sit beside the bed with my own toast and tea, and we will say good morning, wide awake

and you will have twenty points for averting panic even though the moment came when you were only half awake, even though it caught you and swung you deep into the trench that is the past.

•

If your mouth has moved lightly from breast to breast and found its way down my arm, past the flickering of passion on the inside of my palm, to thigh and thigh again, and then to opening thighs and the place within that is like a hidden stream that murmurs under moss, and you move your tongue in a joyous, first gentle, then wild rhythmic thrust...

If your mouth has moved lightly from breast to breast and found its way down my arm, past the flickering of passion on the inside of my palm, to thigh and thigh again, and then to opening thighs and the place within that is like a hidden stream that murmurs under moss, and you move your tongue in a motion that is hard and harder like his beat...

if I whisper "Checkpoint" you will pause, kiss my thigh, my arm, my shoulder, take my head against your shoulder, and wait until I turn again to kiss...

and I will have thirty points for saying no even though I knew you were deep into your pleasure, even though I knew I'd welcomed you, even though I was afraid you'd think I meant a different, larger no.

•

Checkpoint: A Lovers' Game

If I am sitting with you watching television and I put my arms around you, touching your breasts with my curved palms the way I would touch water in a mountain stream, thinking to bend to put my lips there soon, to suck in the sweet fresh water gathered in my cool cupped hands...

If I am sitting with you watching television and I put my arms around you, touching your breasts with my curved palms the way I would touch water in a mountain stream, thinking to bend to put my lips there soon, to suck in the sweet water gathered in my hands that for you are huge and glossy against your tiny breasts, that chafe as against concrete when you skin your knee...

if you say, "Checkpoint," I will stand and stretch, go for popcorn, and remember that circling you from behind that way is not okay, for which I get ten points

and you will have thirty points for interrupting such sweet pleasure as we both might have had even though you're wide awake and could persuade yourself that it would have been okay.

•

I will find the places he never touched on you. I don't think he ever stroked his fingers through your hair. I know he never held you safely in his arms. I will hold you in my arms forever, safe and still, with only my hand gently moving through your hair, only my heart matching your heart's beat, until every atom of your being is your own again.

•

If you grab your jacket as you head out the door, saying, "Let's take a walk down by the lake. We might catch the cranes. I packed a lunch," and the day spreads ahead of you a blaze of sunlight on the water, as hand in hand we watch the trees, the birds, and lie beside the lake, lips finding lips...

If you grab your jacket as you head out the door, saying, "Let's take a walk down by the lake. We might catch the cranes. I packed a lunch," and the day spreads ahead of you a blaze of sunlight on the water, as hand in hand we watch the trees, the birds, and lie beside the lake while the story I've been writing fades off into the past, momentum lost, the feeling of that passage gone beyond recall...

if I say checkpoint and ask for an hour in which to do my work, then I get ten points for telling you I need that time...

and you will go to find the cranes alone; then you get ten points for understanding, and when you return we can lie beside the lake, lips finding lips...

•

If I choose a tape of love songs, light the candles, and tell you dinner's ready; if the music lays time under us like warm sand at the shore so we can look at one another through the candlelight, with love, knowing that a night of lovemaking will fill that stretch of time as naturally as the tide moving in gentle swathes higher and higher up the shore...

If I choose a tape of love songs, light the candles, and tell you dinner's ready as the music lays time under us like warm sand at the shore so we can look at one another through the candlelight with love, and you know that familiar wheels are inexorably turning, carrying us toward bed where expectations will grab hold like vises on a rough workbench...

if you laugh and say: Checkpoint—we'll choose a different tape or talk instead and both of us will know that we will wait and see what the evening and the long night hold, and you get thirty points for desisting from romance

and I get thirty points for laughing back and knowing that it's not an ending to romance, only that we need to feel free and somehow you felt trapped instead.

•

If you glide across my lips, arms, breasts like an evening breeze and I am wild with desire for your tongue and you lay your cheek against my thigh and with your fingers find a path your tongue will follow, expecting me to rise and rise with you...

If you glide across my lips, arms, breasts like an evening breeze and I am wild with desire for your tongue and you lay your cheek against my thigh and with your fingers find a path your tongue will follow, trapping me to holding still beneath your weighted touch...

Checkpoint: A Lovers' Game

if I allow myself to breathe and watch your face that I find beautiful, and I feel your hand as yours, as loving touch, and know I can lift two fingers any time and in an instant the touch will pause, and if I then stay with delight and claim my own desire as my own and I stay with you as your desire and mine conspire to delight...

if I do that I don't need points: I'll settle for delight.

•

If I come to you at dawn and take you in my arms and kiss you with the joy of having you another day close enough to see, to touch, to love with hands and lips and eyes and ears, to celebrate our love...

If I come to you at dawn and take you in my arms and kiss you with the joy of having you another day close enough to see, to touch, to love with hands that you feel insinuate their way between your clenched and confused thighs...

If you trace my contours with your fingertips and feel my thighs as mine, perceive my eyes as my blue eyes, my hand in yours as mine, and if you are ready to claim your body's desire as your own and kiss me in your own joy, knowing that at any second you may lift two fingers and I will draw away from you in bed and we will lie listening to the songs of birds, watching the morning light, but instead you stay with your own joy and welcome mine as we celebrate our love...

you will have no points but pure delight.

•

It is time I want with you, my love, day after day. I want us to walk beside the lake for many hours, day after day, with only your hand in mine, my hand in yours, to signal our hearts' intent.

I want time in which to know we can take forever if we want before we kiss and forever after that to stroke and touch and kiss again.

It is time I want with you, my love, day after day.

It is time I want with you until you know my voice is mine, until I know your touch is yours, until you know the morning light belongs to you and me, until I know my body mine to sometimes meet with yours in love, until you know your spirit is as free as any hawk's, to light near me when that is your heart's choice and to soar alone and high when that is your heart's choice, as I will soar at will when I have need.

•

The pledge I crave is that the time be ours.

Fantasy

The Wind Between the Stars

by Cris Newport

Cris Newport turned thirty and got her bachelor's degree all in the space of one month. She's now working on a master's in teaching and hopes to impart her enthusiasm for writing to all those eager high school students. She has a novel forthcoming from New Victoria Publishers entitled Sparks Might Fly *and her dream for the future would be to live in a world where the canon of literature includes works by* all *people, not just white men, and be able to talk about cultural differences, class and sexual preference issues in the classroom without fear of losing her job. In her copious free time, she and her lover Diane read, write, take long walks, sleep as late as possible, spend time with "the girls" (Deilhia and Chelsea) and try to cope with the chaos of living in the adult world.*

The Wind Between the Stars

The two women moved against each other in the darkness. D'Anna was pale as starlight and her steel grey hair slid across Marta's breasts like a piece of soft cloth. D'Anna drew her tongue down the faint dark line of hair on Marta's abdomen that led to the darker triangle below. The low thrumming of the star ship's engines was a soft counterpoint to Marta's soft moans as D'Anna settled herself between Marta's thighs.

D'Anna paused for a moment, lifted her head and looked past Marta to the convex window above the bed. The stars slid past, and in the far distance, she could see the sun of her own solar system, a brighter fire in the pinpricked sky.

Her broad flat hands, rough and scraped from handling engine parts, lay still on the cream colored smoothness of Marta's thighs. D'Anna pushed them apart slowly and bent her head like a traveller thirsty for drink.

Below D'Anna, eyes closed, Marta felt herself spiraling out, as if she were caught on the edge of the swirling arms of the Crab Nebula, flung out from the center of the fire into the dense blackness of space. She had never imagined anyone could make her feel this way. It was as if a wild storm of chaos had suddenly blown up within her, and she, unable to do anything but lean into the wind, let herself be carried deeper into her body, further from her thoughts.

At this moment, her long held resistance to taking a lover seemed foolish, as did her attempts to tame this wildness within her. Her mind spun away from the well-worn reason: top Security Officers are always in control. This experience, this moment, was unlike anything Marta had ever known. Her hips rose, pushed against D'Anna's hungry mouth. Maybe she had been waiting for this stranger, this woman who had dropped into her life not forty-eight hours before, to touch the chaos within her and bring it to the surface in a crazy rush of wind.

Hours later, exhausted and content for the first time in years, as Marta drifted towards sleep pillowed against D'Anna's soft breasts,

The Wind Betweeen the Stars

she heard again D'Anna's smoky voice floating in her mind. They'd talked of space for the past two days, the many places each woman had seen, each experience savored like sweet wine, held for a moment under the tongue until the fullness of the flavor seemed to seep into each separate cell of their bodies. D'Anna's restlessness had been like a small whirlwind in the midst of the huge and quiet ship. "You have to see it as I have, Marta," she'd said. "Close up, I mean. Not like in this ship. You could come with me. Be an explorer, like the ancient fliers on Souma Three. You know them?"

Marta had nodded. A race of people with papery wings growing out of their shoulder blades who lived on a planet of water and small islands with no means of transportation other than the winds.

"You can't taste that wind on a ship this size."

"I've been to hundreds of planets, including Souma Three. How can you say your little solar system would house the wonders of the Universe?"

"But it's different, Marta. You're so isolated. This ship's too big. You can never hear the wind between the stars."

Even though Marta knew space had no wind, no currents of air that swirled between planets, she wondered how this imaginary wind would sound. Would it be like a great rushing of air, so strong it seemed to lift the ship on invisible wings? Or would it be something softer, like a breath exhaled in sleep?

And as sleep finally overcame her, Marta wondered why D'Anna had chosen to break her silence with her, a silence the Captain had assumed at first to be a language barrier. But D'Anna, Marta came to find, spoke not only her native language but the Union's Standard as well. She was a woman with a secret Marta wanted—needed—to share.

Later, Marta was awakened by the soft swooshing sound of her cabin door closing. She struggled to the surface of wakefulness, her first thought a tactile memory of D'Anna's hands and mouth, her second dismay, then anger. D'Anna was gone. And Marta was responsible for knowing her whereabouts at all times. Cursing, she sprang from the bed and struggled into her clothes. She punched the communication console next to her bed while fumbling for the light switch. "Connors, here," she said. "Seal off the hanger deck."

"What's the problem?" a sleepy voice drawled.

"Just do it." She severed the link.

On the way to the hanger deck, she berated herself for letting her guard down. A good security officer was always on duty, always alert. A good officer never gave in to the chaos within. Marta saw herself as a finely tuned machine. Vulnerability, she believed, led to clouded judgement and was something she could not afford to indulge.

D'Anna wasn't exactly a prisoner here, but the unusual circumstances surrounding her arrival had raised suspicions, Marta's most of all. There was something about D'Anna that made the hairs on the back of Marta's neck prick up. And it wasn't just the physical attraction.

Marta bolted out of the elevator and collided with another security officer. "Hanger decks secured," he said. "There hasn't been any activity here all night."

"Are you sure?"

"Well, that woman came down a little while ago to work on her ship, but that'd been cleared so I didn't think it was a problem."

"She didn't try to open the hatch?"

"No, Ma'am," he said. Marta could feel him looking at her disheveled hair and rumpled uniform.

Disregarding his stare she said, "That's all. Dismissed."

He got into the elevator and the door swished closed behind him. Marta walked across the half lit hanger deck towards D'Anna's craft.

The work lights illuminated the small single pilot ship, throwing shadows across the cement floor and the steel struts like bones that formed the cavernous hanger deck. The sound of Marta's boots bounced off the flat walls.

D'Anna strolled casually into view from the other side of the ship."Didn't mean to wake you," she said. Marta studied her loose jointed pose. D'Anna's casualness was deceiving. She had none of Marta's muscular tension though she was easily as strong.

D'Anna's hands hung loosely at her sides and she tapped the end of a wrench against the grease smeared leg of her coveralls. She leaned against the pitted shell of the ship, her blue eyes almost colorless in the hard white light.

"I hope you weren't thinking of going out for a spin in that thing," Marta said, forcing a casual tone she didn't feel.

D'Anna laughed. "I'd have to push this 'thing' out the hatch with my bare hands." She pushed herself away from the ship and came toward Marta. "I can see in your eyes what you're thinking. Shame on you."

"Don't patronize me," Marta snapped, taking a step back from D'Anna's outstretched hand. "I'm not stupid enough to let you seduce me so you could make your escape while I slept."

D'Anna's eyes hardened to the color of ice. "Are you saying I'm a prisoner here?"

"Just don't get any ideas about slipping away before we've had a chance to sort this whole thing out."

"What's to sort out? I sent out a distress call. You answered it."

"You were out of fuel, nearly out of oxygen, thousands of miles from the closest planet in this system. What the hell were you doing so far from home?" Even as the words tumbled from her mouth, she knew that this was exactly the wrong approach. She hesitated, wishing she could push the words back in. They hung in the air between them like a bad smell.

D'Anna didn't reply. Only her eyes betrayed her rage. She turned around and walked back toward her ship. Marta saw her shoulders tense and D'Anna draw a long slow breath. Touching the shell gently D'Anna said, "You wouldn't understand."

"Why don't you try me?"

"Not now. Not when you're angry and feeling betrayed. I didn't make love with you in order to gain advantage. I did it because I wanted to." She turned around to face Marta again. "And because I thought you wanted it, too."

Marta reddened.

"Come inside. I want to touch you."

Marta hesitated, wanting to go to D'Anna and push aside this burden of responsibility. She didn't want to sever the thread of tenderness that had been woven so recently between them. But the wildness had frightened her and she retreated into what was familiar—the comforting role of the aggressor, the always-in-control Security Chief—a woman with a deadness inside where the wildness was covered over.

The role of Security Chief gave her life the structure it had lacked during the various academic pursuits of her youth. It was the need for a harsher self-discipline that had led her to Officer's school at the Union's home base on Earth, and her rapid rise through the ranks was a testament to the dedication with which she embraced the Union's code of honor and obedience. But, having recently tasted what else was possible, she felt pulled between the two worlds, sensed the tension between her desire to release the chaos inside her and the self-imposed restrictions she accepted as part of her job, now part of herself as well.

She walked to D'Anna, and touched her hand, mindless of the oil and grease that seemed permanently embedded in the lines and whorls of her skin. "When are you going to tell me what's going on?" she asked, trying to temper her voice to get the answers she wanted, but still pushing against D'Anna's frustrating silence.

"Soon."

"How about now?"

"Our intimacy hasn't given you the right to know."

Marta snatched her hand back, stung by the way in which D'Anna seemed to read her unspoken thoughts, to be always one step ahead of her.

D'Anna turned away, the corners of her mouth pulling down in a half frown, and disappeared around the back end of the ship.

Impotent rage surged like fire through Marta's limbs. She had to know the truth. Duty demanded it. Her fists clenched and she strode after D'Anna. Catching D'Anna by the arm, she spun her around. D'Anna smiled slowly at her. "You've got a hell of a temper," she said.

Marta raised a hand to strike the smile away, let it drop. "You get under my skin."

"I know. I knew that from the moment I laid eyes on you. It's not intentional, you know."

"No. I don't know that. I don't know that at all."

D'Anna didn't try to move away from the iron grip that held her arm motionless, but glanced down at Marta's hand. "You don't have to cut off the circulation in my arm to make your point."

Marta let her hand drop.

D'Anna's short, strong fingers touched Marta's cheek. "Come to bed."

"Here? Are you crazy? What if somebody found us?"

D'Anna laughed. "Shall we retire to your cabin, then?"

"I never invited you back."

"Now's your chance."

Marta closed her eyes. I've finally met my match, she thought. She looked at D'Anna, saw that her eyes had regained their smoldering blueness, so pale. Pale against pale. Eyes almost colorless in a face like a silver moon. The only color in D'Anna's face was a slight blush of rose across her cheekbones, and the hint of blueness in her eyes was a reminder of a faded winter's sky.

"All right," Marta said, turning away. "Come back, then."

"Don't do me any favors."

Marta spun around again, an angry retort on her lips. D'Anna was laughing at her, her wide soft mouth spread in a grin. "You take yourself too seriously, Marta. I intend to change that."

"Don't do me any favors."

D'Anna laughed again. "Touché."

•

"Let's review what we know so far," Captain Pilar said. He pushed himself back from the black shellacked conference table and ran his fingers through his thick blue-black hair.

Resident Historian Sam Chui punched up a report. "I believe D'Anna Severns' ship's home port is the planet Tendra," he began. "It's in this system, fifth planet out from their sun. Their native language is Tendrian, but they adopted Standard as a primary language when Tendra was accepted into the Union fifty years ago. Tendra's had a long standing trade agreement with the fourth and sixth planets in the system. Ships like D'Anna Severns' are used for short interplanetary supply runs. What she said about her radio is true, they're basically useless until she's within planetary orbit. The sensors are pretty sophisticated, though. Have to be, considering that's their main form of navigation. The Trade Council, which monitors the movement of Traders and handles the business end of their transactions, is headed by Margaret Danang. She came to power last year promising sweeping reforms. Apparently, there've been a lot of incidents of corruption within the Trader's ranks, and she wants to change all that. Needless to say, according to our sources, there's been a lot of resistance to her iron-handed rule. Now, there's a network of 'Renegades' who are continuing trade between the fourth and sixth planets from their base on Boscan—planet six—who bypass not only the Council's regulations, but also the planet itself. It's a risky business because these ships can barely carry enough fuel to make it from Boscan to Notha, what we call planet four. If a Trader runs into trouble, she or he would be essentially marooned in space until help arrived. Which," he added, "could account for D'Anna Severns' appearance in this sector.

"I sent out a message this morning to Ms. Danang telling her we may have one of her traders on board and requesting information. We should be hearing from her any time now. Maybe she'll know what D'Anna Severns was doing nearly out of her solar system."

"Why did you assume she was Tendran and not a Renegade?" Marta asked.

"I plotted her drift pattern," Sam said, "and it seems to originate from Tendra, not Boscan or Notha."

"But if she's a Renegade, wouldn't we be putting her into essentially 'enemy' hands?"

"It's not our function to mediate intra-system disputes," the Captain said.

"And if she's a Renegade?"

Captain Pilar spread his hands and shrugged. As he rose, the meeting adjourned. He stopped Marta in the doorway. "I'm counting on you to keep an eye on her," he said. As Marta nodded, she felt an internal mechanism click into place. All the uncontrolled feelings of the night before were pushed away, neatly locked again in their Pandora's box.

Marta found D'Anna in the hanger deck. She was lying on the cold floor half under her ship. "I have to talk to you," Marta said.

"A simple 'hello' would be nice," D'Anna replied, her voice muffled.

"Come out here, will you?"

D'Anna pushed herself out from under the ship and stood up slowly. There were smears of grease on her face and arms. "I think I'll have this old clunker fixed up soon. Then it's back to work for me."

"Don't count on it."

The lines around D'Anna's eyes hardened and her lips drew together in a tight line.

The Wind Betweeen the Stars

"We've contacted Margaret Danang."

"Mother Margaret." D'Anna laughed, but her eyes betrayed her uneasiness.

"I know about the problems with the Traders."

"What problems are you referring to?"

"The corruption. The Renegades. By your silence, you've given us no choice but to turn you over to the Trade Council."

D'Anna's eyes blazed with sudden anger. "If your Union had kept out of this, I could have been on my way by now and spared you a lot of trouble."

Marta felt a sudden surge of adrenaline rush through her. She thought she might be getting close to the truth. "Maybe you don't understand the implications of being picked up by a Union starship," she retorted. "We just can't send you back out there without going through proper Union channels."

D'Anna looked at her for a long moment. Marta sensed D'Anna's confusion. "You seem like a different person," D'Anna

"I have a job to do."

D'Anna said nothing.

"Why are you so far from home in a ship designed for short interplanetary runs?" Marta pressed.

D'Anna looked suddenly tired. Old. For a moment, she seemed to shrink in stature, to bow down under a great weight. Then her eyes hardened and she said, "That's a very long story. I'm sure Mother Margaret will tell you all of it."

"Why won't you tell me?"

"Because I know you will wonder—even if I tell you everything —what I am holding back."

"I give you my word."

D'Anna smiled. "And I can see your honor will bind you. No, Marta. I'm sorry. I have my honor to protect as well." D'Anna turned away, replaced the rag in her tool box and snapped the lid closed. She slid it into the open hatchway and pushed the hatch into place. "I'll be in my quarters if you need me." She paused and for a moment, as a smile touched her lips, D'Anna was the relaxed and confident lover Marta had so recently known. But Marta could see a sadness in her smile as well, as though Marta had disappointed her in some way.

Startled, Marta felt the tension she'd wrestled with all morning reassert itself. She opened her mouth to call D'Anna back, then closed it. The elevator doors swished closed and D'Anna was gone.

When Marta returned to the Bridge, Sam had just patched Margaret Danang's image onto the main screen. Margaret was an imposing woman, even sitting behind a desk. Her long black hair was streaked with silver, and her face was composed of hard, harsh lines.

"I hear you have one of our Traders aboard your ship, Captain," she said, her voice raspy with exhaustion.

"Yes," he said. "A woman named D'Anna Severns."

"As you know, Captain, Tendra has fallen under evil corrupting influences. In an effort to root out these problems, we've cracked down on many supposed 'accidents' among Traders. D'Anna Severns is wanted for the murder of her Trader-partner, Silva Morgan. She's also wanted for evading the Trade Police and leaving Tendra without a permit. As Tendra is a member of the Union, I expect your full cooperation in returning her to us."

Marta was stunned by Margaret's words. She'd imagined that D'Anna had violated some trade agreement, broken some law which, in her culture, carried a heavy punishment. But this was far worse than she'd anticipated. Her heart cried out in denial, but she held her tongue.

"Is her ship operable?" Margaret asked.

Marta found her voice. "She said that she'd have it running again shortly."

Margaret smiled coolly. "If nothing else, she's a good mechanic. If you'll send us your coordinates, we'll send a police freighter to pick her up."

"We're nearly within planetary range now," the Captain said, "Wouldn't it be easier—"

"No. It would not be simpler for you to bring her here, Captain," Margaret snapped.

Captain Pilar nodded. "I'll have them sent to you directly." He gestured to a man sitting at the navigation station. "When can we expect you?"

"In twenty-four hours," she said and the screen went blank.

The Captain turned to Marta. "Have her confined to quarters," he said. Marta nodded silently and strode from the Bridge.

•

D'Anna was lying on her narrow bed with her hands behind her head when Marta came into the room. "They're sending a freighter for you," she said.

D'Anna did not look at her. She spoke towards the ceiling. "I thought they would."

"Why didn't you tell me you were wanted for murder?" Marta tried to still her anger, but the words came out sharp and hollow.

"Is that what Mother Margaret told you?" D'Anna's voice was even, but Marta knew that she was frightened. "It's a lie, of course."

"Is it?"

D'Anna shifted her long limbs on the bed, but didn't look at Marta.

"Why didn't you tell me this before?"

"I had hoped, however foolishly, to bypass any dealings with the Council." She paused. "And I wasn't sure I could trust you."

"But now is too late."

"Is it?" D'Anna asked, her pale eyes flitting from the

Marta didn't reply. She hoped it wasn't, but felt the great heavy wheels of the Union bureaucracy turning around her, threatening to crush them both.

D'Anna took a slow breath. "On Tendra, most of the traders work in pairs. Supply runs are handled by two ships—a convenience for the Trade Council. Freighters are too slow and two of our little ships can carry a large load in half the time.

"Silva and I had been working together for ten years. Been friends longer than that. Neither of us liked the work much. But it's good money. We figured we'd retire soon.

"We made this run—our last run—out to Boscan. Right after lift-off Silva's ship—" D'Anna stopped suddenly and sprang to her feet. She towered over Marta's chair and said in a low angry voice, "They say I killed her. That I wanted the money for the run. It *was* an incredible payoff. But I didn't. I hated the fucking Trade Council, with their corrupt officials that'd arrange for you to have an 'accident' if they thought you wouldn't play their games. So we played. But the only thing that ever mattered to me was Silva."

She stepped back and paced across the floor, then flung herself back onto the bed. She sat crouched on the edge, like a caged animal who knows there is no escape. Her voice, when she spoke again, was so quiet and full of anger it struck Marta like a fist. "They will find me guilty. Do you know what the death penalty is for murder on Tendra?"

Marta, pinned to the chair by the force of D'Anna's words, shook her head, unable to speak.

"They cut you loose. They take you up in one of their ships and cut you loose. You float away and when the oxygen in your suit runs out—" she spread her hands, "you die."

She jumped up again. "I hate those goddamn people in the Trade Union who don't give a damn about anything except their precious cargo and their paper reforms."

"Why didn't you tell us this before?"

D'Anna was silent for a long moment before she answered in a voice subdued by resignation. "I am a small insignificant trader subject to the rules of my planet. We both know your Union has no power here."

"So you were trying to fix your ship and escape."

"Of course. Why should I die for a crime I didn't commit? Silva's ship exploded just after we left Boscan. There was nothing I could do. She'd given me all her credits to deposit in an account because she was stopping off before she went home. So the Council thinks I set her up.

"It's not as though something like this hasn't happened before. Most Traders are corrupt. Real partnerships—like the one I had with Silva—are rare. A lot of traders have 'accidents.' Aside from the Council's manipulations, we've managed quite nicely to kill each other off over the years. But ever since Mother Margaret became head of the Council, every real accident, every move a Trader makes is now suspect.

"But it *was* an accident. Margaret Danang hopes to undo years of corruption by framing me for a murder I didn't commit instead of addressing the corruption within the Council that made these conditions a reality in the first place.

"Ever since she came to power, Traders have been defecting by the dozens. The Renegades have set up a competitive system that makes runs without even stopping on Tendra. If I'd been picked up by a Renegade, I could have been dropped down in some insignificant hole and disappeared forever. But my luck didn't run that way."

Marta didn't say anything when D'Anna was finished. D'Anna looked at her for a long time. Then, she reached out and took Marta's long fingered hands into her own. "My ship is ready. Open the hatch and let me go."

"I could be court-martialed."

"I'm as good as dead if you don't."

"Don't ask me to do this."

"I already have."

Marta pulled her hands away and stood up. "Are you sure that you'll be found guilty?"

"The death warrant has already been signed. I was running from the Trade Police when I ran into trouble and you picked me up."

D'Anna rose and put her hands on Marta's shoulders and turned her around gently. "Please. Marta."

Marta felt the tears start and she pulled away. Stumbling, she turned and fled the room. She ran until she reached her own cabin and locked the door behind her.

There had been times, over the years, when Marta found herself confronted with the necessity of making difficult and unpopular decisions: incidents of corruption she'd been forced to report, friends court-martialed and dismissed. Each of those events had taken something from her, had created the tight place inside herself where all her unresolved feelings, all her deep desires resided. And every time, she'd vowed not to let herself become vulnerable, not to put herself in positions where she would be called upon to betray someone in order to fulfill her obligations.

Life on a starship was a series of decisions, made under the auspicious weight of the good of the many versus the needs of the few. It had never been easy. She'd watched Captain Pilar abandon a shuttlecraft full of scientists in an ion storm so that the five hundred-odd members of the ship could escape destruction; watched his face as he stumbled through the wreckage of a mining colony whose lives had been balanced against an outbreak of fever in another part of the galaxy.

Facing the reality of D'Anna's story, laying it side by side against Margaret Danang's, Marta knew it was one of those moments where she had to put personal feelings aside and bow to the will of the Union.

But this time was not the same. No one had ever touched her as deeply or as tenderly as D'Anna had. No one had ever listened so intently to her stories, laughed in all the right places, touched her hand out of compassion in others. No one had ever taken so much time to love her, to touch every centimeter of her body with gentleness and reverence.

It was as though Marta had been waiting for someone to draw out the memories, the pain, the passion she'd locked away for so long. D'Anna was not afraid of that wildness. In fact, she seemed to welcome it.

Marta thought of the fliers of Souma Three, how much they knew and trusted the winds, how much they trusted each other. A society without war, without strife. A society that had no desire for the Union's protective hand, but had accepted it, as they accepted everything else—because someone else wanted it enough to make it important.

This time, the choice was even more muddled in her mind. She knew, with a kind of stunned certainty, that she loved D'Anna. And had even tested the words on her tongue that morning when she awoke. She could feel the barely restrained desire to jump up, run down the hall and confess her love send shock waves of trembling through her body. She wanted to go, felt obligated to stay.

Great sobs tore from her mouth and she pressed her face into the pillow to muffle them. Finally, exhausted and unable to think anymore, she fell asleep in her clothes.

When she awoke, her bedside clock showed that the night was far advanced. Marta rose stiffly and stripped for a shower. A few minutes later, before opening the door to her quarters, she took a deep breath, reached inside for the strength she would need, then stepped out into the hallway.

Marta knocked again at D'Anna's door. Before she was halfway into the room, she said, "I'm not convinced you're telling me everything."

"Marta, when we were together last night, did you believe that I wanted you?"

"Yes."

"How did you know?"

"I could feel it. I could tell by the way you touched me."

"If I could touch you in that way—unguarded, truthfully—what makes you think I would lie to you with words?"

"Words are different."

"Everything I've told you is true. I said last night I didn't think you'd understand. And I was right. You don't understand because your life has been here—full of structure and codes and rules. My life has never been like that. Silva and I were free, together in the vast incredible beauty of space, roaming together from place to place, restricted only by a loose schedule of departures and arrivals.

"I've had a hard and violent life, Marta. Our culture isn't like yours—we're less refined, more prone to corruption and aggression as your people were hundreds of years ago. But I've seen things you may only dream of, even on my simple journeys within this system. I've been closer to the universe than you can ever be in this huge ship. I've touched the wind between the stars." D'Anna paused, looked at her hands again and spoke to them and to the floor. "I loved Silva. I would never have done anything to hurt her."

"How do I fit into all this?" Marta asked softly. "Was I just some distraction, then? Something to fill a night? To stave off some demon that haunted you? Like Silva's ghost?"

"No." D'Anna shook her head and smiled sadly. After a long moment, she looked up. "I want you to come with me."

Although Marta's heart jumped at the words, she forced herself to respond almost angrily, testing the truth of D'Anna's words. "You just want a guarantee. If I come with you it'll be an interplanetary incident."

"We could disappear before they ever found us."

Marta turned away. Her hands trembled. The longing inside her to succumb to the chaos was growing stronger, to give into something that was bigger than she was and to lose herself in it. D'Anna had become part of that something. Long had she imagined what it would be like out there—alone against a backdrop of the starfilled horizon—with no responsibilities but to herself. She wanted to be consumed by the vastness of space, by the hunger she felt in D'Anna's touch, by the passion that burned like cold fire behind her eyes. She wanted to see what she had never seen, to feel the imaginary pulsing winds of space, to fly close to the sun.

Yet even as she felt these desires churn through her, her inner voice cried out for calm. Be reasonable, it seemed to say, you are who you are and you can never change that. Don't throw this life away for something you know nothing about.

Marta pressed her hands together to stop them from shaking. Tears threatened to spill from her eyes. She straightened her back and turned, "I—" she began.

"Let me go." D'Anna stood and gripped Marta's shoulders, turned her around. "You are all that stands between me and certain death. Marta, please."

Silence.

"Come with me. Throw this all away. Think of the things we would see..."

"I don't want to be a fugitive for the rest of my life."

"You'd prefer to be a prisoner of your fear to take a chance instead?"

"I have to go." Marta pushed against the air between them with her hands.

"There's still time. Before the freighter gets here. Marta."

Marta hesitated at the doorway.

"I won't let them take me," D'Anna said.

Looking at D'Anna, Marta saw the cold determination in her eyes. She turned away without another word.

Hours later, Marta rose from her bed without having slept. She dressed slowly and took the elevator down to the hanger deck. It was deserted.

D'Anna's ship gleamed dully in the amber safety lights that filled the deck with soft shadows and golden highlights. She went to the ship, ran the palms of her hand across the battered hull. She could feel the power of the ship, a deceptive strength that was so much like D'Anna herself.

She remembered the incredible freedom she'd felt in D'Anna's arms and wondered if she could feel that every day. Not the sexual connection, but the feeling, instead, of a spirit that has been released.

When she'd joined the Union, Marta had never thought that one day she'd consider leaving it, and certainly not under these circumstances. Here, under her fingertips, was her passport to freedom, to a different and unstructured way of life.

I could have been like her, Marta thought. I could have chosen another path for myself. But I was afraid of living without the singular focus the Union offered me: safe inside a huge powerful ship in a fleet that roams the galaxies commanding respect by reputation alone.

And now, she thought, here is my chance. And I am afraid to take it.

•

The freighter arrived ahead of schedule.

Marta was on the Bridge when the freighter's captain established radio contact. Captain Pilar turned to Marta and said, "Escort D'Anna Severns to the hanger deck."

Marta didn't speak as she opened the door to D'Anna's quarters. She tried to look D'Anna in the eye, but the other woman turned her face away. D'Anna rose slowly from the bed and picked up a battered silver duffle from the floor. They walked together to the hanger deck.

"I'll take it from here," Marta said to the guard on duty. He stepped aside. "Connors to Captain, ready to open the outer hatch."

"Proceed." His voice sounded tinny over the intercom.

Marta punched the buttons on the console and gestured to D'Anna. They walked down to the ship together. D'Anna opened the hatch to her own ship, stepped up and inside.

Marta took a radio from her uniform pocket, showed it to D'Anna and smiled.

"Got room for one more?" Marta asked.

"But how are we going to get out of here? Don't you need to be up at the console?"

"Modern Technology," Marta said. She climbed into the cabin, aimed the radio transmitter at the console and pressed a button. "I rigged it up last night."

D'Anna sealed the ship's hatch.

"You better have some pretty good tricks up your sleeve, D'Anna."

D'Anna grinned. "You're in for the ride of your life."

The inner docking doors slid open, activated by the transmitter Marta held in her hand. The stars loomed before them, bright points of light with immense blackness between.

Marta could hear the confused stream of voices as the ship's engines fired. As the ship shot forward, she thought of her resignation lying in a sealed envelope on the desk in her cabin.

The radio crackled with irate voices from the starship and the freighter. Marta leaned forward and snapped it off. She threw her head back and laughed. They flew past the freighter in a rush of light and a roaring of wind. Out into the darkness and the wind between the stars.

Intrigue/Erotica

Heat

by Caroline Halliday

I am sitting in Peckham Park, South London and a strident blue jay just walked past me. I am a white, older, lesbian and a mother. To me, sex is an intriguing mystery, which is not to be confused with violence or pain. I believe in taking risks in writing about difficult areas, there isn't time for anything else, and most often I write more seriously than this story (which was written 'to see if I could do it'!) My most recent writings are in Whatever You Desire, In and Out of Time, *and* Lesbian and Gay Writing *(all 1990).*

Heat

Sometimes they met at the Baths on a Thursday. If both of them could get away.

Mel had flung her flannel and shampoo in the bag, swung her car into reverse, then out into the street and made it in ten minutes.

She smiled at the woman behind the glass partition, and could see her own face, the angle of her beret, in the reflection.

Joel wasn't there, two hours till closing time.

Heat seeped into her thighs, her cheekbones. It made her breathing shallow. Women chatted, then an empty room. Then the room would fill up again. Women wandered into the steam room.

— Oh, it's perfect in there.

— Find it too hot myself.

— Put the flannel over your face.

Mel looked over all the breasts in the place. Bursting ones and tuppenny ha' penny ones. Brown and pink. Wrinkled ones that floated in the cold plunge.

She looked down the length of her body at hair crisped up, black and curly, between her legs. Her armpit hair was long and jagged. Joel's body was shapely around the bum, her thighs flaring out like a dancer's. Hadn't seen her for over a week. Mel slipped her hand along the side of her belly. She wanted to reach down to her cunt, and she wanted Joel's cheek lying there.

Mel lay back, letting go. Flannel folded over her eyes. Darkness.

A honeycomb of hot places, sweat trickling down her groin and armpit.

She fell asleep once, drifting off on the wooden bench.

•

Two women in the room gathered their things to go home. Another went for a massage. The door swung closed. Empty room. Everything quieted. Silence. She could feel her lax body, nakedness, her legs slightly parted, letting the heat in everywhere.

Heat

There was no one in the room, but unexpectedly her breasts quickened. She checked round, keeping her eyes closed. No one there.

Did it matter anyhow? Her mind drifted off into unconsciousness.

She switched awake with a mouth firm on her breast, a strong swift suck. Her breast leapt alive, taut flesh and sharper points of recognition.

There was a hand on the flannel over her eyes, gentle pressure downwards.

Other fingers licking down, bit by bit, ribs, hip. Raising wet heat from her flesh.

Then nothing.

Mel lifted her hand to move the flannel and turned her head quickly to look round the room, swinging her legs to the floor. Dizzy.

There was no one there. The plastic curtain to the next room made a dry twitch. Two women pushed open the door from the steam room and walked through to the next room.

— Not in a place like that, one of them said.

— You'd never be sure, would you?

Mel got up unsteadily. As she reached the curtain they were settling on the bench.

— D'you want some of this cream? one of them was asking.

The room was full. Six women. Two black women, one reading. Four white women, two younger, two older. None of them looked up. Mel swallowed and stepped back.

•

The shower was hot and she let it drum on her back, her breasts and face. The touch on her thigh remained. Her breathing was uneven. One breast was humming, the nipple a queen of dark against brown aureole and milky brown breast. She squeezed her nipple. It was hard. She brushed the other nipple up and down. Joel had been away last week.

She inched into the cold plunge. Three of the women from the middle room had emerged and she caught their eyes as, in turn, they all looked her way.

The cold water stroked icily up her thigh and she gulped.

She lay down again. This time in the middle room. Perhaps Joel would arrive and...she'd be...amused?
Joel's eyes. Wow. Did you like it?
Swish of dry plastic curtain. Movement of bodies. In. Out. Mel looked round the room a couple of times. An older woman with firm jaw and humorous creases round her eyes smiled at her.
— Hot enough for you, is it?
Mel closed her eyes, wondering if she was waiting.
Nothing happened.

•

A woman in the shower smiled at her.
A woman in the cold plunge dived under like a seal as Mel came to the steps. The woman came up close to her, blowing and laughing and shaking a wet head. Black-brown eyes looked at her keenly. Mel returned the gaze. The woman climbed the steps, her bottom swinging wide and drips of water falling from her. Lips against skin, cheek against dark curve. Oh, to feel it.
Mel floated on her back, the soaping and turning and swishing of the showers in her line of sight. She twisted herself this way and that in the water. Her pubic hair crested the surface of the pool as she arched her body backwards.

•

She went into the hot, hot room. Empty. It filled up as she lay there, her body growing heavy and drowsy. The voices came and went.
— It's always on a Thursday. Did you see it last week?
Loud, then soft. Bits of conversation she heard and then didn't hear the rest. Private then public.
— She used to keep going there, you know. She carried an orange umbrella and...
Voices and bodies. Voices and bodies. The room emptied again.
A woman in a plastic crinkly wrap came in and heaved and sighed with the heat of her wrapper. She waved her magazine in front of her face and made a face at Mel.
— These things make you sweat.
Mel thought of herself curled up in the sweat beneath: sweat between bodies riding against each other.

Another woman, almost breastless, lay down beside her, knocking her towel to the floor.
— Sorry, she murmured, and handed it back, their hands touching. The woman lay still for a long time.

•

Mel showered and was shampooing her hair.
— Ouch. The water went hot, then cold. She groped for the knob and couldn't find it.
— Can I help? A broad arm reached past, knocking against her breast in passing. The woman didn't say sorry. Her strong hand adjusted the heat. Water sluiced down Mel's body, running between her legs. The woman paused, close up.
— Alright?
Mel pushed shampoo off her face. Her body prickled with goosepimples. Was this the woman? Was someone watching her? She wanted the hand to circle down her skin, settle below her black hair and reach inside her, soaking and resolute. The woman still paused.
— Okay?
— Thanks. Mel felt cold strike her as the woman's close breasts and belly moved away.

•

Only half an hour left. It wasn't going to happen again.
— Would you like a massage?
Mel swallowed. It must be... Her belly tensed and she turned to respond.
— Well?
— How much is it?
— Fiver.
No hint of mischief. The woman's green eyes were smiling, that's all. No tremour in her gaze.
— Haven't got it, Mel shrugged.—Nothing comes free, does it!
— Oh, some things do, the woman replied, and went into the next room.
— Anyone want a massage?

•

Mel sank back onto the bench. Can't have been.
A woman with fluted thighs slipped past the corner of the open

door.

—Joel?

There was so many corners and doors and alcoves.

•

It was too hot in the hot room. Besides, nothing doing.

She lay in the middle, cooler room and sweated. Her cunt was large, and her breasts tingled. Better to go home and...

I give up. She turned over to lie on her stomach, face to the wall. Her legs parted. Weightlessness. The heat made her sleepy again. Her thoughts wandered to bodies in the shower, to full curves of stomachs, seen from below. Her feet itched and she rubbed one toe against her heel. Joel and she were...

Swish of curtain, pad of feet. Towels lifted and put down. Silence.

•

There was a touch on her thigh and stroking up the line between her buttocks. A hand crept over her eyes and a voice murmured,

—Don't look.

The hand slipped inside her thigh, touched her inner lips. A rush of moisture expanded in Mel's cunt.

The woman's hand made soft patterns on her shoulders and buttocks, while the other hand played with the silky line. Mel let her legs shift open.

She opened her eyes.

She could only focus on the wall. Blue tiles. A shadow behind her.

The woman was gone. This time the curtain to the hottest room swished violently and was still swinging as Mel pushed herself up on her forearms and looked over her shoulder at an empty room. Two chatting women came in. One of them handed the other a sweet. Mel pushed herself further up and then sank back. Why move? Her cunt hummed deliciously.

•

She went back to the shower, avoiding the hot room entirely. She walked slowly, her body light, her legs feeling all her cunt thicken. Her body was ringing. Any of these women could have light firm hands. She invited them to look at her. She wandered slowly round the cold plunge, paused at the top of the steps, dove in. Cold hit her swollen flesh. She floated and closed her eyes. She wanted the warm hand to reach through the water, sudden and quick.

•

The attendant came in calling her number. The two hours were up. She delayed at the mirrors, rubbing her hair.
She ordered a coffee, found her cubicle and sat down.
— Oh, sod it.
She wrapped the big towel round her and lay back on the chairbed.
7:30. Time to go to the Pizza Hut and maybe meet Joel. It was their usual time.
She put the flannel over her eyes again and breathed evenly. It was over. There was a clatter of noise outside her cubicle.
— Your coffee, dear, the attendant called out.
— Thanks.
The attendant disappeared, pulling the curtain carefully into place.
Mel rested.
She slipped her hand inside the big towel and smoothed over her breast, her nipple hard as a button. She circled her hand on her belly. Wait. There's no hurry. She was aware of her toes, the weight going off her shoulders, and her cunt waiting. She moved her hand over the wiry hair and plunged into her cunt. Ohh, thank god... Her head pushed back, thrusting her fingers again and again.

•

A slight noise.
— Don't move, okay?
It was almost a whisper. Mel pushed her fingers deeper.
Warm hands slid under the big towel, cupping and squeezing her breasts hard, then they moved down the line of her belly. The woman's fingers caressed around her clit without touching it.
The woman's hand brushed hers and Mel bit her lip with an indrawn breath. The mouth covered her own fingers, licking between them, as she lifted them away. Wet fingers swept slippery against her ass.
Oh, to make a sound in this oh, so quiet place.
Mel's buttocks scudded on the big, rough towel, which lay open round her.

Mel swung her bag over her shoulder, pushed her beret to one side and stepped through the revolving doors. Her tee shirt was sticking to her breasts. She was smiling.

Opposite her, Joel was leaning against the balustrade, a bag between her thighs. Her tousled hair curly and damp. Mel stared at her.—Joel? Where...? Mel gestured questioningly towards the doors behind her, aware of her breast beneath the thin tee shirt.

Joel glanced at her, raised her eyebrows, grinning.

— You look good. Joel looked Mel all over.—You look refreshed.

— Where have you been? Mel came in sharply, holding back a smile.

Joel frowned.

— I had a Turkish Bath and then I went for a swim. Why? She raised her eyebrows again. And grinned.

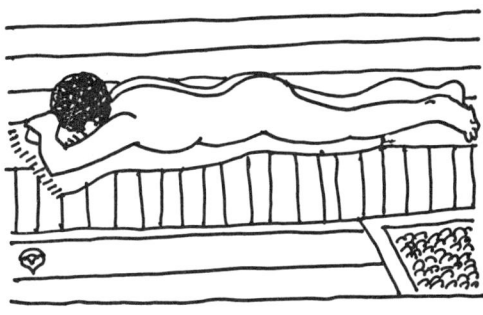

Relationships

A Second Time

by Candis J. Graham

I, Candis Jean Graham, am an Aquarian, with skin the colour of aging unfinished pine and lots of white hair. I live in Ottawa with my companion Wendy Clouthier.

The idea for this story came from a casual comment about me that a woman made to Wendy shortly before we were introduced in 1979. From that kernel, the story took on a life of her own. It was one of those rare gifts, a story that flowed on to the pages.

I support myself and my writing by doing part-time work for a national association that lobbies for quality non-profit child care. I also do the bookkeeping for Wendy's business. Thanks to her financal support, I do not live in poverty. One of my dreams is to be able to write lesbian fiction full time. Another dream is to live and work surrounded by dykes—upstairs, next door, across the street. A book entirely of my own stories, Tea for Thirteen, *will soon be in print. This will bring to sweet reality another of my dreams.*

A Second Time *is dedicated to my friend Barb Augustine.*

A Second Time

"She has quite the reputation."

I turn to look at the woman beside me. "She does?"

"Yes," she says. "She's here every week. She's always alone. She was involved with a woman for years, three or four for sure. They split last spring."

I watch her walk across the room, winding her way around tables and clusters of women, saying nothing to the woman beside me. The band has taken a break and the silence is heavenly. Not silence, really, but women's voices rather than loud music. The heavenly sounds of women talking and laughing.

She stops to talk to someone. After a brief conversation, she resumes her trip across the huge room. She walks slowly, with a lazy stride, as if she has all the time in the world.

"Do you know her?"

The woman beside me lifts her glass mug of beer. "No, not really. I know about her. I know her name." She drinks from the mug, knowing she has my attention, deliberately taking her time. "Her name is Erin."

It suits her. Erin. The perfect name for this woman with short curly hair and over-sized purple glasses. Erin of the lazy stride.

"She sleeps with everyone."

My mouth falls open. "How do you know she sleeps with everyone?"

She gives me a pitying look. "Everyone knows."

Everyone knows she sleeps with everyone. Everyone!! Rumours. Innuendoes. Gossip passed from woman to woman, and presented as fact. Don't we relish the distorted details, speculating about the lives of one another. It entertains us, as long as it isn't about us.

"Yes, she has quite the reputation." There is a sense of satisfaction in her voice.

I want to scream, want to yell at her, want to shake her. She

sleeps with everyone, does she! Well, I'd bet my money that she was celibate, that's what I'd bet, that's how much faith I'd put in idle rumours! Instead, I ignore my inner voice and ask, "Do you want another beer?"
    She smiles. "Sure."
    I walk away quickly. I have no intention of getting her a beer. She can faint from thirst before I'd get her a beer. I want a beer, myself, so I head for the bar.
    I join the line up, standing behind Erin. I hadn't planned this. I am thirsty. I'd watched her walk in the direction of the bar, true. But I am here only because I'm thirsty.
    I'm not angry anymore. I feel excited to be standing close to her. I look down at the floor, trying to calm my racing heart. She's wearing bright yellow running shoes. I have a friend who says you can tell a lot about a person by her shoes. Do women who wear yellow running shoes sleep with everyone? I almost laugh out loud.
    "Why are you smiling?"
    I look up. Erin is grinning at me, waiting for my answer.
    "I had a funny thought, that's all."
    "What were you thinking?"
    Her eyes are looking into mine, warm hazel eyes behind the glass, inviting me to look back. Usually I am tongue-tied, especially around women I admire, but words come easily. "You wouldn't be amused. Trust me."
    She laughs. "Try me."
    It's her turn at the bar. She orders mineral water with a slice of lemon and produces the correct amount of money from a leather pouch on her belt. I am in a state of panic, afraid she will walk away.
    I order my beer and call after her, "Wait!"
    She turns, still grinning.
    "I'll tell you."
    She laughs again. "I can't wait."
    I take my beer from the counter. "Come out here, in the hall, where it's quiet."
    She follows me. She follows me! My heart is thumping. What can I say to her? She would not be pleased if I said I'd been told that she had a reputation for sleeping with everyone.
    The band starts playing loud energetic dance music as we leave

the room. Maybe I'll ask her to dance, after I've figured out how to explain why I was smiling at the bar.

The hall is deserted. We stop at an alcove, beside a water fountain, and I turn to look at her, to see if those hazel eyes are still warm and inviting.

She bends forward and kisses the end of my nose, then she laughs. "I couldn't resist. Do you mind?"

I shake my head, speechless. She kissed my nose. What did it mean, that she kissed my nose?

"Why were you smiling back there? You said you'd tell me."

I nod. What if it is true, her reputation? What can I say to those hazel eyes? No lies. The truth is, the truth...

She leans toward me and puts her lips on mine, warm lips, my heart pounding, open lips, searching tongues. I want to shout for joy. I want to put my arms around her and hold her close to me.

"I've missed you," she whispers.

I put my arms around her, trying not to spill any beer and wishing the mug would vanish into the air. "I've missed you, Erin."

"So, why were you smiling?"

I move back a little, to look at her. "I was thinking your yellow runners should be scarlet, to match your reputation. Did you know that you sleep with everyone? That's what I've been told." I hadn't meant to blurt it out like that.

Tears fill her eyes. Wet hazel eyes. She was always able to express her emotions as she felt them. I'm more inclined to control my feelings. I move her close to my body again.

"I sleep only with myself!" She cries the angry words against my cheek bone.

"I thought so." Her smell is just as I remembered. A hint of soap and freshly-ironed clothes. "Let me put this beer down so I can hug you properly."

"You never do anything properly."

I grin. "Wanna dance?"

"I have missed you."

I feel warm all over. "Me too. Let's dance."

She laughs, takes off her glasses and wipes the tears from her eyes and cheeks with a forefinger. "You want to dance with a scarlet woman?"

"I'd be honoured."
She laughs, puts her glasses back on, and takes my hand.

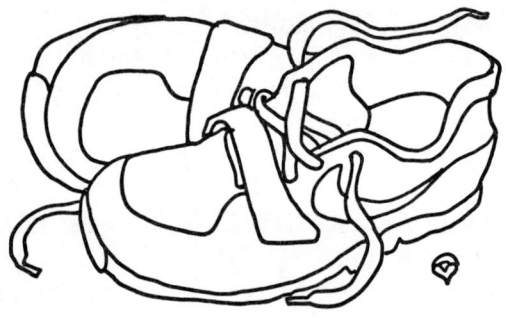

Relationships

Carpentry

by Lida Dowlearn

Lida Dowlearn spent her early childhood years up to age 33 chasing wild women in Texas. Much to the chagrin of her ex-lovers, she has lived to write about her formative experiences. Lida now lives in northwest Arkansas with her two dogs, Edward and Gertrude, who are very well-behaved and she is, too, most of the time. Carpentry *is Lida's first published work. Thank you, Tough Doves. Dreams can come true so be specific.*

Carpentry

I am a worker in wood and a student of architecture. The carpentry pays the bills and the architecture keeps me thinking. I concern myself with houses and what they say. Last year I tried fixing up a house all by myself. I do only minor repairs these days.

As I walk out of my last class for the day, I tell myself it is a wonderful thing to be hit in the face by a brilliant blue sky. Spring is putting me on advance notice. The trees are no longer a simple gray or brown: they have impatient orange and red swellings all over their limbs which are going to burst forth any day now into a shock of green. I am not ready for this. I do not even have my sunglasses in my backpack. I stumble home in the brightness, pick up my carpentry tools, and load them in my truck to go see Judith Garson about a repair job.

I glance in the hall mirror on my way out the door. I have lost a lot of weight in the past year but I would not recommend the "Lose Your Lover, Lose 20 Pounds" diet. My face looks gaunt with the cheekbones I inherited from my mother even more prominent now than they were that night Lisa said I looked like Katherine Hepburn. How could I not love a woman who told me that? I am 34. I have a still new to me streak of gray emerging in my brown hair. I tell myself to get used to it.

Last Spring I was packing my bags and moving out of Lisa's house in Austin. That was the house I tried to remodel. She had a cozy bungalow which was just right for one but I never could find space in there for me. I thought I would try to add some on but she liked the original floor plan better. I guess it was best. I am not the cozy-bungalow-in-the-center-of-a-city kind of girl anyway. I am more the cabin-in-the-middle-of-the-woods type. Cities give me the feeling that I cannot breathe so I try not to stay in them for too long anymore. My remodeling for Lisa's house would have included moving the entire structure to Arkansas and nestling it in these mountains.

Land in Arkansas is cheap. A year ago, I bought 40 acres of it and tried to talk Lisa into leaving with me to build a new home together here. Lisa almost went for it but at the last moment she refused to sign off on the plans in my mind. Her fifty-thousand-dollar-a-year job at the bank and all her friends telling her she was right to stay were too much competition for my personal vision of Better Lesbian Homes and Gardens. Lisa's refusal to join me hit me like a major earthquake with its epicenter in the region of my heart: a zone admittedly full of many faults.

So here I am this Spring with my land in Arkansas which I have not built on yet and no Lisa. I keep thinking Lisa is going to come to her senses, leave Austin, and come live with me and be my love but she laughs when I tell her this. She tells me I am really very funny.

I back my truck out of my driveway and head for Judith Garson's house, determined to concentrate on anything but Lisa today. I drive north out of town past Forest Oaks, Big Oaks, Copper Oaks, and Golden Oaks. I envision a new development, Jo-Oaks, for all the trees with a sense of humor. Finally, I turn into that place most unique among suburban developments, Many Oaks. Trying to get my mind off Lisa, I have started having fun with fantasies about the women I encounter. A voice, a look, a movement can set me off. I had great expectations for Judith Garson but my fledgling fantasy flies right out my old truck's window as soon as I see the territory I am entering. I watch it fly and know I was wrong about Judith's voice. Over the phone, the way she spoke had made me want to take a look at what she needed.

"Hello, is this Beth?" she had asked. "Rena Spencer recommended you to me. The water pipes to my washing machine in the garage froze while I was out of town two weeks ago. I need some sheetrock replaced and some woodwork refinished. Rena told me you could do the job."

It had not been the words, exactly. It had been the tone. The authoritative, self-assured dispensation. Almost a command to appear.

"Well, I'm fairly busy with school right now. But if it's not too big of a job I guess I could fit it in," I had responded.

"Fine. I live on Countryside Lane about five miles out of town. You have a map, don't you?" she had said in the way of directions.

The map in my mind had immediately gone to a winding dirt road on the edge of town where Judith would live in a fine old Arkansas farmhouse with ten acres around it and all the necessary books in her study which would cause us to have an instant recognition of each other. The integrity of her character would be reflected in her honestly weathered, finely chiseled face, her clear blue eyes, and her warm, inclusive smile. After giving her a quick estimate on her repairs, I would spend the rest of the afternoon with her drinking Southern Pecan coffee and discussing Virginia Woolf, Carson McCullers, and Anais Nin. At sunset she would take me on a tour of her property and introduce me to Spiked Punch, her horse, and invite me to return and ride.

But Countryside Lane is a paved road running straight down the middle of Many Oaks. Judith's house is brown brick, two blocks down on the right. It looks just like the third house down from it and the sixth and the ninth. No horses in the backyard.

"I'm glad you found my house," Judith says as she parades me into her living room. The high price of having a rich fantasy life is knowing how much less you have to live with in reality. I am not glad I found her house. I want to go home and crawl back into my fantasy and ride Spiked Punch.

I study Judith, sizing up her actual structure. She is in her early fifties and about my same height, a few inches taller than average. She is bigger than me with a Midwestern strength of frame that has been settling around the edges for a few years now. She has blond hair done up in a conservative wave, possibly assisted by Miss Clairol. Not the Barbara Stanwyck of my fantasy but she did offer seven dollars an hour and I am not really all that busy.

Judith got my name from Rena who was too busy to help her and passed her on to me. Carpenters and plumbers are doing all right these days after that week of below freezing weather that took everyone by surprise. Busted water pipes and damaged woodwork all over town. I prefer building new rooms or designing furniture with clean lines and smooth wood—so smooth if a fly lands on it he will slip and break his neck. But I have not been able to draw up any new designs lately. Oh well, repair work is a living and flexible enough for a student.

"I'll take you around and show you what I want done," Judith says.

That voice is still good at giving commands even though it is a little meeker face to face. Almost as if it senses my disappointment.

The phone rings.

"Excuse me." Judith smiles.

I take the opportunity to survey her living room. All the furniture matches in a predictable way. The stereo cabinet and the television console are oak veneer. The beige carpet looks like nobody ever walks on it. Several fairly tasteful prints of garden scenes hang level on the walls. Judith has one of Georgia O'Keefe's flowers but it is not one of her hot ones. This one looks like a bunch of Kleenex tissues falling in on each other. Not a bad image but not exactly "Black Iris III" either. A navy blue leather (oh, that is somewhat curious) recliner and a contemporary sofa accompany a Queen Anne armchair in a resolute staring match with a vacant fireplace. You can tell someone lives in this house but not very much. No custom touches anywhere. Most of Judith's life must be someplace else. Probably the office.

"Okay. I'll pick up the tickets. See you Saturday. Bye." Judith hangs up the phone and returns to the living room. She is the type who takes business associates to basketball games and dinner afterwards at the Hilton on Saturday nights and considers that a good time.

"Want a cup of coffee?" Judith asks.

We go into the kitchen, another immaculately ordered room. Maybe the microwave has seen some recent use. This house makes me want to go out, get some mud on my shoes, and walk back in.

Judith is getting the personal goods from me now. What are you studying. Where are you from. I am doing the same with her. It is like a giant "Let's Make A Deal" game we are all playing. Everyone wants to know what is behind the doors they did not pick.

I have given up any effort towards disguise. I cut up all my pantyhose when I moved here and used them in my garden to tie my tomato plants. I keep my hair cropped short the way I like it, do not use make-up, and am not afraid to wear my old softball shirt that says "Hill Country Dykes" anywhere I go. Judith is old enough and I think aware enough to pick up on these things. She is not asking the usual boyfriend questions. Still, there are those Baptist Church manuals on her kitchen table. She could be totally unaware of anything. Hard to believe but this is a small town in the bible belt with its full share of tediously repressed people.

"So what brought you to Fayetteville?" she asks.

I do not want to tell the Lisa story so I think of the other reasons I am here. "It is a place where the unknown sometimes happens," I say.

Two sides to Fayetteville. Small, sedate town and then a flash of mountains black against a pulsing orange at sunset. Secretive owls screaming at midnight and a million stars when you go out to look. Tough land dykes and intelligentsia from the university. It is a place where I can live for now and be fairly true to myself. No one tries to sell the American Way too hard here. Judith draws her brow up into two uncomprehending lines between her eyes.

"Oh. I came here on a job transfer," she says.

Judith is one of those rare exceptions. She is someone who was paid to come to Arkansas. By now I have heard that she works for the Wal-Mart General Office as an accounting manager and has been there for 15 years. That could do serious damage to anyone. Yet those blue eyes still have a lot of flash and sparkle to them. Almost making a connection with me. Like seeing another lesbian on the street and smiling in recognition of each other. What an innocent Judith is. She has no idea she is emitting these kinds of sparks. No sense in trying to tell her anything about them. I am here to make repairs but I have my limits. If I told her what I am thinking right now she would probably faint. I walk over to the bay window, coffee cup in hand, and look out at the manicured backyard.

"Nice deck," I say.

"I had that built when we put in the hot tub. More coffee?" Judith asks.

"No thanks." Whoa. A "we". A "we" and a hot tub. Could it be the Royal We? I wake up. An item of excitement in Judith Garson's life after all. She put in a hot tub with someone. What a relief. I imagine a kindly traveling computer salesman with IBM. Maybe he sold Judith a new system at the office. Things went from there. He still comes through town once a month or so to adjust her system. There is something after hours for the Wal-Mart woman after all.

We leave our coffee cups in the kitchen and Judith leads me

around her house showing me everything she wants done. We stop back in the living room and she goes over to her Queen Anne chair. She picks up a broken chair leg from the seat.

"Also, I broke this chair leg when I was moving furniture to clean the carpet. I guess I bumped it or something. It was broken once before in the same place. Can you fix this, too?" she asks.

I take the chair leg and look at it closely and think about this. Do I really want to work on her chair leg? Maybe if it had been some unique piece of wood, I might have been willing.

"I doubt this leg will hold up to another repair," I tell her. "It would be better if you took this chair to a furniture repair place and had them order a new leg."

Judith fixes a quick look on me and I catch a slight glimmer of something, almost a smile, but I am not sure.

"Do you think they could match this leg?" Judith asks.

"They could find one in a catalogue. It's a fairly common type," I say then bite my lip. Well, I cannot help it. Judith seems to want me to take an interest in her furnishings and I just cannot do it.

Judith takes the chair leg back from me. "Rena told me you could fix anything."

Rena and her big mouth. She is always setting me up. Judith looks so worried about her chair. I know she must be disturbed about having anything broken in her house.

"Oh, I could fix your chair leg," I tell Judith. I do not want this woman to think I do not want to help her with her leg. Even if it is true.

"But it would always be weak. It would really be better if you just replaced it," I add. In this way, I subtly remind Judith that one must do the very best one can to have everything perfect as I know Judith will not be able to resist this line of reasoning.

"I guess you're right. I'll just take it someplace. The insurance company is paying for it anyway," Judith says.

Good. We can let the leg go and I can do everything else for her. I go in the garage, measure the sheetrock for replacement, and tell Judith I will be back on Monday to start work. It is Friday night. I call Rena and we meet down at the Restaurant On The Corner to drink coffee and watch women coming in to drink coffee and watch women.

Carpentry

No one hardly ever speaks to anyone except the people seated at their own table but everyone looks around. This is a regular happening on Friday nights. Sort of a lesbian happy hour. Happy just to see each other's faces and know we are surviving here.

I try to tell Rena about Judith but she is not very interested because the story does not involve any sex. It does in a way but I cannot get Rena to visualize that surviving 15 years of Wal-Mart and a lifetime of the Baptist Church well enough to put in a hot tub with someone is pretty damn racy stuff for a woman like Judith.

"So what does it matter? When are you going to stop analyzing every life you come across and start doing something about your own?" Rena prods. Every 34-year-old woman should have a 23-year-old mother hen.

"I am doing something about my life. I am going back to school. I am working," I say.

"Romance-wise I mean," Rena pushes.

"When is romance ever wise?" I ask.

"Don't get philosophic on me. Look, you've lived in this town for a year without asking even one woman out. Women are starting to wonder. I know Lisa is a tough one to get over but your life is here now, not in Austin."

"I guess I haven't been totally in the here and now," I say.

"Listen, there's no cure for an old girlfriend like a new girlfriend."

"Who are you? My Bluebeard of Happiness?" I ask.

"Don't knock it. I've seen two or three women in this town looking at you. If you would bother to look back something might happen. Take tonight. There's Jean Halton, two tables down. Cute. Very cute. Do those lips make your blood run hot or what?"

"I don't know. Maybe."

"Maybe? Maybe is for thinking about going to the grocery store or doing your laundry. Maybe is not for lusting after those lips."

"Maybe some of us are not into lusting," I say.

"I hope I'm not half dead by the time I'm 34. Look, she works at the bookstore on Dickson Street. You go in there all the time. Why don't you open your mouth and try talking to her next time you go? It's easy. You do it like this," Rena says. Rena proceeds to model several inviting smiles and says "hello" and "hi" in ten different sexually suggestive tones.

"Be patient with me. Lisa's been the last six years of my life," I say. I'm trying but it's hard to break out of that."

"How much longer are you going to live your life on hold?"

"I don't know." Sometimes I feel like my heart is caught like a permanently stuck pause button on a VCR. I keep pushing on the button but the frame stays frozen. "I need more time."

"Time for what? What are you waiting for?" Rena asks.

I am waiting for the mysteries of the universe to be revealed to me. I am waiting for the waitress to bring more coffee. I am waiting to feel my heart move again. "I'm just waiting," I say.

"Jesus, get a girlfriend."

"That is what I wanted to say to Judith. Judith, all you really need is a girlfriend. Can you imagine? Besides, it looks like she's pretty happy with the IBM guy," I say. Rena pats my hand.

"Beth, you're mixing again. LaLa Land and reality are not the same."

So what? Why should I totally give over to one reality when I can be in so many others at the same time?

"It doesn't have anything to do with you," Lisa had whispered to me at least four or five times that last weekend we were together. I kept trying to talk to her about how we could build a home together. How anything could work if we wanted it to. But I think she had already moved me out in her mind, and wanted her house to herself. All there really was for us to do that final weekend was to make love together one last time like a long and sad goodbye.

I have a 19th Century rosewood bureau that is with Lisa now in her house. When I moved out I left it because I want something of mine to always be with her. My grandmother told me that the rosewood bureau rode to Texas all the way from Alabama in a covered wagon. Even the mirror made it without cracking so you see it is a survivor. I used to stand before that bureau and stare, stare, stare at all the swirling patterns in the wood and marvel at how it formed beauty out of such mystery.

I'd stared and stared at Lisa, too, and finally she pulled me into her house and we lived there quietly for a time. But I am not one to sit still in a house. I take on projects and look for repairs to do. I like a real, strong house. When I started walking around in Lisa's house I tested doors, threw my weight up against walls. I think Lisa was afraid it would collapse; it was the only house she knew. She refused to abandon it. So I had to leave without her.

I left Texas and I left Lisa's house. I also left my rosewood bureau with Lisa and I will always think about her and dream of Texas roses. Roses with their thorns and deep red flowers.

Rena has continued the conversation without me and is now launching into the intriguing subject of tomorrow night.

"Women will come out of the woodwork for this one. I expect you to be there," she says.

"Yeah, I'll be there."

Martha Benson, a feminist folk singer from Minneapolis, is in town for a concert. This will be one of the two "gala" events so to speak of this year's lesbian social season in Fayetteville. Sweet Honey in the Rock is next month. For the remainder of the year, we will limp along with private parties, pot-lucks, and a benefit dance or two at the aerobics building. I am not complaining. I like things homespun and the Fayetteville scene sure beats hanging out in country-western beer joints. Women make things happen for themselves here and that takes the kind of strong women I like being around.

The next night I find myself standing in the lobby of the Continuing Education Center in the bosom of a powerfully gathering crowd of women. Rena is right. When a beautiful vision is before you, it is a sin not to look. As long as you do not do it like a vulture. That's what men seldom get. The subtleties. Women are here from as far away as Missouri and Oklahoma. They have been drawn to the oasis of lesbian culture Fayetteville women manage to maintain. No matter how small an oasis is, it is a welcome sight to the thirsty.

"Hey, babe, how's it going?" Rena asks as she walks up and gives me a big hug. She is decked out in her black leather jacket and red silk pants with a blazing yellow t-shirt that says "Women Unite To Take Back The Night" in bold black letters. I have on a nice pair of pressed khakis and a slate blue sweater. Rena and I talk for awhile and then she is swept away by Skylight who has just returned after spending the winter in Tucson living in a tipi at Adobeland. She is full of desert tales and news of travelers on the dyke highway.

Elaine Forest skips up to me looking like the main character in her latest collection of stories: a woman who dances for the Goddess before the time of patriarchy. She is adorned in long turquoise earrings, a flowing pink skirt and some kind of soft purple blouse. She dances all over, even in her eyes. She invites me to a Spring ritual out at her house next weekend then she waltzes on to someone else.

I get into a few conversations with some other friends but mainly I am just standing around watching and getting my batteries recharged by all the energy that is surging in this lobby. I am starting to think about focusing on individual faces. Jean Halton is here but I cannot decide what to do about that. We sort of smiled at each other earlier. Just as I am thinking I might start looking around for Jean someone comes up behind me and touches me on my arm.

I turn around with a pleasant smile on my face. I turn and there before me, standing next to another well-dressed fiftyish suburbanite woman, is a smiling Judith Garson. And I thought she was going to the basketball game with Mr. IBM tonight.

"Hi, Beth. This is Karen. I'm so looking forward to the concert tonight, aren't you? We missed her last year when she was here," Judith beams.

So this is the "we" of the hot tub. Karen. This is good for Judith, better than I had imagined. She did customize her house to some extent. I am happy for her. Judith strikes me as being brave in a Barbara Stanwyck kind of way after all.

After seeing Judith with Karen, I am fully charged by the energy of this night. I have been shown that reality can outclass fantasy at times. Suddenly, a vision flashes before me and I believe that what I see is about to happen. I do not have time to stand and chat with Judith and Karen. I must run for the front door of the Continuing Education Center because I have seen that Lisa is going to fly through the door to be here with me. I forget for a moment that people in this culture rarely fly even though a few of us continue to dream about it.

"No one ever gets everything they want," Lisa told me once.

Maybe she was right. Maybe not a single person in the world ever does. Still, I refuse to give up. I run for the door and stare at it like a hungry dog outside a supermarket. The front door is closed and Lisa is not there. No, Lisa is still in Texas, alone in her house or with one of her two new lovers she tells me about over the telephone. I do not believe they are real but I make myself listen.

Lisa is not going to walk through that door. Should I jump in my car and drive back to Austin? Go back to a life that never felt like mine? Then I feel it. The pause button holding down my heart gives way. My vision of Lisa coming to me will not materialize into this reality but somehow the force of it kicked that button loose. I take one last look at Lisa as she exits the frame and the tape moves forward.

What do I do now? The tape is running. Well, I am a carpenter and I have my house to build. I want a house full of light and wood. Nothing fancy but a house that is solid and aerial all at the same time. A house where I can sit securely in these mountains and fly, too, all at the same time.

The house that Lisa and I could have shared will never be built and I cannot fix that fact in any way. Yes, I have to start thinking about my own house and where I will site it on my land for the best view possible of these crazy mountains. I stare at the blank front door.

This same unyielding door I have been begging at for what feels like an eternity now flies open and Rena sails back into the lobby.

"Girl, do I look like a ghost or something?" she asks.

"No, I was just thinking about one," I say. Rena takes my arm.

"Guess what. Jean Halton just asked me if I knew anyone who could build a platform for her futon bed. I told her you were a genius at bedroom furniture."

"If you're so brilliant at it my small project may not be much of a challenge," Jean says as she joins us, picking up the conversation where Rena so indelicately left it. Those lips up close and moving all at the same time could be impossible to resist someday. I think about what I am thinking about and turn beet red. I remind myself I have my house to build. Still, that does not mean I have to turn down all other projects. I open my mouth to answer Jean but Rena beats me to it.

"Beth was telling me just the other day that she has drawn up some new designs for bedframes she'd like to try out," Rena says.

"Why don't you come over tomorrow afternoon and I'll go over them with you. I want something unique," Jean says.

Lida Dowlearn

"Sure, that'll be fine," I say casually. That gives me all of tomorrow morning to come up with something.

"While you're at it, I have a table..."

"With a broken leg?" I ask. I am warming up to this project.

"How did you know?" Jean asks.

"Legs are usually the first things to go. They can weaken quickly."

"Do you do that kind of work, too?" she asks.

"It depends on the leg. I'll be happy to take a look at yours," I say.

Rena laughs. Now Jean turns red. The lights in the lobby go off and back on again. We stop our conversation and start to head for the auditorium. It is time to go in and listen to Martha Benson sing about the amazing sense and never-ending magic of women.

Fantasy/Humor

An Improbable Parable

by Chris Sitka

I am a thirty-eight-year-old lesbian activist of working class migrant parents living in Australia. My full time job is working as an (unpaid) lesbian researcher promoting lesbian culture. I compulsively write lesbian poetry, songs, stories, theory, articles and news for lesbian and women's publications.

I am engaged in researching parthenogenesis and lesbian herstory in prehistorical eras in order to help revive the memories and knowledge with which we can create a world-wide lesbian cultural revival. I hope that soon it will be possible again to live as simply and freely as Tumbalina Copperhead does in this story.

An Improbable Parable

Once upon a time, in the olden lands of Europe, there lived a lesbian called Tumbalina Copperhead. Tumbalina Copperhead had the longest, curliest, copperiest red hair you've ever seen. It radiated out from her head and tumbled in great locks all around her—right down to the ground! And it wasn't just long and curly and red; her hair was also incredibly tangled and wiry and tough.

Tumbalina Copperhead *never* combed her tresses, and she never brushed them, and she never washed them. She just let her hair grow wild and free. This lack of the usual limitations that heads of hair suffer from seemed to inspire her hair to grow unusually fast. It was as if it was trying to get somewhere, and get there in a hurry. Sometimes it grew inches a day.

But Tumbalina Copperhead was different from her hair. She wasn't in a hurry to get anywhere. She liked to take her time, wander, look around, and take things in slowly. For that reason she was strangely fortunate to have a head of hair with such a forthright mind of its own.

You see, Tumbalina Copperhead didn't have a job or a career or any vocation as such. Well, actually, she lived in a 'once upon a time' era when those things didn't exist. Tumbalina Copperhead was not the stay at home type; so she simply became the wandering possessor of a flamboyant head of hair. She walked from village to village, resting sometimes in the woods or by a stream or quiet pond.

Though Tumbalina travelled alone on her journeyings, don't imagine she was lonely. For one thing, she regularly encountered other lubricious lesbians at the seasonal lesbian festivals of yore. These great gatherings were no disco dabblings, where you danced divorced from elemental contact. Closing time never came as moon-touched lesbians danced up frenetic frenzies. Tumbalina's fiery lesbian passions were so inflamed that the times in between were a haven of memories to smoulder in.

Tumbalina's favourite everyday activities were contemplating life and watching all the wild creatures and birds. Never having read biology she was blessedly free from misconceptions in her perceptions; seeing two lesbian lizards embrace brought a happy smile to her face.

Such natural liveliness kept loneliness at bay. Tumbalina often hummed along with the bees. It was a humbling experience listening to their constant conversation on collective co-operation. She always marvelled at how skilled they were at running their busyness.

But business was not Tumbalina's forté. Her's was an idyllic life, even in the days of yore, because she didn't have to make a living. It wasn't that in those days lesbians didn't need to work (she certainly was no privileged upper class twity-flitty); it's just that in those days things were more flexible and undefined. And, you see, Tumbalina Copperhead had a natural talent. Well, it wasn't so much a talent as an attribute.

Tumbalina certainly didn't raise finances by appearing in the newspapers or on television or in films and documentaries as "A wild red-haired woman who wanders carefree in the countryside". They didn't *have* those sort of things then. Tumbalina Copperhead made her living, or better said, survived, in a much simpler way than that.

For one thing, Tumbalina's wondrous head of hair was so tangled, and so dense, and so plentiful, that while she wandered the woods and fields of yore, whenever she wanted to lie down and have a sleep she didn't think "I should have kept up my mortgage payments". No. She only needed to arrange her hair about her in such a way that it made a completely impenetrable, weatherproof shelter. It sufficed in most weathers.

I know women's hair is supposed to be soft and flowing and glowing as a shampoo commercial. But they didn't have shampoo in those days; things were different. Women weren't so particular about hair care. What's more, before the witch burnings lesbians could wander about the highways and byways in a downright carefree manner. Should they encounter evil in the usual male form there was the art of witchcraft to hold before one. There was great safety in it.

Should the lesbian leavenings of Tumbalina's thoughts or her resting place be disturbed, her wild woolly looks also served her well. She'd leap and burn about like a brush fire; red hair swirling in heat waves; flamboyantly excorcising her space.

Now I'm not saying that Tumbalina necessarily was or wasn't a witch. That's not the point of the story I'm telling. She certainly was a wise woman, and she certainly became ever more so from living wild and contemplating life all around her. She had no commitments, no responsibilities and plenty of time to enjoy herself. She did what she liked most: she travelled. Not travel as we know it: zoom, zoom, zoom at great expense. She never paid a penny, and she didn't have any luggage to carry either. That might be hardest of all for the reader to understand. So let me set the scene a bit more.

For one, we're talking about a long ago European setting. Dotted over the misty, green countryside, within reasonable walking distance of each other, were little villages connected by footpaths or dirt tracks. Villages were just a small collection of cottages and barns surrounded by fields. People in them were pretty much self-sufficient, growing and making everything they needed. They bartered and traded just a bit of extra stuff, especially at monthly markets in a slightly larger town nearby. Things were pretty simple and there wasn't any money to speak of. Two chooks were worth a goose and a bucket full of apples was worth one wooden shoe, even though you might need two. Throw in a bushel of wheat if you do. That's sort of how it worked.

Everyone knew each other and that was helpful in some respects, but rather boring too, because no-one moved around much. It was easy to become sort of stuck at home because you had to milk the cow, herd the goats, plant the barley, make the candles and all that. There wasn't money to take travelling and you couldn't just expect to be put up for nothing at all: life was pretty tight. Well, not tight, but you only produced as much as you needed, and it didn't stretch to entertaining lots of strangers who might drop in for a bite to eat while just out wandering the countryside. And it wasn't practical to walk long distances carrying, say, 65 pounds of butter or 25 wooden buckets to trade. One just couldn't manage it.

The only practical way to travel was to be free from the responsibilities of a farm (you just can't leave a milking cow or laying chooks to be preyed on by wolves) and so you needed to have a skill to offer in exchange for a bite to eat. Some lesbians used to travel carrying only a spindle. At night they would seek shelter and food; in exchange they would spin wool for the woman of the house.

An Improbable Parable

This was very helpful, as you would know if you've ever tried to hand spin enough wool to weave a whole blanket. And that's what you had to do if you wanted to be warm.

But travelling spinsters is another story. So don't let me digress. Tumbalina Copperhead did not carry a spindle. She didn't carry anything. Well, you might be thinking, she at least needed a blanket or something. During some times of year that might be true but travelling was made much easier in those days by the fact that they didn't go so much for fashion as for practicality.

Clothes were woven from pure wool replete with natural oils that repelled rain and retained body warmth. Lesbians, including Tumbalina, wore cloaks and things; it was a cold climate, there's no doubt about that. Still, lesbians were tougher and weren't so sooky about being caught out in the rain, and they didn't have to worry about their make-up running and that sort of thing. That would never have happened to Tumbalina Copperhead.

But sometimes it did snow. And I'm not pretending that Tumbalina Copperhead, fire woman that she was, could always take the cold out in the open. Nor, might I add, that she always wanted to be alone. Besides the many friendly creatures, there were lots of interesting lesbians to meet in the villages and market towns. She liked to discuss the meaning of life and sing songs with these women around a warm fire inside cosy walls on a winter's night. She also loved to snuggle up in the hay either alone or with someone she'd just grown fond of: be it a cow, or a horse, or a cat, or one of the village women.

A song which she often sang on such nights went:

> "Life should be easy, life should be fun.
> If something's not easy, it shouldn't be done.
>
> There is no basis
> in wild places
> for feeling dread
> of where to bed.
>
> I'm always burning I'm always learning.
> But I'll never do what makes me blue."

Not everyone thought life so easy. Of course in those days one didn't have to work and save for a new stereo or an as yet unrusted car. Still it was amazing how much was asked in exchange for a new carthorse, and how often you had to comb the sheep to get silkier wool. Cleanliness was not yet next to godliness; so the vacuuming could be left to another century. But having a house to keep you safe from the elements meant you had to keep replacing the thatch and then, should you decide to whitewash the walls more often than the neighbors, well that would well and truly keep you off the road. You'd only have time to play with the fairies of the forest at festivals. No gamboling in between.

But at least an industrious villager was assured there'd be food on the table. What, you might ask, did Tumbalina eat when she was out and about? I can tell you, she foraged in the woods for acorns, hazelnuts and berries. She also gleaned from the fields after harvest, but she never stole. She didn't need to. And she certainly didn't—it's almost too crass to mention, but as some cruder readers will think of it I must say—she didn't kill animals for food. No way.

Certainly being a skilled forager and herbalist helped Tumbalina Copperhead, but it wasn't her only resource. Just as the glowing aura of her flaming red hair and her serene self-assurance weren't all that protected her from the elements, it wasn't mere foraging through the four seasons of that clime that provided her food. And it wasn't all witchcraft. It could have been, but it wasn't.

No, Tumbalina Copperhead was unique. What she had to offer no-one else, in those times before factories, delivery trucks and supermarkets, or even corner shops, had. She became renowned for it. Women of the villages she sometimes passed through, or villages where they had heard of her, would often sigh and wish to see before them the vision of Tumbalina's hair curling and swirling down to the very ground approaching them, silhouetted against the backdrop of the sunset sky and the dark, mysterious village wood, while they sat wearily on the doorstep, scrubbing the pot in which they'd burned last night's barley gruel.

Most nights Tumbalina did appear at some lucky village and the women would warmly invite her in for dinner and company. Probably because she was so free and carefree, she had a generous

An Improbable Parable

spirit and a good sense of humour. But she didn't presume to impose on their hospitality just on that basis. She knew how hard they worked to get the food on their oaken tables.

As I said, Tumbalina Copperhead did have something useful to offer. And it was precisely so useful because no-one else could offer it; or even knew how to make a poor imitation of it.

Alright. I'll tell you what it was. It was her hair of course. Her hair would have been unique anywhere. There was no-one with hair quite like hers. What's more; it was so long, and so curly, and so fast growing; and so tangled, and so wiry, and so tough, and so proliferous—and so coppery—that wherever she stopped, she more than repaid any hospitality by simply cutting off handfuls of her hair and giving it to the women to use as pot scrubbers.

Humor

Weaver Loses Her Wa

by G. D. Rose

Ginna Dinah Rose, whose great-great-grandmother Dinah was the actual and very Dinah mentioned in "I've Been Working on the Railroad," is a tall, handsome, and wonderfully intelligent Celtic-descended witch especially devoted to the Lady of the Lake (who is Herself as nimble with a sword as many a Lezzie is with a pen). Before that she was a priestess of Seto in pre-nuclear Crete. What would make her whole century would be that Jesus, Mohammed, Marx and all those other male sky-gods would (should! please!) show up and take their left-brain crazed fanatic followers to Heaven, leaving the Earth to the rest of us creatures who like Her and appreciate Her. So be it!

Weaver Loses Her Wa

Weaver switched her tail irritably. Those two pussies were at it again, whispering to each other just outside her door. Weaver thought the two voices might as well belong to one cat, dementedly sing-songing to itself: psssb-psssb-psst-PSSSTBT! Mmmmrmmr? Hmnnnmn. Mmrt? Hmmmmn. But clearly there were two cats out there. The door made it impossible to understand what they were saying. Not that it mattered. Weaver knew it would be nasty comments.

After all, Weaver was New Cat in the house. She knew prior feline occupants always object to having their territory diminished, even if by just one room.

Weaver's golden eyes swept lazily across her New Room. From her perch on Mama-Marta's and Tabbitha-Mate's waterbed, Weaver felt pleased to count two large dressers, two cluttered bedstands, one rocking chair and one straight-back chair draped with jeans and rumpled undershirts: plenty of good lounging-spots for a big orange cat. Plus, a big beautiful east-facing window, open slightly to let in the luscious spring air, showed the branches of a majestic old pecan tree. Weaver's only objection to the place was its carpet, its stinky new carpet, which smelled somewhere between vinegar and burnt rubber. Being a connoisseur of scents, Weaver detested even walking on the vile stuff to get to her dish, litter box, or the door. It smelled up her paws and made licking them unpleasant. And so Weaver was keeping her big, bodacious, yellow-striped body on the bed, which was full of *wonderful* fragrances: Mama-Marta's, Tabitha's and her own. As time passed, the bed was also getting full of wonderful hairs: black, brown, yellow—some curly, some straight—but all of them short.

When Mama-Marta had first brought Weaver into this room just last week, there had been only Tabitha's smells—garlic and chocolate—punctuated by New Carpet. Right away though Marta had carried in familiar things, full of her own scent to add to the room.

Well, it was certain then, Mama-Marta had taken Tabitha to mate. The two wimmin must have read Weaver's cat-mind. They made strange cries, and grappled with each other all over the bed—purring, growling, and marking the sheets with their scents. All this made Weaver happy: nothing like good smells to bring sweet dreams and facilitate quiet afternoons contemplating the ineffable serene presence of the Dearest Goddess Basht, Queen of Cats, Divine Nature Unhindered and Unfolding. Weaver valued peace, harmony, and *wa*.

Which was what she'd been doing when she was so *rudely* interrupted by whispering pussies: fine-tuning her *wa*. Whispers. How juvenile. Out in the nut tree Basht was manifesting Herself as three gray mockingbirds. The sun had shone warm and lovely all morning, and now a tender breeze sifted through the windowscreen, mixing sounds of bird gossip with tree smells. Weaver especially liked that the leaves of Marta's potted rhododendron, recently placed on the window sill, were swaying faintly in the foreground. An excellent composition, visually serene in an Oriental way. "So beautiful..." she murmured.

Then, Weaver's moonyellow eyes narrowed. There, beside Marta's rhododendron, was a catrump's width of empty window sill. Though it might be a bit of a balancing act, Weaver thought she could fit there, to better appreciate the Goddess' birds.

It pleased Weaver to think of herself as a spiritual cat. Blessed with great size and strength, she tried for great self-control to match: in short, Weaver tried to achieve great *wa*. The idea of balancing on the window sill intrigued her.

Except...how could one properly focus the mind when one's peace was disturbed by ignorant turd-heads like those presently outside her door? Well, she grumbled, maybe it's time I do something about their bad manners.

Jumping from the bed, Weaver found herself wading through the acrid-smelling carpet pile, which did nothing to improve her annoyance, as she stalked to the door. The turd-heads must have heard her coming, because their whispering stopped.

"Hey you two mousies," Weaver growled, using the pejorative that all cats found offensive. "Back away from my door! You're interfering with my *wa*." She crouched down to glimpse their paws beneath the door, but New Rug filled in the doorcrack. There was no view, but phew! Weaver blew air out her nose. It certainly stank.

More whispering. Finally a high pitched voice, full of bravado, hissed back at her, "You're on *our* turf! We don't want you here! You better not come out or we'll fight the fur off you!"

Oh how original, thought Weaver disdainfully, as another voice, distinctly that of a youngster, chimed in, "Yeah!"

Weaver yawned and grated back. "Listen up, you two juvenile delinquents! I'm not scared of you. My Mama's taken your Mama to mate so that means I'm here to *stay*. You've got your territory and I've got mine. This is *my* room now. Besides," she paused and lowered her growl dramatically, "I'm a BIG CAT."

"Yeah, well there's two of *us*," Voice One spit back.

Big deal, Weaver shrugged, not dignifying the exchange with a reply. When the time was right, she'd show them. But for now she only wanted to get her over-sized extra-toed paws out of smelly carpet and back to comfy bed.

"We're not scared of Big Cats!" shrilled Voice One.

"Yeah! We're not scared of you!" squeaked Voice Two.

They were pissing Weaver off, not so much because they kept challenging her, which was only to be expected, but because they sounded so...so...je ne sais quoi...*stupid*! Weaver almost never had to actually fight other cats; they usually took one good look at her bulk, her breadth, her flashing tallow eyes and peace would come wafting through the air as if by magic. When persuasion was needed, she'd spread out her talons, six on one side and seven on the other...but with adolescents you never knew. They didn't always have good sense. Sometimes you'd have to knock them spinning.

If that's what it's going to take to harmonize with my new house-mates, Weaver grunted, I'd just as soon do it and get it over with. But there was that door between them. Full of pent-up belligerence, Weaver knoshed down a mouthful of kibble, chomping rather viciously, then looked up just in time to catch a flash of mockingbird-tail-white out in the nut tree. Her big tail lashed. Spontaneously she jumped for the window ledge.

If Mama-Marta had been a bit more tidy when moving her things into Tabitha's house, she'd have cleaned up the vermiculite that fell when she'd set her rhododendron on the window sill. And if she hadn't been tired—and more than a little eager to hop into bed with her sweetheart—she would have done something about that screen being popped out a bit in the corner; she was usually a neat and orderly person.

But since Mama-Marta had done neither, when Weaver's big, multi-toed feet hit the sill, vermiculite when flying, she hydro-planed against the screen, its other lower latch snapped open, and despite Weaver's frantic back-paddling the screen gave way, sending her soaring between the house and the nut tree!

Like frenzied windmills, Weaver's four legs were twirling, but there was nothing for her to grab onto. Twisting her big yellow body, she slapped past tree-leaves, entering a whirlpool of smells as she dropped: tree bark, car exhaust, bird dung, leaf mold, marigold—and, above all else, the overpowering odor of Dog. Dog! DOG!

Thunk! Weaver hit ground like a fur-covered stone, dizzy, fighting for balance, fortunately cushioned on impact by sweet, lemony, spring grass. But as soon as all four feet were securely under her, and her stomach stopped spinning, Weaver gagged: Dog smell.

Yet she kept her wits about her.

Flattening down like a badger, she looked around. Overhead the screen hung precariously, but she ignored *that*. The main thing was to find where Dog was—Dear Basht, may there be only one!

Starboard was the house. In fact, not ten pounces away she saw the main door with—of all things!—a pet door in it! Its hinged metal flap was small, cat-sized, perfect! To her left was the nut tree. So far, so good; two escape routes close at hand. The yard was a big one. After a moment's search, she saw a chain-link fence. Looking down its course led her to a dark-colored lump, far off to her left. That must be Dog.

Dog was looking her way, but above her.

Maybe Dog watched birds, too.

(Willow, Tabitha's good-natured black dobie, was actually watching the screen teeter back and forth and wondering if she should go investigate.)

Weaver decided to make a run for the pet door—a slow and sneaky run. Maybe Dog wouldn't see her. If she couldn't get in, she'd backtrack to the nut tree and hang out with mockingbirds until Mama-Marta came to rescue her. Mockingbirds would be rough, but she'd take them over Dog any day. If the pet door were locked, she might have to. Weaver wriggled her tiger-striped hips getting ready to dash.

Just then the pet door flap moved a little.

A distinctly pointy-chinned little cat-face showed its fangs and made a nasty grimace at her through gray and white fur.

"You don't look so tough!" Grayface sneered. "Don't come this way!"

"Yeah!" came the echo, chirping, "Don't come over here!"

"Being a Big Cat can't help you now!"

"Yeah! You don't look so Big anyway!"

Swaying, the pet door parted slightly farther; in the crack Weaver made out a second set of quivering whiskers and blink of evaluating eyes. Little Miss Echo sported the same pointy face as her gray and white mother, only hers was black. They both had white paws which were hard to ignore because they were pushed all the way forward to block Weaver's entry through the pet door. The pair stared at her malevolently, silently, daring her to come their way.

Under any other circumstances, Weaver would have charged and ripped the whiskers from their smug faces, but at the moment she was more concerned about Dog. It would be upon her before she could win a cat-fight and get in to safety. Dogs could be mighty fast if they wanted to, and they had big crocodilian teeth.

A big dog had done her in, third life.

She tensed. No time to reminisce! The lump by the fence was slowly hunkering to its feet. To the tree!

Pow! OUCH! Something ripped at her head! What in holy catdom...???

With a burst of staccato screams, one of Basht's mockingbirds triumphantly skimmed the grass in front of her, white tail flickering, a tuft of yellow head-fur in its beak. Fast as a flash, dazed and furious, Weaver lost her wa and instinctively lunged forward...

...where she found herself nose to nose with Little Miss Echo. From her crouch behind the pet door, the young black kitten had also lunged forward, reacting from her feline genes to the mockingbird's close pass. Startled, the little midnight cat looked into Weaver's

G. D. Rose

rugged Bengal face, then off to her right.

It was a moment Weaver would never forget. Little Miss Echo spat then danced up on her toes, every hair slowly standing straight out. Seven leaps away quivered the pet door, Grayface peeking anxiously at them both. Then came the percussion of galloping feet. Weaver didn't take time to look. She charged the pet door like a locomotive, not caring that she knocked over Echo-Cat, who hit dirt then frantically somersaulted in behind her. The Orange Express whacked open the pet door with her solid pate, ears straight back, then collided head on with grayface, who was backing up, but not fast enough. In a moment, all three panicky cats tangled like yarn, spitting, yowling, and hissing like teakettles.

A screaming, scrabbling ball of fur, each cat desperately sought to dig claw into something that would propel her *away* from the pet door. It swung back and forth, one ominous time, showing daylight, then suddenly burst inward. The ugliest monster-face Weaver had ever seen pushed its snout and snickering teeth to within inches of her legs. Hurtling themselves outward, the two smaller cats skidded across tile, away and out of reach, while Weaver flew straight up, an orange rocket.

Suddenly it was quiet.

She dared breathe and look.

Below, on her left, snout-nose was snuffling up the scent of cat. The monster's muzzle seemed to be stuck in the pet door, its toothy jaws and palpitating schnoz uselessly, horribly, drooling. But she was safe. Weaver took a shaky breath. She feared and hated dogs as much as she loved the Goddess Basht. Dogs were evil. Cats were good. How could it be that Tabbitha, whom Mama-Marta had taken to mate, kept such evil so near at hand? Weaver realized she would have to re-evaluate Tabbitha. But later.

Where were the mousies? Oh, right in front of her, down and center. Cautiously, for the second time within a few minutes, Weaver took her bearings. She was midway up a stairs, couldn't remember exactly how she got so high up, but she was glad to find herself in a good defensive position. With a loud snort, and to every cat's great relief, dog-snout finally withdrew. Only a gleam of saliva remained. Grayface, five feet away from the first step, started making a show of cleaning her front paws, while Echo-Cat crouched nearby.

Weaver spat, showed her fangs, and puffed up for their benefit. Of course she hadn't looked like much out in the yard, all scrunched down—let them get a look at the real her!

Grayface paused and they both stared. This time neither one seemed to have a word to say.

Weaver, satisfied she'd made the right impression, rotated her shoulders. Dog had scared her more than she wanted to admit. She felt tight all over, something no cat likes. She flexed her neck and relaxed enough to notice that here on the stairs the carpet was worn down and didn't stink at all. In fact, it smelled rather pleasant with an odor she couldn't quite place.

Just below her nose, resting on the third step, was a small fuzzy torpedo-shaped thing, dangling a string, and sending out an alluring, spicy fragrance. Weaver extended her neck so that she could get a big inhalation. Wonderful!

Down on the kitchen tile, watching, gray-faced Hera whispered to her midnight-black daughter, Sugar, "Look! She's gonna get snockered!"

"Holy Hannah," Sugar gasped. "She's one BIG CAT, you know?"

They both were smarting in a few places where Weaver's claws had dug in during her desperate climb up the stairwell wall. To preserve their dignity, however, both refrained from licking their wounds. Neither wanted to give Weaver the satisfaction.

"She's big," agreed Hera. Even though she was street-smart (a life from which Tabitha had rescued her before Sugar was born), in all her life Hera had never seen a cat as big as Weaver. She'd seen meaner-looking ones, but not bigger. "In a few minutes that catnip is gonna knock her silly." Hera didn't say so but she thought it could make Weaver dangerous as well.

By this time Weaver had rolled down a couple of steps and was on her back doing her best to disembowel the fuzzy-fragrance thing. Raking it with her back claws caused a most delightful cloud of incense to waft all around her. A few more kicks, and the incense thickened almost into an airy gel. Through it she peered outward. She remembered the beautiful face of Basht, looking like an elegant Egyptian short-hair, seated on the crescent moon. Supplicants had entered the temple.

"Minions of Basht!" she wailed, whiskers quivering, "I will receive your gifts!" She tried to get herself upright, into a beatific pose, but couldn't quite succeed. That's all right, she consoled herself, I'll be gracious to my worshippers no matter what triflings they bring me. Two skinny little things they were, these supplicants. They seemed bashful.

"You may approach!" she growled. Where were the priestesses, anyway? If there were supplicants, there should be priestesses around somewhere. Well, she knew the lingo. If it was the priestesses' day off, she could fill in well enough without them.

Weaver cleared her throat and began yowling out the Great "Basht is gracious! She is the light of the eternal! She is life! She is force! She is the wind that carries scent!"

Hera recognized Weaver's chant, having also, like so many reincarnates, spent one of her lives in Ancient Egypt. "She is the beauty of the green earth!" Hera rejoined.

"She is the source of all mice!" bawled Weaver.

"She is the source of all birds!" sang out Hera and Sugar.

"Fish!" yodeled Weaver.

"Lizards!" cried Sugar, surprising herself.

"She is the pale light among the stars!"

"She is the joy in the heart of all cats!" Weaver sang out, "Beloved and blessed Basht, smile on us!"

Weaver lay panting. She couldn't remember any more. It seemed her petitioners couldn't either. Where were those damn priestesses?

"Bring me your gifts," she growled, flexing her front paws.

"Sugar, quick," whispered Hera, "Go get some kibbles."

Sugar turned her pointy face up in question but Hera hissed, "Don't waste time! Do it!"

Hera had just counted the claws on Weaver's magnificent fists. She'd also just figured out that Weaver was bigger than the two of them put together.

Sugar reappeared pushing kibbles, skritch-skritch, in front of her.

"Oh excellent Cat, beloved of our dearest Goddess Basht," extemporized Hera, "Be pleased to accept our most humble gift."

To her daughter, Hera raised a whisker and muttered, "Stand back now."

Weaver condescended to inspect and then accept the gifts, humble though they were. A fresh mouse would have been more fitting an offering, but then, these petitioners looked hard up. Kibbles were probably the best they could do. Perhaps they could improve their gift with quantity, since the quality was lacking.

"More?" she inquired hopefully. The adrenaline was wearing off along with the catnip and she was hungry.

"Sure," said Hera, lashing her tail for Sugar to stay put. "Just follow me." Already the mother-cat, who was indeed small and lean, but nobody's fool, began thinking of what Weaver could do for her.

Five minutes later Weaver, having eaten her fill from Tabitha's ten-pound bag of Friskies, (Hera showed her where it sat and looked the other way while Weaver gnawed a hole through the paper), prepared a nice blessing for her new housemates. They'd risen to the occasion after all. Her *wa* was back, they were all safe, and she hadn't had to fight. She was happy. She smiled.

"You will live to an old age. You will grow fat and sleek. No dog nor crocodile shall injure you. You will enjoy peace in your household." Weaver felt expansive. "And now, dear Hera and Sugar," she murmured, "It's back to my wa for me. See you later." Tail raised, she ascended the stairs and curled up on a chair in Tabitha's vacant office.

Hera shook her head and murmured to Sugar, who was eagerly chowing down from the hole in the bag that Weaver had left open: "Holy Manx, can you beat that?"

•

Marta got home first, leapt up the stairs as Lesbians are prone to do, and threw her knapsack onto the bed, oblivious to Weaver wandering in through the open door behind her. Marta's mind was on getting a shower before Tabitha got home. She stripped off her work clothes, threw them in the laundry basket, and turned just in time to see Weaver jumping up on the big unmade bed.

"So there you are!" She smiled, rubbing her yellow-orange tiger under the chin. Weaver purred a little in her usual Mama-Marta greeting. Absent-mindedly, Marta put a few kibbles into the cat dish, which today was fuller than usual. Carefully, she closed the bedroom door behind her as she made her way to the shower.

"It's too soon," Marta thought, grabbing soap, "Too soon to try to introduce Weaver to Tabbie's cats. We'll give her more time to settle in."

•

It was Tabitha, that evening, who saw that the screen was almost falling. She noticed it when she went to close the window for the night.

"Wow," she sighed to Marta, who was looking most inviting stretched out across the waterbed. "Look at this! Good thing we caught it before it came all the way undone!" Conscientiously, she pulled the frame in and re-latched the fastenings, making it secure. Then, turning to Weaver who was sound asleep at the foot of the bed and lost in cat-dreams, she murmured, "Wouldn't want you to fall out, would we?"

Tabbie went downstairs and said goodnight to Willow, her dobie, Sugar and Hera, her cats, then rolled into her own dream-land with Marta. They nuzzled each other.

"Goodnight, sweetheart."
"Goodnight, love."
"Goddess bless."
"You too."
"Meow."
"Meow."
"Meow."

Erotica

Fair Play

by Rae Wheeler

Rae Wheeler is the pen name of Molleen Zanger, who invented her as she invents her own life: making it up as she goes along then making it true. Molleen would like to stand alone, but Rae won't have it and besides, the name has been lucky. Rae has been published in Common Lives/Lesbian Lives *and* Erotic Fiction Quarterly. *Rae (which Molleen consistently mistypes as Raw) is working on a poetry manuscript and has written a novel which Molleen is trying to market.*

Molleen writes for a weekly newspaper (births, deaths and infinitives) and longs for a time, say noon next Tuesday, when everyone everywhere will suddenly be able to drop all their masks and pretenses and just be who they are. Against that day she toys with names for her new self: Molleen NLI, maybe? Molleen Ladydyke? Molleen Molleen? In the meantime she is considering enrolling in barber college. Trim, anyone?

Fair Play

Make love to me! I scream at her silently. *Touch me!*

But her hands are on the steering wheel, driving competently, confidently.

She thinks she would not know how to, but I know she would. In her secret heart she already knows and would be as skilled and competent at loving women, at loving me, as she is at driving this car.

I steal another glance at her hands. She is keeping time to jazz with her right hand now on the shift lever. Her hands are so beautiful. They fascinate me: such feminine hands on such a guy. My heart catches every time I see her. She swears this is all new to her but it is so hard to believe. She exudes butch. It is how I made this ghastly mistake.

This ghastly mistake has led us to going away together for the weekend. To a jazz concert, but I am already so jazzed I can barely talk.

We are going to make love on this weekend. This has been decided. She has made all the decisions from the beginning—at least from the night I came out and on to her. She said it had to be this way. Because I've wanted her so intensely from the moment we met, I have forced discipline over my impulses. Impulses have dictated my entire life until this woman.

We met on a fluke, the exact kind of fluke I expected to happen someday, in a few years maybe. I was doing my job, going about my business, always hoping but not looking. I have always believed the best things are found by not looking for them and this time I was right. But first she had to decide.

Decide what?

I have never asked.

Decide to experiment?

Decide to explore?

Decide to admit?

Would it matter? We are here now, going away together to hear jazz and make love in another town. After all the restraints, after all the holding back, I am now supposed to teach her. It must be some kind of karmic thing, for me to be always teaching someone how to love, how to show love, make love, live love. It wearies me, some years. Some years I have taken sabbatical. But it seems I must always return to this. Even now.

As I watch her lovely hand keep time to the music I cannot help but notice the distance that hand is to my knee, an almost equal distance to my...oh, god, there I go again. Hot. I get so hot just thinking about her touching me. In discomfort I cross my legs, holding in the want.

I can hear her smile and I glance again at her profile. A grin is there, a knowing grin. She knows what she does to me. I don't know if I do the same to her. Although we have kissed and groped a little, I am not convinced that I arouse her. I feel like I am in this heat alone.

Selfish bitch that I am, it is enough.

I reach and curl the back of my hand into her palm. A submissive gesture. Submission is so new and scary to me, more threatening than lust or love.

I love her. I would not have to love her to want to make love with her, but I do. I try to not let it show, but I suspect she knows.

I suppose I like complexities or I would not have sculped this life for myself. Contradiction, complexities and controversy. The three C's. I could create an entire seminar around them.

Her hand is on my knee now, casually, like it just drifted down there like a feather or a falling leaf. A bonfire is loosed under my skin.

I am a sensualist. I have told her that the best way to teach someone anything is to show them, not tell them. And that what drives one person wild will put another to sleep. And that the first time with any new person is often not totally fulfilling, is seldom totally fulfilling. But I tell her this so that she is not disappointed in me.

My secret, my private shame, is that I am never disappointed. I am so embarrassed by this I cannot tell her although I believe she needs to know. But I am afraid she will quickly tire of me when she learns what a weak challenge I am.

Hair trigger is what I call me. Maybe that's why a year or two of seduction followed by about a month of foreplay is so important to me. Without long lingering glances, deep slow kisses and sensual strokings it would all be over for me in sixty seconds flat.

Fortunately, this flaw has been more than compensated for by a gift for multiple orgasms. I once tried to measure my capacity but gave up, gasping.

Her casual hand now curls and she slowly draws her closely clipped nails up my thigh. Maybe she knows. She knows so much more than she admits, even to herself. I reach across to her lap and she pulls her hand away, removing mine with the same motion.

Not yet, she says, her face going stony as it does when I have, once again, gone too far. She torments me this way. Come here come here come here go away go away go away. I have relinquished my title to her; now I am the hungry one. Hundreds of half forgotten names and faces cheer to see me sample my own medicine.

The highway seems endless. Our conversation is strained. With no one else do I have such difficulty talking. I suspect it has something to do with wanting to end each sentence with I want you.

Did you get that shipment straightened out, I want you.

How was work, I want you.

Any promising applicant yet, I want you.

I want you.

I want to take your face in my hands and kiss your lips and your eyelids, and the line of your jaw. I want your earlobes. I want to unbutton your shirt and slide it off your body. I want to touch your skin, slide your bra straps off your shoulders. I want to massage you: your shoulders and neck and back, your arms and your breasts, I want to tweak and kiss and suck your nipples until you moan, moan with wanting me. I want to unbuckle your belt and unfasten your pants. I want to wrap my arms around your waist and kiss your skin, and to trace the round softness of your flesh with my eyes closed, memorizing your body. With my hand flat on the inside of your thigh I want to move up and touch your mons. With aching fingers I want to explore the inner folds of your damp private parts and feel them slick and hot on my fingers. I want to probe with one finger then two then three intertwined then none, to hear you moan again, and then with my thumb I want to slide into another opening, as with tongue and teeth and lips and hands I pull you toward your orgasm and then...

"We're here," she says, pulling into the parking lot.

My knees are weak from the force of my fantasy and I nearly stumble as we check in. We carry our bags to our room. We have hours before the concert, hours to explore the town. Windowshop, sightsee, scope a likely restaurant for dinner.

I am preoccupied with my decompression and barely notice our surroundings. I am trying to clear my mind as she shuts the door behind us and takes my bag from me, placing it beside hers on the floor.

"Hey," she says, "talk to me." Then taking my face in her hands she kisses my lips, my eyelids and the line of my jaw and nuzzles my earlobes.

She unbuttons my shirt.

Relationships

Unlikely Places

by Ann Tabachnikov

Ann Tabachnikov is a native New Yorker, and a thirty-eight-year-old Jewish lesbian with a Russian temperament. She dreams about leaving for a nice quiet place with a green yard and a white picket fence. But this nasty, gleaming city is still too hard to leave. Ann spends most of her time teaching, writing and madly adoring her lover of more than two years. Unlikely Places *is her first published work. She thinks that being exactly who you are should be everyone's life's work.*

Unlikely Places

That I should have such feelings for her—a German girl, a kraut, my little Panzer-head. She's beautiful, sure. But that *I* should have such a weakness for her strictly Aryan good looks (which have kept me in this cursed Fatherland for nearly two years now), I feel sure is causing my sweet little Bubby Rivkah to turn over in her grave and spit three times. Ach, ach, ach. But really, it's pretty great. Except for the guilt, of course—a great, terrible sword in the belly and crotch at the first hint of arousal: the sight of Nina's thin lips, always a little wet, or her breasts, possibly her best feature (except for her mind), mainly because they're so strangely large for such a thin girl, like two healthy tomatoes on a too-fragile vine. Oh yes. I often tell her, "Nina, you really could have been a model, if not for these astounding titties of yours." I do it to make her scowl at me. Nina scowls magnificently.

Nina insists that the guilt is what I love the most about us. "After all," she says in her best upper-class British accent, "you *are* Jewish, my dear girl." This incites me beyond belief. I yell, call her an arrogant fuck. "And what about *your* guilt, fraulein? You're telling me you love me just for my sunny disposition?" "What you think?" she asks, wide-eyed now, the little milkmaid, which turns me on like crazy. Sometimes, though, there's nothing I can do about it, not till I've had a few snorts of Slivovitz.

If I overdo it and get too looped (or just too nasty), Nina sees only the gruesome specter of her alcoholic father, and stays away.

But most times I'm pretty friendly, drunk or not. So she might sit on my lap and I'll pet her, giggling and whispering tentative endearments and insults. My favorite is "zeesn courveh," Yiddish for "sweet whore," but which any German will understand. Nina insists that she hates it: "Now that is dreadful, it's awful. It's really going too far." Does she ask me to stop? What you think?

My first week here, I ran around the dark, rainy streets, the picture of tormented youth in my distressed leather bomber jacket and silver star of David, which I displayed with studied unconsciousness to any shopkeeper or museum guard I came in contact with.

But the fact that I was in Germany (ostensibly on vacation) was not the only thing behind my crisis of Jewish identity. There had been no woman in my life for so long that the blonde beauties who now surrounded me were provoking sudden, feverish staccatos across my whole over-stimulated little frame. Treacherous renegade that I was, I had no choice but to become this silent, scowling keeper of the Judaic flame. Finally, I found the perfect outlet for my positively frothing Jewish agonies: a program of sacred songs by the Cantor Shmuel Grossbach at a little Jewish center across town.

I sat in the last row, rocking and nodding at a big black beard from which emerged a truly stupendous baritone. When he began belting out the Kol Nidre, I thought I wouldn't last. Strange, unrecognizable passions were being torn from me. They came from ancient cities, long buried in desert sands. (I know now that these are the same passions that Nina draws from me, every time she moves her long fingers across my cheek, or lays her breasts exactly against mine. Go figure.)

I *did* last though, right through to the end, beating my breast and tearing at my precious leather jacket. I was sore afflicted, and loving every minute of it. On the way back to my hotel, I passed an old Lutheran church I'd been meaning to see. Perverse little soul that I am, I went in.

Before I had a chance to sit, I was drawn to a still figure towards the front. Her smooth blonde hair went at least halfway down a straight, slender back. Aha, I thought. I imagined cool blue eyes focused directly on the altar, forthrightly confronting a stringent yet reasonable Protestant God.

I walked down the center aisle and sat across from her. Looking out of the corners of my eyes I saw tears, large and profuse, running down pale cheeks blotched with red. "I have to," I thought. Then began one of the many internal dialogs which were to become a daily staple of my first months with Nina.

"After all," I said, "Why not? Why else did I come to this strange and terrible place but to consort with the enemy?"

But How? Will you sit next to her and offer her a hankie? Wait outside and follow her home, skulking in and out of shadows?

You're no good at that; she'll see you. No matter what you try, she'll think you're a twisted, dangerous character. Go to a bar if you want to meet a woman, not a church.

I countered: "You have no adventure, no romance in that dry, dusty soul!"

Look, I snapped back rudely, I've been putting off telling you this, but now that you're haunting churches, I feel I have to be blunt. This is not healthy, this obsession of yours with these German broads. It is weird and sick and it makes my skin crawl to be in the same body with you!

Now, I figure that weirdness and obsession are about as Jewish as circumcision or guilt. But sickness implies something sticky and yellow, like the inside of that caterpillar my brothers insist I ate when I was four. (I only pulled it apart.)"Look," I said reasonably, "Don't you see the possibilities for personal growth here? For great spiritual catharsis?"

Of course, it could be you're not yourself, on account of being so close to so much shikseh nookie for the last week, but—

"Oh, Christ, is it just me, or is everyone nauseous?"

—to paraphrase that other weird, obsessive Jew you secretly admire so much (and remember, the Goyim crucified him), let's shake the dust of this crummy little town from our collective feet and direct them to the nearest airport.

No chance. Now I had something to prove.

The blonde got up, wiping both cheeks with long, graceful fingers. As she moved towards the door I noticed something I'd missed before as I'd studied her tears: She was beautiful. She wasn't "pretty" or "striking." She was the essential Shikseh Goddess and—

—and oh boy, is she gonna jump at the chance to meet a morose, neurotic, slightly fat Bronx Jew!

As she passed, she darted her eyes—such deep blue ones, dark ones—over me then away from me several times. I decided to be encouraged by this.

I walked out of the church behind her. I couldn't be doing this, I thought. It was very heady, this ghastly freedom. Outside, I didn't waste any time. "Look," I said.

She did. All around. "At what?" she asked. She had answered me in English with no hesitation at all.

"Eh no. I mean, can I—uh, talk to you?"

The back of my neck was sweating ice. I hadn't even considered making up some pretense, just gone and spat out the truth.

No one but Nina can look into a person with such stillness. Then she gave a little nod and just the beginning of a smile. I considered asking if anything was wrong, that I couldn't help but notice her crying. But that wasn't why I approached her, and something in her bearing told me I'd never get the chance to lie to this lady twice.

"No, no. I mean, I just—I just want to talk to you. For awhile, you know. Just for a few minutes. Not—not about anything specific."

She kept the little smile, but raised an eyebrow. Talk fast, kid. I gave what I hoped was a relaxed, charming grin.

"You see, I've been here about a week, and I don't know anyone. Also, I speak no German, really, and well, gosh, frankly it gets just a bit lonely. And to be perfectly honest, I'd like to have a nice conversation with a friendly person. It's embarassing, ma'am, but there you have it." (Well gosh-oh-gee, ma'am, it's the All-American dyke!)

"Well OK. But we must avoid sex and politics, because then it wouldn't be a nice conversation."

"Ah, you're very kind to a lonesome traveller." I realized I had just about quoted the title of that old folk song and bit my lip hard to keep from laughing.

"Not at all. I spent three months in the States for my work. If some people had not been so kind, I would still be looking on Fifth Avenue for the Empire Building."

"I'm sure you'd have found it eventually. It's kind of hard to miss."

She looked down at my feet as I shifted from one to the other. She said, "So, we can have a cup of coffee?"

I accepted gratefully, introduced myself and stuck out my hand, much too intensely. She asked, "What is your last name?"

When I told her, she looked delighted.

"That's so beautiful, so Russian." So Jewish, I thought, But really only to a Russian, kind of like the Soviet "Goldstein." I also don't look the part, with my blue eyes and little shikseh nose. And the perpetual Star of David around my neck was hidden beneath my jacket just then.

"Now you have me at a disadvantage, madame."

"My name is Nina. But since we're being formal, you can call me Frau Wagner."

"Fine. And you can call me Comrade."

"I will call you Tovarich. Or is it Tovaricha?"

"Whichever you like. Whichever you think fits."

Out the corner of my eye, I could see her face grow thoughtful. I soon learned she often looks this way.

She took me to a cafe she said she liked. "Great coffee—you'll see. Not like in America."

On the way, Nina speculated as to the obvious inability of Americans to make a decent cup of coffee, and I scoured her landscape for hardness, for some strange, unforgivable Nazi trait: a taut, stern face or the fast, cold step of a big black boot. Nina turned her head in my direction and smiled that little smile.

We sat outside. Although the seats and tables were wet from the constant rain of the last week, the smell in the air was irresistible. We wiped off some chairs with a newspaper and sat carefully.

Nina had merry eyes—always very active, very bright, even when the rest of her face was downright sombre, which it often was. This appealed to me enormously, like a lot of things about her. In fact, in two years I haven't found a single thing to dislike about Nina. Even the things that make me spit venom all over the house, I like. Especially these.

We talked quietly. She had a still, penetrating stare and asked me a lot of questions. Again and again, I was struck by how beautiful she was. She seemed genuinely impressed when I said I was a writer, but not surprised, as if I were only confirming a suspicion.

I can't say I fell in love with her that day, or any particular day. But I found myself wanting to tell her things. I went on and on, about my work, my family, especially my mother.

"Why (the poor woman must ask herself daily) am I not a devoted Jewish daughter? *(There, it's out!)* Why am I not married to a doctor, making smart Jewish babies?"

She put one hand on her hip and frowned. "Yes, *why* aren't you?"

"Because I'd rather be here talking to you."

"Ach! I can just imagine what your Mama would think about *that*. What did she say when you told her you were coming to Germany?"

I may have flapped my lips a few times. But mainly I remember staring down at the table, where my hands were very busy tearing my napkin to shreds. I watched open-mouthed as her own calm hands covered mine, quieting them.

"I see. Where does she think you are?"

"Paris," I said miserably, sure that she found me a useless wimp. *Any second now, mameleh, she's gonna remember a previous engagement; she's gonna get up and—*

That little smile again, somewhere between sadness and irony. "Well, then you better remember to bring her the six-inch Eiffel Tower."

I laughed too long and too loud.

It suddenly became my mission to see her teeth—I wanted to make her smile so wide that her face cracked. I wanted to hear uproarious laughter from her.

"And have you considered, Frau Wagner (I made sure to pronounce it "Vagner"), *why* there is only one Eiffel Tower? No? Because it eats its young."

I didn't get the laugh but her eyes widened and she *did* smile in a strange, intentional way, almost like she was really displaying her teeth for me. They were the teeth one would expect a girl like Nina to have—very white and even, except I could've sworn one was missing.

•

We met many times that week, and the next. We always parted with careful nonchalance, then found a reason to ring the other up later that day or the next morning. Nina showed me her town, and what it had to offer. We took an early train to Berlin and stared blankly at The Wall.

"Nina, as an American, I find this incomprehensible."

"Then as an American, I am sorry to say, you are very naive."

I just grunted and shook my head, neither a yes nor a no.

As a woman, I told her, I understood walls and prisons very well.

"But then—" I shuddered.

"You're cold?"

"No."

"Then what?"

"As a Jew, I see this and it's—more than fair. In fact, it's not nearly enough."

"Still," she murmured.

"Still? Oh, Nina, talk about naive! Look, I have a South American friend who will never go to Spain. And she's hardly the fanatic type. But just suggest that maybe it's time to put the events of 400 years ago in a different perspective, and she rattles off a list of old atrocities against South American Indians, make your hair stand on end. Look at Northern Ireland, for God's sake. And do you think slavery is a dead issue to Black Americans? Should American Indians be all ready to forgive and forget? 'Still,' Nina? Try *forever*."

"You paint a terrible picture. How can there ever be peace if all the evil done in the past can't be resolved, finally, and forgiven?"

"Maybe there can't be."

I wouldn't look at her for a long time. I knew if I did, I couldn't hold on to my hatred.

On the train ride back, I went into the bathroom and leaned my head against the cool glass of the mirror. I heaved some dry sobs and thanked God for the four little walls of my apartment, and the prosperous inertia they shared with me. I threw some cold water on my face and went back to my seat. Nina followed me with her eyes and I stared at her openly.

"I am sorry if I seem—not to understand why you feel as you do. Believe me, I have learned all about the holocaust, and it has given me great pain. But I must believe in a future."

"I'm glad you do. I mean it. Someone has to."

"You look profoundly sad."

"Something else I wanted to tell you back at The Wall, before I started lecturing. As a Jew, there are places I don't want to go."

"But you *do* go. You came here. And you came as a Jew, didn't you?"

•

Nina was a music therapist by profession, and by nature. Once at a concert, as we listened to a dark, ominous piece by Beethoven, she began whispering to me excitedly that she "must, simply must" use that piece for one particular patient of hers. "He's so depressed, the poor man, yet he tries so hard to pretend to energy, to optimism. I'm convinced it's a result of behaviorist treatment. Those fascisti!" A few people began shushing in our direction. Nina smiled at them, apologized profusely, then went on: "So I think if I use this magnificent, terrible piece on him, he might begin to surrender to his sadness. It's the only way, the only way..."

She adored the song *Let It Be*. It had an eerily calming effect on her. Her eyes got misted over and she would start to rock and hum softly. It's all the reference to Mother Mary, no doubt, and Nina's unfulfilled yearning for Catholicism, nurtured by her beloved Italian grandmother.

"It's funny," she once told me, "I've always read a lot about Judaism, and felt—ach, what is the word for it?—like respect, but more, you know? Humility?"

"Awe?"

"Ach, yah! Das ist. *Awe*. Because it's so civilized, I think. Also, the Jews don't have this—em—*afterlife*. You're not obsessed as we Christians are with living forever. I mean it's ashes to ashes and the rest is a big question. It's like to me a certain maturity. No need for fairy tales. But for this same reason, I couldn't have more than a—a desire of the mind, of the *intellect*."

"Nina, do *you* think the afterlife is a fairy tale?"

"I don't know. I just know I can't give it up. In fact, some place in me wants more. Something more—I forget—primary?"

"Primitive? Primal?"

"Primal, yes!"

Nina explained how the Catholics really understood the need for ritual, for living mythology.

"So, Ninotchka, if you feel so strongly about it, why don't you convert to Catholicism?"

"Ach, are you kidding? It's so *stupid*. And all that *sheise* about abortion. No, I couldn't. I'd lose all respect for myself. I'd rather stay bored but reasonable. The perfect Lutheran."

For a second, I was tempted to suggest other ways one might attain the passionate transcendence she craved so. I'm glad I didn't. With a woman like Nina, timing is everything.

A little later I told her, "Nina, I think you're wrong about

Unlikely Places

Judaism; it's more than 'civilized.' The real *passion* of Judaism is buried under tons of mystical crap now, but there *is* the Kabbalah. That's if you're really interested in spiritual passion. And ecstasy." I drew out the word ecstasy as long as decently possible, and stared into her baby blues. "But then maybe not, maybe not."

Oh, her interest was more than piqued. "*Why* not? What are you getting at?"

"Well, it still doesn't give you answers, you see. If anything, it makes the mystery of God even more intolerable. No, you goyim can't take that. No Nina, on second thought, *don't* read Kabbalah."

I smiled what I hoped was my most ingratiating. Nina, for a change, was stunned into silence, wide-eyed and truly outraged. Suddenly, she tilted her head coquettishly and returned my smile.

I was thrilled and a little frightened. I took great care to treat her very gently for the rest of that day. When she left to meet a friend, I took her hand in both of mine.

"Thank you, Nina." It felt like taking a liberty suddenly, to say her name.

Nina's facial expressions were those of a cat. "Thank *you,* my dear."

She walked away from me, waving backwards Italian-style. Again, I was seduced by the way she moved: she was graceful, expansive, and the way her beige skirt played over her hips made me think of a mother caressing her favorite child's head.

I was surprised when she turned back and said, "I'm glad you didn't say you're sorry."

"Yeah, well, I'm *not* sorry." Not if you don't want me to be.

•

On Sunday, we decided on a light breakfast and a trip to the zoo. Nina called it "The Big Zoo." I explained to her that there were no big zoos in this city. "Where we're going is the little zoo. The other one is the littler zoo."

"Ach, the American has spoken. The New Yorker."

"Well, c'mon Nina," I whined good-naturedly, "if this is the big zoo, what do you call the Bronx Zoo?"

"Noah's Ark! One can hardly appreciate it, it's so big."

"Well, ya gotta walk fast."

"Yah, well today we walk slow and enjoy ourselves, OK?"

"I guess I can handle that."

"Gut."

She slid her arm through mine, and pressed close. There was no doubt that the constant press and rub of her breast against my arm was intentional. But of course *I* doubted it. She couldn't want *me*, could she? Not me.

There had been no more rain for at least a week, and the air was in that transitional April stage, neither warm nor cold, but incredibly sweet. I tilted my head back to see a clear blue sky. The word *romance* came to me. I could die now, I remember thinking.

Surely it was time to tell her, to show her my open heart? I kept silent, and a sadness filled the wide space between us.

Nina, with what should have felt like blessing, but instead surfaced like diabolical timing, said, "I love you, you know, dear." Sure, I knew that.

Something live was uncoiling within me. In a high, tinny voice, I managed, "I love *you*, Nina." Yes, it was true, and so what? The air was suddenly damp and oppressive, and the streets cockeyed. There would be barbed wire around the next corner. There would be guns and uniforms, a line of half-starved animals in prison stripes, and a prettily-lettered pink sign: Arbeit Macht Frei.

"Why did you come here?" Her voice was sad and almost resentful.

"I can't answer that, Nina, except maybe I came to meet you."

She went on as if I hadn't spoken, or I'd said something so stupid that it would have been bad taste to acknowledge it. *The bitch,* I thought.

"You hardly talk about it. And you *know* it's strange, especially for someone like you, to just say one day, 'Well, I'm going to Germany,' and just fly off—"

"Well, it wasn't exactly like that. I mean, I read a few brochures, developed a taste for strudel." I was outraged. If it occurred to me that this should have still been a happy moment, I don't remember it. Pain, passion, paranoia: the three Jewish P's—these I remember.

"So why does a Jew come to Germany, hmm, fraulein? This is what you want to know? Why does a Jew have the audacity to come to Germany without a very good reason?

"Well, I just had to convince myself that it was real, as real and ordinary as any place on earth. Also, I didn't *like* it that there was somewhere I couldn't go. It bothered me, OK?" There was definitely something wicked and gleeful in my voice.

"So, the experiment is a success? Are we real, the same like other people? We eat, we sleep, we work, we fall in love the same? Yes? Gut! Now you can go home. Now you'll just go—"

She broke off, keeping her face turned away from me, but I could see her eyes were brimming. I suddenly remembered that the first time I'd seen Nina, she was crying, and I'd never asked her why. We had stopped walking sometime between "love" and "leave."

I turned her to me. She resisted half-heartedly, head down, like a sullen child who just needs a reason to get over it.

"I don't want to leave you. Nina, please don't let's do this."

I held her by the arms over soft white cashmere, and gently rocked her, right to left and back again. I stared at her until she looked me in the eyes and smiled. Damn tooth really was missing.

"And anyway, you know, Jews wander. I think it's genetic at this point. We just wander."

"To some very unlikely places, I must say."

Once at the zoo, I bought her food obsessively. She protested, but it did no good: every kind of junk food on earth eventually went sliding down Nina's lovely white gullet. I wooed her with ice cream, potato chips, hot dogs, french fries and caramel popcorn.

We were idly watching some species of animal which seemed to be a cross between an ox and a deer, in a depressing but hilarious dance of courtship. The male would patiently chase the female around the pen, both of them going at a nice steady trot. She would let him get close enough to mount, then she'd trot away again. It seemed as if this had been going on for hours before we got there, and would continue for hours after we left.

There was something strangely compelling about it, and disgusting. I looked over at Nina to see if she found it offensive, but she was already looking at me. "The main thing about this is that it's *funny*, don't you think? It's *so funny!*"

As I looked at her dark blue eyes, which was like looking into the bottom of a well, and her straight, white teeth with the one impertinently missing, I grew enraged. Suddenly, it was me she was laughing at. When she took my hand and led me cheerily away to see the monkey house, my fury left me, and was replaced by pure, sweet arousal.

Later on, under a small bridge that led from the mammals to the reptiles, I caught her hand and pulled her to me. I turned her around and kissed her neck. Her hands were planted firmly against my shoulders. She was surprisingly strong, and I couldn't hold her any closer. But she didn't push me away, just whispered "Ach." Then, "People will see!"

"Let them see, Nina, my sweet, let them see."

I was enjoying her discomfort immensely. My tongue found her ear and I circled it lightly. I bit the lobe. "Let me kiss you," I blurted.

"Nein. No, not—"

"What?"

"Not here."

I groaned, mostly with relief. I guess she thought it was flaming, horny impatience and smacked my arm, not altogether playfully.

This set the tone for the rest of the day. She ran a lot, but never too far.

We got to her apartment as night was falling. I was tired and riding on adrenaline. I walked in carefully, wondering if I were welcome. The couch was incongruous in that sea of old, polished wood and carefully placed antique miniatures—it was black leather, with the lines of a puma. I wondered if it were an accurate reflection of Nina's libido. I settled in and looked around. On the end table to my right were three books on Kabbalah.

Nina became the cordial hostess, offering coffee, water, anisette? I shook my head at everything, and finally said in what I hoped was a convincing and sensuous growl, "Nina, there's just one thing I want. Now, stop running from me and *sit down.*" She looked at a chair nearby. "Don't even think about it," I warned, wagging my finger then using it to point down at the couch. She nodded slowly and sat by me.

I waited. Her head fell to my shoulder. I told her I loved her, this time with some heat. I told her again, with more than a bit of annoyance. She looked at me miserably and I took pity: "We'll work it out, my beautiful Nina. We'll work something out." Then I buried my face in her breasts and started to cry.

Unlikely Places

Now when I come home from the copy shop, Nina is sprawled out on the couch with her legs spread and her hands cupped beneath a very pregnant belly. I stare, and marvel that a visit to a nearby church some two years ago has kept me in Germany all this time, except for a brief sojourn back home to sublet my apartment and take a hasty, guilt-ridden leave of my variously shocked family and friends.

Sometimes, Nina just stares at the TV; other times she cries softly. Her oversized green T-shirt is covered with patches of sweat and her long blond hair is mussed and greasy. My mouth goes dry with desire.

I smile cheerfully. She scowls. "No, no Ninotchka, little Noonie. Lover *good*. Lover bring Haagen-Dazs. See? Don't cry, my apple strudle, my little Valkyrie."

One time, she screamed at the top of her lungs, just once. Another time, she picked up my mother's heavy brass ashtray from Israel with the lapiz lazuli. I thought she might fling it at me, or the wall. Instead she threw her head back and put it to her mouth. I took it from her before she broke a tooth.

Mostly though, she's quiet and tries to shush me so she can finish watching her game show. I chatter on during commercials and she slowly comes around, as if only just figuring out who the hell I am. Occasionally, she curses me in German, looking very fierce as she calls me "shveinhundt," but with a very different light in her eyes. I cluck and spoon chocolate-chocolate chip into her mouth. I sing, "Let me call you shveinhundt, I'm in love with you," until she giggles.

I've noticed that as her pregnancy progresses, she seems only interested in sex as a way to calm me down. Nina's a great believer in neutralizing stress to avoid illness. I don't mind. I suspect it's a bit of transference of her maternal instinct (which is mighty—I've known the woman to take us a block and a half out of our way in freezing sleet to get a closer look at a tiny form passing by in knitted cap and booties). And I guess she knows it wouldn't do to have the breadwinner laid up.

Some nights I feel the terrible, clammy progress of doubt up my spine. I wonder if Nina hates me, whether I've somehow destroyed her. We fight and bicker a good deal, but it never seems to last—at times, I think it's because we're blessed. Other times I worry that it's due to some creeping couple apathy. But when Nina wakes in the deepest night, and clutches me ferociously and tells me how happy she is, how she adores me, and how I must never, never leave her, and I feel that unbearable life in her body—her own and the new one shivering and thumping inside her womb—I feel sure someone like that must know what she's talking about.

Relations with my family have been strained, to say the least, but I think they're coming around. At least when I call now, they ask politely, if not warmly, about Nina's health. Possibly telling them that the baby has a Jewish father (I avoid calling him "the donor" when I speak to them) has helped. My brothers have begun referring to Nina by name, and my mother has at least stopped calling her "the Shikseh." My Dad's been great, but wants us to live in Florida. Anywhere but here, is what I think he's trying to say. I don't tell Nina this, but I'm thinking he has a point.

Last week we went to The Wall again; this time to catch great chunks of it falling into our hands, as the hordes of young people swarmed on top, their fists and voices and pickaxes raised. Only a fool wouldn't find them beautiful. Nina's eyes glowed with some future light; mine narrowed with confusion and trepidation at a past I never knew, but can't forget.

We're planning a trip to the States when the baby's here. We might even settle there, back in my old digs in the East Village. There's only one thing left to say, but I'm not sure I can choke it out. Not that it's a crime to be happy.

Erotica/Relationships

Summer Thunder

by L. A. Patterson

L.A. Patterson is a writer who lives in Pasadena and wishes the world the joy and peacefulness she discovered this winter when she fell in love all over again with her lover of twelve years.

Summer Thunder

The rain snuck by our house, tiptoeing fast around the hills that border our domain. I can smell the clouds separating, spreading wide and loud above me. Midweek July rain, the wind heavy with liquid heat, the clovers in the fields next door hum with expectation, shimmying in the breeze, lifting their heads up for a taste of water.

You left only an hour ago. You are still in town, I think, though maybe you're on the road back already. Stores don't glue your feet to their floorboards like they do mine. I hope you remembered cream and fresh coffee. Tomorrow's Sunday, you know.

Still in line at the market watching old man Kutchman squinting at the price tags and rolling your eyes, is it raining where you are now? It's getting dark here. I've switched on the porch light for you. I like it in town when the neon signs and the street lights lazily sentry the quiet stores. It's a tiny town, to be sure, but it has what I want and right now it has you.

Maybe you are on the road, in that old car of ours, sweaty and grubby, your legs sticking loudly to those old taped up seats. Your shirt is open to the waist because you love the breeze from the open windows. Bits of dirt and grit fly in and try to hide in the hollow above your collar bone. The waistband on your shorts is soaking wet.

I look out and watch for your headlights to crest the last low hill before our house. The big oak tree that marks our driveway would see you first and I am suddenly jealous. I run for the door and burst out of the house, my heart pounding in my ears: make it to the tree, make it to the tree, make it to the tree first.

You kissed me under this tree once. You pulled me close and safe when the sky turned as it is now. It could have been just two minutes ago if it hadn't been a year.

You had been working in the garden, the dirt was thick in the creases of your hands. I called for you when the first thunderclap hovered over our house and I was scared. Oh, fear. I needed your arms around me so badly.

You hid from me; teasing and calling after me until I was almost in tears. Then I leaned against this dear old tree and you had me in your arms before I knew it.

I could barely breathe you held me so tightly. Your hair smelled like freshly cut grass. Your skin was hot velvet. The rain came down around us, pooling near our shoes then scuttling down in rivulets at the last minute.

You moaned into my ear as you tugged my shirt out of its tuck, your tongue homing in for my nipple. Salty, you muttered, and bit playfully into the hardened flesh. I reached for you but you pushed my hands away. I smiled and obeyed.

My jeans were at my knees in one quick move. Your fingers found my clit waiting, wild and wet for your touch. My private smell rose high and it peppered that tiny slice of air between us, fighting for top billing over new rain and wet dirt.

I pressed hard against you, disobeying your silent command and not caring. Kiss me there, I screamed with a caress. *Now.* You pulled yourself away from me for a moment, just a small moment, but long enough to shout to me the miles of love in your eyes. I sealed that look in my heart as you leaned me against the tree and sank to your knees. You nudged my legs wider apart with a kiss on each thigh then pressed your mouth hard against my mound. Your tongue found its favorite rhythm within seconds of tasting me. My juices ran into your mouth and down your chin, settling finally in that long valley at your throat.

I steadied myself against the tree, its roughness etched itself into my back. The moistening air around us dizzied and danced with the rising heat of our passion. The rain soaked the world around us, but only your touch triggered the torrents that ran so freely from me.

I came hard and heavy between two thunderclaps, and my cries outshone the best nature had to offer that evening.

Is it raining where you are now, my love?

The road from town is lonely and dark, selfish with its clues. Black clouds are doubling back and I can see the curtain of rain closing tighter around me.

I breathe in deep and whisper your name. I stand defiant under the greying sky, my face slick with the licks of new rain. I stare hard into the rolling, sharp edged line of land until the blur of a thousand splintering points of light carve deep halos into my eyes.

Your headlights rise bright and eager at the top of the hill. Finally.

I tear off my shirt and let the quickening rain dance down my chest. It catches momentarily at my nipples then falls gracefully to the ground, rinsing away the sweat my reminiscing has triggered. You see me and stop, not turning off the lights. I pull off my jeans and kick them into a puddle. I close my eyes and wait against our tree. The car door clicks open but doesn't slam shut. You look at me frozen in the spotlight of our Chevy. As you turn, the headlight hesitates, then dims, at your touch. The ground crunches under your feet as you walk slowly toward me.

The radiator ticks and hisses a backdrop protest under the battering rain. The leaves above me hold their water for a long moment then break under the strain, splashing my bare feet with the warm water. Then silence. I hear only the rush of your breathing close to my body. My skin burns from the heat of your approaching lips. I lean against our tree as I listen for the thunder you create within me.

Coming Out

Santa Claus at the Right Moment

by Elaine J. Auerbach

Born in Passaic, New Jersey, Elaine Auerbach was named by a nun and raised in Nutley by a second-generation Polish-German-Hungarian working-class family. She wanted to be a writer since she was ten. With the support and encouragement of her lover, Viviana, her voice is slowly emerging. She believes anyone can be creative with words provided they are willing to work hard. She dreams of going to the corner store to pick up her favourite lesbian-feminist magazine.

Elaine moved to Canada in 1975 and now lives in Waterloo, Ontario, where she is a freeelance writer and custodian of wildflowers and herbs. She is proud to be part of a tradition of women, including her grandmother, who have donned the gay apparel of Santa Claus.

Santa Claus at the Right Moment

Claudia was living with two cats and hordes of roaches in a three-room apartment above Mario's Deli in Passaic, New Jersey. She had just quit her job after three years as a hospital emergency room equipment aid. She'd felt she needed a change. And for the first time since she'd quit high school, Claudia began to think seriously about her life.

The only person she'd ever really admired was the red-haired charge nurse of the Emergency Room, Miss Wirtminer, a feisty RN dedicated to keeping people alive as they hovered on the brink of life and death. Claudia, without really knowing her, would have trusted Miss Wirtminer under any circumstances. She had watched her ordering lab tests and starting I-V's while Dr. Rich, inadequate at handling emergencies, fumbled with charts and threw up his hands in defeat. Claudia and Miss Wirtminer had spent a couple of coffee breaks together, but neither had gone any further in establishing contact beyond the work environment. Claudia already missed their connection, casual though it had been.

Remembering Miss Wirtminer made Claudia suspect that her preference for solitude was only a last refuge, a fortress she would quickly abandon when the right moment arrived. So far that moment hadn't materialized and she was wondering if it ever would.

She was out of work, yet she was an inveterate believer in purpose. Everything, to Claudia, had a purpose. But finding purpose—a job or a cause or a life partner or something—might be as difficult as coming up with the proverbial needle in the haystack. Because she couldn't find the needle didn't mean it wasn't there.

When she thought of sharing her life with someone, the idea of marriage always popped involuntarily into her head. Most of the women she had met believed that the trek down the aisle was the best path to take, so Claudia had an inkling where this idea had come from. But was she a candidate for marriage? She was twenty-two, tall, well-built and congenial. There was only one problem she fixed on when she thought of marriage: men—in fact, people in general—were scarce in her life. She didn't know why she had no close relationships. Social workers would have attributed her isolation to feelings resulting from her childhood in foster care. Claudia, however, was not the kind of flower whose being could be understood by analyzing the fertilizer.

She loved ideas and took particular delight in tuning into a listener-sponsored radio station from across the river in New York City. She could identify with those women and men with thick accents, both local and foreign, as they discussed Latin American politics, feminism, pacifism, homosexuality, ecology, economics, and other topics ignored by the mainstream media.

After one particular discussion on women in non-traditional occupations, Claudia realized that despite her lack of a high school diploma, she could get a job doing anything, even a job that "belonged" to men.

She had finally discovered a purpose, but it was a purpose that was composed of a good helping of impracticality seasoned with aspiration. But this didn't stop Claudia. She wanted a non-traditional job and now she knew she wanted an alliance with women; she wanted a relationship with someone who would feel for her something of what she had felt for Miss Wirtminer.

She was scanning *The Star Ledger* classifieds, when among the seemingly endless positions available for waitresses and cashiers, and ad for temporary work caught her attention:

WANTED: Part-time Santa Claus for Department Store. Training Provided. Thompson Temporaries. Applications and Interviews at the Essex Hotel, 100 Broad Street, Newark, Sat., October 24, 10-1.

Claudia knew right away that this was it. Here was a way she could begin to crack the patriarchal system. Going for the Santa Claus job would show them, she told herself, uncertain as to who exactly she was going to show and what exactly it was she was going to show them. Recalling Miss Wirtminer's flashing red hair as she purposefully darted in and out of the E-R treatment rooms, Claudia didn't see anything beneficial in being stopped by a little uncertainty.

"Is this where you apply for the Santa Claus job?" she asked in the middle of a room full of men at the Essex Hotel.

A burly, middle-aged man, obviously the manager, bellowed, "And what can I do for you, honey?"

"I'm here to apply. I want to be Santa Claus."

"Go on! You gotta be kiddin'! *You?*"

Claudia did a couple of rounds of ho-ho-ho, sang *White Christmas* like Bing Crosby, and was promptly handed an application.

"Well, you're tall enough."

"Five foot ten to be exact."

"My name's Garth Thompson. I run this shebang." With a nice plump pillow, some white stick and gloves, this babe'll fit the part, Garth thought to himself, shaking Claudia's hand. Her strength convinced him she would probably last longer than some of the rummies and lazy college kids who were also applying.

Claudia believed in her heart that being Santa was the right and moral thing for a woman in her day and age to be doing. She would be paving the way for those who would follow her, row after row of women donning their beards and red suits.

At first it was exhilarating. After years of watching TV comedies and musicals, Claudia had no trouble lowering her voice and thinking up witty Santa things to say.

But she was disappointed with her posting. Instead of sitting on a red velvet throne in the middle of an alpine scene, facing a line of children streaming to her knees, she had been assigned to a cardboard and brick-papered chimney behind glass in a Penney's display window at an outdoor shopping mall off Route 46.

"This is where you work," said Alice Major, the assistant store manager and her official guide.

She took Claudia to the back room of the men's department.

"I hope you don't mind using this as your dressing room," Alice said in an apologetic tone.

Claudia had to put on her suit and make-up surrounded by shelves of jockey underwear and sales clerks dressed in the latest men's fashions. It was a test, Claudia decided. She was going to have to prove herself before being presented to the kiddies in the toy department.

"So," Alice directed, "here's the window entrance. There's your microphone. It's hooked up to a loudspeaker so you can be heard all up and down the main mall. You won't be able to hear anybody outside, but they'll hear you. Now since only half your body'll be seen, you won't have to wear pants and boots. I'd keep 'em here, though. Nobody'll touch 'em."

Great, Claudia thought, staring at Alice's crooked red lipstick. She would be Santa from the waist up and herself from the waist down. No one would get close enough to her to even suspect she was a woman.

But despite Claudia's misgivings, people found out her secret. Alice was so impressed with Claudia's performance—and so guilty about the store's discrimination against her—that she spilled the beans and soon word spread all over the mall. People were incredulous. The Santa singing *White Christmas* like Bing Crosby couldn't be a woman, they said; he was too real. He was too much like what they imagined Santa would be like if he were stuck in a chimney trapped behind glass in a department store window.

There were interviews for UPI. She made the *New York Times*.

"SANTA CLAUS IS A WOMAN" the headlines read.

Bob Roberts from WCWX TV came by to interview her.

"Why does a woman want to be Santa?" he asked, shoving a microphone in Claudia's face.

"Well, Santa's a good guy. He drops presents down chimneys rather than bombs on houses," she answered, surprising herself with her own spontaneity. Her popularity with the press quickly ran out.

Although she attracted curiosity seekers to the store and felt a twinge of pride in her work, she felt let down, as a woman, as a newly awakening feminist. She wondered if she had done the right thing.

Maybe she should have thought things over more carefully. Stayed at the hospital, where the pay was a lot better, until she could have saved enough to go to vocational school. Then she could have qualified for training as a carpenter or a heavy-duty mechanic. Had she acted too quickly? She wondered if she had taken this job so that she could be loved. What better way to receive love than to play Santa Claus? She had expected that her job would bring camaraderie with people, especially women, but she was as solitary as ever.

She thought back over the relationships in her life. Had anyone cared for her? Certainly not her parents, who had given her up for adoption when she was born. Certainly not her first adoptive family, who had abandoned her to foster care when she was eight. And of all the foster homes she had been in, the only people who had shown any real interest in her were Mabel Stoner and her sister Clara, two schoolteachers who were austere but fair. Completely fair, Claudia thought, but definitely not loving, at least not enough to convince Claudia she had much to give.

Claudia was surprised to discover that she was indeed looking for love and acceptance. But who, she finally asked herself, was going to take seriously a woman who impersonated Santa Claus?

As the holiday season wore on, Claudia felt blue. Christmas had always been a depressing time for her. She didn't like the commercialism or the phony family togetherness, although she sometimes imagined the togetherness might be real, that only the foster families she had lived with had pretended a loving spirit during the holidays.

She listened to the radio every night when she got home, wondering why so many were descending on toy departments and nosing around perfume counters when the sky was falling in the Middle East and the water in their taps was turning to poison. Claudia decided she would put as much of herself as she wanted into her job. She started to lace her ho-ho-hos with other than the usual Santa things.

"Merry Christmas, ho-ho-ho. Don't forget the less fortunate."

"A tree in the forest is worth twelve in the house. Ho-ho-ho."

"Rudolph says fur coats are for animals. The elves are working on a special Christmas gift—food for everyone. Nobody starves this year!"

The first few times she delivered her messages, no one seemed to be paying attention. She was almost convinced that her efforts were wasted when she noticed something unusual. People were beginning to listen to her.

•

Santa Claus at the Right Moment

Claudia didn't see her in the beginning, intent as she was on communicating the lines that mattered.

The woman stayed in the background. In the middle of the afternoon, she would stand near the reindeer trough, staring at Claudia, munching on a pretzel from Woolworth's, her hooded parka closed tightly around her neck. At mid-morning, steaming coffee in her hand, she leaned against the talking Frosty a few stores down, watching and obviously listening. Sometimes she wore a hat and Claudia had to strain to recognize her curly auburn hair beneath the unfamiliar headgear.

Claudia had the urge to say something personal to her, to let her know she saw her, her devoted listener, but she didn't have the courage.

The woman never came close to the window, so Claudia never got a good look at her face. Did she work in one of the shops at the mall? Did she work for Penny's? She didn't dress stylishly enough to be in cosmetics or clothes. Maybe the credit office. Maybe the cafe. Maybe she was a spy for Mr. Christianson, the manager, one of the store detectives checking her out. But Claudia knew all of the badge people; she arrived at the same time they did every day. Most of them were former police or army officers, women in short, close-cropped hair, men in crew cuts. Was this woman from the FBI? The CIA?

One thing was sure, her observer was always alone, as solitary in her position as Claudia was, propped in her chimney.

A week before Christmas, at the start of her shift, Alice came to see her.

"Don't suit up yet, dear."

Claudia knew what was coming. The woman in the mall had taken notes on everything Claudia had said and now she was going to be fired. Too subversive. Too un-commercial. Oh well, it was only a temporary job anyway. So what if she lost the job a week earlier than she expected?

"They want you upstairs in toys today," Alice announced, beaming.

"Upstairs?"

"Yup. You're the real Santa from now on. Olive's taking the pictures. She's your little Elf. Lunch is from two to three. Can you stay on to do the second shift? It's not too busy then, but it's up to you."

"Sure. No trouble."

"Great. Now when you're upstairs, make sure you always wear your gloves. Don't let your hands show. And keep that voice low."

For the entire day, Claudia coddled and cooed and winked and popped her cheeks and softly laughed and gently ho-hoed and quietly sat while girl after boy after girl smiled and wailed and fought and looked stunned and ran away and threw up and blushed in shyness and giggled while their mothers—nine times our of ten it was their mothers—stood by, sometimes keenly or idly observing, sometimes pushing and pulling their children toward the throne of Santa Claus.

Claudia found that repeating over and over again, "What do you want? And what do you want? And what do you want?" was getting to her. She still wasn't sure what it was that she herself wanted, if want was the right word at all. It was about time, she figured, that she stopped asking questions and provided some answers, not for others, but for herself.

Then the moment of her last refuge arrived. She knew it was her moment when, a half-hour before quitting, with no children left, and Olive, the Elf, half asleep hunched over the camera, the woman she'd seen from the window paid her a visit.

"Do you want a photo with Santa?" Olive asked the woman, rubbing her eyes.

"No. I'd just like to sit on Santa's lap."

"Sure. Hey Santa, this one just wants to sit on your lap. No picture," Olive said, wandering off to chat with Sybil in notions.

The woman slowly walked up the red carpet and eased herself onto Claudia's knee. She was smaller than she had appeared wrapped in her parka in the mall; she was almost as light as a child.

"Santa, I've wanted to meet you for a long time."

"I know," Claudia kept to her deep voice, "I've seen you from the window."

"I thought you might've. My name's Mona. I do inventory in the stock room."

Smiling within inches of Claudia's face, Mona appeared celestial, her auburn hair haloed in a silvery glow reflected from the tinseled trees surrounding them.

Santa Claus at the Right Moment

"I hate Christmas," Mona declared.

"Me too," Claudia confessed, rapt in wonder.

Did Mona's brown eyes sparkle like that, or was it the lights and the fact that Claudia was dead tired from 14 hours of playing Santa? No. The sparkles in Mona's eyes radiated from within, from some deep and enchanting source.

"When do you get off?"

Did Mona know she was a woman?

"In twenty minutes."

"Would you like to go out or come over to my place for a snack—you must be exhausted after all this."

Claudia hesitated at the invitation. Hadn't Mona heard the news—that she was not a man?

"Santa Claus is a woman," Claudia whispered in her own voice, expecting Mona to jump up in alarm.

"Yes, I know. And quite a wonderful woman. I've heard you. I like what you have to say. I like you."

Claudia could feel herself blushing, hoping the colour couldn't possibly show beneath her heavily rouged cheeks and snowy beard.

"So what about it?" Mona asked. "Want to drop by for some holiday cheer?"

"Sure!"

"Meet me by the reindeer trough."

Claudia hesitated. "How will you know me? I won't be wearing my suit."

"But you'll know me. I'm not wearing any disguise. You can remember what I look like, can't you?"

She would remember, Claudia thought, taking into her heart this very right moment, and she would never forget.

Romance

In The Woods

by Barbara Harwood

Barbara Harwood lives in a rustic cabin in the woods on the Mendocino coast of California. She has written numerous plays and short stories. She has just finished her first novel.

Barbara actively strives and hopes for a world in which people recapture their natural love for all living things. A world where quality replaces quantity and the killing stops.

In The Woods

Michelle was just a bit nervous as she approached the cabin. Her first serious photographic assignment for *Women Alive* magazine and they had to give her the notoriously difficult Meryl Brannigan. She guessed they wanted her to pass some kind of litmus test.

The well-weathered cabin was falling down rustic—almost buried in a massive tangle of wildflowers, weeds, and blackberry vines—something terribly chaotic about the whole place. Michelle wondered if this was a symbolic manifestation of the woman she was about to meet. If so, it was time to become a lot more nervous. She suddenly yearned for her own tidy designer garden and the familiar comfort of her small house on Collins Lane.

"You the photographer?"

Michelle's skin prickled with instant adrenaline as she turned to face the woman who had so quietly approached her from behind. It was true, the short curly hair tangled itself in every possible direction, and the worn and baggy overalls barely covered the slender torso of this ageless woman. But it was the eyes—the dark piercing eyes that nailed her speechless to the spot.

"You the photographer?"

"Yes...yes I am." Michelle said, almost choking on her voice.

"Name?"

"Michelle...Michelle White. And you're Meryl Bran..."

"Yep," Meryl interrupted. "Shall we go inside and get at it?"

"Sure."

"What kind of pictures you want?" Meryl asked as they strolled the few remaining yards to the cabin.

"Well, I don't really know just yet."

"You don't know?"

"I sort of have to spend a little time getting to know my subjects before I can sense the direction I want to take." Michelle felt more centered now that she was focused on something familiar.

Meryl opened the door and let Michelle enter first. The interior of the one room cabin was simple, uncluttered, clean and primitive. The few pieces of furniture appeared to be handmade. In the far corner stood a large oak desk with a computer on it. The desk was piled high with books and manuscripts.

"You want some tea?" Meryl asked, putting an ancient kettle on to boil.

"Love some."

"Mint or Chamomile?"

"Both, if you don't mind."

"Great combination," Meryl affirmed.

"Where's the bay window?" Michelle asked.

"Bay window?" Meryl questioned as she stoked the fire.

"I thought all brilliantly creative writers sat at enormous oak desks facing huge bay windows with magnificent views while they watched the autumn leaves fall."

"You're right. Better for you to get to know your subjects. Bring you down to earth a bit," Meryl teased.

"Do you honestly sit in that dark corner facing that blank wall?" Michelle asked with sincere wonder.

"Yep. Keeps me honest."

"What do you mean?"

"If I sat at your big bay window I'd be writing story after story about autumn leaves. This way I'm forced to search out the truth—inside myself."

"That's great." Michelle was surprised at how quickly Meryl was willing to share her secrets. "Is that where you wrote *Life Images?*"

"Where else?" Meryl set out mugs and poured the tea.

"I really loved that book," Michelle said as they both sat at the kitchen table.

"Yeah. Me too," Meryl said. "I still enjoy reading it."

"You read your own work?"

"Sure. How else am I going to learn about myself?"

"But you wrote it, you must know what it says."

"Do you ever study your photographs? Ever wonder why you like one better than another?"

"Sure. Funny thing. The best ones are frequently the ones I didn't plan."

"Spontaneous shots?"

"That's right."
"Almost like someone else took them?"
"Yes. How'd you know?"
"When I'm really tuned in it's like someone else has borrowed my body and is writing the story. Then I have to go back and read what they've written."

•

Michelle was totally confounded by the contradictions between the reputed Meryl Brannigan and the woman sitting before her. Where was the brusk and uncooperative hermit she was led to expect? This woman was warm, friendly, open and wonderfully real.
"Can I ask you some personal questions?" Michelle said.
"Maybe. Depends on what you ask and how you ask it."
"Are you a hermit?"
"Selective."
"What?"
"I'm not a hermit. I'm just selective. You've been reading my 'grouchy hermit' write-ups haven't you?"
"Well...yes. I read a few articles."
"And they said I was difficult, unfriendly and strange. Right?"
"Yes," Michelle felt a bit embarrassed.
"Well they wrote the truth. At least they wrote what they saw. I'm all those things when I have to spend time with idiots and poseurs."
"Poseurs?"
"You know. The ones who think writing is more important than ditch digging."
"Well isn't it?" Michelle asked, hesitantly.
"You ever try to dig a ditch with a book?" Meryl smiled. "More tea?"

•

Michelle was already liking Meryl too much. She found her to be as wonderfully outrageous and special as her books. "How do you feel about my being here?" Michelle asked.
"I like you." Meryl smiled warmly.
"I'm not an idiot or a poseur?"
"Are you?"
"No."

"Do you have a portfolio with you?" Meryl asked.

"Yes," Michelle answered, curious.

"May I see it?"

"Why?"

"I want to know more about you." Meryl gazed intently at Michelle. Michelle handed over the portfolio. She watched as Meryl opened it, and slowly turned each page with care and obvious appreciation. "This one, where was it taken?" Meryl held up Michelle's favorite.

"On a reservation in Southern Utah. She's a Piute medicine woman."

"It's absolutely wonderful." Meryl enthused. "She has such a spiritual radiance." Michelle felt her chest fill with intensity as she watched Meryl finish turning the pages. She could barely avert her eyes from this woman.

"Do you think we ought to get started?" Michelle forced herself to say the words. She needed to be doing something, put her focus somewhere away from the fantasies that were forming in her mind.

"Sure." Meryl closed the book, stroking its textured surface with obvious respect. "How you want to do this?"

"Why don't you pretend I'm not here. Just go about your daily routine."

"I don't have a routine. I just do what needs doing by the mood, what feels right at the moment."

"So what's your mood right now?"

"You don't want to know." Meryl's eyes glowed with a teasing radiance.

"What?"

"Let's chop some wood," Meryl said, heading for the door. Michelle was delighted at the prospect of Meryl doing something potently physical. She set her camera to automatic as she caught quick successive shots of Meryl's smooth muscles responding to the challenge of hard physical labor. Working up a sweat, Meryl stopped to push the overall straps off her shoulders which caused the bib to fall away from her breasts. She tied a scarf around her waist to keep her pants from falling and went back to work.

The whirring sound of the automatic advance seemed to have a rhythm of its own as Michelle caught the inspiration of Meryl's

In The Woods

beautiful breasts from every possible angle. Finishing the roll, she allowed herself the luxury of just sitting and watching, letting her fantasies float freely. It was wonderfully erotic to watch the rhythmic sensual movements of Meryl's body as she crashed the ax into the wood.

Michelle felt a surge of warmth in her crotch, the juices starting to flow. She felt her breath quicken each time the ax struck home. The power of it was hypnotic—powerfully, sensually, wonderfully hypnotic.

Meryl struck the ax into the chopping block and left it there. She turned to look at Michelle. Seeing the transfixed passions in her face, she walked the few paces that separated them. She gently reached her hand to Michelle's cheek, stroking it softly as she pressed her lips to the warm waiting mouth. Michelle moaned as her arms reached around and pulled Meryl's body close. They stood there, holding each other, letting their energies blend.

"I guess we better keep on with the assignment," Meryl said reluctantly as she stepped back and returned the straps to her shoulders.

"Right," Michelle agreed, finding her knees a bit shaky.

"Let's go in the house and get the 'famous writer at work' shots over with," Meryl teased as she went through the door.

Michelle followed, her mind overwhelmed by the passions surging through her. How quickly Meryl had wiped away any barriers that might have been.

Michelle dutifully loaded her camera with fresh film and moved around, pretending to be a photographer.

Meryl sat with her feet propped on the desk, the keyboard resting in her lap. She slowly pressed her fingers to the silent keys and the screen came alive with little green letters:

        MERYL WANTS MICHELLE!!

"Oh god!" Michelle breathed as she bent to circle her arms around Meryl's neck, pulling her head back against her breasts and pressing her lips lovingly into the mass of chaotic curls. "I can't stand this," Michelle exclaimed, turning Meryl's chair, kneeling and burying her face in her lap.

"Patience now. You've still got a job to do." Meryl gently stroked Michelle's hair.

"Fuck the job!"

"That's not exactly what I had in mind," Meryl teased.

"You're right! Damn it!" Michelle moaned with frustration. "So what now?"

"Well, I generally go for a swim in the lake before the day's over. Shall we?" Meryl said, heading out the door.

•

The lake was shimmering blue in the late afternoon sun. Orange and yellow wildflowers spilled along its shore.

Meryl stood on a rock ready to dive. "Your magazine going to print all this nudity?" Meryl teased.

"It's for my private collection," Michelle teased back.

"And how big is your private collection?" Meryl asked as she dove in.

"Not big enough, Michelle thought as she waited for Meryl to surface.

Meryl's head broke through with a yell guaranteed to let the whole world know how cold it was.

"Can't be that cold," Michelle challenged.

"Course not," Meryl shouted. "I'm just practicing for the opera. Why don't you join me?"

"I gotta take the pictures, remember?"

"You're a chicken. Put the camera down. You can take the pictures later."

"No, ma'am. I'm going to finish this assignment if it kills me."

Meryl began stroking away toward the center of the lake. Michelle quickly switched to a zoom lens but it just wasn't working. Not enough subject above the water line.

Michelle put the camera into its case and began to strip. The warm sun pleasured her body as the clothes dropped away. She walked to the edge of the lake, bent down and splashed a bit of water onto her skin. Too cold. Not for the likes of her. She climbed onto a large flat rock and lay down, closing her eyes against the sun.

•

The first drips of water made her think of rain, gentle drops splashing down from the sky. She opened her eyes to see Meryl's still wet body standing over her.

"You're beautiful," Meryl said. "You should have been born on this rock." Meryl knelt and pressed her lips gently to Michelle's breast. "You're so very beautiful."

Michelle reached to pull Meryl onto her, holding her as a riot of desire coursed through her body. "I want you," she said. "I want you so bad."

"I know," Meryl whispered, "But I think we should wait."

"Why?" Michelle groaned.

"Ancient Chinese proverb." Meryl smiled. "Cut flower dies quickly."

"Meaning?"

"Meaning I think we should let what's happening between us have a chance to root itself."

"We don't have to cut the flower," Michelle said urgently. "We can let it blossom."

"Why not have the pleasure of experiencing it from the sprouting of its seed to the falling of its petals?" Meryl said as she looked deeply into Michelle's eyes.

"I can't stand you," Michelle complained and pulled Meryl tight against her.

"Why's that?" Meryl teased as she nibbled lovingly on Michelle's neck.

"I can't stand people who are always right."

"Yeah," Meryl said, "Me neither."

•

"Can I at least say the words?" Michelle asked as she packed her camera and perpared to leave.

"Please do," Meryl said as she reached to stroke Michelle's hair.

"But we're not supposed to say them," Michelle said.

"Do you feel them?"

"Yes."

"Then say them."

"There's an ancient proverb," Michelle teased.

"Yeah?" Meryl waited.

"Can't think of one." Michelle grinned as she turned to embrace her.

"I love you," Meryl whispered into Michelle's ear.

"Me too! " Michelle breathed as she felt the roar of desire come charging into her chest.

They stepped apart and stood looking at each other. Michelle was once again fixated by the piercing dark eyes of this woman.

"You'll come back on the weekend. For sure?" Meryl asked.

"Yes," Michelle said. "But you better arrange for separate beds."

"Not on your life." Meryl grinned.

"What about the proverb?" Michelle asked, confused and excited at the same time.

"My guess is that by the time you come back the roots will be reasonably solid."

"And just to give them a good start..." Michelle said as she took Meryl's face in her hands. They kissed passionately, patiently, thoroughly.

Walking away down the path, Michelle stopped and turned for one last look. Meryl had removed her clothes and was standing naked inside a massive bower of brilliantly pink wild roses. Her legs were parted and her arms reached up toward the sky. She looked like a winged dancer about to take flight.

"You're wonderful," Michelle yelled as she etched the scene into her minds eye.

"Aren't we though," Meryl yelled back.

A Chant

The Chant of the Women of Magdalena

by SDiane Bogus

SDiane Bogus is no stranger to lesbian women. She has been writing about, to, and for us since 1971. Her books include Dykehands, Sapphire's Sampler, *and* Women in the Moon. *She is represented by W.I.M. Publications. She performs, teaches, dances, chants, makes love, and listens to music to preserve and buoy her soul. She insists that you read* The Chant of the Women of Magdalena *aloud. This excerpt is just a hint of the power the full poem reveals. In general it is a modern metaphor for the female response to patriarchy and an exploration of the moral nature of women. It is meant to loan visions of lesbian personal power, to delight, and to instruct. The full book is now available.*

The Chant of the Women of Magdalena

An Excerpt

I

In the labrys of the mountain
In the circle of their communion
The women of Magdalena gather near...
The daughters of the mothers
The sisters, and the others
Chant this tale of woman strength that you will hear:

During the English Protectorate
Still accused by church and state
An unformed coven of women chose to flee
They'd not be made slaves and tarts
Accused of Satan's darkest arts
They cloaked their whispers, made a plan to get free

From the prison, they tunneled like moles
With dirty bedding they hid the holes
And in time, inch by inch, they all crawled out
One by one, they snaked and stole
Refusing to eat to fit the hole
But they dared forest nights despite their doubts

On a chosen moonless night
Led by eyes of deadly light
They stole a whaler, drugged the sailor who watched the deck
Hardly knowing the sea or compass
But knowing neither winds or morass
Would ever leave them lost or awreck

Thirty-two souls in weeds and wool
Thirty-two souls who knew the world
They'd left behind would bring them death or cause them pain,
Across Southeast watery shoals
Across its straits, gulfs, and corals

The Chant of the Women of Magdalena

Thirty-two souls rode the waves, a sea near Spain

Though some of them were hurt or ill
The trip nor waves did neither kill
For the hope of a better place inspired their health
Where some blazed crimson fevers,
Were wounded deep, there was a healer
Magdalena's touch allowed no death

II

Not long were they out, adrift
Afright with questions, unsure, makeshift
Not much known of the gifts they had
How to govern their several ways?
Or live loveless throughout their days?
To understand the different, the shy, the bad?

But evoked as need can do
Those gifts arose as they were due
The response to duty, to lack, to want...of heart
Like Magdalena's useful healing
Or Yamasee's able reeling
Of the wheel which she wielded with natural art

Yes, Yamasee had taken the wheel
Strong her arms, bold her zeal
For she had been sold as slave from ship to ship
Mustee freed on English shores
Herself's own master for evermore
Never again to feel the white man's whip

Merci Crevecour, Canadian fish maid
From Northern port where sailors stayed
Yamasee's mate, for she knew of sailors' tasks
Their stories in her father's store
Had made her want to experience more
So she stowed away; found trials and much unasked

Monifa from the Americas coast
Abducted from her trading post
Was purveyor of that which met the designs of men
She knew their lack, their need, their virtues,
She knew their ways, their wants, their culture:
A captive coquette playing in a pirates' den

These the helmsmates, its threesome-master
Assigned the duties, midship, and after
From the tally, to the galley and the bunks below
Their work let no fear increase
It gave mind and body a busy peace
As each woman did what she could or did know

Ling Ping, private, wise, and small
Her gift to know the tongue of all
Translated the sense, intent, where English failed
Student-agent hidden away
Mystic rebel from Cathay
Her story nor her mission she n'er detailed

She skirted busily from aft to bow
First there then, below deck now
Her speed the job more job than the foreign tongues
French, English, Spanish and Creek
The signs of Ann who couldn't speak
Swahili, Hausa, Italian—languages coined

She made the strange seem commonplace
Connected languages race to race
Her gift like Magda's touch made them all belong
Sonal helped—she heard their minds
If they were busy most worked out mimes
Or called someone whose study was coming along

But a girl, yet assigned up high
Sonal served sentry in the sky
Atop the foremast she leaned back listening
Condemned to die, her village burned
When of her gift the authorities learned
She could hear the sound of soundless distant things

She heard the dawn when light first broke
Heard when Ahemsa and creatures spoke
They followed the sound of wings and songs of whales
For Ahemsa could change her voice
To that of seal, or gull—her choice
Their gift together made easy the ship's travail

Sonal's mother helped move the whaler
Through stiffened waves—hardly a sailor,

The Chant of the Women of Magdalena

Yet Protecta's power a kinetic energy
Thus with Yamasee's able arm
These boatswimmin through rain and storm
Kept certain the course, their discovered mastery

The women discovered their course and mastery.

III

Sometimes the sea was painted glass
Upon which none but these could pass
For no ship of men nor any encroached the scene
Ruth the pub maid, Merci, and others
Detached one of the whaling luggers
Dropped lines for fish, the catch they also cleaned

When nights were long not filled with stars
And the water, misty-cold, splashed dark
Some sat on bins or leaned against the rails
Others lay in sleepless bunks
Some searched the hold, the endless trunks
For clothing to assuage the stinging gales

Elizabeth stoked the willful fire
Vengeance and purpose bespoke her ire
For she was third generation of a captive tribe
Native Creek raw and staid
One of four new-world maids
To England brought, forgot, novelty aside

Namaste whittled but spoke to none
Some said the jailers'd cut out her tongue
They'd burned her face for acts assigned to man
But dark Namaste understood
The nature of stone, fiber and wood
Her knife she handled with deft and bitter hands

Emily Griswold muttered alone
Because they took the babe, her own
Born out of wedlock and put her in a cell
Much like the trail of the nun
Sebastiana whose virgin womb
Was filled with the roguish seed of a hapless hell

She prayed while others talked or sang

She mourned the womyn who had been hanged
For crimes of faith, of art, for gifts from God
"As almost I was," Aveda'd say.
(She chronicled each passing day)
Told them tales and kept a gay ship's log

"My only sin in this creation
"Is knowing women's situation"
"Be married, behave, or be made to fornicate."
"If you talk or speak your truth,
"You'll be damned for being uncouth,
"And dragged as I was before a magistrate."

Yet, the rock and tumble of the boat
Wrest hopeful songs from their throats
Then Kundegi upon pot or crate would drum
African servant inopportune
Held like Tsembaga for gold doubloons
At the Newgate jail for a bidder's sum

"Sebastiana" was one night's tune
That drew them all into commune
To imbue her unborn babe with special charm:
"To walk the earth like land is air!
"To know herself from toe to hair.
"Upon the earth, to walk, without alarm!"

Kundegi's drum's deep vibrations
Drew into their celebration
Ann the deaf mute who took Tsembaga's waist
More joined in arm in arm
To dance itself a welcome balm
To minds and bodies needing this lilting grace:

Josephine, a jeweler's daughter Claire, the painter,
Eve the potter Adama, Esperanza's child and friend to Ann
Stopped what they were busy doing
Weaver Mary stopped her sewing
To watch the mincing of this mirthful band

Creole Monifa uncorked a wine
Said to the gardener, "Just this time!"
Then they passed the bottle from mouth to mouth
Mary the gardener someday'd make
A vineyard full of wondrous grapes

The Chant of the Women of Magdalena

For she had saved some seeds from France's South

The boots, and moccasins, and bare feet
Beat out a tune both fierce and sweet
As the twins clapped hands and sang their made-up song:
"She is big with hope and faith!"
"Let our new home be just as great!"
Lost echoes pierced the hard night on and on

Across the tides to homeless shores
Across the miles where no ships moored
  Their hope for a place unlanded, unknown to man.

Their hope for a place unlanded, unknown to man.

IV

A foggy morning, a gray midnoon
No sounds to hear, no whales, no tune
Tsembaga, Protecta slackened the longish ropes
Ahemsa summoned a school of eels
Whose light and length helped guide the keel
Through that fateful morning of everyone's hopes

"And so it shall be!" cried Delaware
Whose eyeless trances and blinded stare
Saw times to come and mysteries to unfold
"We are near, within this moon;
"We will find a shelter soon;
"A treasure more precious than oil, silk or gold."

Through the day they plod each wave
The time too long that Delaware gave
They watched her or the eels who made the trail
When Rebecca cried out, "Damn this ship!
"I'm tired of every rise and dip;
"Another day and I shall leap the rails!"

"Gentle Becky," Grace took her waist
Swabbing her tear-stained Irish face,
"Come sit and talk while we sew and dye."
"'Tis but the darkness before the sun;
"Watch, before event this day is done,
"We'll heave the anchor o'er with a thankful sigh."

Grace and Becky joined some at the bales
Drinking Magda's chamomile
In the silence it made them feel warm and whole
Sewing, hearing the groaning rudder
Deep they looked into each other
Each contemplating the tale of the other's soul:

Weaver Mary's craft with cloth
Called bewitched, bedamned, near lost
A plot against her land in lawless times
No one's the gift like Magdalene's
Whose hands, and thoughts, and potent dreams
Were possessed, by spirits blessed, powers most sublime

Bastard blood of a Spanish crown
Whose place at court was soon withdrawn
When it was learned her touch and brews could coldly kill
Accused, condemned without appeal
Never seeing her touch could heal
The crown denied the promise of her good will

'Twas said her heart was badly bruised
That final night when she'd had to choose
To fell the guards, like trees, from jail to ship
To her there was neither leaf nor spice
That could forgive a curtailed life
Even taken by hands from hands with knife or whip

"...Let us ask the blesséd sea
"To rinse our flesh of dirt and flea,
"To wash away the past, the pain we've seen."
Magdalena's eyes—from dark and grim
Shone sun-bright upon the whim
"How simple!" she said, a sleeper roused from a dream.

The word spread from deck to hold
Then nearly every blesséd soul
Lined up to wash their weathered bodies down
Merci Crevecour jumped the line
Joked in French, "It's about time."
And Ling Ping laughed passing the words around

First by ones, then by twos
The entire blesséd dirty crew

The Chant of the Women of Magdalena

Stood chilled and naked laughing gleefully
They passed round newly sweeted oil
From the whaler's gruesome toils
First oiled themselves then others timidly

"Ahoy, Ho, Wims!" then cried Yamasee
"Aground, we don' run; the fog...couldn't see."
"Drop that ankha, look lak home's yon dis sand!"
The bump and halt stopped those yet dressing
What lay beyond? Curse or blessing?
How here to realize the victory of their hands?

V

Wet and weary from the voyage
Much determined to fiercely forage
Out a new life inside the caves of Magdalene
So they called those immense crags
After she whose own two legs
Put forth first sturdy feet upon the terrain

She, like the host who had come
Weathered and brown from the sun
Was not too proud, nor too tired to give thanks
They joined hands in the full moonlight
Embraced the base of the mountain's height
They blessed the moon, the mount, the sea, its banks

Then they found atop the mount
Growing foliage, a flowing fount
A garden haven nourished by sun, mist and air
In the beginning they covered the walls
With wools they'd dyed, designéd clothes
From the ship they brought up stools and chairs

Took the captain's wines, his covers
Took the stash of loot for lovers
Meant to be brought home for favors in ladies' beds
Took the cook's preserves and pans
Took what treasure from exotic lands
That was saved in chests, on shelves, beneath bedsteads

Salted whale, beans and bread
Silks, and sashes, wool and threads
The womyn took for life all that they found

Tallow candles, whale oil lamps
Fires burned to kill the damp
All about, and throughout, the blessed ground

Once settled, needing nought
They took apart the ship that'd brought
Them to this uncharted haunt across the sea
Long they burned the whaler's wood
Long it made their new lives good
It was years before they ere touched virgin tree

And so life within the mount began and flowed

VI

Standing watchful upon the deck
England's lands at his back
The red-haired Whytehall looked afar with glory's hope
Through his telescope he had spied
The distant mount, his hoped-for prize
Discovered, he thought, at last, for English claim

But watchful gulls above them hovered
Screamed a warning to the coven
And the daughters heard—at Magdalene
"Let us climb and seek to discover
"What can be returned to Charles' coffers
"Let us see what this mountain will offer up."

"But, my Lord, Sire Whytehall,"
The First Mate dared, of them all
"Might not this mount have its dangers, such to fear?"
Whytehall, haughty, determined said,
"I'll have the sailor's very head
"Who fails to make the Mount fear us first.

"We will kill beast or savage.
"This mount will be mine, I must have it,
"And no thing can defeat our minds' intent!"

And so armed, they set forth up the mount.

VII

In the labrys of the mountain

The Chant of the Women of Magdalena

Where the women often gathered
Sat the eldest, grown-gray woman Magdalene
Stirring in a caldron hot,
Enchanted logs burned and shot
Fearsome cinders, crackling plot, Mother Magdalene

Hardly cautious, and too daring
With dreams of the booty they'd be sharing
The crew followed Whytehall, their minds engrossed
At the lead of their search
Whytehall climbed each ledge and perch
Expecting animal or wildman at the most

Disconcerted, stopped in his tracks
Feigning composure, Whytehall asked,
"How now, sailors, ho now sailors, what have we here?"
"An old woman!" murmured back the crew
All through them, twenty-two
Their amusement and surprise a derisive sneer

"Hovelled here, among these crags,
"A withered, bedecked, olden hag,
"An only woman living lone upon this mount!"
"How is it, fair beldame,
"How is it that you came
"To be alive among these wet and moldy haunts?"

Sitting ireful in the captain's chair
Magdalena's dreadful stare
Brought the men's dauntless steps to a halt
No one moved, no one stirred
No one uttered a further word
No one believed his eyes, nor hardly what he thought

In youthful voice, to the crew
"Sit," she said, "I do bid you."
Then Magdalene watched as they and Whytehall sat
This Whytehall watched as did his men
Who gaped unshamed to take the place in
Surely so much more this cave would beget...

Next, she rose and took down bowls
From long shelves against the walls
Of the cave while their eyes followed relentlessly
Giving one to each stunned man

Filling each with steady hand
One by one she poured a brew deliberately

"Aye, Captain, to the beldame's health!"
Cried the mate, dismissing a death
Before imagined much more dreadful as they climbed
He raised his cup, the others as well
Each relieved to find no hell
Nor savages, nor demons in these craggy climes

"By the crown of King Charles II.
"To his health, and to his crew!"
Then, irreverent, they drank the brew, bold Whytehall
 "We now claim in England's name,
"This mountain's treasures and its game.
"Old woman, treat us to knowledge of here and all."

Sitting, without a smile, said she,
"I tell you no secrets for King or thee
"For what you find here is not yours nor his to claim."
Whytehall's sneer, and the crew's wild laughter
Did not echo, did not matter
For the wizened woman's face remained unchanged

"You will go from whence you came,
"Or you'll die upon this mountain
"Because its owners are not disposed to give it up."
Master here, to his own thinking,
Whytehall signalled the men, "Stop drinking!"
Stood to challenge Magdalene, discarding his cup

"You speak as if there are others;
"Are they aged like you, Mother?
"Are there men here who will fight for your claim?"
Womyn's voices from high up walls
Echoed laughter and despising calls
Unseen legions for the Mount took their aim

Angry, Whytehall drew his knife
Beset the dame to take her life
Leapt behind her with the blade close at her throat
"I will kill her, hear me heathen!
"Come out now, or watch the bleeding!
"Bleeding like a sacrificial goat!"

The Chant of the Women of Magdalena

At that moment in the high-domed room
Began the rain of Whytehall's doom
A storm of fiery spears sped from unseen bows
The crewmen scattered and they ducked
They flew for fear, ran amuck
Except for those who were in horror froze

Some caught arrows in the neck
Others caught them in the back
Still others hid behind a nearby cache
Magdalena, the adept elder,
Whose very flesh was charmed, was sheltered
Did not flinch nor even bleed at Whytehall's slash

He aghast with fright and horror,
Never knowing woman nor daughter,
Who could withstand nor oppose the will of man
Cried out, "Witches!" convinced and stricken
That unfair word had long since been
Left behind when these endowed had left his land

"Sons of England, remaining living,
"Mercifully, we are giving
"You your leave but you must go and ne'er return.
"That you live is the wish of few;
"Treachery requires death for due,
"But your dead have paid for what you learn.

"You must take your master bound
"Back to English shores and Crown.
"Let no man speak the words to change your minds."
"Aye, we promise!" the cry of ten.
Lacking but one voice of the men
Stubborn Whytehall swallowing their and his own brine

"Let me warn you before your going,
"We have powers and ways of knowing
"That will insure you keep your given word."
Then, again, pledging, "Aye!"
Each man's grateful reply—
Unbothered Magdalene watched their ship unmoored

And so they left.

VIII

Yes, they muffled their threats and cries
But they could not feign or disguise
That most, at whatever post, had eyes for home
But as distance 'twixt ship and womyn
Grew great and wide, the mountain dimmer
Whytehall then made his secret scheme known

"Only women would lack the wit
"To fail to kill and then acquit "
When we can return armed and then surmount."
"Aye," said some prideful others
"We but played weak, did we not, brothers?
"For freedom, to return more armed to the mount."

On the bow with telescope,
In his breast relentless hope,
Whytehall viewed the distant mount with maliced gall
"They have conquered but a day.
"They have no means to long stay
"On that mountain, I now proclaim, Mount Whytehall!"

"Mount Whytehall!" the men hailed and cried
Forgetting how they'd nearly died,
Trying to get that womanned peak within their grip.
Then, upon their very words
As if the very sky had heard
The echo, "Whytehall!" thundered about the ship

The sky darkened as the sun
Was covered with clouds dark as dung
Then the wind whipped about an angry hail
The center masts cracked and fell
The men surprised, ran pell mell
While high waves rose and beat against the sails

The men scattered and they ducked
They flew for fear, ran amuck
But they could not dodge the falling masts
As in the caves of Magdalene
Laughter again from forms unseen
Rang our angry and derisive—a new spell cast

"Whytehall!" "Whytehall!" echoing thunder
The sailors' dreams dashed and plundered

The Chant of the Women of Magdalena

"Whytehall!" whirling, piercing, ringing far, then near
Ringing, ringing no sirens calling
Drove them stumbling, fearful, falling
Powerless hands against assaulted ears

O'er it all Magda's voice,
"Sons of England, you forfeit choice.
"Here's the due your faithlessness makes erupt!"
Then the ship rose in the air
Then it hovered unearthly there
Then it slowly rolled and turned bottom up

Out spilled Whytehall, his masts and men
Their guile and ropes, and empty bins
Split the sea and splashed like a sperm whale's fluke
It sank sails first in the water
Hulk and hull to Poseidon's slaughter
The closing whirlpool not the sea's rebuke

The closing whirlpool was not the sea's rebuke.

IX

In the labrys of the Mountain
In the circle of their communion
The womyn of Magdalena gather near
The daughters of the mothers
Among the new and surviving others
Go on living, made immortal o'er the years

Las mujeres de las Magdalenas!
How they stand for what's between us
And offer dreams of strength and woman power
Their many names are written down
Beneath the stones upon the ground
Where they sit to talk and laugh at any hour

They dance, sing or play the drums,
Bring news of what it is they've done,
At days' end, or decide their ways and means
They pass by word, by gift, and sign
The words you hear, I swear, not mine
They sent to me this Chant of Magdalene.

They sent to me this Chant of Magdalene.

Romance

INSIDE YOUR HEART

by Jackie Manthorne

I, Jackie Manthorne, am a Lesbian of 43 living in Montreal, Quebec with my lover of 17 years. I've been a writer all my life and a feminist activist since the early 70's. I write to celebrate our similarities and diversities and to explore how we relate to each other in friendship, love, lust and sex. My fondest hope is for the end of all forms of oppression and for a cure for AIDS.

Inside Your Heart

A nanosecond is just long enough to fall in love. At least that's what you tell me as you pull your old, battered suitcase out from under a dusty pile of old shoes and orphaned socks and yellowed paperbacks and bent coat hangers which have accumulated on the floor of your closet over the past four years.

"What on earth is a nanosecond?" I ask, deciding to be obtuse, unwilling to admit that under the circumstances, obstruction may be a lost cause. But my blood is up, and I feel determined. I will fight hard for you and I want you to know it; after four years, giving you up quietly and politely to another woman would be in incredibly bad taste.

"Don't get smart," you warn me. Your stare was meant to shrivel, but I brazenly wait you out, knowing that I can't become any more insignificant or miserable than you've already made me feel. "And anyway, she's going to be here in ten minutes," you warn me, sighing as you recognize my mood.

"And how many nanoseconds are there in ten minutes?" I ask sweetly, implying that it might as well be forever as I block your way to the living room. It's all mine anyway, my gestures inform you; you can take your clothes, a couple of records, a few books. The rest is MINE. If you want to use it, you'll have to stay here, because I sure as hell am not going to let you take any of it with you.

"I mean it," you snap. "She's going to pick me up here in ten minutes, so let me pack."

Who is this mysterious SHE, anyway? Some super intelligent computer whiz you fell in love with one day when you happened to glance over the top of your screen? One of those haughty, handsome businesswomen your partners are always introducing you to, the type with long, tastefully painted fingernails who drives a popular but expensive sports car and never, ever utters the word lesbian? A fluffy-haired puppy dog type who clumsily tripped over your big feet in the subway and then not-so-clumsily placed her hand on your breast or your groin to keep her balance and make you lose yours? Or did you actually have the nerve to fall in love with a mutual friend or go sniffing around one of those idiotic bars when I wasn't looking?

"So tell me about your incredibly exotic nanosecond," I cajole, mixing myself a stiff drink while watching your every move, just in case you try to stuff something that isn't yours into your suitcase.

"What are you talking about? It wasn't exotic, it was —" you pause momentarily in your packing, obviously trying to think of just the right word, one which you can safely utter in my presence.

"Erotic, then," I suggest, taking a painful breath as a bolt of jealousy strikes me right between the breasts.

You blush and pack faster, tossing in one thing after another. I can see that everything will be wrinkled, but this will serve you right, and that's about the mildest thing I want to call down on you for even thinking of leaving me.

"How could you do this to me?" I wail so plaintively that I'm half embarrassed. The other half is feeling quite righteous, possessed with determination.

"You don't understand how it was," you reply quickly, rushing to defend yourself. "You see, I fell in love."

Love? Huh! Lust, most likely. A flirtatious smile probably caught your fancy, or a fictitious compliment hit the mark, or the sight of a pair of rather shapely, unfamiliar breasts set your blood pounding in your veins, or the way she walked or touched you with her fingertips went right to your cunt. In short, somebody sold you a bill of goods about the grass being greener, the bed being bigger, the sex being hotter, the orgasms longer, more intense, guaranteed to take you somewhere I couldn't or your money back. I thought you knew better, I imagined you were getting enough at home, but no. My heart shrivels in just under a nanosecond as rage, jealousy and despair rivet me to the spot. I wish I could die and be reborn with a lover who never made me feel bad. My mouth grows dry and my hands and feet chill. Perhaps you'll reconsider? After all, lust is not love, and a couple of super-duper orgasms do not a relationship make.

I watch you take one of my favorite videotapes and push it to the bottom of your suitcase, and open my mouth to tell you to give it back to me this very minute, but you turn to me and shrug. "I really did fall in love."

I open my mouth again, this time to lose my temper, since everything else is already seemingly lost to me, but you're already halfway back into our bedroom, so I snap my mouth shut and follow you.

"How in hell could you fall in love without me knowing it?" I challenge you.

The radio is on and you're only partially listening to me. I don't believe it—you're going to walk out in what, half a nanosecond now—and there you are, sitting on our bed, listening to the news!

"You don't know everything," you reply finally as I reach over and turn off the radio. "Not even the half of it."

What am I going to do with you, I wonder as I move closer to the bed, intending to sit down. And how can I get through this dangerously feverish lust you've surrendered to and touch four year's worth of meaning before you slam the door on our relationship?

You smile up at me but I could be anybody, and that makes me want to groan.

"Don't make such a fuss," you say, and that does it: I really do lose my temper, and before either of us realize what's happening, I rush you, pushing you back on the bed and pinning you there.

"Don't be silly," you say unnecessarily, since both of us know that you're perfectly capable of tossing me to the floor with a flick of your well-developed muscles. But you don't, and we lie there together for the good part of a nanosecond, me panting from an excess of anger and hatred and love and desire and you holding your breath for reasons known only to yourself. The comingled breaths of Buddha and the raging prophet, I muse inanely. Are you meditating on the meaning of your impending release from our relationship? Was it humdrum, lacking in stimulation, old hat? Was the sex starting to lack some of that old je ne sais quoi, some spark of vitality? I feel this impulse to tie you down on the bed, to make sure you can't escape, to do something dramatic to bind you to me, to leave my brand upon your body, mind, soul.

Of course nothing suitable comes to mind, at least not until I start feeling that old, familiar warmth spreading out in hot, pulsating whirls wherever our bodies are touching. I look at you to see if you feel it too, but you jerk your head away.

"Look at me," I whisper with some urgency.

"No," you reply rather vehemently.

"Why not?" I ask, a smile growing somewhere deep inside.

"Let me up. I have to finish packing," you tell me, still avoiding my gaze.

"You don't really want to get up, do you?" I say, in a bad imitation of my normal tone of voice.

"The hell I don't!" you exclaim, and then we are kissing, deep, hard kisses coming one after the other, building strength, making claims, opening doors, sliding away from obligations, promises, accountability. I'll take it anyway, just like I'll take you now, right now. There's nothing like a good fit of jealousy to make me really want you, to make the shedding of our clothes extremely urgent, to harden my nipples, and yours too, I see.

"You are one hard bitch," you utter with no little respect as I lower myself on you, my body, hands, mouth, tongue rapidly spreading fire.

I smile and kiss you for a long, long time, and then slide further down, visiting your breasts for a short eternity. And only when your breath is coming in short gasps and your nipples are taut in my mouth do I move lower yet and open your legs, gently parting those smooth, swollen lips, bending to taste you, to slake my thirst on your wet need. I want to consume all of you, to fuck the distance away.

"You—"

"Yeah, it's me all right," I reply, groaning as I feel you straining urgently up to my touch. And as I slide three fingers into your cunt and increase the tempo of my stroking tongue, the doorbell rings.

You freeze. I slow down, still holding you close to me, my fingers gliding into you in long, slow thrusts, my mouth closing over your clit and sucking. I will you to forget her, concentrate on making you mine, struggle for possession of your body and your

"I've got to go," you say half-heartedly.

"You've got to come," I counter.

"No," you whisper. "I can't now."

"Look at me," I urge, reluctantly rising from between your thighs.

We stare at each other as my fingers continue to play sweet music on your clit and I touch your sensitive flesh, inserting only my fingertips into your quivering vagina every so often. I want to wipe the image of her face from your mind, to erase the succulent promise of new love which I know is exciting you precisely because it's so new. I want you to want me so much that you forget all about her. I want you to remember only me, remember only my touch.

"You don't really need her," I assert.

The doorbell rings again, its shrillness demanding a response.

"She's expecting me to answer," you whisper.

I hear the mute pleading in your voice and feel your body begin to withdraw, to reject my caresses. Your nipples shrink and flatten out and your vagina grows dry and narrow on my gently thrusting fingers. I remove my hand from your cunt and admit defeat by moving far enough away that our bodies are no longer touching.

"Do you really want to go away with her?" I ask, my desire waning to bitterness, my own juices curdling. This is it, I think. It's up to you now; I can't do another damn thing to keep you here.

"I love you," I hear you say. "But I love her too," you add after a pause.

Shit. And there goes the doorbell again. I think she's leaning on it now.

"I wonder what she's going to think when she sees me like this," you say as you rise from the bed.

"She'll think the truth," I reply. "She'll think you've been fucking," I add, reaching out and brushing a strand of hair from your face.

"And you? What do you think?" you ask cautiously, your eyes searching mine.

"I think that you don't love me enough," I tell you truthfully, putting all the games aside, admitting my vulnerability, no longer hedging my bets.

You nod as if this is exactly what you expected to hear. I watch you remove your housecoat from your suitcase and slip it over your naked body, and then you leave the room and close the door behind you without looking at me.

"Well," I say to myself. "Well, well, well." Because there's really nothing else to say, not when you shoot for the stars and end up with your ass in a deep mudpuddle. I pull the sheet up over me and try not to listen to the voices coming from the living room. And since you have to come back in here for your clothes and your suitcase, I concentrate on not starting to cry.

How can you love another woman when I love you so much? How could I have given you so much room, so much empty space to fill with someone else? And what are you actually talking about out there? Are you telling her why you're still wearing your housecoat when the requisite number of nanoseconds obviously passed some time ago? Are you trying to explain why you look like you've just had sex? If you weren't about to leave me, I'd really enjoy finding out whether you've managed to talk yourself out of that particular corner.

Hundreds of nanoseconds pass before you open the door again; I sit up as you approach the bed, afraid to interpret the expression on your face but yet unable to avert my eyes. You look sad; breaking up is always hard, even when you're the one doing all the breaking. Four years is a long time, isn't it?

"Move over," you say.

"What?"

"I said move over," you repeat, dropping your housecoat to the floor.

I'm stunned, although not too stunned to move, and before you can change your mind, I slide over and make space for you in bed beside me.

"What's going on?" I ask, feeling breathless as hope expands and battles with despair, with the acute sense of loss which had nearly overwhelmed me just moments before. We pull the covers up to our chins and you move closer until your warm, naked body comes into contact with mine.

"I like your foreplay," you reply, a slightly wicked smile toying at the corners of your mouth as you turn towards me and grasp my breasts in your hands.

"Is she gone?" I whisper, my body swiftly growing aroused from your rapid-fire touches.

"Uh-huh," you answer, your voice muffled against my neck.

"But what happened?" I manage to utter as your hand slides down over my belly and promptly discovers just how wet and ready my cunt is.

"Shhh," you scold, and then I know that you have no intention of telling me anything, that your persistent love making is your way of changing the subject. But what can I do? I've never learned to resist your caresses, to counter the insistent touch of your skin, lips, hands, tongue.

"She is gone, isn't she?" I finally utter.

"Yes, of course she's gone," you hiss as you lift my leg and wrap it over your hip.

"For good?" I ask, as you rub the back of your hand over my exposed cunt.

"Uh—" you reply as you start rubbing yourself on my thigh. So you like my foreplay. I ponder this knowledge as our bodies surrender themselves to the comforting, primal rhythm of good, hot sex.

"Oh!" I gasp and then I come. As soon as I can see straight I eagerly move over you, wanting more than anything else to feel you take your own release on my mouth and tongue.

"That was so good," you sigh when you're finally exhausted, and I slip up beside you and cuddle you in my arms.

"Yes it was," I reply, deciding there and then that you simply must love me or you wouldn't still be here.

"I love you," I say sleepily.

"Me too," you whisper.

So just remember that next time then, I think as I possessively pull you closer just before I fall asleep.

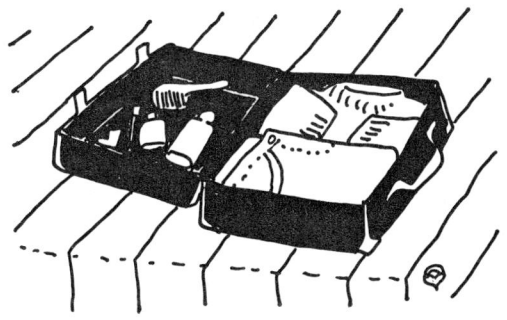

Humor

The Thing That Would Not Hide!

by Julie Blackwomon

Julie Blackwomon is a poet and fiction writer who lives and writes in Philadelphia, Pennsylvania. Most recently she has been published in the humor anthology Women's Glib, scheduled for publication in the Spring of 1991 and Voyages out 2.

She freely admits her warped sense of humor and believes that people will not only listen to your message longer if you make them laugh, they may even hear you better. She sees humor as a subversive activity and envisions a world in which the nasty isms are erased because the practitioners are all busy laughing at each other while engaging in the art of masturbation. Unfortunately, she also envisions a world in which some humorless explitive deleted will use this tongue-in-cheek biographical note to prove she is or she is not...fill in the blank. Just keep laughing.

The Thing That Would Not Hide!

"I've got something in my closet besides clothes," the client said.

The psychologist leaned back in her black leather arm chair, and nodded for the new client to continue. The client, a distraught woman of about twenty-eight, sat crumpling tissues onto the plush brown carpet.

The doctor took note of the fact that the cleaning lady would not approve. She reached over and picked up a pen and a yellow legal-sized tablet. "Continue," she prompted.

"It's a dildo," the client said as if she'd just admitted to a weakness for rare pork, topped with white sugar, to a new and deadly serious jogging-four-miles-a-day type health food junky.

The client took a deep breath and hurried along lest she bolt from the doctor's office in panic. "I have a dildo in my closet," she repeated. And only because she'd practiced saying this repeatedly at home in the privacy of her bedroom, was she finally able to resist an intense urge to reach for the ruler on the doctor's desk to give her own knuckles a sound rapping.

"I see," the doctor said. She stopped writing and put down her pen. She checked the room for electronic bugs. As casually as she could she got up, walked over and closed the blinds to her ninth floor office. This disclosure was top secret and the doctor did not want the client's shameful secret overheard by someone who might disclose the information to the lesbian feminist community. There could be retribution. The doctor then looked sereptitiously around her small office. She started back to her desk then stopped short. For extra measure she went back and closed and locked the windows. She did this despite the fact that it was 92 degrees in the office and the air conditioner was not working.

Back at her desk, the doctor again picked up her pen and note pad. "What about it?" she asked, feigning an air of nonchalance.

"Then you've heard about them?" the client asked cautiously.

The Thing That Would Not Hide

"Is that important to you?" the doctor asked in that maddening way therapists have of answering questions with questions.

The client stared at her.

The doctor stared back but she had her soothing, "everything-will-be-alright" smile on her face. The client managed a weak smile in return.

The doctor cleared her throat and wiped her wire-rimmed eye glasses on a tissue that she pulled from a box on her desk. "Now, tell me, Ms. Jones..." she began again.

"Oh please call me Jennifer, Dr. Harris," the client said.

"Alright, Jennifer," Dr. Harris continued. She was so focused on the enormity of the client's problem that she forgot to tell Jennifer that of course it was okay to call her Laura. "It says here in your intake file that you're a lesbian feminist. Is that accurate?"

"Yes it is."

"Can you tell me why you feel you fit that classification?"

The client immediately rose to her feet, slapped her hand over her heart, and said as if reciting a learned text: "I've been lesbian for ten years, dyke for seven. I spell women with O's and I's. I go to women's conferences, march in lesbian and gay pride rallies, dress dyke chic: jeans and sneakers, no bra, no polyester. I took separatism, collectivism and non-hierarchical revolutionary movements 101 through 199. And I call men 'boys' and 'mutants.'"

Dr. Harris smiled and nodded her head as she took note of Jennifer's nervous twitches and signs of "acute anxiety." The doctor had been counseling lesbian feminists, like herself, for twelve years and this was the most severe case of dildo panic she had ever seen. Dr. Harris realized it was induced by dildo guilt. "You have impressive credentials, Jennifer," Dr. Harris said.

"Oh I'm serious about my politics, alright."

"So where exactly in your closet is this, ah, thing?"

"It's in the linen closet, hidden down between the white sheets and an old down comforter I use when it's really cold. At least that's where it was when I last saw it," the client said, her upper lip quivering. "Trouble is it won't stay there. It likes to stick it's little brown head out between the sheets and say 'boo!' to everybody. I can't let my friends use the bathroom any more."

"However do you explain that?"

"I say, 'You can't use my bathroom because the toilet's stopped up.'"

"This sounds like a serious situation, but let's back up a bit. You say you're having auditory hallucinations?"

"I beg your pardon?"

"You indicated that your dildo talks to you."

"It does, doc, I swear it does!" the client said, raising her right hand, as if taking an oath. "I was totally shocked. It wouldn't be so bad if it confined its comments to me, but it's freaking out my friends too."

"Embarrassing is it?"

"Extremely," the client lamented. "I'm a radical lesbian feminist with separatist leanings. This could ruin my standing in the community. Last year I tried to give it up for Lent. I figured if that worked then perhaps I would be able to wean myself of it entirely."

"But that didn't work out?"

"No, I kept waking up in the morning with it in my bed, it's cute little head on my pillow." The client sat back in her chair and relaxed a little. "You see, doctor," she continued, "intellectually, I realize that dildos are just another form of penetration. The problem is that somewhere lurking in the back of my mind is the suspicion that there is a progression here—or rather a regression—like first penetration, then dildos, then men. See what I mean?"

"But that isn't the case, is it?" the doctor asked kindly.

"No, of course not, I'm a dyke because I love women, because I love the way women look, and feel and smell. But most of all I love the way women think.

The problem with penises is that every penis I ever ran across has been attached to a male head. Inside that male head is a male mind. That's what I really cannot deal with, the way men think, the garbage you have to go through to relate to one. And frankly I also find semen rather gross."

"But you still like dildos, which you see as a substitue for the male penis?"

"No, not so. A dildo is a substitute for female fingers, another woman's fingers inside me. It's the penetration I like. I mean, gosh, I didn't invent the damn thing, they could change the shape for all I care. It's just that dildos are the only things which are

The Thing That Would Not Hide

created for penetration. When I make love with a woman using a dildo I think about the woman I'm making love with. The dildo is an extension of her, not some bone-headed man. When I use it alone, I'm still thinking of a woman's fingers, a woman's body."

"You seem to be fairly comfortable with the use of the dildo, so what brings you to my office?"

"Well, the problem all started when I got this vibrator which I keep by my bed on the nightstand. Sometimes, when I'm making love with another woman, we use the vibrator. Well, to tell you the truth, lately my dildo has been getting jealous. It seems to feel that I like the vibrator more than I like it. Now I can't make love with another woman in my house anymore. When I do, the dildo makes rude noises from the closet."

"What sort of noises?"

Jennifer turned a bright crimson. "You know...sexy noises."

"Could you be more specific?" Dr. Harris had laid down her pen and tablet and now watched intently as Jennifer ran her hands up and down her own thighs. Obviously the mere thought of it was getting Ms. Jones all stirred up.

"Do I have to tell you?" Jennifer asked.

"Not if you really don't want to," the doctor replied.

"Well," the client said, relenting, "she imitates the sounds I make when I'm approaching orgasm."

"Do you do a lot of oohs and ahs?"

"Well...yes."

"A few 'Oh baby, Oh babys' interspersed for variety?" Dr. Harris found her legs drifting apart, then abruptly remembered where she was. She reached for her pen and pad again and cleared her throat."

"So when your dildo makes rude noises what do you tell your lovers?"

"That I've got rats."

"Rats," Dr. Harris repeated, incredulous, her silver pen now poised over the yellow tablet. "They can deal with rats better than a dildo?"

"Of course, at least rats are normal."

"And you feel that dildos aren't normal?"

"Well, it's just that all the women I respect feel that dildos are the toys of heterosexual women and gay men. And that any decent, self-respecting, politically correct dyke should be able to enjoy making love without penetration. They say if the Goddess had wanted us to enjoy penetration, dykes would have been born with six-inch forefingers or at least cucumbers. Have you ever tried cucumbers?"

The doctor ignored the last question. "You have problems with thoughts of penetration too?" Dr. Harris asked.

"Politically correct dykes say the Goddess gave us fingers for stimulating the clitoris."

"Oh, I see," Dr. Harris said, making a few notes on her note pad. "And you're having trouble with this?"

"Yes, if the lesbian feminist community found out about it they'd call me names," Jennifer said plaintively.

The doctor made more notations on her note pad. "What kind of names?" she asked when she looked up.

"Well, you know, horrible names like 'heterosexual,' 'bisexual' and, worst of all, 'male identified.' I keep having this nightmare in which I'm giving a large potluck dinner for something really important like raising money for legal defense of lesbian mothers, or to help support pro-choice candidates or something, and all my lesbian activist friends are there. Suddenly my dildo comes downstairs and materializes like a roach on a white table cloth. All the polite dykes continue on with their conversations, convinced their eyes are deceiving them. But then some curious soul reaches over and touches it and the dildo writhes with pleasure, while all the radical dykes run yelling and screaming from the table in horror. It's just awful," Jennifer said with her eyes bugged out. She paused and absent-mindedly chewed her fingernail down to the quick. "And there's something else too." She paused again, then continued without additional prompting. "Listen, I have to tell you all of it right? I mean, it won't do any good if I hold things back?"

"Feel free to say whatever's on your mind," Dr. Harris said, encouragingly.

"I'm afraid they'll torture me."

"You mean, beat you?" Dr. Harris asked, slightly alarmed.

"Worse!"

"How then?"

"Guilt tripping! Do you have any idea what a burden it is to feel

The Thing That Would Not Hide

that one of the ways you make love oppresses all lesbians? That your orgasm perpetuates the stereotype men have of lesbians?"

"It really gets to you, huh?" the doctor said.

"Damn right!"

"It appears that you have two choices, Jennifer: either you must stop internalizing bad feelings about your desire for a dildo, in which case you'll stop feeling badly; or you can give up your dildo."

"It's not that simple, doctor. You see my dildo is well..." she looked around, flushed. "You see, my dildo is not like any ordinary dildo. It has a mind of its own. Last week I used the dildo in the privacy of my own bedroom, and then I went to a concert. Alone. When I looked around my dildo was lying on the chair next to me as brazen as you please. Fortunately, I was able to snatch it up and place it in my coat pocket before anyone saw it. When I got home it went quietly back into the closet, but not before it said to my vibrator, still lying on the nightstand next to my bed, 'See, I bet she never took you to a concert!'"

"Then you still keep your dildo hidden in a closet?"

"Where the hell else?" Jennifer asked, exasperated now.

Dr. Harris looked thoughtful. "I see," she said. "That might be the problem."

"I beg your pardon?"

Dr. Harris made a few additional notes, then looked up at the client.

"Does your dildo have a name?"

"Of course not."

"What's your vibrator's name?" the doctor asked, playing a hunch.

"Sappho," the client replied matter-of-factly.

"What's your car's name?"

"Assatta." Jennifer looked puzzled.

Ms. Jones, your dildo is acting out because it obviously feels it's not getting it's proper share of attention." Dr. Harris stood up now and checked her watch. Time was almost up. "I think if you treat your dildo just a little bit special, you won't have any more trouble out of her. That will be sixty-five dollars please."

As Dr. Harris walked Jennifer to the door, the client stopped and said, "Maybe next week I can make another appointment to talk about my black leather harness..."

"Anything you want to talk about we can handle in here in strictest confidence," Dr. Harris assured her new client.

"Can we talk about condoms and rubber dams?"

"Whatever is on your mind," Dr. Harris said just before she closed the door to her office.

She then went back to her desk, got her purse, then unlocked and pulled out the drawer on the bottom left-hand side. There, lying nestled in the drawer next to a pink vibrator was the cutest, most well-trained lavender dildo any radical lesbian feminist would ever want to know and love. She reached down and petted it.

"Did I do alright, Taboo?" she asked her beloved dildo. She gave it a platonic kiss on it's inoffensive head and stood admiring it while the theme song from 'Dr. Zhivago' played softly in the background.

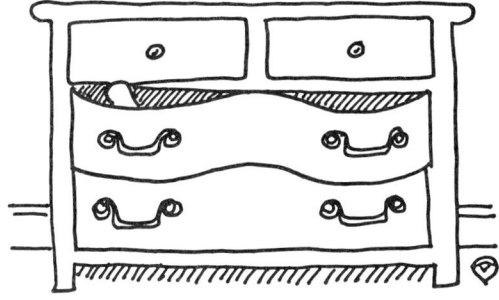

Relationships

HOWL

by Penelope Pratt

Penelope Pratt is not a real lesbian. She is a nomme de plume. Penelope wears make-up and dresses when she damn well feels like it. When she does so, men don't realize that she feels like she's dressing in drag.

Penelope is a big woman; she loves living in the woods. Like so many lesbians she is now ready to transform the self-healing 80's into the planet healing 90's. Oh yes, we should make them the gay 90's as well.

HOWL

It started off being a normal day, and it eventually turned out that way, I guess, but out here on women's land "normal" has broad meaning. Broad meaning is like this blessed open ground we live on, high up the south slope of a small mountain in a big natural bowl. It's poor country here, but it's wild country, too. Living and being together, on land, is what makes us rich women, I think.

Quite a few years ago some practical, idealistic women joined monies and bought this spread. Now, in so-called legal terms it's a landtrust—none of us "own" it but by a lease that each of us can sell or swap we can be here for life—if we want to be. Longevity of lesbian land groups is about the same as the longevity of our personal relationships though, and I think the reasons are similar. It has something to do with our long snarly teeth that only come out when we're feeling like sweet little lambs.

My lover, Dorr, had gone off with Bo to do a town trip. I thought I'd take an easy day; I must have been clenching my teeth again in the night, my jaw was real achey—more than usual. It was the day of full moon. No sooner had I arrived at the main house to get myself tiger balm for my jaw than I heard loud voices. They were coming from the back porch and they were rising.

Uh-oh, I thought. Louise has the kind of voice that increases like earthquake numbers: from one to five isn't much; six to eight is devastating.

"So you're telling me I can't be here?" Louise was bellowing. "I LIVE HERE, GODDAM IT!"

Not backing down, in her most leisurely upper-class Southern drawl, Gene reiterated, "It's Sappho."

"You're telling me Sappho has no right to live here?!"

"I'm telling you to supervise your dog!"

"Sappho is not my dog! Sappho is her *own* dog! She has just as much right to freedom as any woman does!"

"But she snuck up on me! It terrified me! Doesn't that infringe on *my* freedom?"

"Sappho is not an IT!" screamed Louise.

"Gimme a break! It doesn't fucking matter *what* Sappho is. Nobody has a right to show their teeth and growl at somebody else, especially for no good reason. I was at my own cabin! Keep your goddammed 'it' on a goddammed leash!"

"Sappho is not an IT!" screamed Louise.

I peaked out the back window and though Louise was restraining Sappho, Sappho was being pretty wild. Picking up the energy, she began snarling and snapping the air. Gene is afraid of dogs. Yukky gilrhood stuff, I guess. She ran into the workshop, slammed the door and cried for help.

Taking immediate, decisive action, especially to end a fight between women, is not one of my fortés. Though I know shepherd/wolf dogs can be pretty scarey, I didn't think Sappho had ever bitten anyone. I didn't think she would, especially not Gene. I found myself thinking: *Oh great. What is this gonna do to tonight's fire circle?* I knew none of the fightees would attend. Three women missing out of seven makes a big dent.

Instead of acting, I stood there and began to fret. Louise is our best story teller and her lover, Bo, is a great drummer. Wherever Louise won't go Bo won't, either. Gene would be staying by herself, 40 acres away, based on some vague and important personal principles, I was sure. Gene is by far and away our best singer. Without her there we'd be as good as without songs.

I bravely peaked out the window. Nothing much had changed except that Sappho was sitting down. It was obvious to *me* (leaning against the kitchen wall) that all Louise had to do to end the altercation (and Gene's entrapment) was to take herself and her non-dog Sappho away from the house and the back porch area. Something about Western culture has always made it difficult for one person to share the obvious with another, however. This was especially true since Louise was looking meaner than her dog.

Just then, as must only happen on women's land, two women I'd never seen before burst into the main house, walked right up to me and stuck out their hands in unison. The first said, "Hi, I'm Carol."

"And I'm Brook," said her companion. "We're from Missouri and did we ever get lost finding this place. We got to hear coyotes but we meant to get here last night instead of sleeping on top of that mountain over yonder." She pointed.

"But we're glad to be here now," chimed in Carol. She was a short, muscular, anglo woman who was still decked out in her silky green-and-blue traveling clothes. She had some kind of green stones hanging from not only her ears, but also from her wrists and neck.

"My name is Casey," I said. "Is anybody expecting you? She should be the one to welcome you and show you around."

"Louise," they said together.

"Oh, that's good." *A goddess send,* I thought. I invited them to our usual, monthly, full moon circle that night. When I opened up the back porch door these two effectively and totally distracted Louise. Also Sappho. Sappho jumped up on them and wagged ferociously. She even rolled over on her back for them. Canines have a way without words.

I released Gene from the workshop, where she had been hiding. I ascertained that she was allright, then I hugged her. "Are you still going to the circle tonight?" I asked hopefully.

"Nope."

"Aw, c'mon," I whined. "Sappho won't be there."

"No, she'll probably be at my house," Gene said ruefully.

"Nah. She won't bother you. Why would she bother you?"

"Cuz she likes me."

"Then why'd she growl at you?"

"Cuz I shooed her with a broom," Gene admitted.

•

It was still being a normal day; I'd asked Gene if she wanted to do some planting with me, so we could chat, but Gene said no. Gene's a burly, butchy woman, brown-haired and hazel eyed—tall and luscious and partly everything as far as stock. She's strong willed, righteous, and you probably don't know a more committed feminist, although there're lots of us. She's lived on the land as long as anyone. At one time I think she'd been Alpha Female, but now, except for the woman who sometimes visited her from Syracuse, she mostly stayed by herself... I know I'm not the only one who tried hard not to take her newfound unpersonableness personally.

I headed for the garden. I *adore* our garden. Not only is it centrally located, that lush, loved, half acre of women's ground is the hub of our land community. It's our economy and meeting place. We even have some benches under the apple trees for when we get tired. Just that day Rhon and Carlita had held hands and talked for some time there after they'd finished weeding and foraging. I gave them plenty of space. They're so sweet and new together.

It was a gloriously beautiful summer day. How could I forget to mention that? I gazed over at Bear Butte, then further, out into the layers of forested hillsides. I strolled around our bulging beds of beans, brocolli, and squash. Although the greens were on the wane, the corn was more than waist high.

I thought it would be good for us to have more carrots. To eat them raw is very good for jaw problems, you know. And though I try to restrain my superstitions, I kept thinking that if we had more carrots a juicer would "come to us." It's difficult to squeeze the little buggers by hand.

I love to dig, and I had lots of energy, so I thought I'd just go ahead and prepare a brand new 5 by 15 foot bed for more carrots. Though full moons are supposedly not a good time to plant they are very good for opening... for changing things.

I saw Louise briefly as she dumped the compost bucket and gave the whole pile a turn. Louise and I waved. Sappho and the new visitors weren't with her.

Louise is a large woman, with big hands and big feet. She's got black hair, a rugged complexion, close set eyes and a good sized nose. As she turned away I caught a profile of her jaw. Such determination. Such strength! Even though Louise has a well-earned reputation for her horrible temper I've always been friendly towards her. I figure there're a lot worse things for lesbians to have than anger.

Energetically at first I dove into the unwatered, hardpanned rock and clay soil. While I was digging I sortof started thinking about Louise's jaw, her firm, dark Italian line. Then I had a vision. Just like in a nature movie, only in my head, I saw a shark open its mouth, roll its eyes all the way back and then bingo, ATTACK! Then the vision filled my mind of a dog—a wolf descendant like Sappho— its jaws locked into the leg of an obviously bad man who was futilely beating and kicking and walloping the beast who just *would not* let go. I admit it. I found the idea not the least bit unpleasant. But where is this coming from? I thought. I'm not really the psychic type so I didn't get an answer. But then, as I worked, I entertained myself thinking of all kinds of bitey things: of coons and snakes and squirrels, of wolves and bears and bobcats. I tried to imagine the strength they must have in their jaws that allows them to really hang on like that once they bite down. No, I don't have a bad attitude. I'd just say it's high time for the empowerment of nature and animals and women... What we do have on our side is powerful tenacity.

The more I thought of all of this the more I thought it was definitely something to think about. I thought of black ants' humongous mandibles, who I can't really say are bad for successfully defending their homes against all odds. I bet wild and toothy creatures depend, probably even thrive on the release and temporary insanity they use to really clamp down when they have to. When a dentist told me about 12 years ago to quit clenching my teeth she didn't tell me *how*. While I let myself think of things that bothered me— especially since nobody was around in the garden with me—I put my lips back and sortof snarled for the rest of the afternoon.

Gee. It felt great.

By dinnertime, sweaty and dirty and leaning on my shovel more than into it, not only had my teeth stopped hurting but I'd created a weed-free, double dug, unraked and unplanted 3 by 13 foot bed for future carrots. Satisfied, I wanted to bathe and eat before Dorr got home and we went to the evening's circle. Dorr would have eaten in town; french fries, certainly. I munched a raw carrot and ran down to the swimming hole. I plunged in and screamed happily.

I know lots of lesbians think full moon circles are flaky, but being with a group of good-humored lesbians, sharing, in harmony, around a flickering fire has helped put more joy in my life than I ever even hoped for back in my isolated and unhappy beginnings in Straightville, PA. In fact, maybe the moon has nothing to do with it, but coming out as a lesbian is the best thing I've ever done in my life. The best thing that's ever *happened* to me is experiencing the love of lesbians, and living within this country lesbian community.

When my darling Dorr got home she told me all about our new solar-powered water pump and I told her all about our new 3 by 13 foot carrot bed. We decided that we still felt like going to the moon circle. Fights on women's land are almost as common as sunrises so we determined not to let other women's fussing spoil our evening. On the other hand, fights between Louise and Gene were becoming almost as much an institution as these two women were on Howl Farm: and we all hoped they'd work it out soon. Without forgiveness and compromise habitual tensions can escalate to eventual disaster for land groups. Maybe that's why so many lesbians are living in cities during this part of the century.

By the time we got to the circle Rhon had already built the fire and Carlita, who lives in the uppermost tipi, was flossing her teeth. They'd both heard the fight had been a pretty bad one. The way they'd heard is that Louise's yelling had echoed over the entire land via the river canyon.

It was early; the newcomers weren't there yet. They were probably still making a camp and besides, when the full moon first comes up through the pine trees in the back meadow every woman is bound to start looking real good to her lover. If those two got to celebrating the full moon just between themselves I knew there'd be a good chance they'd never show.

I'd brought my drum. Dorr had brought her sticks. We sat down and started in. One drum sure isn't the same as drumming with Bo or with an entire circle, but even in the diminutive, drumming is the goddess's gift to country women.

We started low and easy, like always, and let the rhythm build. Drumming builds just like emotions do but a whole lot safer. Drumming is also the doorway to other worlds. Drumming suspends time and brings stars down to our level. Or is it us up to theirs?

Rhon was making some pretty good sounds with her tambourine; Carlita put her floss into the fire and started to dance. Carlita has a body like an hour glass. It was quite a warm night so she was only wearing a halter top above her full length skirt. She was barefoot. As she danced her feet ran over the earth like rain does: it patters first, before it sinks in.

At the fire circle it takes longer for the moon to rise than in the back meadow. Rhon was the first to see it and then we all joined her in hooting and howling. Hooting and hollering is another fine gift of the nature spirit or whatever you call her. Howling is primal singing. Pure.

In the full moonlight I saw Sappho come running from the back meadow. She was thrusting and churning like a new pump and in no time she was running around our circle. I swear I saw a smile on that companion beast's face before she bounded off towards the north woods.

With renewed vigor the two of us kept clacking and beating. Carlita was flowing around and Rhon took a fire stick and drew it purposefully through the air. I was mesmerized by watching the trails. There is no television on earth that can simulate the red-golden glow of embers against the white and black sky of a full moon. The moon must have disappeared behind some clouds because out of nowhere, to my surprise, appeared Louise. She was wearing her full brown cape. From across the circle she mouthed to Dorr, "Have you seen Sappho?" Dorr nodded, had her fingers do the running, then she shrugged and pointed to the north woods. Louise mouthed, "Thank you ," then disappeared.

Just as I started to wish that Bo would overlook Louise and Gene's quarrel and come and do some drumming (my hands were getting burny but I can always drum forever when Bo's around) Bo approached the circle from the west. Good old Bo. Just as if we were only sewing or sawing wood Bo said outloud, "Has Louise been here?"

Our racket dropped way down and Rhon said, "Yeah. She's looking for Sappho. They both went thataway." Rhon pointed to the north woods and then in mass realization our jaws dropped. Rhon was pointing in the direction of Gene's cabin!

Bo took off running. She's built for it and has championed in it. It was as if she flew by pumping her legs. Mine was the only drum in the circle and I knew not to let that energy wane. My hands followed Bo's feet. Lightly.

One of the new women approached the circle from the moonside. Her body was a silhouette against the moonlit forest. Even in the moonlight I could tell she was still wearing all those green stones. She was carrying a conga. Her partner carried a walking stick. She held it up like a staff.

"HAAAAAAAAAAAAYYYYYYYYYYYYYYY" she

bellowed, forever, from a bottomless pit that must have been her lungs. The sound was thin but long, and the sound was like two or three women's voices in one, and sharp like a knife. I noticed more than a couple of us turned, confused as to where the sound was coming from. Were Gene and Louise at it again?

I'm not going to make any outlandish claims about magic, but the sound of the drum I was playing grew deeper and louder of its own accord. With every step they took the women dancing seemed to lift off the ground. I sensed we were all praying. But who knows for what?

The green-stoned Missourian pulled out a rattle, the kind that's made from seeds strung around a gourd. It made a loud scratching sound, the kind that can go right through you, and it did. We drummed and we danced and we rattled: the country woman boogie. We let it go on and on—how long?—maybe 15 minutes; time flies. When I suddenly noticed that the burning in my hands had progressed to numbness and then back to burning we all mellowed out in unison; it wasn't my doing. I stopped drumming and then everything was real quiet. Like when you can hear the forest breathing.

I looked up and Rhon was adding wood to the fire; she's such a good fire woman. She loves trees and derives her power from everything transforming through them. She almost took the name Wood, and then almost Walnut, which she says is hard and burns hot, and has that deep, full color. But to truly take a nature name would mean to become nameless, she says. God, she's so complex!

Dorr and I touched eyes. For a long time. "I pray for strong, sweet, safe, sultry sex. Tonight," she said while holding my eyes. I blushed. I'm shier now than I was with her six years ago. And deeper, further, in love.

"I pray for planetary peace and clean air and clean water and unmolested rainforests everywhere," said Carol while holding her staff.

"And I pray for the prosperity and safety of women everywhere," said Carlita.

"I pray for Gene and Louise to work it out," said Bo as she reentered the circle. She looked tired; the struggle was not new and it looked like, indeed, she'd just left it again. Gene and Louise had been lovers when they'd first come to Howl. They were the only two women from the original land group still living there. When Bo had come, two years ago, the three of them had tried non-monogamy, faithfully, but alas it seems they'd (as usual?) loved and lost.

"I pray somebody figures out some solutions to the dilemmas of lesbian sexuality," said Rhon. We all laughed. Seriously.

There was a pause. It was my turn to pray if I wanted. I pray a lot, and for lots of ideals. This time I said, "I want strong jaws, lots of carrots and a juicer right here at Howl Farm to juice them with."

"We've got a juicer," said Brook.

"In that Honda?" I asked incredulously.

"Yep," said Carol of the many greens.

"Can I use it while you're around? How long are you going to be around?"

"As long as it feels right," they said together.

I looked at Dorr and my eyes filled with tears. Oh shucks.

From outside the circle we heard howling. We all joined in, one at a time. When Gene came into the firelight she looked radiant. We saw that she was accompanied by Sappho who, for reasons beyond my comprehension, was obviously pleased and proud to be at the end of Gene's rope, on a leash. Gene smiled at me. She sat down next to Bo and placed her hand on Bo's knee.

I think it was more than a coincidence that the rest of us started looking around at the moon and each other instead of Gene and Bo and Sappho. I never asked just what exactly had been said and done but a few minutes later, when Louise entered the circle, her eyes looked closer together, her face longer, and her jaw was more powerfully relaxed. She sat down next to Gene and the two of them held hands.

Gene told us a story about an angry woman, lonesome and free, who howled at the moon one night until she became a wolf. She turned in the moonlight and in the shadows she found her old pack, who loved her more dearly than she had ever realized. They ran off together into the mountains and the towering, shimmering pines.

Every full moon the wolves decided to become women together. This way they could talk and have quarrels, sing and dance, and generally just have fun. And that's the way HOWL farm came to be...

    That night Dorr and I made love while growling and snarling and smiling. The next day we installed our new solar-powered water pump and very little went wrong. We had our lunch together at the upper pond. Towards evening, Dorr and I planted our new 3 by 13 foot bed while Rhon and Carlita kissed on the bench in the garden.
    Louise and Gene are friends again and Sappho spends a lot of time with Gene... I just wanted you to know we're doing fine out here on women's land. You could say we're all living happily ever after.

Humor

La Llorona Loca: The Other Side

by Monica Palacios

Hello. This is Monica Palacios. Nice meeting you. Firm handshake. I must tell you the history behind my story. I am a writer/comedy performer and I wrote La Llorona Loca: The Other Side *as a humorous piece for a Latina lesbian event. Since that time, I have been performing this piece and getting great response from lesbians of all colors.*

The original Llorona story is a tragedy from heterosexual Latino folklore. In writing this lezbo version, I wanted to respect my Latino roots by maintaining the tragic sense of it. So I'm sorry my story doesn't have a happy ending. But please note, I am living in LA performing comedy and writing, promoting positive images of people of color, women, gays and lesbians. The time has come to educate the masses and I want to be part of this teaching wave from the shores of Hollywood.

La Llorona Loca: The Other Side

Growing up, my mother told me scary stories of the Latino folkloric character known as La Llorona Loca—the crazy cryer. According to my mother, "...This woman drowned her children because she apparently woke up on the wrong side of the bed—a little pissed off..." And as the story goes, La Llorona, realizing she had done this terrible act, tried to deal with her crazed sorrow by searching and crying desperately for her children. The story also states, as she wailed, she wore a long white gown and I'm guessing—low heels... remember, she's searching.

I have always been fascinated by the legendary Llorona Loca and I knew there had to be more to her.

Was she trying to wean herself from caffeine when this notorious incident happened? What was her astrological sign? And, did she know about networking? My curious mind led me to the world famous Llorona Loca Archives at UCLA and there, my friends, I found a story that was never told to me. And now I present to you:

LA LLORONA LOCA: THE OTHER SIDE

Many years ago in Mexico, lived a very beautiful woman by the name of Caliente (hot)! Every man wanted her—every woman wanted to be like her. She was the essence of cool as she carried herself proudly, even though she had flat feet. Her face was stunning—perfect bone structure, olive skin, pouty lips, sexy nose and dark brown eyes that shot out fire. All these delicious features were surrounded by thick, wavy, dark hair that she tossed as she walked down the street, making the men shout:

"Ay, mamasita!"

"Come here, baby."

"Let me touch your chi-chi's."

Yeah—she was really beautiful.

But there was something really different about her—something that the townspeople could not figure out. As beautiful as she was,

she had not married. She was never seen with a man. And this girl was thirty years old! So it was like—you know—what's up? The townspeople would whisper amongst themselves:
"Lack of male companionship."
"She wears spurs on her house slippers."
"She's always eyeing the senoritas. I bet she's a PE Teacher!"

One glorious day, a stranger rode into town, looking for a woman. The stranger galloped down the main drag when all of a sudden—the stranger caught the eye of Caliente who was sitting on her porch balancing her checkbook. Their eyes locked—Caliente walked towards the stranger. The stranger took off her hat—that's right—I said her hat! Her black curly locks slowly danced all the way down to her leather chaps. Caliente dropped her checkbook! To Caliente, the stranger was looking mighty fine and very voluptuous. The stranger spoke in her best bedroom voice. "If you want something good, you will ride with me and you will be my woman—MI MUJER!" Caliente quickly jumped on the stranger's horse and the new couple briskly rode out of town. They had no choice—they were being chased by many macho Mexican dudes.

The women stopped in Tiajuana, got married by a curandero (witch-doctor) and eventually settled down in Bakersfield; happy, in love and always doing it. Until the morning came when La Stranger (as she was affectionately called by Caliente because her real name was Petronilia de La Chihuahua y que!), when La Stranger took Caliente to their favorite spot by the river. Caliente was looking as radiant as ever—dressed all in white, her skin was aglow and her lips were red with passion! La Stranger put Caliente's hand in hers, "Mi vida [my life], I am like the river. I am happiest when I am moving."

Caliente gave La Stranger a perplexed look and then said, "Cut the crap. Get to the point!"

La Stranger smiled and said, "Mi reina [my queen], every Wednesday during the last six months while you were at your Latina I Am Woman You Are Scum support group, I was having an affair with—with—Trixie!"

Caliente grabbed La Stranger's hand and bit it. "Puta! [Whore—as if you didn't know!] Trixie is such a sleaze ball. She'll do anything with anybody for a quarter!"

La Stranger chuckled and said, "Yeah, that's Trixie."

Jealousy filled Caliente's body from head to toe. La Stranger could feel the fire burning from Caliente's eyes. (She kind of looked like my mom when I came home drunk from my friend's quinceniera [debutante bash].)

La Stranger blurted out, "Now look, baby, let's talk. Let's get into a feeling circle." Caliente slapped La Stranger who then said, "Okay, let's not get into a feeling circle. You can have all the property!"

But Caliente could not control herself. She jumped on La Stranger and pushed her into the river, holding her head down until—until La Stranger's body went limp. Caliente, realizing she had done this horrible, horrible act, started to cry uncontrollably until she fainted into the river and died. I'm sorry to bring you down, folks—but that's life.

Two hours later, a group of women on a boat (they were returning from a sexual healing weekend) spotted the two floating bodies, figured it was a "love thang" and buried them together by the river bank. A week after the burial, a villager was getting water from the river and was startled by an eerie cry of a woman. At first the man thought it was really loud Carly Simon music, but as he listened closely, he could hear something about "a stranger." The villager walked towards the cry and a woman appeared from the bushes, dressed all in white and wearing clogs. He jumped back and gasped, "Clogs?! That's so 70's."

The ghostlike woman sobbed to him, "Have you seen La Stranger?"

The man ran back to the village to tell the others what he'd seen. They had also heard the crying even as they watched Wheel of Fortune. From this time on, the people heard and saw this woman almost every night—searching for La Stranger. Her crying was so hysterical, everyone began to call her La Llorona Loca—the crazy cryer. Well, almost everyone. There was this one family who insisted on calling her Loretta.

Humor

Connexions

by Joell Smith

Joell Smith has just been given the opportunity to introduce herself to the entire Lesbian community (practically) and she has suddenly developed a severe case of writer's block. So I, Jojo, Lesbian Mutant Ninja Escort and secret alter-ego of Joell, am stepping in. Joell is 24, or was in 1991, if you're reading this in some future time. She is a graduate student (and probably still is, regardless of when you're reading this) with no real plans for the future except to continue avoiding the real world for as long as possible. She apparently has a problem with any job that doesn't offer two weeks off for Christmas and four months off for summer. With her wonderfully ugly dog (a Brussels Griffon, if there are any dog fanciers out there), and a black rat named after a tall, stunning blond, she lives the highly transient life of a student quite merrily. One of the things she loves best about being a Lesbian is the sense of having a culture, since she actually did grow up in the Cuyahoga Falls of the story, a remarkably culture-free Ohio suburb. At this point in her life (regardless, again, of when you are reading this) she is probably plotting to get into a bigger and better graduate school, pining over a certain handsome, dark-haired woman, and celebrating the connexions inherent in women's culture—in other words, doing exactly whatever the hell she wants. Her hope for the future is that everyone else can and will do likewise.

Connexions

Restless and frustrated. And depressed. I would walk the spring nights, the streets and the campus and the grocery stores looking for something that wasn't so stiflingly familiar. Of course there wasn't anything. I'd pace libraries and malls and bookstores, but it was all the same stuff I'd known forever. People are the only things that are different. They don't really change, but they're always different. But back then I didn't know me so I couldn't know them, and there was no connection. And it was disconnection that put me on the street and in the clean, well-lighted grocery stores.

Now I know me. I'm a dyke. It's a good, square word, with a definite start and a solid finish—I love the sound of it in my mouth, in my friends' mouths. It suits me. 'Course it took some getting used to. I got into some weird relationships, lost some people I thought were friends, found some I know are friends—and in the process I paced the whole city almost moaning my restlessness and frustration. And depression. When Spring Break came, I bolted.

I'd become obsessed with a vague memory of a tall dark Ms. Z. My sixth grade teacher. I was convinced that she too was a dyke. Compelled to find her, I had to know that my conviction was true. My belief wasn't based on the little I remembered of her. It had come one night in the Kroger produce aisle, I'm not sure from where, an instinctive hunch about a woman I had barely known and hadn't seen in twelve years, and then I started remembering. I remembered that it was always Ms. and never Miss, and she lived alone with a cat and she was strong and dark and her hair was short like a man's and she never wore make-up. I started remembering and re-ordering and deconstructing and then I was convinced. I'd built myself an obsession and when I got a break I bolted.

I drove five hours to Cuyahoga Falls, Ohio, the white-bread suburb of my youth, and got there Saturday afternoon. She wasn't in the phone book and out of my motel room I paced my old child place with my new dyke feet for two days, grumbling for Monday and school to start.

I got to J. Alfred Newberry Elementary School at 8:00 a.m. and stood in the hall watching the herds of babies and envying their intensity of purpose. I could see the door standing open to the room that had been Ms. Z's just down the hall. Six giant dyke steps. Mother may I? No, you may not. It wasn't hers any more—the red poster was gone. Every school day for seven years I had marked time by that poster: "Smile. Relax. Be Happy. Only [139] more school days left until summer." I wondered if, when she had left and taken her poster with her, if the other teachers had kept looking to the door, looking for the number of days left, and being surprised for a microsecond that it wasn't there, and not knowing that they'd looked or expected until they were surprised at their surprise, and then forgetting the whole thing and doing it again the next time they passed the door and looked to mark the day.

When I saw the secretary was free I stepped into the office to ask her something—I wasn't sure what yet—and the office was small and comfortable, but the bench was still there where they had let my sister sit for two hours with a concussion and I remembered that and then I was uncomfortable so I think I sounded stupid. "Do you know what happened to Ms. Zientara? When did she leave? Where did she go?" I felt like my voice was high off the ground, zipping over the heads of the babies still in the hall, skittering in and out of the office. I wondered if they'd grow up to wonder what happened to all the tall people too.

"Gretchen Zientara?" I was startled. That she'd have a first name hadn't occurred to me. "She left two years ago. She's teaching in Mansfield now, at Taft Elementary."

I bolted again. It was too weird. Too familiar and too small. Unchanged and utterly different. On the way out I passed a little girl coming in late, looking terribly frightened but otherwise looking just like my second lover must've looked at nine years. Tracy would never have been afraid to come in late though, or at least never would've looked it. Even at nine years. She would've looked just like this girl but not afraid, more defensive and opaque. Tracy was born opaque and would've been opaque even at nine.

Fifteen giant dyke steps to my car, parked right where my mom used to wait for me on rainy days. Back then it was 28 baby steps from door to drive. I drove to Mansfield, only 45 minutes away. She must like Ohio, I guess. I was pretty lucky she hadn't moved to Nevada or New Hampshire, I never could've afforded to find her. I found the school's address and a map of the town in a phone book in a phone booth and ripped the pages out. I imagined people wanting to look up the phone numbers to other schools, high school kids playing hookey and looking up the number to call each other in sick and not finding the page and running for another phone booth, angry frustrated excited. I found the roads on the map and folded the pages crinkly up and put them in the glove box.

Howard G. Taft Elementary School was set up different from Newberry. When I looked for the red poster I saw the doors were shut up and down the hall. The secretary was young, but still older than me, and pretty, with one eye blue and one brown. I wanted to think of something to say so that she'd look at me, and know me, and want me to know her, but I couldn't think of anything at all. Except, "Does Ms. Z teach here? Do you know when she has a break? I was in her class twelve years ago and I thought it'd be cool to see her again." Cool. Why did I say "cool?" A master's candidate in rhetoric and comp and with this beautiful woman in front of me all I know is "cool."

Ms. Z had a break at 11:30, and then only a half hour. School was out at 2:48. Weird time. 11:30 was two hours away. They had a bench in that office just like the one at Newberry, and I thought of my sister sitting there, a baby with her head scraped and her pupils dilated and I went outside and drove around. I found another phone booth and tore the page of bookstores out of the phone book. There was a women's bookstore in Mansfield so I found it on my yellow map and went there for an hour. I browsed and found a book by a woman I'd met at the Michigan festival, and I bought it when my hour was up. I went out the door and came back in and asked if they knew Ms. Zientara. "Gretchen? Yeah, we know Gretchen; she's in here all 'a time." Eight giant dyke steps back to the car.

In thirty minutes, I think. In thirty minutes I'll see her and what will I say? How will I say it? I have nothing to say. I have a million things to say but nothing I can say to this woman I've never met.

I'm thinking I'll have to ask the secretary which room is hers but I get lost driving back and pull in at 11:45. In the hall the babies' voices echo from a place that sounds and smells like a cafeteria even from the other end of the building. Ms. Z's door is open and the red poster announces, "Smile. Relax. Be Happy. Only [57] more school days left until summer."

Eight giant dyke steps. Mother may I? Yes, you may.

She's sitting at her desk and she's not so tall or dark as I remember. She's gone quite gray in fact. I wonder if her cat is still alive and if it isn't if she got a new one and if she still threatens to go home and kick it when the students are bad. I wonder if there ever was a cat.

She looks up from her desk when I step through the door. I saw 'the look' cross her face. Family knows family and I often get the look from dykes behind counters or on streets; I'd often felt the look on my own face. I felt it there now. With the look she said, "I know you." With my hand out I said, "You probably don't remember me. Joanna Davis. I was in your sixth grade class in '76."

She shook my hand and looked blank but 'looked,' "I know you sister." I said, "On Valentine's day I hit my head in gym class and only got one Valentine and I cried in class." She remembered that. She said, "I know you" with that look, she said, "You look like you probably get plenty of Valentines these days."

The babies were about to be set free from the cafeteria noise and smells. I said, "Can I call you? I'm in town for the week, on Spring Break, I'd like to talk to you more. Can I call you?" She said, "Yes. My number's in the book." I said, "Tonight then. I'll call you tonight." And I bolted. Only six giant dyke steps back to the door. To my left the babies were coming down the hall, just like a wave comes to the beach, sucking what's in front of it back into it, lifting it and throwing it forward and creating a curious noisy vacuum of tiny sneakers and soft fine hair.

I found a phone book and I took the page of Z's. I imagined the friends of the Zarkas' coming into town and trying to look them up and I laughed out loud to think of them talking to each other and flipping from Mansfield Y to Canton A and then going back again and their consternation when they see that the Zarkas and none of the Z's are there. I spent the afternoon finding her house from the address in the phone book and then going to the mall. I bought new clothes to wear for her, hoping I'd get to wear them that night, and at

3:15 I called her house. And again at 3:20 and 3:24 and 3:30 and finally she was home. She said she'd like to go to dinner with me that night. I changed into my new clothes in the bathroom at the mall and went to her house.

And that night we ate dinner at the nicest restaurant in Mansfield, and that night I spent at her place, and I called her Ms. Z while I made love to her and she laughed and called me Jodi which no one had done except distant relatives since ninth grade.

In the morning she went to school and I went and checked out of my motel room in Cuyahoga Falls and brought my stuff back to her place and I lay on the couch until 3:00 reading my novel and playing with her cat, who certainly didn't act mistreated. I didn't pace the streets or go to a grocery store until she came home, and then we went out and bought stuff to make stir fry and we bought wine, and then we went back to her place.

And I stayed with her until Spring Break was over and I kissed her good-bye and went back to school. We still write to each other. On the outside of the envelopes below the return address we write, "I know you sister."

humor

you've got to be kidding

by tova

tova is a jewish working class aquarian librarian alien to this planet dyke who presently lives in the northwest loving the lushness the rains bring while trying to make various and sundry deals with the slugs not to eat up everything in her garden. she's working on a novel, has had some stories and poems published around and about, has had and plans to have some more readings, hopes to have more of her "stuff" out there in the universe, and is starting to work with the editorial group of bridges, *a jewish feminist journal. she hopes having this story published in* lesbian bedtime stories 2 *will permanently help her insomnia.*

you've got to be kidding

"hello."
"hi. martha?"
"yes. this is martha. who is this?"
"don't you recognize my voice anymore?"
"well...i guess i don't."
"it's joyce, you fool!"
"joyce? joyce?"
"joyce. joyce patrolli."
"joyce patrolli??????"
"uhhhhh-huhhhh."
"oh, uhm, how are you?"
"oh, i'm just fine. listen, i'm flying into albuquerque for a work conference and i was wondering if i could stay with you for a few days next week, tuesday through sunday."
"next week, you mean this coming week?"
"yeah, i know it's short notice and all so i hope it's not too much of an inconvenience. it'd be great to see you again."
"oh, uhm, yeah, next week, uhm, sure, next week will be okay."
"great, i'll just call you when i get in, tuesday nite at six. is that okay with you? i don't want to ruin any plans."
"Plans, oh no, i don't have plans for tuesday. tuesday at six will be okay."
"good, i'll see you then. it will be so nice to see you again."
"yeah, uhm, it will be nice to see you too."

shit. what was that about? i swear i must be dreaming. it's been twenty years since i've seen her. twenty years since i drooled over her incredible lay ups and hook shots. twenty years since i stood in her doorway dreaming of what it would be like to be with joyce patrolli; twenty years since joyce patrolli was all i could think of every day after junior high school. wait a second now. how did miss patrolli, i mean joyce, know i was in albuquerque, get my phone number, have the nerve to casually call me up and ask if she could crash at my house? it's true i did see her a couple of times since junior high school, but not in these eight years i've been in albuquerque. for goodness sake, what does my junior high school science teacher want from me after twenty years? maybe she's a dyke and wants to reconnect? does she know i'm queer? maybe we have mutual lesbian friends. the lesbian community is after all like that, friends of friends of friends' ex-lover's ex-friends' lovers always crashing at someone's house. why does joyce patrolli want to stay with me? i was so stunned to hear from her that i didn't ask her any questions at all about what she was doing or how she got my number or anything.

well, she sure sounded friendly enuff on the phone. maybe she has a crush on me. yeah, maybe she has had a crush on me for the last twenty years and just never did anything about it because of the age difference, which seems less consequential now. yeah, maybe she was looking through some old junior high school photos, saw a picture of me, got all excited and spent weeks, maybe even months, trying to find me, and then waited patiently for some excuse, like a work conference, to come out to albuquerque. waited for an excuse to come out here and throw herself in my arms so we could furiously make love for days only stopping long enuff for me to watch her shoot lay ups naked on a deserted outdoor basketball court in the albuquerque sun.

yeah, right, martha. your junior high school science teacher spent months trying to locate you and then found some ridiculous school conference to come to in albuquerque just so she could come make passionate love with you after twenty years of waiting for the right moment. lets get real here for a moment. where do i pick up these incredible fantasies from anyway? i've got to stop reading those trashy lesbian romance novels. they are eating away at my brain cells. on the other hand, why is miss patrolli—joyce—coming to see me and why after twenty years do i still feel my heart in my stomach when i speak with her? tuesday, tuesday at 6 p.m. that's five days away. am i going to live through this?

<u>later</u>

you've got to be kidding

"hi martha. how's tricks?"

"chris!! you are NEVER going to believe this. my junior high school science teacher called me up this morning and wants to stay here next week for a few days when she's in town for a teacher's conference. i was so shocked i forgot to tell her i had to okay it with my roommate. i hope its okay with you."

"your junior high school science teacher? oh c'mon. what third rate lesbian romance novel did you pick that up from?

"i'm not kidding, chris. she called up and casually asked if she could stay, as if she was some friend i hadn't seen in a few months. i just don't know what to make of it."

"really? that's amazing. if you wrote a story about this one no one would believe you. i can just see the lesbian eyes rolling now. who could believe every dyke's fantasy coming true? speaking which of, what kind of relationship did you have with old...what's her name, anyway?

"joyce, joyce patrolli. and what kind of relationship do you think i had with my junior high school teacher? i was in absolute love and lust. i used to hang out and watch her shoot baskets in the school yard. she had a great hook shot and hit every lay up i ever saw her attempt! and then i used to hang out after school, waiting to talk with her, to tell her all my adolescent problems, how my family was freaking out cause i hung out in greenwich village all nite, how confused i was about drugs—once i even gave her some drugs i got just to prove to her that i was trying not to take them. of course, on the other hand, i used to sit in the back of her class and drink. creme de menthe, if i remember correctly. and she taught us sex education. we had to get permission slips from our parents. it was the first sex education class they taught in the school district the first day of it she shut the blinds, locked the door, and wrote every curse word i had ever heard on the blackboard and asked us to tell her what they meant and what we had done and..."

"allright, allright martha, spare me all the details of your drooling adolescent trip down memory lane. obviously, you must have made some pretty intense impression on her for her to still remember you. have you seen her lately?"

"a few times, but not since i've been in albuquerque. and those

tova

times were just a simple hello on the street, though once i saw her in the village when i was with an old lover and we asked her to join us for a drink at the duchess, which she graciously declined. and then i did write her a letter about ten years ago. remember that stage i told you about when i was unemployed for a really long time and living by myself in that cabin way deep in the woods? i sat and wrote letters to all these people from my past, telling them what my life was like. well, i wrote her too, care of the junior high. i even included a picture of me and asked her to return it, in the hopes she would be more apt to respond. she never did and i never knew if she really even got it or not, though it never got returned to me. chris, what am i going to do? she'll be here in less than a week. i don't even know if she knows i'm a dyke. where should i have her sleep? on the floor? in my bed?? what if she eats red meat and potatoes every day for breakfast and is a member of some fanatic christian sect and wants to convert me?"

"hold on there martha. i realize that this might be a scene, but lets not make it entirely into a soap opera. it could be simple. really simple. maybe she was just coming to the conference in albuquerque, remembered you lived here, was feeling really broke, thought you were a nice kid who she'd like to see again, and decided to call you up for a place to stay."

"yeah, simple, keep it simple. it sure doesn't feel simple to me. i just don't know what i am going to do if i start to drool all over her at first sight."

monday

oh my goodness, joyce patrolli is going to be here in less than 24 hours and there's still fingerprints on the fridge, and the fireplace needs to be cleaned. i don't want her to think i'm a slob who can't even take care of my own house. and what do i think about all the photos of naked womyn i've got hung up all over the house? maybe i should take them down. geez, i don't even do that for my family anymore, with my rough and tuff attitude of this is who i am, accept it or shove it... but then again truth is they haven't been here since i

you've got to be kidding

put those photos up.

and dinner. i wonder if she'll want dinner. i bet she eats. i should go to the co-op today. what does she eat though? i haven't the faintest idea. i guess i just never thought about the great joyce patrolli doing anything as banal as eating. are we going to have a quiet dinner together; i don't think i can stand it. i wish chris didn't have a meeting tomorrow nite, at least then i wouldn't have to face miss patrolli alone. now, that's definitely out, i better call her joyce; i would just die if miss patrolli slipped out of my mouth. keep it simple, just keep it simple. maybe a nice generic casserole, but what if she's allergic to dairy? stir fries and rice. that's it, stir fries and rice, not too heavily spiced. everyone likes stir fries and rice, don't they? what if she ate on the plane? oh, that wouldn't matter, i know what they serve on planes. this is not a fantasy, martha, this is really happening. your junior high school science teacher is coming to visit.

<u>tuesday evening</u>

"hello."

"martha?"

"yes, this is martha."

"it's joyce."

"oh, uh, hi joyce."

"i just got into the airport and i forgot how to get to your house."

"forgot? forgot? oh, that's okay, i'll come pick you up, i forgot to ask you about your exact plane schedule last week."

"you don't need to do that, i'm sure i'm inconveniencing you enuff; i can take a cab or something."

"really, no problem, i'll just pick you up. why don't you go to the bar near the luggage pick up and i'll pick you up there. i can pick you up at the bar."

"are you sure?"

"really, no problem,, it's only about twenty minutes by car, but forever by bus and the cabs are miserable here."

"alright, i really appreciate it."

"sure, no problem, i'll just pick you up."

"okay, bye."

tova

"bye."

she's here. i can't believe she's really here. so it wasn't a dream after all. i cannot believe how many times i said, "i'll pick you up." what could be behind that statement? i wonder if she sensed my nervousness? she sure seemed cool as a cucumber. now don't use some euphemism every second sentence when you see her; you know how that annoys people. and my car. i didn't dump the ashtray. what if she's severely allergic to cigarette smoke and starts having an asthma attack? what if she hates the color blue and refuses to be in a foreign car? oh please, martha, she is after all human. and what did she mean that she "forgot" how to get to the house?"

<u>at the airport</u>

okay, martha, i think that's her sitting there at the back table. is she beautifull or what? it's no wonder i used to lust after her so much. now calm down, martha. don't act so nervous. just act as if you're seeing an old acquaintance you haven't seen in a while. and remember no euphemisms and make sure to call her joyce. *hi joyce. did you have a nice flight?* no, that sounds ridiculous; too formal. i wonder if i look ok? not too casual, not too dressed up. stand up straight; i know teachers have a thing about posture and mine is terrible. huh, it looks like she's not through with her beer. maybe i should join her for a drink. maybe it would be better to be in this neutral territory for a little while before we go into the confined privacy of my car, and then my house. yeah, that would be good. some re-acquainting before we get to the house. now don't drool, remember to breathe, remember she's human and you are too. here it goes.

"hi!"
"hello."
"how ya' doing?"
"fine, thank you."
"uhhm, i see you're not done with your beer yet. maybe i'll

have one with you, if that's ok."
"what?"
"i said, maybe i'll have a beer and join you."
"no thank you."
"what?"
"i said, no thank you."
"oh, uh, ok. well...do you just want to go back to my place now then."
"what?"
"i said, do you just want to go back to my place now then?"
"no, i don't want to just go back to your place now, and i don't want you to join me for a beer."
"oh, uhh, well, didn't you want me to pick you up?"
"no, i didn't want you to 'pick me up.'"
"but i thought you wanted me to pick you up. i really thought you wanted me to pick you up."
"where did you get that idea from?"
"well, i got that idea from you."
"from me. well, i'm sorry if i gave you the wrong impression, but i'd really rather be by myself."
"you want to be by yourself?"
"yes."
"but i thought you wanted to be picked up."
"not right now."
"oh, well, uhh, maybe i'll go to the bathroom."
"suit yourself."

ok, martha, what is going on? your dream is quickly turning into a nightmare. first she calls all excited and says she's going to stay with me, and then calls from the airport and we agree that i'll pick her up in the bar, and now she acts totally weird. she doesn't want me to join her for a drink and doesn't want me to take her home. i don't remember her being this weird. maybe she's changed a lot. maybe she's just moody. maybe she gets nuts after she's on a long flight, and she has pms on top of it. maybe she's having second thoughts about staying with an old student and is going to stay at a hotel or something. that's ridiculous, martha; i'm sure she'd have the decency to say so. maybe she's just as nervous as me and

tova

some time to calm down, or is acting weird cause she's nervous; i'm sure acting weird. maybe that's not joyce at all. no, i'm sure it's her, she really doesn't look that different. maybe i'm not martha. wait a second, i know i'm martha, but maybe she doesn't know. maybe she doesn't recognize me and thinks i'm some weirdo hanging around the airport. yeah, that must be it, and if it's not it, well if it's not it i just don't know what i'm going to do. but that must be it, i think. now, just throw some water on your face, take a couple of more deep breaths, and go out there and act calm, friendly, and mature. remember, you're not in junior high school anymore.

"hi."
"hi."
"how are you doing?"
"i'm fine, thank you. listen, you seem like a pretty nice womyn and all, and maybe this airport bar is a known lesbian hang out, but i'm really not interested in being picked up tonite. i'm waiting for a friend of mine to come get me."
"i know."
"what? what do you mean? really, i'm not interested."
"i mean, i'm the friend, i'm martha. aren't you joyce patrolli?"
"huh?? uh, yes, well, i am joyce patrolli, but you're not martha."
"i am martha. we just talked on the phone. you're here for a work conference, and you're supposed to stay at my house, and i told you i'd meet you at the bar here."
"you did?"
"yeah, don't you remember?"
"well, yes i do remember, but you're not the martha i thought you were."
"well, maybe you just don't recognize me. it was over twenty years since i was in your science class at erasmus junior high."
"my science class...erasmus junior high...twenty years ago."
"yes, erasmus. my name is martha, don't you remember me at all? we did run into each other once in the village; you remembered me then."

"oh, yeah, i do remember you now. how are you doing? what are you doing here? what a coincidence. i'm waiting for a martha too."

"you're waiting for me. i'm the martha you talked to."

"what? wait a second, let me look at this paper. do you live at 6210 43rd street?"

"yes."

"and is your phone number 633-0221."

"yes, but you should know that already. you've called me twice."

"but you're not who i thought i talked to. wait a second. who's your roommate?"

"chris."

"chris? chris who?"

"chris bordens."

"huh. i don't know a chris bordens. have you two been living there long?"

"eight years."

"eight years. eight years. huh. let's see it's been about nine years since i've spoken with martha. do you know who lived there before you and chris?"

"well, chris really found the house and talked to the two wimmin who lived there. i had just moved to town and they were moving to denver. i only met them briefly once. one was named, uhhmm...robin, i think, and the other one was named, uhhmmm..."

"the other was named martha. martha berkowitz."

"oh yeah, that's right. we all thought it was funny that another martha was moving into the house. ohhhhh...i see, her name was martha too."

"yeah, she was an old friend of mine, but i haven't seen her for about nine years. i thought your voice was different, but i didn't know she moved to denver. i took a chance and called cause i needed a place to stay; i thought it would be nice to see martha after all this time and i always prefer to stay with dykes. when you said you were martha..."

"and when you said you were joyce patrolli, i couldn't believe you even remembered me, but you seemed so friendly and casual."

"well, i do remember you now; you were a hard kid to forget.

this one's going to grow up to be a dyke, i used to tell myself, i guess i was right."

"well, uhhh, well, if you still need a place to stay you're still welcome to stay at my house."

"sure, that would be great. let's get out of here."

"ok. uh, by the way, what's your schedule like?"

"i'm at the conference most of the days, but i have most evenings free."

"well, there's a wimmin's basketball game tomorrow nite. they're a great team, and i'm going with a few friends, and we could get an extra ticket, if you'd like to go."

"wimmin's basketball. that sounds great. i'd love to go. i love wimmin's basketball."

"yeah, i, uh, sort of remember."

Political Humor

"One of Them"

by La Verne Gagehabib

La Verne Gagehabib is a Black/American lesbian, living in the Northwest with her partner of 10 years. She describes herself as a fat, Black nappy-headed woman, with a tendency to be domineering. She has started a group in her community of similar women of color. They get together often, but mostly keep in touch via telephone. They call themselves the Chatty-Cathy Club. She writes western stories about women during that time in our herstory. She also writes erotica and is published in the 1990 Lambda Award winning anthology, Intricate Passions, *edited by Tee Corinne. La Verne's story "One of Them" grew from her many years in the women's movement, and her impatience with minor changes, where "isms" are concerned, especially among women. She has also grown tired of educating Euro/Americans on these "isms" and dreams of starting a business such as "One of Them." She has a book completed called* Jonny and Vera, *in search of a publisher.*

"One of Them"

Ring...ring...ring...
"Hello?"
"Hi. Is this 'One Of Them?'"
"Yes."
"I desperately need your help."
"Ok, what can I do for you?"
"Oh...yes...well...I need several of them...(nervous giggle) I mean...ah..." "Maybe it would be easier if you would just say what you want."
"Why...yes, of course. I need two Blacks, and one Asian, maybe throw in a Hispanic, or Mexican."
"Alright. Would that be two Blacks with afro's, dread locks, braids or exactly how would you like them?"
"Oh...I'm not sure how to order, maybe you can help me."
"Sure. We have two fat, Black, nappy-headed women available, but they have a tendency to be domineering. Would that suit your needs in that race?"
"Well, the tendency to be domineering might not set well with some of the women, but if that's all you have right now...I guess that will have to do."
"Fine. Now the Asian woman is somewhat submissive, but does talk back if provoked, she can be persuaded to be quiet if made to feel welcomed."
"Oh, that would be perfect. Now back to the the two Blacks, if I throw in a bonus, do you think that they could be more accommodating, and hold their tongues? And also maybe straighten their hair some? Oh yes, and can they sing, dance or entertain at all?"
"Well..."
"That would mean an extra, extra bonus. And make us very happy."
"I could speak with them, but no guarantees. If you want to wait another week, our meeker ones will be available, but they are in much demand these days."

"One of Them"

"No, I need those Blacks now, I can't wait. So I will just have to take my chances with them. My courier will have your cash to you within the hour. I need those women by this evening. The courier will also give you the address of the event. Thanks ever so much for your help. You come highly recommended."

"Thank you. 'One of Them' is pleased to be of service to you. Please call upon us again."

"I will." Click.

•

Ring...ring...ring
"One of Them."

"Yes, hello. You were recommended by a friend, who said that you might be able to help me out of an embarrassing dilemma."

"Maybe. How can we help?"

"Well, our women's group has been accused of racist practices by other women of color and white groups in the area, and we are not that at all. It's not our fault that we haven't been able to find any suitable women of color to participate in our activities. So...I was told to call your agency and hire some women of color to attend our group events, then maybe other women of color would see them, and feel safe enough to join us in our celebrations. Can you help us?"   "Why yes. Specifically what type women of color are you looking for?"

"We sort of need to break into this slowly, and many of the women have requested that I not order those women of color who would upset the group too much, but are willing to teach us how to unlearn racism, if we are in fact...racist, and learn how to interact with women of color on all levels."

"I understand totally."

"Wonderful. Now, what we are interested in are some fair skinned Blacks, Native Americans and Mexican descent women, and with no accents, no ethnic hair styles or clothing, such as rings in their nose, or combs in their hair...but for them to sort of blend in with us. Is this possible?"

"Of course. Will they be required to sleep with the women as well? That will cost extra."

"Well, some of us might want to try it, but many are totally repulsed by the thought, so maybe a lesbian or two is ok, but nothing

nothing too obvious. The women who may want to sleep with them would require absolute discretion, and perhaps rejection of their advances in the beginning."

"Fine. Now what exactly are your choices, and when do you need them?"

"Well...we have a large group, so one of each per hundred would be fine. Say, six...mixing them up with two from each racial group. I need them within the week because we are having our annual conference and we want to look good. I will have your check in the mail within the week."

"No. We have to be paid in cash prior to the event, and if our women are insulted, are harmed in any way, and are forced to insult anyone in your group, our services will not be available to you again, plus you will hear from our attorneys."

"Now wait a minute. I can't promise you that women in my group will not be racist, or ignorant in their treatment of these women of color intentionally. I can safely say that they probably won't become violent, and that we will pay in cash, but that's all. Can you promise that any of your women won't be rude or insult any of us?"

"No...I cannot, because that's part of the package. 'One of Them' not only provides women of color, but we also train our women to educate and work with the white women on their racism, whether it be through their supposed submission and silence, or their vocal rejection of all white people. We are working towards total social justice, and equality of the races through our services. Many women of color in the community have grown tired of educating white women on racism, and that is how our agency came to be. We are not here to fill a need, but to educate and maybe change some opinions about women of color. We don't just provide a splash of color for white women to hide behind, but an integration of the races, for a price."

"Right. I understand, and I have read your brochure and we will try to comply to your rules, but change...where race is concerned doesn't come easy."

"We know that, that's why we have this service in the first place. This way you can learn at your expense. So, are you still interested?"

"Yes, absolutely. Are you available too?"

"One of Them"

"Only for very special occasions, but not very often."

"Oh I see. I would like to continue this conversation with you over dinner if you are available tonight?"

"Well..."

"Think about it and get back to me. I would be honored to be in your company."

"Ok, I will think about it. Now I would like to complete our business first."

"Of course. Just arrange for those six women, and I will have the messenger deliver the fees within the hour."

"Thank you. Now, about dinner. Are you a lesbian?"

"Yes. Are you?"

"Uh-huh."

"Good. So, how about you call me later, and let me know for sure if you still want to meet for dinner someplace, your choice. Should I just include the fee for your time also? You can return it if you decide not to join me."

"Sounds fine, good-bye."

"Bye."

•

Ring...ring...

"One of Them."

"Yholbine?"

"Yes."

"This is Gloria Geraldo. Girl...have I got some juicy stuff for you."

"What?"

"I have just about had it with some of those white women with their birkenstocks and bull shit."

"What happened?"

"I can't talk about it over the phone, but can you meet me for lunch at Cabby's, within the hour?"

"Sure. I'm leaving now."

"Ok, bye."

•

Ring...ring...

"This is 'One of Them,' we are not in the office right now, but if you leave your name, phone number and the time you called, we will get back to you as soon as possible. If you have an emergency, and need one of them immediately, please stay on the phone, and your call will be connected to our emergency beeper number. This service will cost double the regular price. Thanks so much for calling 'One of Them.' Leave your message after the tone."

Relationships

The Gift

by Amanda Hayman

I, Amanda Hayman, believe that the only way Lesbians get anything in this world is by making it happen for ourselves. I live in Tokyo with my lover, Linda Peterson, and delight in being part of a community of wonderful dykes from all over the world. These include the writing group dykes, whose critiques of The Gift were invaluable. They are Laura, Lynn, Eve, Suzanne, and the above-mentioned Linda.

I've written lots of short stories over the past three years, and have had two published. I'm also working on a novel, about dykes and timeslips in Wales, which is nearing completion. Discovering a talent for story writing is undoubtedly the most exciting realisation of my thirties.

The best thing I can imagine for the future is that we lesbians start valuing ourselves and our precious space, and stop making compromises.

The Gift

As she climbed the narrow flights of stairs leading to her apartment, Imogen heaved a sigh of relief. Busy days she was used to, but the dripping heat of summer made them hard to handle. Her dress had been sticking to her back since she'd gone out that morning, and it seemed the most productive activity of the whole day had been mopping her brow. Everyone was affected in this way, of course, but somehow she was always waiting for someone to giggle behind her back about how if she wasn't so fat she wouldn't be sweating "like that". If anyone had warned her about just how hot and oppressive Tokyo summer could be, she might have thought twice about taking this job. Probably not though—four years ago her first priority had been getting away from England, where everything had reminded her that Jill was gone.

Imogen was older than most of the teachers at the elementary school. Her colleagues, with the exception of the principal, seemed to consist of lithe, long-limbed twenties, some of whom had taught all over the world. Forty-two wasn't old, but everything was relative. She would have to admit these young women were mostly pleasant and friendly, often extending invitations for her to join them in their out-of-school plans. Like today, for example. Rosemary and Candy had asked everyone over to use the pool at the American Club. There was nothing Imogen would have liked better than a swim to relieve the sticky heaviness of the day. In England she'd gone swimming every day after work, delighting in the way her body cleaved through the water. Twenty years ago her powerful strokes had made her a champion, and it had been disappointing to find that Japanese public pools were crowded beyond belief. There was no room to really use her abilities.

Now she swam infrequently, and though a visit to the American Club pool had sounded wonderful, she had refused. A scene with a cartoon-like quality had flashed through her mind, of Candy and the rest displaying tanned, firm flesh inadequately covered by minuscule

The Gift

swimsuits. Imogen alone would be pale, her flabby muscles a blemish on the American dream of blue sky and palm fronds reflected in the glassy water.

She sighed again, this time from the everlasting disappointment of living in a world that set such limited standards for bodies. Recently she had become aware that even in Japan the words "thin" and "beautiful" were beginning to be synonymous. If she could change just one thing about her life, Imogen would choose a more universally acceptable body—she was so tired of the pitying glances that came the way of a fat, middle-aged schoolmarm. As a prize-winning swimmer she'd been admired and envied, despite the roundness of her body, and she had revelled in that attention.

The heavy bookbag was cutting into her shoulder, a reminder that there was still work that had to be done before the day was over. But not yet. First she'd have a cool drink and a shower, take half an hour to sit on the balcony with her feet up, do nothing except enjoy the breeze that sometimes cooled the sweltering city as the sun went down.

A door opened, and Iwasaki-san, Imogen's next-door neighbor, appeared, holding a package. Imogen took it eagerly, thanking the old lady while trying to work out where it had come from. She hadn't realised, before she lived abroad, how important a lifeline to the familiar world the post would become. But this parcel wasn't from home—the stamps were wrong.

Inside her flat a wave of hot, damp air rushed to meet her. Obviously the timer on the air conditioner had failed again. Imogen took off her shoes in the pocket-handkerchief-sized entry hall, and padded inside. The kitchen-dining room was neatly fitted out with the usual accoutrements, all scaled down to fit into the space of a large dining table. At first she'd been appalled by such cramped living conditions, but now it just seemed normal.

Despite the newness of the building, fungus was creeping under the window-frames, and she'd already killed three cockroaches this week. Nevertheless, Imogen knew she was fortunate to live in a flat owned by the school; such luxurious (by Japanese standards) quarters in the middle of Tokyo would have been unthinkable if she'd had to pay the full rent.

She dumped her bag on the table, together with the package and a handful of post she'd taken out of the mailbox downstairs. The morning's *Japan Times* lay where she had left it, and using this as a fan she went to see about the trouble with the air conditioner.

Well, she couldn't figure it out. She thought she'd chosen the right setting, but even after four years those kanji still all looked alike. As soon as she'd turned the dial, cool air had drifted towards her, bringing a much needed cloud of relief. That was better, but she'd have to hunt out the piece of paper which deciphered the confusing characters, or she'd never survive the summer.

Still sweating, but not quite so profusely, Imogen went back to the kitchen, took orange juice from the pale pink doll's refrigerator and drank it straight from the carton. My, that tasted good. Already the discomforts of the day were beginning to recede. Impatiently she wriggled out of her navy cotton shirt-dress, which fell like a limp dishcloth to the floor. She discarded the restricting bra too, resenting the too-tight garment that held her pendulous breasts to a 'respectable' shape. The seven-year-olds she taught couldn't care less what she wore, but their mothers did, and a thin summer dress required regulation underpinnings.

She stood contemplating the jumble of possessions she had dropped on the table, scratching absently at the welts the elastic had cut in her midriff. By far the most interesting thing was that package. It was bigger than a shoe box, wrapped in an unfamiliar type of brown paper and then tied tightly with green twine. The stamps were unusual, and the whole exuded an atmosphere of faraway places. Who on earth could it be from? The handwriting was indistinct and the ink smudged, but she could make out Yolanda's name, and the word "clothes" on the customs form.

For a moment she toyed with the box, wondering whether to open it now or later, amazed that she'd been remembered. Whatever it was wouldn't fit, of course, and she mentally steeled herself to accept the inevitable disappointment. No, she'd wait until after her shower, when she had been soothed by the water into a state of relaxation. Briskly, Imogen turned her attention to the other items in her mail, aware of this action as a deliberate diversionary tactic. The international phone bill—had she really talked so long?—a notice of an upcoming shakuhachi concert, and a form letter she couldn't understand because it was written completely in Japanese.

The Gift

The needles of water coursed over her skin; first cold to combat the stickiness of the day, and then hot for cleansing. Carefully Imogen soaped every inch of her body, the desire to be clean overcoming as it always did the distaste she felt for her exuberant curves. Gravity dragged the rolls of flesh downwards, creating folds and pockets that had not been there in her youth.

Today as she bathed, Imogen remembered Yolanda and the brief time they'd spent together. She'd felt different about her body then, seeing it almost shyly, through Yolanda's approving eyes. And to think that she had been in two minds about going to that smart cocktail party, knowing she would feel out of place in her colleague's sleek world of executives and designers, but tempted by the chance to visit the sumptuous New Otani hotel.

She *had* felt awkward, her crisp linen trouser-suit dowdy among the silk polo shirts and tight-fitting leggings. Miserably she'd sat on one of the few available chairs by a wall, clutching her drink and smiling brightly every time anyone came near her. They didn't stay though, swanning on instead to the next breathtaking encounter.

She was just about to give up and go home when a small, dark woman came and stood disconsolately by the wall beside Imogen. She looked as if she were not accustomed to being bored, and wrinkled her delicate nose with distaste as she watched the world whirl by. Imogen had noticed her as she mingled with the other guests, primarily because of her dark hair, which was thick and lustrous, and even in a complicated braided style reached well below her waist. She was dressed completely in black: textured suede boots, twill jeans, matte silk shirt open at the neck to display a heavy silver chain, an outfit defying the peacock mood of the party. Could this attractive woman be a lesbian?

She smiled at Imogen. "Terrible, isn't it? I don't know why I come to these things."

"Me neither." Her own voice sounded cracked to Imogen, as if rusty from disuse. Well, she hadn't spoken for nearly an hour, so maybe it was.

The woman offered her hand. "My name's Yolanda. Do you work with Don?"

Imogen shook her head. "No, with Theresa," she said. We teach together at St. Monica's, the international school. I'm Imogen

Thomas."

Yolanda surveyed her coolly. "You don't look like a nun."

Imogen laughed aloud, amused by such a possibility. "It's you that's wearing black," she pointed out.

It was Yolanda's turn to be amused. "True enough," she said, touching Imogen's arm gently. "And I even considered the possibility once, many years ago."

Imogen was intrigued. "Oh, really? What happened?"

Yolanda's black eyes were mischievous. "It's a complicated story—do you really want to stay here that long?" She indicated the drinking, laughing melee disdainfully. "Or would you prefer to hear it over dinner?"

•

They'd eaten shabu-shabu, at Imogen's favorite restaurant, which looked nothing from the outside, but was famous for its sesame sauce. At their table they cooked paper-thin slices of beef and delicate vegetables in a fragrant broth prepared for them by the Mama-san. They'd eaten slowly savouring the flavours and talking.

"So tell me about your call to the convent," Imogen said through the steam.

Yolanda sampled a mouthful of Chinese cabbage. "It started when I was five," she began. "My mother and I were living in Malaysia. She worked for a while at a hospital run by the nuns, and when she was on duty they took care of me. I thought they were wonderful, so calm and dedicated. I was quite sure that it was what I wanted to be when I grew up." Her face wore a dreamy expression. "Of course my infatuation with the underwordly life didn't last—thank goodness."

"I thought you said it was a long story," protested Imogen.

"I could embroider the tale a little, if you like." Yolanda's dark, dark eyes opened wide in innocence. "But as you must realise by now, my dear Imogen, it was merely a ruse to get myself a dinner partner—I am so very tired of eating alone."

"Oh?"

"A woman doing business in Tokyo cannot casually accept the offers of an evening's entertainment from her customers, the way a man might. I find it preferable to turn down all such invitations, rather than putting myself in possibly compromising circumstances,

The Gift

and losing a deal into the bargain." Yolanda shrugged, but Imogen could tell that such vulnerability irked her.

"What do you do?" asked Imogen.

"Oh, I run a small import-export business based in Hong Kong. I love the freedom of working for myself, but there's no-one I can trust to send on these business trips."

"How often do you travel?"

"About every six weeks or so. I get to Tokyo once or twice a year, then there's Manilla, Taipei, Bangkok, and Seoul to be kept happy, not to mention the U.S. and Australia."

"Wow!" Imogen was impressed. "It sounds fabulous."

"It can be exhilarating," Yolanda agreed, "but when I'm tired, or a flight is six hours late, it's just another job." She searched in the broth for a morsel of river-shrimp. "Now tell me about yourself—so far all I know is that you're a teacher and you don't like cocktail parties."

"There's not much to tell."

"Where did you grow up?" Yolanda would not be brushed off that easily.

"Oh, in the south of England, a small town called Winchester. My father was a bank manager, and my mother teachers piano. I think my childhood was absurdly suburban semi-detached."

"I'm sorry, I don't follow you." Yolanda looked puzzled.

Laughing, Imogen explained, "It's a colloquialism for being as boringly middle-class as it's possible to be. In England, that is. Refers to the house we lived in, joined on one side to another exactly the same. I went to the grammar school, belonged to the church choir, and swam three nights a week at the local club. Year in, year out, until I left for university when I was eighteen. You can't get more ordinary than that." She was amazed to see how eagerly Yolanda was drinking in her words.

"I used to dream about staying at the same school long enough to make a real friend," Yolanda reminisced. "Do you know, Imogen, I went to eleven different schools between the ages of eight and seventeen? Your life sounds like just what I always wanted."

Imogen shook her head. "That's hard to believe, when you've lived in such fabulous places. My sisters and I used to imagine..."

"Sisters! Oh, how many do you have? What are their names?"

Imogen was again surprised that Yolanda could be so interested, but she answered the questions anyway.

A waitress in a blue-and-white kimono knelt before their table, adding pinches of different spices to the broth their meal had cooked in.

"In a minute we can drink the soup," Imogen translated haltingly for her new friend. "And these noodles are to go in now." She indicated a heaped bowl.

Watching Yolanda, she considered the wistfulness of the delicately-featured face. "How did you feel about being an only child?" she asked.

"I was lonely," said Yolanda simply. "Mama was my best friend, and being a doctor she worked very long hours." She reached for Imogen's hand across the table. "Tell me more about being an English schoolgirl."

Later, as they sipped the green tea which signalled the end of their meal, Imogen asked, "Which is your hotel?"

Yolanda made a face. "The Century Hyatt. Oh, I know it's very luxurious, but it's not home. All I ever see of Japan is hotel rooms, offices and restaurants..." She finished on a lingering note.

Why, she wants to stay with me, thought Imogen, amazed, and shyly she offered her new friend the use of a futon in the living-room.

Laughing, Yolanda kissed her on the cheek. "I thought you'd never ask," she said softly.

•

Imogen turned off the water and grabbed a towel, tousling the fine pale hair reaching to her shoulders. Grey showed quite clearly, though Yolanda's midnight plait had hardly been touched, and she was a year or two older. The only photograph Imogen had of Yolanda came to mind, the six months that separated them only served to sharpen the image. In build Yolanda took after her Taiwanese mother, whilst the wide, sparkling black eyes and ruthless business acumen were probably inherited from the Turkish father his daughter had never known. She barely came past Imogen's armpit, and to Imogen her slenderness seemed to border on fragility. They had laughed at their differences and agreed that it was all of no account if the mood was right.

The Gift

•

Of course Yolanda didn't sleep in the living room. At Imogen's apartment she had taken the lead, kissing the big woman again, this time on the mouth, and with much passion. Imogen had felt a part of her soul, which had been ignored and coiled tightly in the pit of her stomach, awaken and soar upwards. Tentatively at first, half afraid she might be dreaming, she'd kissed Yolanda, catching her breath as the seeking fingers ran fairy circles around her nipples.

It was Yolanda who had led the two to Imogen's tiny bedroom, her hands all the time stroking and searching, the gentleness by and by becoming demanding and imperious until Imogen too began a journey of exploration. And as they became bolder with each other, sensation and excitement heightened, catching them together in a mesh of lasciviousness from which they had no desire to extricate themselves.

Three days, and then she'd gone. In an effort to make the most of that time Yolanda had cancelled all but the essential appointments, and Imogen had called in sick to school, an unprecedented event. Once, they'd forced themselves to go out for longer than an hour, and had visited a graceful park in the west of Tokyo. That was when the photograph had been taken, by an obliging tourist, capturing the image of the two of them in front of a rustic shrine. The rest of the time they'd stayed home, needing nothing but each other. Even now Imogen blushed, remembering the long hours spent in bed, and how very skillfully Yolanda had drawn orgasm after orgasm from her luxurious and responsive body. Imogen had done her best to return the favours, but had been frankly overwhelmed by her body's capacity for pleasure after all this time. For five years, since Jill had gone off for a wild weekend and never come back, Imogen had denied that sex had any place in her life, and had all but convinced herself that she had no need of closeness to a woman's body. Yolanda had proved this conclusion mistaken, and when she had left there had remained inside Imogen a confusion—of emotions and physical desire.

•

Imogen took a second towel and wrapped it round herself, tucking in the edge above her cleavage. She had told herself not to expect Yolanda to write—what they had had was a passing affair, a swift and loving encounter, but nothing more. A woman so desirable and worldly-wise could not be expected to make room in her life for a shy schoolteacher. Forever she would have the knowledge of the sun-splattered, miraculous hours they'd spent together, a concealed diamond to take out and wonder over on the darker days. But in her secret heart Imogen had hoped, and now it looked as if her optimism had paid off.

The brown paper was sealed with heavy tape, the type that would not tear, which necessitated a hunt for the scissors. When at last she got it off, there was more wrapping underneath: this time turquoise blue with Chinese characters repeated at intervals—the name of the shop where whatever it was had been bought, Imogen surmised. Inside this was a white cardboard box tied with string, and when she opened it all that she could see was a froth of white tissue paper. Holding her breath Imogen lifted the layers and peeped beneath them.

Something was dark pink, and wine coloured, all shades of red, silky to the touch, and shot with gold thread. Delight and disappointment mingling, she lifted the garment from its nest. Such beautiful colors, and it was bound to be too small.

The mounds of fabric billowing in her hands proved to be pants of an unusual and intricate design, gathered and tucked beyond belief. A great pleated fullness formed the legs, caught at the ankles into wide cuffs, which were fastened with buttons and tiny loops. Something fell to the ground, another piece of the same material, but this time a double thickness had been used to fashion a short bolero, styled to barely reach the waist. A charming outfit, in fact, the likes of which Imogen had never seen before. Too bad she couldn't wear it. Sadly she held the pants in front of her as she looked in the mirror. What wonderful colours!

But wait a minute! With all that stuff in the legs, the pleats and gathering, perhaps there was just a chance...? She dropped the damp towel hastily, and loosened the drawstring that ran around the waist of the lovely garment. Hardly daring to breathe she stepped into the pants, expecting that at any moment they would refuse to rise over her ample thighs and hips. But then they were on. Imogen tied the tasseled string in a bow, bent to button the ankles, then stood back to consider her image in the mirror.

The Gift

The pants foamed and billowed over her curves, disguising them not at all, and yet she looked wonderful. Not quite able to believe what she saw, Imogen turned this way and that, viewing herself from every angle. They fitted! They really did! Oh, if only Yolanda could see her now. She'd wear them the very next time one of her colleagues had a party, that'd show them.

Then she spied the bolero, lying discarded on the floor. Could she wear that too? She slipped her arms into the holes, enjoying the feel of the fabric on her naked back. Why, it was perfect, everything was perfect except for...what was this? Oh, a pocket, with something inside—what could it be?

Imogen took out an envelope, and smiled. Now she had everything she could wish for. The thickness of paper she pulled out was a surprise, but there was less than a page of Yolanda's elegant handwriting. The rest of the envelope was filled with a narrow booklet of flimsy pages. An airline ticket lay in her trembling fingers. What did it mean? The letter—that would tell her what she needed to know.

"Dearest Imogen," Yolanda had written. "The enclosed has been made especially for you, by my good friend. It should fit perfectly, as I described your luscious body in all the detail my hands could remember. A little different from the rest of your wardrobe, but I hope you will be able to find a time to wear it. I would like so much to see you again—would you consider visiting me here sometime soon? In this envelope you'll find a roundtrip airline ticket, Tokyo to Hong Kong, one year open. If only I could get a letter telling me when you'll arrive, I'll be so happy. I just can't get you out of my mind. Do you miss me too? Love, Yolanda."

Half laughing, half crying, Imogen pressed the letter to her lips, her heart filled with joy. Already a plan was forming in her mind for an early departure to Hong Kong. Wildly she began to dance, whirling and twirling, breasts flying, revelling in the glory of the gift.

Relationships

Angel Toes

by Heidi K. Pfeuffer

Heidi K. Pfeuffer recognized her lesbian identity around the age of eight and can't imagine why any woman would want to be anything else. She is a church organist and choir director and writes both sacred and secular music as well as short stories. She is currently working on a novel. Heidi lives and loves with her life partner, Amy, in Thomaston, CT. Their tiny apartment is crowded with books, music, stuffed animals and several whimsical creatures peering out from various shelves. Together, Heidi and Amy fight chocolate attacks and dream of owning their own home with enough room for one or two Labradors.

Angel Toes

"I hate my feet," said Ariel. "They're big, wide, hard to buy shoes for and I have fat ugly toes."

I drew my attention away from *Jeopardy* and looked at the feet that had walked into my life little more than one year ago. I smiled.

"Your feet aren't fat or ugly," I told her. "You have cute little chubby angel toes." I bent and kissed each toe. Twice.

There had been several others before Ariel. Seventy toes worth, in fact. But none of them had stepped so completely into my life as had Ariel and her C.L.C.A.T. (cute little chubby angel toes).

Ariel turned back to watch *Jeopardy,* but I continued to look at Ariel. Logically, the odds were stacked against this relationship. I was her first (last and only?) lover. She hadn't even internally recognized her Sapphic self before meeting me. And of course, our almost 18 year difference in age often made even sister lesbians shake their heads. Illogically, none of these things seemed to matter to us. (The age difference is actually 17 years, 8 months—not that it matters, of course. And yes, I'm the one whom strangers mistake for "Mom".) She smiled in my direction during the commercial break. It was just before the determination of the winner in final Jeopardy.

"What're you grinning at?" she asked.

"You. Your C.L.C.A.T.," I responded. She looked puzzled. I could tell that she had not yet adjusted to the fact that the digits she had so disparaged were to be forever cherished as ten little cherubs. My eyes traveled to her feet and then back to her eyes. She grinned as she understood.

"You say such sweet things. You always make me feel good about myself when I'm down. No wonder I love you."

"Ditto," I said. Toby, our chocolate Labrador, licked the toes in question. I reached down to pat that noble head.

"How did we ever manage without a dog?" Ariel said. Toby pricked her ears and raised her doggie eyebrows. I kissed her wet little nose. (Toby's, that is.)

I remember how we used to dream of owning our own home and getting a chocolate Lab. Sometimes, even now, I think that it's all too good to be true.

"Tell me the story about how you would never become involved with me," begged Ariel. I grinned.

"Silly. You know how it goes," I chided.

"Yes, but I love to hear it." She gave me one of those teasing little pouts specifically designed to melt my heart and win any and every difference of opinion.

"Well, the first time I ever saw you I thought you were cute and hoped that you were gay." Toby snorted a doggie sigh and rested her nose on her paws.

The first time I'd seen Ariel, I was immediately attracted. I knew she was younger, but she conducted herself in such an assured manner that I completely misjudged her age. I also remember silently admonishing myself that having recently ended a relationship I was very vulnerable. I should be cautious in evaluating my feelings, not only to protect myself, but also not to hurt, inadvertently, a sister.

As I got to know Ariel I discovered that she was evidently not a lesbian (sob!), but neither was she dating men (yay!). We became good friends and went to an occasional movie or dinner together. I learned her actual age (and sprouted three more gray hairs that night—I swear it). We discovered so many common interests. It got so that we could complete each other's sentences and anticipate each other's needs.

I've always hated the problems caused by society's homophobia, but I loved Ariel's friendship. I decided to risk it all and share my orientation with her. She was honest. She asked for some space to think about this revelation. I was crushed.

I was elated when Ariel re-connected. She invited me over to meet her parents. I thought I had experienced almost everything, but somehow it had never occurred to me that her parents would be my contemporaries. It felt so weird! I felt like the proverbial teenaged male squirming through the ritual pre-date parental inspection. I must have passed. We began seeing each other more and more often.

When did the touching begin? Slowly, we touched more often...more intimately. Forget those previous 70 toes. I experienced love as if it had never happened before as Ariel gave me her first (last and only) love.

Now to digress for just a moment. In several of my earlier attempts at cohabital bliss I was accused of being an animal, a beast...sexually insatiable. (Before all of you hot and horny dykes start panting and thinking "Right! I could live with that!"—let me modestly confess that while I am quite *sensual,* I am no sexual Wonder Woman. All that trauma and drama had simply been a matter of incompatible levels of libido.) In Ariel I had finally found a libidinous level to equal my alleged lechery.

Toby's paws shuffled on the braided rug and she wooffed deep in her throat. Ariel and I looked at each other and smiled. "Must be dreaming of delightful doggie dykes," we said in unison and giggled.

"I wanted you to make love to me but I didn't want you to think I was a slut." Ariel always took-up the story at about this point. She told about how frustrated she got while I was forcing myself to proceed slowly so as not to frighten her away.

Of course, by now we were punctuating our story with looks and touches and kisses. We found ourselves heading for the bedroom.

It never ceases to amaze me that someone as wonderful as Ariel could find me desirable. I see myself as very intelligent, very warm, very sensuous...very short, rather chubby and not so young (but only 17 years and 8 months of my accumulated 40 years really bother me).

Ariel gently strokes my face. She traces my eyebrows with her fingertips. Her lips touch mine...softly at first, then with enough pressure to force open my mouth for her tongue to probe. Her taste is so sweet. She frames my face in her hands, then slides them down to my breasts. She is so skillful and knows me so well; she can make me come without doing anything more. But she does do more. Much more.

Later, we play our private game. For those who shake their heads at our age difference, we imagine scandalizing them with our possible scenarios.

"You could have been the toddler sitting on your mommy's lap that I once entertained while we waited for sodas at a crowded lunch counter," I told Ariel.

"I might have been throwing spitballs in your junior high classroom when you were a substitute teacher," confesses Ariel.

We both get the giggles when I pull my "Sophia" routine. (You know, from the *Golden Girls*.) "Picture it: Connecticut, 1967. A young woman holds an infant in her arms, gazes into those already incredible eyes and says 'I'm going to leave for college, graduate school, a career and some screwing around. You learn to walk, talk, go through puberty and get an education. In about 22 years we're gonna be lovers, baby!'" We laugh until our sides hurt. It does sound kind of depraved.

In truth, we are the same age. We are the age of lovers in love. Often, I am more startled than insulted when someone says that my "daughter" can have a seat right over there.

Sleepy from our passion and our laughter we cuddled together and drifted off to sleep. Sometime during the night Toby joined us and stretched across the foot of the bed. Ariel stirred and snuggled into the blankets but never wakened. After trying unsuccessfully to follow her example, I decided to get a book and read myself back to sleep.

On the way to the living room I stopped in the kitchen for some juice. Toby, of course, deserted the sleeping Ariel and joined me in the kitchen as soon as I opened the refrigerator door.

"Don't you tell Ariel I gave in to your begging again," I warned Toby as I tossed her a piece of chicken. "She'll put you on a diet: no scraps, no dog biscuits...nothing." Toby didn't hear me as she practically inhaled the tidbit in two chomps. She looked for more. She wiggled her eyebrows, plopped her rump on the floor and smiled at me.

"No. I'm in trouble already if she knew," I whispered. Toby followed me to the living room as I let my eyes cruise shelf after shelf of titles. Occasionally I'd pause to mentally sample a familiar book.

I made my selection, offed the light and headed down the hallway. Toby had remained in the living room intrigued by something. She was investigating what seemed to be a dark spot in a patch of moonlight framed by shadows. Fearing that it was perhaps a piece of contraband chicken betraying our refrigerator raid, I went over to see what had caused Toby's nose to go into overdrive. It appeared to be something on the hardwood floor. Had I spilled something? No. I bent closer. What was that smell? Something familiar...just can't seem to place it. I sniffed again. Toby wagged her encouragement. I placed one hand gently on her nose to warn her not to bark in her enthusiasm for this game. Ariel. Something about the smell reminded me of Ariel. Toby backed away and lay down to watch me. I lay down, too. Stretched-out and belly down to the floor, I sniffed the darkened area in the wood. Aha! Ariel's body oil.

I decided that the mystery would be answered by tomorrow's sunshine, but at that moment the clouds parted and the room was flooded with moonlight. There, as perfect as a snapshot was the solution to this oily aromatic mystery. It was the perfectly detailed outline of a very familiar foot...and five of my darling Ariel's cute little chubby angel toes.

I smiled. I knew exactly where to find the owner of those toes. Replacing the book on the shelf, I tip-toed into the bedroom and slipped under the covers. I began kissing Ariel's ears and the back of her neck. She stirred in her sleep and turned toward me with a smile of welcome already on her lips.

This relationship is the one I was searching for with all those others. It wasn't that I didn't love the others. It was because we were each so busy giving our love away, no one noticed that it was not in the form our partner was capable of accepting.

It is not only knowing *what* your partner needs, but *how* she will accept it. This is the chemistry responsible for the ink eradicator which permanently removes the sum from the "difference in age" column. Now enter "0."

Ariel needs to receive love in the way I need to give it...and returns her love in exactly the manner I need to receive it. That is the whole secret. That is what Ariel taught me...and I was supposed to be the one who was experienced.

Well, maybe this old wise one still has a few aces up her sleeve. I nuzzled Ariel's breasts and gently sucked a nipple. Feeling my passion rise, I knew I was about to show her there *is* that which only grows better over time.

Relationships

Badwater

by Sharon Gilligan

I, Sharon Gilligan, am a forty-seven-year-old white lesbian, born and raised in Chicago. In 1989, my life partner and I resolved not to start another decade in the city and moved to the North Coast of California. This story, while fiction, was conceived during a trip we took years ago to the sweeping vistas of Death Valley. From 1973 until 1988, I spent my energies in pursuit of "equality" through the women's movement. Most of my previous published work may be found in newsletters of a major women's rights group. Now I want most to celebrate loving women by telling our stories. I always cry when I hear the song The Ones Who Aren't Here. *As we dare to flourish, we are warned we have little chance for happiness, let alone peace. My goal with this story and much of my other writing is to dismiss that lie and affirm our right to the love and the light beyond the closet.*

Badwater

Carrie welcomed the sound of her sneakers crunching the salty path. The silence in this place was startling. Moments earlier she had turned off the car and stepped out. It was almost as if she had lost her hearing.

She glanced back toward the car and beyond to the steep foothills of the Black Mountains and above to the sign about halfway up. She couldn't read it, but knew from the guidebook that it marked sea level. She stood nearly 280 feet below; the lowest point in the western hemisphere. 'How appropriate,' Carrie thought bitterly.

She looked ahead to the strong, supple back about a hundred feet in front of her. With Rachel's long legs and swift gait she easily left Carrie behind. Sometimes Rachel would check her pace, and if Carrie picked hers up a bit, they could walk side by side. But today, Rachel, caught up in the spell of this desolate place, was striding briskly to reach the salt flats.

'How'd we get here?' Carrie wondered. It was a double question: how had their lives together reached this nadir, and why did she agree to this trip?

•

Winter in Detroit could be bleak, but post-holiday doldrums couldn't fully explain Carrie's feelings about her life with Rachel. Sometimes, she blamed apartment living and talked with Rachel about how they should think about buying a house, but Rachel usually said something noncommittal and changed the subject. Carrie, unable to articulate her feelings and unwilling to "rock the boat," would go silent.

One evening Rachel was leafing through her professional journal for school administrators. She studied one page a long time then said, "Hey, this sounds interesting." She read aloud about a seminar for educators in Las Vegas. A packaged travel plan and the anticipated tax break made the trip sound reasonable, but Carrie wasn't so sure.

"Las Vegas? Yuck! All that gambling, noise, gaudy architecture and rude men. Sounds awful."

Rachel chuckled. "You've seen too many movies. It can't be that bad. Besides, the conference is only two and a half days. After that we can see some sights, maybe rent a car. At least it'll be warm. Come on, think about it. We need to get away. Maybe that's what we need, a little fun. I know this place is small, but do you really want to get tied down with a house?"

Carrie knew Rachel was trying to fix things between them. They needed something, but Carrie wasn't sure it was a few nights at gaming tables. Reluctantly she agreed to the trip, then said, "It's getting pretty late; why don't we hash this over in bed? We used to do some of our best planning there."

Rachel shook her head, "Can't yet. I've got a meeting early tomorrow. I need to work on the agenda." As Carrie turned toward their room Rachel added, "And I'll probably be gone when you get up. School starts a lot earlier than pet parade."

Rachel's name for Carrie's job at the veterinary hospital usually made Carrie smile, but tonight it sounded scornful, like her job was not important. She wondered if anything could help if that was true, if Rachel had outgrown her.

•

As they were riding in the taxi from the airport, Carrie's skepticism about the trip deepened. Despite the welcome warmth and bright sun, she was chilled by the stark, angular buildings, the tawdry lights, and most of all by the flashy billboards and signs with nearly naked women.

'We can find enough sexism at home,' she thought. 'We didn't need to come this far to be offended.' After checking in, Rachel immediately left to register for her conference. Carrie went to the gift shop where she bought a map of the area and picked up some local papers. She went outside and walked a short way down the strip. Her senses were assaulted repeatedly by the noise of the traffic, the quickie marriage parlors and the rampant flesh-peddling.

Disgusted, she returned to the room, read the papers, flipped the TV channels, and sorted through the books she had brought from home. Nothing held her attention very long.

By the time Rachel returned, Carrie was pacing amid the debris she had strewn about in her restlessness. Rachel, clearly stimulated by the contacts with her professional peers, greeted her. "Hi, hon. Ready for dinner? I've meant these neat women from Seattle, and they'd like to eat with us."

"Us? Don't you mean you? They don't even know 'us.'"

Rachel turned sharply. "Hey, what's up? I just got here. Yes, I mean they invited me to join them, and I told them I was travelling with someone, and we'd be having dinner together."

"Travelling with someone. That sounds innocuous enough."

"Carrie, I just met these women. What am I supposed to say? 'My lover's upstairs, and we don't go anywhere apart after dark?'"

Carrie knew she was being foolish, but she was too embarrassed to admit it. "Why don't you just go on without me? I can call room service or go to the coffee shop."

"I don't want to go on without you. I know I should have asked you first, but there wasn't time. If you want I can call them and cancel—"

Now completely chagrined Carrie said, "No, don't. Just give me a few minutes to clean up." Quietly, she added, "I'm sorry."

Rachel looked around the room. "Have you been up here all day? Why didn't you get out a little, see some sights?"

"I saw quite enough, thank you. Rachel, maybe I shouldn't have come to this thing. I don't know if it's going to work."

"Give it a chance to work, Carrie. I've seen you exactly ten minutes in this room." As always, 'it' was undefined, and neither quite said what they meant by 'working'.

Over dinner Carrie was quiet, partly because the conversation was out of her realm. School budgets, discipline problems, merit pay for teachers were topics quite foreign to her. But she was also watching; watching Rachel make her points, listen to her colleagues, expand on their thoughts, and receive recognition for her ideas. Despite their current crisis, Rachel was still her woman, and Carrie

Back in the room, Carrie was still bathed in the glow of that love and pride as she reached for Rachel. They kissed briefly, then Rachel twisted away, saying, "I've been in these clothes too long. I've got to change into something more comfortable."

Smiling, Carrie said, "Why don't you change into nothing more comfortable?"

Rachel grinned back, "Some things never change. You're right though. Might as well get ready for bed."

When they were together in bed, Carrie wrapped her arms around Rachel and kissed her hungrily. Rachel responded warmly for several minutes, then laid back with a sigh. "That was nice; it felt real good. But honey, I'm worn out. Can we—"

Without waiting for a further word Carrie turned away. "Alright, good night."

Rachel was silent for a long time, then said, "I love you, Carrie."

Carrie said simply, "I know." For the first time she did not finish the now familiar, painful scene with 'And I love you'. Her pride, that fierce feeling for Rachel she had known just moments ago, was now being saved only for her own hurt. As much as she tried not to measure their relationship by how often they had sex, the lovemaking was important to her and the loss of it was enough for her to question Rachel's professions of love.

The following day, Carrie tried again to "see the sights" but they affronted her—the wanton waste of money and time, the conspicuous capitalism and, most of all, the blatant symbols of heterosexuality. She and Rachel went to dinner with the women from Seattle again, but Carrie's dark mood deepened, and she excused herself early and walked back to the hotel.

When Rachel returned much later, Carrie was already in bed, feigning sleep, but she heard the door and every move Rachel made getting ready for bed. She felt her slide in beside her. Carrie felt hot tears stinging the corners of her eyes, but she couldn't think of anything to do or say to reach out for Rachel.

In the morning, Carrie sensed Rachel moving about for a long time before she woke up fully. What finally did rouse her was Rachel talking on the phone. Finishing her call, she said brightly, "Well, you are going to get up this morning. I've got an idea."

Carrie was quiet, too stubborn to respond to attempts to cheer her up, but she listened. "It's pretty clear you hate this town so I just called to reserve a car for the rest of the week. A hundred miles free. We can go a little way into the mountains and get away from the city and still not go over our budget."

Carrie was touched by the plan. Rachel hadn't even had time to see the city much less dislike it, but she was willing to give in to

Carrie's distaste for the strip. Rachel went on, a little too cheerily, "I've still got the breakfast meeting, but that ends the conference." As if trying to get away fast before Carrie refused, she said quickly, "Can you pick up the car by yourself? Then we can check out right after the meeting and start enjoying this trip."

Carrie, holding back, said off-handedly, "Sure, if that's what you want. I'll finish packing and find us another room."

"Yeah," said Rachel, "This one will sure cost too much after the conference rates end." Rachel paused, swallowed hard, "I'm glad you're here on this trip. I missed you after you left the table last night."

Carrie, still embarrassed by her petulant behavior, said, "Yeah, well. That wasn't too smart. It was a long walk back."

Rachel's face stiffened, wounded by the off-hand reply. "OK, see ya later." She hurried out the door.

'Damn,' Carrie thought, 'Can't we talk at all anymore without inflicting pain?' She wondered how, if they could not even exchange a comfortable sentence, they would get through the rest of the week. And if this week didn't somehow change something, what about the rest of their lives together?

Trying to shake off her bleak thoughts, Carrie got started on her assignments. The car rental place was at another hotel down the strip. She produced the required bits of plastic and was about to leave when the agent asked, "Is there anything else you need? Maps, directions? Where are you headed?"

Carrie shrugged, "I'm not sure. I just want to get away from this city." Not wanting to explain a lot, she lied, "I've been here on business, but now I've got a few extra days... I just want to see something different, quieter."

The agent asked if she skied, and when Carrie shook her head, she offered maps to a few of the more popular spots around Vegas, then said, "And then there's this one for Death Valley. It's a longer trip, and most folks like to go later in the spring when the desert flowers bloom. I don't know if you're interested..."

Carrie accepted the maps with thanks and returned to the room. As she went over them nothing seemed much to interest her, and she wondered if she was just refusing to like any of them. But she kept going back to the map to Death Valley; she especially liked what the agent had said about it not being very popular this time of year. She was drawn to the somber-sounding locales: Dante's View, Devil's Golfcourse, and those that evoked a sense of folklore: Emigrant's Pass and Twenty Mule Team Canyon.

It seemed ironic that she was looking for hope for the future amid these melancholy names that echoed only of the past. She didn't know why it attracted her except that she and Rachel shared an interest in history and loved wilderness. She called the number in the brochure about accommodations and made a tentative reservation. She checked the route, nearly 200 miles one-way, and they would still have to come back to Vegas to fly home.

Four days. Could they really do or say anything in four days to make up for the hurt they'd been heaping on each other? And if they had to come 2000 miles to fix their lives, what would going home mean—more of the same? Carrie shook her head. Questions. Too damn many questions. The first thing was to get through those four days.

Whether Rachel caught Carrie's enthusiasm for the drive or just gave in as a peace offering Carrie didn't know. But by late afternoon they were on Route 95 out of the city. Conversation was limited to remarks about sights they passed and Rachel's liking for the conference. They stopped in Beatty, Nevada and picked up ice, a bottle of wine, snacks and a cheap cooler. By the time they reached Stovepipe Wells it was very late.

•

Looking up now at Telescope Peak more than 11,000 feet above her, Carrie's memory of arriving last night was fuzzy. They had checked in and fallen into bed, exhausted.

Catching up with Rachel, who was shading her eyes to get a better view, Carrie was overwhelmed by the warmth she felt approaching this woman she had shared so much with. She thought, 'No matter what, I love her. If I have to settle for silence, or bickering, or even absences, we have to find a way to stay together.' But Carrie choked off that notion. No, settling for so little was no way to save a relationship that had once been so full.

"Lord, this is beautiful, Care. I sure wish we had remembered to bring the binocs."

"Yeah, it's incredible. Even after reading all that stuff I got yesterday I'm amazed. It's so vast and rugged.

They walked back down the path together. Just as they were getting into the car, Rachel glanced up toward the mountain at a deep crevice above the rocky fan. "Hey, do you want to go see what's up there?"

Carrie shrugged, "I don't know, do you?" They both paused, afraid the fragile truce was about to dissolve into a foolish dispute over nothing.

Finally Rachel said slowly, "Let me put it this way... If I go up there, will you come along? Or will you be pissed if I leave you down here while I check it out?"

"I'll come." Carrie looked at the steep path and grinned. "But leave it to you to pick a hike where my short legs put me at the disadvantage."

Rachel glanced warily at Carrie, but when she saw the smile she said mockingly, "Always got an excuse. Come on, the exercise will be good for both of us." Comfortably they walked to the trailhead side by side, but once they started climbing Rachel's natural advantage again put her far ahead.

By the time Carrie met her on the ledge outside the crevice, she was saying, "Oh well, maybe it wasn't such a great idea. Just a cleft; I was hoping it would be deeper, maybe a cave."

Carrie turned back toward the salt flat, then said, "No, I think this view was worth the trip. Come here." The shoulder of the hill in front of them and a ridge next to it formed a V-shape that framed the flats below. The sun glancing off the salt crystals created a hazy, ethereal scene.

Rachel came up behind Carrie and rested her hands on her shoulders, viewing the scene from over her head. "Wow, that is nice." Out of habit, Carrie looked around, as they always did when they were `in public,' to be sure they were alone. Then she took a step back to press into Rachel's body like a pair of spoons. "So's this."

They stood like that for several moments, as if neither knew how to break the spell without offending. Suddenly the sound of a car door slamming below made them both jump. They exchanged startled looks then laughed.

Later, on a hiking path by the Natural Bridge, Carrie stayed back to get a picture of Rachel standing under the massive span of rock. When she hurried to catch up, she stumbled. Reaching for a nearby ledge, she was able to steady herself but bits of the ledge broke off in her hand.

As dusk approached, they pulled back into the parking area at the motel. Carrie was sure she was done for the day, totally worn out. But she showered and slipped into her robe, then laid down while Rachel cleaned up. By the time they were dressed to go to dinner, she felt refreshed—and anxious. She was afraid now to feel so good, so close to Rachel, afraid it wouldn't last.

Their rubber-soled shoes were almost silent on the wooden planks that led from the room to the adjoining restaurant. The amber lights bathed the rough-hewn sidings and posts in bronze tones as Carrie and Rachel found the stairs to the dining room. The menu offered standard American fare—fried chicken, pork chops, some fish entrees. Rachel chuckled, "No exotic stuff here. Remember the time we tried Chinese food in Arizona and the vegetables were all celery and carrots?"

"Sure, that's the same trip where I took a whole roll of gorgeous sunsets with my lens cap on. At Christmas you got me this camera so I couldn't do that again. Wasn't there a promise of a return trip in there somewhere?"

"Yeah, I think there was. We sort of ran out of time, didn't we?"

Carrie had no answer, but the question sounded so sad she lowered her face in her hands.

"Tired?" Rachel asked.

"Not really. I'm surprised. We did a lot of walking today. I was hoping..." Carrie hesitated, not sure she could say what she was feeling without sounding full of self-pity and reproach.

Rachel looked at Carrie steadily, refusing to let her remark pass. "You were hoping what, Carrie?" When she was still quiet, Rachel persisted, "Tell me, talk to me. Please."

"I thought if I wore myself out I'd be so tired...so tired that I'd just leave you alone."

Rachel closed her eyes, pressed her lips together for a moment, then said softly and very deliberately, "Is that what you think I want? To be left alone? Good God, Carrie."

"I don't know what you want. And I haven't been able to get you to tell me if you still want—me."

Rachel didn't reply right away because their food arrived. When the server was gone, she said, "Have you been paying attention here? Three sentences ago I was begging you to talk to me and now you wanted me to tell you something I've tried to say a thousand ways. What's happening to us? When did we stop talking to each other? And when did we stop listening?"

"I don't know what's happening. But I'm scared. I love you so much, but lately I've questioned if you still love me."

"Carrie, I don't know any other way to say it. I've never stopped telling you how much I love you."

"I've heard you, Rachel. I just have trouble believing it when you don't seem to want me very much. I've even wondered if there might be someone else, someone you could share your work with..."

Rachel reached across the table and put her fingertips on Carrie's lips. "Don't say that. Don't demean your work. If I'd wanted a colleague, there were plenty to pick from—in school and later at my first job, before I came to Detroit and found you."

Carrie thought for a long time as they ate in silence. Finally she said, "Then I don't understand what's happening."

"Maybe that's it. Maybe nothing's happening between us. I know this damn job gets to me sometimes, and I get preoccupied, but you used to talk to me about the things that mattered to you. We haven't really connected lately."

"I don't know how. You've been so busy, and your work is so demanding. I haven't wanted to bore you with my inconsequential stuff."

"Oh, Carrie, I need you to pull me out of that morass at work. Just the way you used to need me to hold you when one of those furry patients died after you and the docs fought to save him. I can't remember the last time we shared anything like that, or even played the fool for each other. And when we can't connect with words, lovemaking just doesn't feel right. It's just fucking, and it's no substitute for what we used to have." Rachel blinked back tears as she finished.

Quietly Carrie asked, "Are you ready to go back?" When Rachel nodded, she paid for the meal and they left, Carrie holding Rachel's arm on the boardwalk back to the room. She knew Rachel didn't need support, but it felt good to hold onto her.

Back in the room, amid an awkward silence, they undressed shyly, unlike women who had known every pleasure-giving site on each other's bodies. Rachel, wrapped in a warm, nubby robe, settled in on the bed, her back propped against the head-board, feet stretched out in front of her. Softly she said, "Come here, Care." Carrie climbed in next to her, then slid over until her back rested against Rachel's breasts. Rachel said, "You know, back in Vegas when we went out with those women, I was having a great time playing the know-it-all academic. That is, until you left. With you, I feel capable of anything. Without you, I just feel empty. Somehow, we've got to make this work."

"Rachel, today out on a trail I stumbled and grabbed a shoulder of rock for support. It crumbled under my hand, and I was shocked because it seemed so rugged. Maybe we're like that. For a long time we, and even our friends, believed that nothing could ever hurt us or change us because we've been at it so long. Maybe we forgot how fragile this is."

"We really did reach bottom. Not this morning in that depression at Badwater. A couple of hundred feet below sea level is nothing compared to the depths we were in the other night. I knew you were awake when I came in. I looked at you, waited for you to stir, hoped for just a word, a sound—anything. It terrified me that we couldn't even say goodnight to each other." They laid together without words for a long time, savoring the closeness that had been stubbornly eluding them. Finally, Rachel said, "This is one hell of a distance to come to find our way home. Right now I feel closer to you than I have since... a long time. If you want me right now..."

Carrie snuggled deeper into Rachel's body, "You're not going to believe this, but could we wait? This minute, this feeling...I just want to hold onto it awhile."

"I believe it. We can wait, maybe in the morning. That's one of my favorite things, waking up to you." As she reached over to snap out the light, Rachel added, "But let's keep that promise. It's been so long."

Romance

The Best Things Happen While You're Dancing

by Su Stout

I am Su. Not Susan, just Su. I live with my three best dog friends in a very large urban area. I earn my living as a copy reader for the Wall Street Journal *in New York City and am presently working my way through my B.A. in Media Studies (journalism/English) at Fordham University.*

I'm working on a lesbian detective novel, short fiction, personal essays (mostly about life with three unique, creative, albeit grouchy dogs) and sometimes op/ed pieces for the university paper. My goal is to add to the growing collection of fine lesbian literature in my lifetime. I look forward to the day when our literature will encompass all sizes, colors and preferences of lesbians, and all will be "normal."

The Best Things Happen While You're Dancing

The music was loud. Jess could feel the vibrations through the Frye boots she had polished to a deep caramel a few hours ago. In spite of her dislike for the song, she began to tap her foot. She was feeling comfortable, even a little happy. The overhead lights were dim. Spotlights flashed in rainbow colors across the dancers in the middle of the floor. Jess leaned her elbow on the mahogany bar and rested her chin in the palm of her large hand.

The dance floor was crowded although the evening was young, but Jess' eyes had no trouble singling out the redhead. She was dancing with a short blond, but seemed oblivious to anything except the music. Eyes closed, her head was thrown back as her body swayed and her feet followed the beat of the song. Jess watched. She imagined her arms around the woman; imagined feeling the music the way the redhead was.

For over a month, Jess had come to CHARITY every weekend. It was one of Portland's most popular mixed gay bars and was almost always packed by 10 p.m. On Friday and Saturday evenings, Jess would polish her Frye boots, press a sharp crease into her Levi's and brush off her brown tweed jacket with the corduroy patches. Each time she was at the bar, Jess watched the redhead dance with partner after partner, yet all she did was watch. Tonight, Jess intended to dance with her.

Jess had been alone for a long time. After her ugly, bloody breakup with Cassie, Jess hadn't been interested in being that vulnerable again. She'd thrown herself into her work and her friends and she'd nursed her wounds. That was five years ago. Feeling stronger, more confident, more at ease with herself and more than a little lonely, Jess leaned back on the barstool and thought, Tonight is the night!

She was brought out of her reverie as the music abruptly ended. The dancers left the floor. To her amazement, the redhead walked right toward the bar. She slid her body between Jess and the guy on the next stool. Jess caught her breath, sat back and tried not to stare. Signaling the bartender, the redhead said, "Another Olympia, Alice?"

Jess opened her mouth to say hello, but before the words came out, the woman walked back toward her table. Jess grinned sheepishly, turned back toward her drink and looked directly into the broad face of the bartender.

"You got it bad, dontcha pal?"

Jess smiled weakly, feeling her cheeks and ears getting warm. "Shows, huh?"

"That one has a real bad rep, y'know," said Alice as she dragged a damp rag up and down the length of the bar. "Goes home with a different one every night."

"Maybe she just hasn't met a woman she wants to settle down with yet," said Jess. "You know her name?"

Alice shook her head, looked away for a moment, ran her hand through her halo of gray curls and said, "It's your funeral...her name is Lila."

Alice walked toward the far end of the bar and Jess said softly, "Lila." She liked the sound.

The music was starting again. A slower song, perfect to dance close to. Jess downed the rest of her Perrier, wiped her lips on the back of her hand and started toward the table across the room.

In front of the redhead, Jess straightened to her full six foot stature and said, "Care to dance?"

The redhead looked up at Jess. Six feet tall with long, wild black hair, Jess knew she always made a strong impression. The redhead stared for a long moment, then smiled, held out her hand and said, "I'd love to."

Jess led her to the center of the floor and pulled her close, wrapping her long arms around the lithe body. Both women responded to the rhythm of the music and the rhythm of each other's body. Seconds later they were moving as one. Jess rested her chin lightly against the top of the frizzy red hair and said, "My name's Jess. What's yours?"

Without missing a beat or looking up, the redhead said, "Lila."

"That's pretty," murmured Jess. "Suits you."

"Thanks."

Jess felt transformed. Senses long ignored were waking. Everything except the rhythm of the music and the swaying of their bodies ceased to exist. Everything was sensual. She felt every inch of her six foot, 220 pound frame come alive and smolder. Gently, she tightened her grip on Lila, who responded by reaching her arms around Jess' waist to stuff her hands into Jess' back pockets. Jess caught her breath as Lila eased her body more tightly against the tall woman. Bending her face to Lila's hair again, Jess inhaled the delicate scent, trying to memorize every sensation.

When the music stopped, Lila looked up at Jess and said, "Join me at the table?"

Jess smiled. "Let me get us some drinks."

Lila made her way across the dance floor as the music began again. Jess watched her walk away, then wove her way through the gyrating couples to the bar. She grinned at the bartender and ordered another beer for Lila and a Perrier for herself. Alice shook her head as Jess walked toward the table on the other side of the room.

She sat down next to Lila rather than across from her and said, "Here you go."

Lila took the Olympia and sat back to look at Jess in silence for a moment. "You've been watching me for a long time. Am I everything you expected?"

Jess blushed scarlet. "I don't know you yet."

"What's to know? What you see is what you get," said Lila. "I saw you talking to Alice. I'm sure she told you all about me."

"I heard the words, but I have a feeling she's all wrong. I'll take my chances."

The smile faded from Lila's face for a minute. "I hope she's wrong too. Trouble is, I'm afraid she isn't."

The pained expression in Lila's gray eyes squeezed at Jess' heart. In the next moment, the pain was gone, replaced by a cold, hard stare that made her eyes look like steel. Jess continued to look into the hard stare.

"What's so fascinating about my face?"

Jess smiled, reached out and gently moved one of Lila's red curls off her cheek. "It depends. Actually, I was watching your eyes. They're supposed to be the windows of the soul. Yours are like doors. They open and I see a fleeting glimpse of you, then they slam

The Best Things Happen While You're Dancing

in my face."

"What do you think you see when they're open?"

"I'm not sure. I usually reserve judgment until I know someone very well. We've got a long way to go. In the meantime, want to dance?"

At the 3 a.m. closing, Jess and Lila were still dancing, talking and laughing. Jess was happier than she had been in a long time, and she felt Lila was losing her tough exterior. Jess searched the gray eyes each time their gaze met. Maybe one day the doors would stay open.

Jess walked Lila to her car. Lila hesitated for a moment, then leaned seductively against the white Camaro and said, "Want to spend the night?"

Jess caught her breath. Every cell in her body screamed YES. She watched Lila. This was part of the act that by now Jess had decided was simply an act. Jess smiled at Lila, leaned close and very gently pressed her mouth to Lila's soft lips. Lila's lips parted as she began to run her tongue along Jess' upper lip. Abruptly, Jess stood back.

There was a pained, confused expression on Lila's face.

Jess cupped Lila's chin in her hand and said, "I want to say yes, very much. But if I do that, I'll be acknowledging that Alice is right. I don't think she is. I want you. I see someone in you that you may not even remember, and I'm willing to wait until you find her and remember."

Tears flooded Lila's eyes and spilled down her cheeks. "So what if you're wrong?"

Jess wiped the tears off Lila's white cheeks and said, "I know I'm right, and when I feel this strongly I won't back down. Go home and sleep on it. I'll be here later tonight."

Walking back to her beat up old Chevy was one of the hardest things Jess had ever done. She waved to Lila as she eased the Nova out of the parking lot, then gripped the leather laced steering wheel as panic and pain washed over her. What if Lila didn't show up again? What if she didn't want a relationship? What if she only wanted one night? Jess closed her eyes and leaned her head against the seat's headrest as she stopped for the last traffic light on N.E. Sandy Blvd. before it became W. Burnside Street. She was almost home and fighting an overwhelming urge to go back to Lila. When she opened her eyes, the light was green. She headed home, where she fell onto the bed fully dressed and slept.

That evening, Jess was at her usual station at the bar, when Lila arrived. Her heart skipped a beat when she saw the red halo. Lila had come in alone, but was greeted by four women at the door. She smiled a perfunctory greeting, letting her eyes scan the bar. When she saw Jess, she shook off the four confused women and made her way toward the bar.

"Hello, Amazon, I was wondering if you would be here."

Jess smiled, then reached out to envelope Lila in a mammoth hug. When she released the smaller woman, Lila looked up into Jess' face and again Jess saw the clear gray eyes. No guards, no barriers.

Lila slid onto the stool beside Jess and smiled as Alice put an Olympia down in front of her. She smiled at the bartender, then turned to Jess. "I'm glad you're here."

Jess took her hand and said, "Me too. Let's dance."

Chicago's "Color My World" was playing as Lila reached up to put her arms around Jess' neck. At five feet five, she had to stand on her toes to do this, but she liked being slightly off balance, depending on Jess' strong frame to keep her upright. The power in Jess' arms and the gentleness of her personality made Lila feel safe and warm. These were new feelings for her.

Lila's was a classic horror story. A new stepfather and an alcoholic/jealous mother left Lila on the street at sixteen. She had learned early on that love was a commodity that she could ill afford, that her body was just a vehicle that brought her money and other necessities. What she had done had kept her alive. Nothing more, nothing less.

Now here was someone she wanted She didn't remember ever feeling this way before. What she didn't understand was what Jess wanted. No one had ever waited for a second invitation. She had stared at her face in the mirror for a long time last night. Even at thirty and a little drunk she was still a beauty. No denying that. So what was the story with Jess? Why bother?

Lila tightened her grip around Jess' neck and swayed to the final strains of the song. Patience had to be the answer.

Again, Jess kissed Lila goodnight at her car with promises to see

her the next weekend. Lila was unsure, but forced herself to be calm.
 Friday night, Lila rushed to CHARITY. At the bar, in her usual place, sat Jess. Lila relaxed.
 At the end of the month, Lila's resolve at patience was wearing thin. They had been to a concert at Mt. Hood, hiking at Multnomah Falls, walking on the beach, sampling exotic restaurants and dancing at CHARITY. Jess was comfortable and happy with Lila. Lila had seen no one else in the month. After their fifth week together, Jess proposed a picnic dinner at Mt. Hood. She picked Lila up at 5:30 and they drove to Mt. Hood National Park. Trillium Lake sat nestled at the base of the mountain. The melting snow run-off fed the lake with clear blue waters, and if you stood in just the right place, you could see the reflection of the mountain on the glassy surface. It was a spectacular view that left Jess in awe every time she saw it. Jess parked her old blue Nova in a clearing. She lifted a wicker basket onto her shoulder, stuffed a couple of old blankets under her arm and started off through the thicket. She seemed sure of where she was going, so Lila followed in silence. After a short walk through the cool brush, they emerged at a cove. Right at the lake's edge the trees and bushes formed a barrier on the right, and a natural rock formation provided a barrier on the left. Jess spread the blankets on the thick grass and pine needles closest to the trees.
 "I like to think that only I know about this spot. I've never seen anyone else here."
 "It's breathtaking! I've never been to the park before," said Lila.
 Jess chuckled and said, "How deprived you are! I come here every chance I get."
 "Alone?"
 "Mostly. I can breathe here. Shake the cobwebs out of my brain and let go of old hurts. It's hard to feel bad when the scenery is so powerful."
 They sat side by side on the blanket facing the lake. The sun was dipping low and reflecting a brilliant orange in the clear, still lake. Jess put her arm around Lila's shoulders and drew her close. Lila rested her head on Jess' shoulder, feeling the strong arm surrounding her, the warm hand softly stroking her arm.
 When Lila looked up into Jess' face, she had a feeling of being home. When Jess kissed her, it was like nothing she had ever

experienced.

Jess lowered her lips to Lila's neck and shoulder. She felt the tremors in Lila's breathing as she slowly lowered them both to the ground. Jess kept looking into Lila's eyes to see if the doors had closed. What she saw was a beseeching, a pleading, a welcoming.

Slowly, deliberately, she opened button after button on Lila's blue shirt, exposing the ivory breasts. Lila sucked in her breath, arching her back as Jess' mouth covered first one, then the other. A moan, barely audible, came from deep within Lila as she grabbed Jess' hair, pressing the mouth more tightly to her breast.

Painstakingly, Jess removed Lila's clothes and then her own. Both women were breathing rapidly, each touching, exploring the other with hands and mouths. In a frenzy, Jess pulled herself away from Lila's hot hands and moved to the center of passion, slowly tasting and dipping, teasing the moaning woman. Lila's rocking body and hands that pressed Jess into her told Jess that the time was right. In the briefest instant Lila went rigid, gasped, then went limp.

Jess crawled up beside her, gathering Lila into her arms to hold, to kiss, to protect, to love. She held her close, kissing eyelids, stroking her back. Lila opened her eyes, and for the very first time, Jess saw molten lava rather than cold steel. The doors had been torn from their hinges. In their places were flecks of indescribable color, beckoning Jess to come in and be at home.

With tears on her cheeks, Jess cradled the fiery redhead and said, "Welcome home, sweetness. I've been waiting a long time for you.." Lila reached out to consummate their growing love.

Relationships

The Wait

by Patty Hennessey

Patty Hennessey has known she was different since she was five years old. When she was eight her younger sister asked their mother, "What is a queer, Mom?" Their mother explained that "queer" was not a nice word and that the proper term was "homosexual."

"Well, what is a homosexual then?" insisted her more extroverted sister. "Well," their mother continued, taking a deep breath, "A homosexual is a man that marries a man or a woman that marries a woman."

"So, that's it!" Patty thought. "What a great idea!"

Patty, now 39, has not changed much. She lives with her lover and their cat Quadraphonic in the mountains above Boulder, Colorado. Her sister is still inquisitive. Her mother, who died in May, 1990, would have liked this story.

The Wait

All we wanted was a puppy. It seemed simple. We had grown enough as a couple to be ready to accept one more living thing into our home. We had been lovers for two years and three months. We had survived working together, the last gasps of my previous relationship, and Alice's grudging acceptance of her dykedom. I had learned to love her enough to respect her proud independence. She had learned to sleep in the same bed with another human being all night and not feel claustrophobic. Life was good. All we wanted was a puppy.

We had both quit our jobs. We were taking the summer off to enjoy the northland, get centered and decide our joint future.

Despite a petless childhood, Alice had taken to my feline housemate, so the cat and I had moved into her apartment. I was writing, sending out resumes and reading. Alice was visiting friends, planning our summer trips and writing letters. I had mentioned a dog more than once, testing the waters.

One day Alice turned to me and said, "I think it's time for the puppy." We were off. We checked out *Dog Breeds of the World* from the library and studied the specifications of each breed appealing to our joint sense of dogness. We made lists of pros and cons, wants and dislikes. Ours was a process you would only believe if you experienced it.

We decided on a mutt. We would get a puppy of mixed origin (they're smarter you know) and train it ourselves. We were tending toward female but interpersonal skills and a sense of humor could win out over gender. A terrier crossbreed would provide the required feistiness. We answered advertisements from the newspaper and bulletin boards. We followed leads from friends and became regulars at the Humane Society Adoption Center. We were serious.

•

Stan is a calm and quiet man. He is the older brother of Fred, our gay friend who regularly attends guy's night at the Women's

The Wait

Room Lounge; their resemblance is striking. The first time Alice and I went to the Humane Society Stan helped us "review the current selection." Our conversation strayed from puppies to brothers to lifestyles and Stan worked his way into our hearts with his obvious love for and pride in his brother. Now Stan expected one or both of us at the shelter on a regular basis and he expedited our visits with a quick review of any new arrival that fit our criteria.

On June 22nd, two days after Alice's birthday, I made my semi-weekly trip to the Society. As soon as I saw Stan I knew something was different. He was busy with two adoptive parents so he motioned slightly with his head for me to wait. I removed my sunglasses and browsed through the pamphlets displayed on the FYI section of the bulletin board. As I read about "Heart Worm and Canine Distemper," I listened to Stan's strained, usually mellow voice as he quickly explained the adoption process to the new pet owners. Something was up.

After the happy family finally said goodbye, Stan rang the buzzer for the Kennel Assistant to cover the desk while he took me to review new arrivals. When we got to the glass bowl that served as the office Stan shut the door behind him, sat gently in the desk chair and leaned back slowly until he rested against the wall behind him. I waited as Stan looked at me thoughtfully over his oval wire rimmed glasses. I smiled. Stan said, "I have a dog I'd like you to see."

"A dog?" I asked.

"Yes, a five or six-year-old German Shepherd," Stan stated almost too matter-of-factly.

"Stan?" I asked with a mixture of confusion and frustration. "We want a puppy, you know that, a little apartment size puppy."

"I know, Pam," he said in a calming tone, "but you should look at this dog." The room was warm. I could feel the heat rise in my face as I sat, gazing at Stan. He was thinking too. We looked at each other, our minds working on opposite ends of a puzzle.

I waited. After several moments I said, "Why, Stan? Why a dog? Why *this* dog?"

Stan took a deep breath, sighed and said, "He's been here eight days, Pam. Ten is the limit. He's been raised by women; it's not that he's mean with men or anything, he just prefers women. He's a good dog. I think you should look at him." In the weeks that Alice and I had been cruising The Society, Stan Davis had never tried to sell us on anything. He had never presented an animal for review that did not meet at least eighty percent of our criteria. He had never used pity or euthanasia to bias us. I realized that I had to look at this dog before I was going to understand.

"Okay, since you feel so strongly about it I'll look at the dog."

The air in the hall was much cooler than in the office. I breathed deeply. The barking and whining became louder as Stan opened the door labeled LARGE DOGS and the warm smell of dog kennel waved over us as we entered the room. Stan stopped just inside the door and looked across the room. "His name is Max," Stan said without breaking his gaze. There was no mistaking Max.

He sat quietly in the middle of his indoor run. He wasn't sad or excited. He was alert, ears cocked, eyes clear. He was waiting. He watched us, or rather, he watched me.

Stan walked across the room and stood several feet to the left of Max's kennel. Max sat quietly. I walked across the room to where Stan stood and Max watched my progress with interest. The hair on the back of my neck raised slightly. I thought, "We just want a puppy."

"How old did you say he is?" I asked, trying to break the silence.

"We think he's five or six," Stan said.

"Didn't his owner tell you?"

"The owner didn't bring him in so the information on him is a little sketchy," Stan offered hesitantly.

I moved closer to the kennel containing Max. A sheep dog to Max's left leapt against its kennel door, whining and prancing in basic adolescent attention seeking. Max and I only winced at the suddenness of the movement, our attention keenly focused on each other.

He was a beautiful dog, tricolored, with a shiny coat. His ears and nose were neither too big nor too small. He was of medium build with a well muscled chest and rump. His tail was unbroken and arched gently off the floor as he continued to sit. And wait.

I glanced sideways at Stan. He was watching Max. "What's the deal here, Stan?" I finally asked. Stan looked at me calmly.

"It's a special situation, Pam. An elderly lady had a car accident over on Wilson Way where it curves by the Seven-Eleven. She apparently had a heart attack at the wheel and instead of heading off into the intersection she turned the car into the trees at Whitley Park. She died instantly."

"So Max was hers, huh Stan?"

"Well, yes, hers and her companion's," Stan said softly, his eyes burning into the side of my face.

"The lady who had the car accident was, Rose Curtis," Stan continued. "The police found a card in her purse about who to notify in case of an accident, the card said Grace Jenson, same address. So, after things were cleaned up, the officers went around to see Grace. No one answered their knock, but a neighbor was out on her porch." Stan paused, rubbed both palms on his pants, shifted his weight and continued. "Things are kind of sketchy here but, to make it short, Grace had a stroke two days before the accident. Rose was headed down to the hospital to see her."

Max still sat in his kennel, watching Stan and I, waiting patiently. I probably only imagined that his eyes looked sad now.

I was suddenly aware of a tightness in my throat. I swallowed hard. I thought about life and death and time rolling by. I remembered my dog Tippie and the fourteen years we shared. I thought of Alice and how much I wanted her to be there. I tried to think of something else, something outside the room, outside the building: something superficial, something mundane, something less real.

I walked to the kennel door and knelt down. I put my fingers through the fence. Max stood and walked to the door. He laid his muzzle against my fingers.

"So then the police brought him here, hey?" I asked, trying to end the story.

"Yeah, the neighbor told them Max was inside. When they checked with the hospital where Grace was the nurse said she wasn't even expected to live through the night." Stan finished.

I leaned my burning face against the cool metal of the kennel gate. Max sniffed around my eyes, nose and chin. His nose was wet. "Healthy dog," I thought. "At least Stan remembered one of our criteria."

"I have to call Alice," I said as I stood up. "This isn't exactly an independent decision I have here." Suddenly the time warp, in which I had been standing, sped up. In less than five minutes I explained the situation to Alice on the phone, then she was at The Society within twenty minutes of hanging up. As she walked in the door she said, "Is this what you want?"

I answered, "Only if you really think it's a good idea. Just look at the dog. If he's not the one, then he's not the one."

It was love at first nuzzle. The dog adored Alice. Though reserved, Alice obviously loved the dog. Stan was happy. Alice was happy. I was sort of numb.

•

The next several days are a blur in my memory. They were days filled with introductions: to neighbors, the cat, friends and the landlord ("That will be an additional $200 security deposit and you're all out at the first complaint!"). We purchased dog food, a collar, dish and bowl. Hours I sat at my computer with Max's head on my leg; he was delighted with every pet, every word, his eyes full of love. We spent priceless moments watching the cat sleep against Max's side and learning that if Alice was in the apartment Max was never more than six feet away.

Just as Stan said, Max was a good dog. He obeyed all the standard verbal commands, "Stay, Max! Come, Max! Heel, Max!" He could have been walked without a leash, but we wanted to be safe so we temporarily kept him on a leather lead whenever he was out of the apartment. He enjoyed being outside and was very alert to the sights and sounds of summer but he never pulled, nor darted, nor whined. Rose and Grace had trained him well.

After the first two weeks life settled into the hot days of August. Our family had worked out most of it's boundaries and mores. Yes, it was okay to sleep on the bed *if* you slept quietly at the bottom and did not roll over the cat. No, you don't eat human food except on rare occasions and *only* if the human offers it first, no begging. Do not bark or whine at the noises on the street at all but if someone touches your doorknob growl like crazy!

I had forgotten we had wanted a puppy and Max's history seemed more a fable than his orphaned past. The feeling of importance I had felt the first day at The Society was much less keen, that aura of destiny, subdued. Those feelings returned, however,

The Wait

when I heard Stan's voice on my answering machine, "Pam or Alice, please call me at the Humane Society Adoption Center at 525-2367. At home I'm at 529-8965 after six. It's about Max."

"What does he mean, it's about Max?" Alice asked repeatedly as I tried to dial Stan's work number.

"I don't know Al, but we'll find out," I answered, feeling less brave than I tried to sound. Ringgggg. Ringgggg. Ringgggg. Ringgggg. "God, this is a place of business for crying out loud! Don't they answer their damn phone?" Ringgggg. Ringgggg.

"Hello, this is the Humane Society, can you hold?" Hummmmmm.

"No, I can't, dumb shit, as though that makes a difference," I mumbled into the receiver. I waited. The battery-powered clock above the kitchen door ticked irritatingly. A fly landed on the top of Max's head and he shook it off. Alice paced. The cat laid in the sun and dreamed.

"Hello, this is Jack, may I help you?" said the adolescent voice.

"Yes, is Stan there?"

"Hold a minute and I'll get him," the voice countered. Hummmmmm. I waited.

"Hello, this is Stan, may I help you?" That mellow voice made me feel better.

"Stan, this is Pam, what's up?"

"Oh, Pam, good. It's about Max."

"Yeah."

"A nurse from Community Hospital called a little while ago, actually about three hours ago. They'd like to have Max visit Grace in the hospital."

"What? Grace? But I thought... Stan, well, isn't she dead?"

"I guess she's still hanging on. The nurse says she keeps talking about her dog. She seems to be worried about him."

"Oh."

"Pam, you there?"

"Huh? Yeah, I'm here Stan. Community Hospital, is that where you said?"

"The nurse said at the Rehab Center. It was the head nurse there, Carey Somebody."

"Yeah, Carey Ludkowski, I used to work there."

"Yeah, Polish name, sounds right."
"Anything else, Stan?"
"Nope, I didn't give her your name or anything. That information is confidential. I just told her I'd give you the message."
"Okay, thanks, Stan."
"Yeah, no problem, bye, Pam." Hummmmmm.

•

Carey met us at the front door of the rehabilitation center. "Glad you could come," she said quietly. Carey always talked quietly, even if she was angry. "Mrs. Jenson is very weak and not making the progress she should, I would like her to see her dog."

"Ms.," I said.

"Pardon me?" asked Carey.

"Ms.," I said again, "Grace Jenson was not married, not legally anyway."

"Oh, you know her?" Carey asked, probably sizing up the situation and coming up with a close but slightly off-target scenario.

"Only from the report the police gave the Humane Society," I said, mustering my best matter-of-fact tone.

"Well, then you know she is gay and her lover died on her way here to see her." Carey was better at matter-of-fact than I was.

My face was warm. Alice was petting Max gently on the head, smiling slightly. Carey didn't wait for me to respond. "Ms. Jenson is stuck, Pam, she is not getting better or worse. She talks about her dog all the time." Carey nodded toward Max who stood by my side, his shoulder inches behind my right leg. "I think seeing him might help."

I looked from Max to Carey. Her eyes were moist and her face, though professionally composed, was filled with understanding. Alice kept smiling, maybe she knew things I didn't.

We had worked with Carey Ludkowski RN for four years. She was head nurse, I was therapy supervisor, and Alice was a therapist. Carey had been competent and proud. Carey had done things by the book. She wore starched white uniforms and always referred to patients by their last name, with a traditional marital prefix properly attached. I knew nothing of her personal life other than that she was unmarried, lived on a small lake twenty miles out of the city and enjoyed fishing. I'd never seen her at the Lounge or at church. She

The Wait

didn't wear a pinky ring or any other symbol and she never mentioned her lifestyle. But, now, her eyes told me a story I had never suspected. Some closet doors are well guarded indeed.

"I see," I said, returning her look. "You seem to know more about the situation than anyone else. She must trust you very much."

"It's a mutual condition, fate is an unusual force," Carey stated in a whisper. "Let's go up the back elevator. Ms. Jenson is in ICU."

The four of us stepped off the elevator at the second floor. Alice, Max and I waited as Carey checked with the nurse at the desk. Then Carey led us to cubicle three and we walked in.

It was a typical ICU unit, lots of tubes and machines surrounded by an easily moved curtain. There was the steady hiss of the oxygen and the blip, blip, blip, of the cardiac monitor. The small white bed was centered on the far wall. The smell of alcohol and powder, urine and disinfectant hovered in the air.

Carey was standing by the bed holding the frail woman's hand. "Ms. Jenson, Ms. Jenson it's Carey Ludkowski. You have an important visitor."

Grace Jenson was of medium build and had fine gray hair that encircled her head like a light mist. Her complexion was now pale and tinged with yellow, her lips were tight and drawn. She seemed to be bearing great pain. She opened her eyes slowly as though being pulled from a deep, deep sleep.

Carey repeated her last sentence. Grace squinted past Carey at the two strange women standing in the room. Grace said, "Visitor?" in a whisper.

"Yes," Carey's voice was excited now, "These two women are Maxwell's new owners, they've brought him to see you!" Grace's eyes widened and she raised her head from the pillow. "Maxwell? My Maxwell? He's here? Maxwell?"

"Yes, he's right here," Carey said as she stepped aside.

I was frozen. Max was wiggling. Carey was crying. Only Alice was able to act. She took the lead from my hand, patted me on the shoulder, and let Max go to the bed. He seemed to know just what to do.

He raised slowly up on his back legs and gently rested his front paws on the bed beside Grace's shoulder. He laid his nose beside her face as her hand found his ears, his head, his neck. "Oh my! Oh my!" Grace muttered over and over.

Alice held my hand. Carey scratched Max's back and explained, "See, Ms. Jenson, Maxwell is safe and well. He has a good home with two women who love him. He still loves you but he loves them too. Just like he loves Rose and you."

"Yes, yes, I see," said Grace after covering Max's nose with neat little kisses. "He looks very well, and happy. Come here please and tell me about yourselves," Grace whispered between labored breaths. I was worried all the excitement could be too much for Grace but Carey didn't seem concerned. I left it to her.

Alice and I moved beside Max and he, as though on cue, nuzzled against Alice's side. Grace smiled wryly as her eyes searched our faces and came to rest on my hand, on Alice's forearm.

Alice explained our lives. Our search for new jobs. The brightness of our apartment in the morning sun. Grace closed her eyes as she listened, interrupting only to clarify a description or murmur approval.

When Alice had finished Grace thanked us for coming and for bringing Max. We promised to come back the next day. Grace squeezed each of our hands, patted Max once again and drifted off to sleep.

As the three of us turned and walked toward the door the familiar blip, blip, blip, became a startling Buzzzzzz. Grace had gone to be with Rose. The wait was over.

Relationships

Margo

by Diana Rivers

I, Diana Rivers, am a 58-year-old woman living on women's land in a house I designed that was all built by women's hands, including my own. I have lived in women's land communities for years and written many stories drawn from those experiences. I have written a novel, Journey to Zelindar, that is a combination fantasy, myth and Lesbian adventure story or perhaps should be called women's alternative history. I am now finishing the prequel to it, called Daughters of the Great Star. It comes 200 years before and tells how it all began. Another side of me is an artist and I am a partner in a women's greeting card company, Willow Moon Designs. We print several other women's designs besides our own and try to create powerful and affirmative images of women.

The most exciting thing in my life right now has been writing what I call performance pieces. I see these as women's empowerment pieces, sortof like the old christian morality plays but with a very different message. This is a totally new form for me, a way of taking ideas I used to mutter around about but never wrote down and giving them a right brain experiential form. These pieces are intended to be read with improv dance providing the action and drum, flute and audience joining in. They are designed so one or two women can go different places, create a cast out of the women there, rehearse a couple of times and put them on—instant theater! It's been a great experience. At the end women in the audience are up on their feet dancing and shouting and full of energy. I want to do much more of this and I'm also starting to get some ideas for street theater.

Margo

Margo loves to be the first one up, loves to greet the morning alone, chopping kindling in the silent house. Before going down, she always stands a few minutes at the upstairs window, watching the new light redden the bluffs. When it touches the tree tops, that's her signal to move.

After Margo has stirred the old coals to life and filled the stove with wood, after its cold metal sides are beginning to heat up and radiate warmth, the others start to stir; women's voices from upstairs, Earth running in from the tipi with her clothes under arm. Every morning she runs in like that, naked and shivering to dress by the stove. "Good fire, Margo," she says each time with her shy, slow smile.

By that time Margo has the cookstove going too, a big pot of water heating for dishes, a pot of oatmeal on, the cast iron frying pan heating for whoever wants eggs and coffee keeping warm at the back. She pulls the old rocker over by the cookstove and sits there rocking, keeping an eye on breakfast and listening to the house come alive around her.

Earth is usually the next one in the kitchen. She sets the table, fills the big honey jar and tries to gather enough cups for them all. Cups have a way of migrating upstairs or to the outdoor kitchen or even further to women's tents and tipis. "How does it happen so fast?" Earth murmurs and makes a little note about cups at the bottom of the meeting list.

Carrie comes down still buttoning her shirt and rings the breakfast bell. Then she cuts thick slices of homemade bread, fitting them in skillfully on the crowded stovetop. "I'll watch those, Margo. Why don't you start eating?"

Margo enjoys being mother of the morning, seeing them all gather for breakfast, hearing women tell their dreams. Afterwards she has a second cup of coffee, a little luxury of time while the dishes are being washed. By then she's ready for the solitude of her workshop. In the evening, as a trade for her morning energy, she likes to be fed and taken care of. It's a silent bargain she's come to with the other women in the house.

The workshop is down a little slope from the house, out of sight but nearby, an old goat shed Margo has converted for woodworking. She walks to it awkwardly. Going down hill always increases her slight limp. It reminds her over again each day that she's still alive when she could have been charred flesh and bone wrapped around a motorcycle. She's learned to accept the limp and the scars too as a part of herstory.

The big oak tree in front of the shop is turning bronze. Autumn, a time of changing weather, a fire in the morning and a sleeveless shirt by afternoon. She opens all the doors and windows and sweeps yesterday's sawdust into a big pile in the corner. The dirt floor shows through again, dark and waiting.

With the end of the broom handle she carefully unhooks a bat from the rafter and shakes it off outside. It flies away drunkenly in the unaccustomed light. Third one this week, she thinks. The shed still has some gaps that need patching. Well, after the craft show's over and before winter...

Sunlight falls on her tool wall, the tools elegantly arranged, each hanging on its own nail against the gray weathered wood. They sparkle in the light, waiting to greet her. "I like to have my tools out where I can see them, makes me feel good." Ever since she can remember she's loved hardware stores, the look and feel of tools. For a while, when she was younger, she went through a stage of pocketing tools that appealed to her, even ones she had no use for—until she got caught. She never forgot that big man looming over her with his hand on her shoulder. "Helping yourself I see," he'd said in his gruff voice, before taking her to the manager. That was the end of her career as a thief. When Green Sister Farm was going through a readjustment there was a lot of talk about collectivizing everything, no personal property. "Look, I'm willing to collectivize whatever else you want, my clothes, my books, anything. Throw it all in a box to be shared. I don't care. [Margo, of course doesn't have much else.] But not my tools! Hell no! I'm not collectivizing my tools. I've had some of them more than fifteen years, longer than I've known any of you. They're my friends. They're part of me. We've travelled all over this country together." She'd say this while clumping around in her big boots, making sure they all heard her. "Any woman wants to use those tools, she can use them in the shop—after I show her how. But no tools out of the shop." For emphasis she'd hit the table with her hand. "No tools out!" That had become the catch-word for a while when someone was taking a tough stand—'No tools out!" Standing square-shouldered and obdurate in the middle of the kitchen she'd made it clear that if she was forced to collectivize her tools she'd leave.

But in spite of what she says, Margo does lend out tools, worrying and fussing the whole time. "Okay, just this once. Make sure you bring it back. It goes right here." A missing tool leaves a gap on the wall, a wound. But she has limitless sensitive patience for teaching women how to work with their hands, even women who've never held a tool before, who feel awkward and clumsy and sometimes cry with frustration. It's worth any amount of time to her just to see that look of pleasure when they finally get the feel of it. They've all learned a lot from her. Except for Earth, Margo is the only woman at Green Sister who grew up on a farm. The rest of them come from cities and suburbs. However much they may grumble at times about her ways, Margo's a valuable resource there.

Margo clears herself a space on the worktable to do some .drawings. The morning light blazes back at her from the paper. Big, rough slabs of wood, yesterday's truck load from the local sawmill, stand waiting against the wall. Make some fine tables, Margo thinks, looking at them fondly.

While she's working, Earth slips in, soundless on her bare feet. She sits against the wall, feet tucked under her, chin on her knees. Her straight hair falls forward like a dark wing almost covering her face. Margo glances around, aware of her presence more by sense than sound. She sees Earth isn't ready to talk yet, is just "being" and so she goes on with her drawing. Margo's in the process of designing joints and notches so her furniture can be disassembled, laid flat in the truck and reassembled at craft shows. She's completely absorbed in the problem when Earth stands up to leave.

Margo looks up in surprise. "Didn't you come to talk to me?"

"No, I just wanted to be here." Earth is shaking her head as she moves sideways towards the door. "Someday I want to start building things, even my own house," she says quickly, speaking so softly

Margo

Margo has to strain to hear her. "First I have to get over my fear of tools."

"Any time you're ready..."

"Not yet. I'm not ready yet."

"Maybe you can help me with this next craft show." "Maybe..." Earth slips out as softly as she came in, seemingly erased from the air.

Margo watches her go down the hill, moving with the lightness of an animal. Earth is the quiet one; she never talks about herself. No one knows what her life was like before she came to Green Sister. Sometimes she makes the others nervous with that way she has of watching things none of them can see.

"Strange woman," Margo says aloud to herself. "That's for sure one strange woman." Earth has disappeared, melting into the little cluster of trees by the pond. "She can bake ten loaves of bread at a time, the seedlings in the greenhouse spring out of the ground for her, she knows where to find just the right herbs to brew when we're sick and she doesn't think she's worth shit." She shakes her head with puzzled fondness.

Margo tacks her drawings on the wall. She gets up and stretches, happily breathing in the smell of earth and sawdust. Such a pleasure to have a real shop. No woman could ever get as much joy from her mansion as Margo gets from that old shed. Moving around it she pets the waiting slabs and runs her fingers across the cool metal of the tools. Such a pleasure after working out of a truck. That truck had even been her home for awhile. What a crazy time that was. Twice she'd almost gotten locked up for vagrancy. "You mean you live in that thing? Well you just drive it away and be quick about it. Go park it in some other state. Next time I find you hanging around here you're under arrest." She'd driven off raging and helpless.

Needing to earn some money, wanting to use her skills and not work a straight job again, Margo had finally settled on making furniture for craft shows. It's been a good bargain but it took her awhile to get there. First she had to escape the family farm. "Hell, they worked me like a boy and treated me like a girl." Trapped back in the hills, the autonomous independence of the city had looked good to her. "I'll never shovel cow shit again in my life!" she'd shouted at her father when she left.

250

But it hadn't been easy. She'd started as a secretary. She was a fast enough typist but had no patience for office protocol. It ended with her shouting at the boss, "You can shove this typewriter up your ass sideways!" There were no references from that one but it didn't matter. She'd already decided an office was too confining. After that there were a few waitressing jobs. On the last one she threw over some tables loaded with dirty dishes and stormed out. At the door, she'd shouted back into the faces of the startled customers, "Good enough show for you? Bet that was better than TV." That's when she'd had her motorcycle accident, zooming off into the night, full of anger.

After she'd recovered or been "patched together" as she liked to say with a funny lopsided grin, Margo bought her old gray truck and some tools. Then she started wandering across the country, doing some carpentry. It wasn't much better. She got hassled by men on the job—even had a few fights. One foreman said to her, "Margo, you're a good carpenter. You work well, you're quick and careful. Everything would be fine if you could just keep your mouth shut."

"Why? Why should I keep my mouth shut? Why not them?"

"Look, they're only kidding around. That's the way men are. You just have to get used to it."

"The hell I do!" Next morning she'd been on the road in her loyal truck. She never worked for a boss again. With the wood scraps she'd accumulated, she started making toys: trains, cars, boats, even a motorcycle, sometimes selling them out of the truck or on the street.

But it was getting lonelier. She felt like she was running and there was no place left to run to. For a while she drank, knocking off a few quick ones at the end of the day and beginning that way the next morning. When she started getting an ulcer she quit. Alone that way she couldn't afford to be sick.

Green Sister Farm had seemed like paradise to her. After she'd heard some men in the lumberyard talking about a "...weird bunch of women living together up in the hills, over by Crawford Gap..." she'd headed that way, not even waiting to buy her wood. Living on the land with all women, doing her own work; it was a reprieve, an oasis, a sanctuary. She was even glad to be back in the country. "Not really the city type after all," she'd say, kicking the mud off her boots. It was as if she'd been saved though not the way they meant in church. "I can for sure see I was headed for jail or the bughouse, one or the other." But she's still a bristly fighter, not an easy person to live with.

"Hell, it took me years to get this way. I'm not going to mellow out overnight. You think this is bad? I used to really be a wild one. There was this one time in Wyoming when I busted up the whole bar: chairs, tables, bottles, everything, and got out of there walking. Here I've never even thrown a plate, have I?" She winks at Carrie who throws plates and anything else at hand when she gets angry.

Margo likes to tell them stories about her rowdy past, sitting around the stove at night, the lamplight shadowing the corners of the room and drawing them together. Then she loves to talk, but not at meetings. She has no patience with meetings. She walks out. If she can't do that, she falls asleep.

"Talk, talk, talk. I just want to be doing something. How can you sit around using up the best part of the day just talking?"

"Margo, we have to talk so we can decide what to do next."

"Well, let me know when you've decided so I can go do it but don't ask me to sit here jawing!" Her energy burns holes in her. She needs to be making, moving, doing.

Sanding a slab, Margo is suddenly aware of Earth standing next to her. She clicks off the sander.

"I came back to help you," Earth says softly. Then she shakes her head, looking at the ground. "No, it's not true. I came back to struggle with it, my fears..." She scrapes her toes in the damp earth.

Margo's delighted. "Doesn't matter what the reason is, I'm glad you're back. Here, I'll show you how to run the sander. You can do that while I notch the legs."

"No, not the sander. I couldn't do that. I'm afraid of machines." Earth is shaking. She seems ready to spring back through the doorway. Margo puts out a hand to hold her and it's like holding a frightened horse.

"So much..." Earth says, shaking her head, "So much ... but I can't talk about it..." Suddenly she's crying.

Awkwardly, Margo draws her into a hug. "Hey, easy, easy." Trying to be consoling, she strokes Earth's back but her own wide, calloused hands seem clumsy to her and out of place. She's not used to physical contact. It makes her feel helpless as if something has come too close and is blocking her movement. Sounding hoarse, almost whispering, Margo says over and over, "It's alright, it's alright." Finally, when Earth doesn't move, Margo pushes her away a little. Earth stands with her arms held stiff against her.

"Look, we'll start slowly, okay?" Margo's still whispering. "I'll do the sanding. You can stand next to me." She shakes Earth gently to get a response. "Just put your hands over mine. You'll see how it feels."

Earth shakes her head. "I don't think..."

"Your hands," Margo says forcefully. She starts the sander. Earth rests her hands on Margo's, lightly, like shy birds ready to take flight.

"Press down a little, get some contact." Earth takes a firmer hold. There are tremors running up from her body through her fingers. Gradually her hand steadies, her arms move with Margo's arms, it becomes a dance, two women and a sander moving in union over the surface of the wood.

"Let's trade now."

"Not yet..."

"Just put your hands here. I'll guide." Again they move together. Very slowly Margo lightens her hands until she's not guiding anymore, she's following. The grain of the wood evolves out of the sawdust.

"That's enough, we're going to sand it all away. I'll use the fine sandpaper on it later." Margo stands the wood up in the stack of finished planks, wiping the surface with her sleeve. The walnut glows back at them, darkly beautiful.

"Are you ready to do it alone?"

"Yes, I think so, maybe...I'll try, but stay right here next to me."

"You can push the off switch whenever you want. You have the control, the last word."

At first Earth turns the sander off every minute or so. After a while she runs it for longer. When she begins humming, moving lightly and loosely, the way she moves around the kitchen, Margo goes to the other work bench and starts notching legs. Soon Margo's humming too, a little off key, unconsciously following Earth's melody. By late afternoon the slabs have shifted from one pile to the other. Earth clicks off the sander for the last time. She's coated with sawdust. The room is getting darker. Autumn coolness comes through the open door.

"That's enough," Margo says. "That's much more than I expected to get done." She hangs her tools back carefully in their places. "Earth, I'm late getting ready for this show. It would help a lot if you could work with me." That's as close as Margo can come to asking for something. Earth doesn't look at her. She just nods, brushing herself off.

Walking up the hill Earth says, "This is the first time I've ever..." and without finishing, she's off the path and into the field. She comes back with flowers and ferns and a branch of red berries bound together by grass. As she passes Margo, she quickly thrusts her bunch of wild pickings into Margo's hand and then goes singing up the path. Startled, Margo stares at this sudden offering. No one has ever picked flowers for her before. With her bad leg, she has to move more slowly, but Earth is waiting for her at the door.

When they come in, Carrie and Sage are setting the table. The lamps have just been lit. The battered old kitchen is lovingly softened by lamplight. They're all transformed by it, made soft and glowing. Earth looks particularly radiant, her face moon-like. Margo feels that inexpressible ache that sometimes comes to her in the evening. Carefully she puts the flowers in a jar of water, sets it in the middle of the table and takes her sweater off the hook. Going out again she hears Earth say, "I used the sander today. I'm going to help Margo work on her tables..." and she thinks, that's the most I've ever heard her say about herself.

Margo sits on the steps with her aching legs propped up on a stump. Her back is against the door jamb. The evening blue fills up the sky and slowly darkens. The first stars spring out. Familiar evening sounds come to her from the kitchen; food and laughter. She keeps thinking, I've never worked with anyone before. When she sees again in her mind Earth's dark head bent over the slabs, a sudden thrill rushes up her spine.

True Love

by Jan Hardy

Jan Hardy is a poet who occasionally fires off a short story when the mood strikes. She came out in the mid-70's when lesbians read, talked about, and published lots of poetry; she misses those days and works to recreate them. Her chapbook, out here flying, *is available from Sidewalk Revolution Press. She is currently editing* Wanting Women, *an anthology of erotic lesbian poetry.*

She enjoys meeting lesbians in other communities, corresponding with other writers and readers, and helping other lesbians fight writer's block and get their words into print. After all these years of loving women, her fantasy of the ideal lesbian future includes: many, many more years with Pat; working with lesbians to fight the "isms" because we want to, not because it's p.c.; writing more; reading more; and tap dancing lessons.

True Love

How did we get together? Well, that's a long story. First of all, let me tell you that at the time, I was living with my parents (by choice, ok?) for a couple of good reasons. I was saving to pay off my car, which on my salary I couldn't do if I was also paying rent. Also, my landlord, in his infinite wisdom, had just built a fire escape from the back alley directly up to my bedroom window—well, the whole apartment was my bedroom, it was one room—and I didn't feel safe anymore. In addition to this, my landlord, whose intelligence just astounds me, raised the rent yet again. One day when his rental agent was showing somebody the apartment, in my presence she gave a figure $50 a month less than what I was paying. I made a scene. Ruined her sale. I hated to take it out on her, I know she just works for this asshole, but I couldn't stand paying an arm and a leg for the privilege of living alone, and having some MAN install a stairway for rapists on top of everything. And the final reason I was living at home—you ever notice, no matter how old some of us get, our parents' place is "home"?—I had just been dumped by this woman who probably went back across the state to *her* parents' and went straight. Yes. So I was feeling pretty poorly and decided to move back where there were some people who loved me. Besides, my parents have always been a lot of fun; they're like a comedy team once they get started, they'll turn somersaults to make you laugh. They also respect my privacy and my life, even though they wish I were straight.

So that summer I lived across town in my parents' attic, played my sax, did stretching exercises and ran up Brownsville Road every day, two miles to the Presbyterian church and back. I laid out in the sun a lot, formulating great theories about True Love—namely that it was all a lie: people just took advantage of each other and lied to get laid, and so on and so forth. I tell you, I was pretty depressed for a while, but I got really good on the saxophone and my body was tan and muscular. And any time I wanted to be with dykes, I could hop in my wonderful new-used car, Chris Cagney (the name, incidentally, was suggested by my father). I'd drive down South 18th Street to the women's bookstore or to Wildsisters and socialize my heart out. If I got depressed there, I could hop back into Chris and drive up Brownsville Road, ten miles to the Mini-Mart and back, and by then I was usually okay.

The crowning finale of all this recovery stuff came in August. I went to the Michigan Wymyn's Music Festival, as always. Oh sure, my parents know about it. They don't like to hear all the little details, but they know what it is. My dad helped me tune up the car, my mom bought me Trail Mix. You know. Anyway, I got up there with my friends, pitched my tent alone, went to the concert that first night with everybody, and I was fine. The second night I got violently ill from some damn thing—no, this wasn't the year of the shigella, it was the food or the water or something. I spent the whole night barfing near my tent and the whole next day crying in the Womb. I know it was something physical, but I'd been feeling pretty miserable looking at all the beautiful pairs of women laughing and loving in such a festive, idyllic setting—I'm sure it was something emotional as well. I was lying in the Womb in a sort of daze trying not to throw up, when this little butch Army nurse came over to me. In the middle of asking about my symptoms, my pains, my allergies, she said in a very flat, matter-of-fact tone, "Did you just break up?" I crumbled right there. I sobbed and sobbed. She patted my hand soberly and just sat with me. When she had to leave, she sent one of those witches from the Emotional Healing Tent to me, but that didn't do any good at all. This woman came wafting over in her robes and crystals and auras, with her tender, sensitive expression, and I clammed right up. It's funny what works with different people.

Back home, I stopped theorizing quite so much about True Love. I finally got to the place where I liked myself again and didn't feel like such a fool after all. I figured I had given my best, and if it wasn't right for this woman she could take her stuff elsewhere. As for me, I would enjoy women for the miracles they are and leave the rest to happen as it might. I was ok.

Right about this time, Susan the pianist started to call me. She cried on my shoulder about Ann leaving her, and about how she couldn't play the piano anymore. I was able to give her shots of self-esteem and yell at her to keep on playing: Never Give Up Your Art. We talked for hours about music and women and love. About the same time—you ever notice how breakups happen in clumps?—my old friend Melissa started calling me in total panic attacks. Pat had supposedly thrown her out.

Melissa and I had known each other for years. I guess you could say we were friends in spite of our differences—she was one of those crystals-and-aura persons and I wasn't. She kept looking for evidence that I was a crystal-and-aura person too; I guess like most folks with a religion, she thought anyone she liked ought to have those beliefs too, otherwise why did she like me? I liked her and we had been in touch off and on over the years, but you know when someone breaks up, suddenly she's "renewing her friendships" all over the place. I've done it too. So Melissa was renewing our friendship, which means she was calling me all the time to see if I knew what Pat was doing, who Pat was seeing, what Pat would think if Melissa called her, and on and on.

Well, I didn't know Pat beyond a couple of dinners we'd all had as a foursome (the three of us and this woman who left me), so I truly didn't know what to say. And I believed Melissa when she said Pat had packed up her stuff and put it out on the sidewalk. I started to snub Pat when I saw her out at Wildsisters, especially if she was there with another woman. I started taking Melissa out dancing so she wouldn't be hysterical on the phone to me as much—I thought dancing cured everything, I should have told her to go to Michigan and throw up. She would have had a better time with those Emotional Healing women, and they could have compared auras and things. But I wanted to comfort Melissa, I guess because I had so recently been dumped myself. And when I went out to Wildsisters, I was still frowning and looking right through Pat, WHO I'D ALWAYS HAD A CRUSH ON.

Yes. Always. Since the first time we met, which was at Player's, years ago, when Melissa had just gotten her hooks into Pat. I shouldn't put it that way. But Melissa would hang on Pat all night, only letting go long enough to fetch a friend to introduce to her. Pat was sort of new to the community; she'd been closeted for years due to her marriage and kids. I'll never forget the moment we met. I was dancing with someone, and at the end of the song Melissa cut in, dragged me over and said proudly, "This is Pat," and I swear, it was exactly like the movies where everything stops. This woman was looking at me as if we shared a joke on everybody else; her eyes and her smile reached right into me and turned me into pudding, warm, sweet, and ready. Mmm.

I shook myself out of it; Melissa was saying something about Pat's marriage and kids, and an old Bisexual Alarm went off in my head: MARRIAGE! KIDS! I blurted some escape line, turned and dashed off to dance. I wasn't going to get involved with a straight woman, WITH KIDS (I pictured little *baby* kids), and I wasn't going to endanger Melissa's new thing. She looked really happy, and she was my friend, and I am, after all, a woman of principle. And there was no way I could be around this woman and not turn into pudding, so I took off. I didn't exactly handle it gracefully, but I was acting on my principles.

Of course I kept running into Pat and Melissa over the years and every time, Pat would look at me like we had this joke between us. Actually, I was afraid she was laughing at me because she knew I was attracted to her. It must have been obvious—I'd either yap and yap, or I'd stand there going "b-duh, b-duh." She'd smile that cool I-know-you smile, with those warm but piercing brown eyes and her fluffy brown hair and a delicious kind of tension in her body—cool, but like an athlete ready to spring. All those years I thought she was as tall as me, just because of the way she held herself.

Maybe when they broke up, I believed those rotten things Melissa told me because I thought I could finally get some control over the way I acted around Pat. I don't know. I should know by now that there are always at least two sides to every breakup. At any rate, by the night Pat and I finally got together, I hadn't even looked at her without scowling for months.

That night, a bunch of us had come to Wildsisters from an erotic poetry reading at the bookstore—is that perfect, or what? We were all high from the reading; I felt revved-up as I usually do, and on top of that I'd worn an outrageous black t-shirt thing that just kind of draped across what it had to—no back to it and a neckline down to my navel. Kind of a V-thing. I had been doing all this running, so I was pretty self-confident, and I'd bought all these femmy clothes

True Love

during my break-up, so I was into dressing up. Jane Street was playing at Wildsisters, and all the women from the reading wanted to get rowdy and dance out all of our raging hormones, so the place was just throbbing with energy, lust, and wild women. What a setting.

As a matter of fact, there was so much energy that women weren't really dancing in pairs, we were just boogying away in groups—and into this group Pat suddenly came, and I saw her REACT to me, not lose her cool but she did look startled at this lack-of-a-shirt on me. I felt so relieved and relaxed and happy that she finally showed something like that to me. Confidence, you know? It's the key.

But I didn't have any plans, mind you. I wasn't there to get picked up, although if you ask Pat that's what she'd tell you. I was just dancing up a storm, and I was happy to be with women.

Eventually the place got too hot, the band took a break, and my friends and I drifted out to the patio for air. I guess Pat hadn't seen the back of this lack-of-a-shirt, and somehow we started to talk about backrubs, and I must have asked her to rub my back—really, is that tacky or what? It was the spirit of the night as much as anything. Anyway, when I turned around I could *hear* this woman gasp, then regain her composure, and once I felt her hands on my shoulders it was all over. My chest was burning, I couldn't catch my breath, I wanted to turn around and take her into my arms...but I couldn't move, her hands on me were magic and I didn't want it to end. She massaged my shoulders, gave me a little athlete-to-athlete pat on the back to signal that it was finished, and I turned around and thanked her. Now I know you're not going to believe this, but after that I gave her the second oldest pick-up line in the book—I actually asked "What's your sign?" It was only because it came up in the conversation. Sherry was talking about the fact that she and I were both Leos, and kidding me about fire and all that; so of course, just to be polite and include Pat in the conversation, I asked her her sign. She said she was a Taurus, and I said, in my best Lauren Bacall voice (well, you try getting a backrub from a gorgeous woman you have a crush on and not sounding husky!) "Ooohh...Tauruses...are very...*earthy*..." Pat looked back at me with her smile and said, "Earthy, huh?" in *her* husky voice, which really laid me out. THAT was when I knew for sure that she was interested. We were finally officially FLIRTING, although me being who I am, with Virgo rising and all, I still had my doubts.

Especially when we went back in, and Mary started dancing at Pat. I remember thinking, Maybe she would be better for Pat; Mary's been married and has a kid, and Pat seems to be responding... I was trying to back down gracefully, holding back and boogying with Sherry. I was determined not to get hurt that night, it had been just too much fun. Then the band sailed into "Would I Lie To You?" and all of a sudden Pat was back, and I was grinning like mad and throwing her my best bumps and grinds.

We sat on the steps to catch our breath, and reflected on the fact that the bar was clearing out and it must be getting late. I started to pout. Well, I've never been very assertive and by this time, I wanted this woman badly. I could have gone home to Mom and Dad, or driven around for a while, but I didn't relish the thought of either option, not after the heat of her hands on my back. So I started pouting about going home alone, and she said in a kind of therapist tone, "Well, you don't have to do that, you know."

I looked at her, hopeful and happy, then doubtful again. She could have meant I could go home with somebody else. "I don't?"

"No, you don't." I sat there biting my lips. She wasn't going to say it and I didn't know what to say. Then it came.

"You could come home with me."

Well, my pulse returned and the world became a sweet place to be and I trusted True Love again. I put my hands up to my heart to keep from bursting and fought the urge to giggle like a kid. "I was hoping you would say that!"

As we were getting ready to leave, saying goodbye to our friends (trying to be subtle), somehow I suddenly felt shy enough to cool out a little and have a drink. After all that, and in that shirt, I still felt shy? You know, our conditioning goes so deep. Pat brought me a Black Russian which I started to sip, and she just watched me, patient and eager at the same time, smiling that cool smile. It felt so good to be finally inside that smile with her instead of embarrassed and outside, I grabbed her into a kiss. Can you believe I could do that? I can't. But there we were, kissing in the middle of the dance floor, and I could feel everybody's eyes popping out of their heads.

Pat says she looked up afterwards and saw Judy in the sound booth among the controls, almost falling out.

Well, of course she kissed just like her hands felt on my back—slow and hot and sweet—and there was no sound or movement in this bar full of women all the time her lips were on mine. I'll tell you, that woman can kiss. Melissa was a fool. Wait till I tell you more and you'll be convinced.

Anyhow, we finally got out of there and into my car, and Pat directed me to her apartment between giggles and necking, kissing at red lights until the car behind us honked. Pat told me months later that the person driving behind us for half the trip home was none other than the director of the Home for Retarded Children where she works! Pat turned around and this woman waved to her. And there I was, with my "WILD WOMEN DON'T GET THE BLUES" bumper sticker, wearing my big shiny earrings and my backless shirt, obviously a woman, but I was oblivious. Pat kept right on kissing me at red lights, too. The car behind us finally turned off into a side street, honking goodbye, and I was still oblivious.

Pat said this woman saw her the following Monday at work and she just smiled. Pat grinned back. Of course she says she was smiling at everybody that Monday, the whole week, whatever happened. She's so sweet.

We finally got to her place, got out of the car, and I heard this low "Oh, no." Pat had stopped dead on the sidewalk with her hand on her pocket. Then she patted her other pockets. "My keys. I don't have my keys."

"Oh, shit."

"I forgot. I got a ride with Sherry down to Wildsisters, and I must have left my keys in my car."

"Oh no."

"Maybe the back door is open." She lived in a first floor apartment so we stumbled around to the kitchen door. She tried the knob. "Nope." She turned to me, and by now our raging hormones were absolutely bursting out of our skins. We'd spent five miles practicing our kisses, we were ready to go on, and nothing was going to stop us! We couldn't go to my parents' house. I would have killed for my little apartment right then, fire escape and high rent and all.

Suddenly Pat said, "I have an idea." She went out rustling around in her little backyard and came back dragging a branch about six feet long and thick as a small log. She hoisted it up onto the porch and said to me in the most delicious, protective tones, "Stand back." And she bashed the window in! Glass all over her kitchen floor before I knew what she was doing. She reached in past her little yellow ruffly curtains, undid the lock, opened the door, kicked the glass aside—"Be careful," she was saying in that same velvet voice, and I was falling in LOVE. I'm serious. A woman that would bash in her kitchen window for me... I am in love.

Pat was going to have dinner with her kids the next day, too. She explained to them why the glass was broken and how happy she was: "I met a very special woman last night," she said. Her kids were happy for her. As it turned out, she had been divorced for years. She came out to her kids long ago, and now they're all grown up with lives of their own—a relief, though I still regret taking off across the dance floor at the mention of them. I've never wanted to be a co-mother, but I like to think I could at least be more polite these days and not run away.

No, I'm not stalling, I'll tell you the good parts. She took my hand and led me to a mattress where we undid each other's clothes and fell on each other like we hadn't made love for fifty years and were just learning all over again. Touching her was everything all her secret smiles said it would be. It was everything I'd tried to play on my sax, every wailing shuddering moan of pure joy I ever felt. Her lips were slow and soft, shaping little kisses up and down, and every part of me opened up to wait for her. My hands on her were like a kid's in a sandbox, I couldn't stop playing and petting. And for sure I couldn't stop smiling. We played and played and I had the feeling that her body, her voice, the way she talked were new and exciting but familiar to me, and right. Like a piece of music you hear for the first time that seems to play your heart back to you. It's right, and you want to cry and laugh at the same time because you've finally found it.

I thought she felt that way, too—I think I would have felt it if she was Just Having Sex. I don't know. But one of the times we were just lying there, holding each other, she said, "I never thought you would even speak to me, let alone this."

True Love

"I know. I'm sorry. But Melissa told me some pretty bad things about you."

"Oh yeah?" Pat ran her fingers through my hair and I shivered and kissed her neck. "What'd she tell you?"

I pulled my head up from her beautiful soft skin. "Well ... she told me you threw her out all of a sudden."

"Huh." Pat laughed a little and then she told me her side.

It seemed Melissa had been lying to Pat and having an affair—with a man she met in one of her spirituality groups. Melissa! The woman I'd listened to for hours on the phone, the woman I'd taken dancing and tried to comfort. The woman I had believed to the point of snubbing her ex-lover. I was furious. Pat was calm, though. "Aren't you pissed off?" I asked her. "Why didn't you tell anybody?"

"Oh, people think what they want to think. And sure I was pissed off, but—" she kissed me again—"I got the best deal."

So that's what happened with Pat and Melissa, and that's how Pat and I got together. Melissa? She's married now, in both Pagan and Presbyterian, and she has a baby boy. She still leads spirituality workshops in Michigan—Pagan, not Presbyterian—and she claims she's 70% lesbian. I tell you, I hope she never becomes an accountant or a bank teller, with that kind of capacity for arithmetic. She does numerology, though, charts of characteristics based on the number of letters in your name. Charges people money, too. Maybe she should work for my old landlord. I dunno.

Pat's wrong, though. I got the best deal. Making love to your crush is one of the best dreams, and mine came true. Finding out that your crush is a woman who would walk across broken glass for you, who still makes you warm and sweet and soft inside with just one kiss—that's even better. And that's what I have. True Love. You bet.

Relationships

Jennifer

by Wendy Caster

Wendy Caster is a thirty-five-year-old Jewish ex-New Yorker who has lived in San Diego for the past eight years. She shares her home with her lover, Liz, their roommate, Karen, and their cats, Lily, Chirpy, and Zina. Wendy's award-winning column, "Double Mischief," is published regularly in six newspapers, including San Diego's Gay and Lesbian Nation. Jennifer *is her first published fiction. She wishes that all writers on earth would have writing groups as supportive, talented, and helpful as Jayne, Julia, Lynne, Gina, and Susan have been for her.*

Jennifer

I'm giving up women. No, *really*. I am. It's not that I don't like them anymore. I do. Always have, always will. I just don't know how to talk to them. I just don't know what to call them.

No, it's not that lady/woman/girl thing. It's not when I first meet them at all. It's later, after—well, you know.

It all started the other night when I met Jennifer. I've been single five years and I wasn't looking for anyone—just went to a party to kick back a little. It was after a softball game, and it was mostly the same old jocks, but I saw this sweet-looking little woman getting a sandwich—and I decided to get a sandwich. We hit it off quickly. Went from "do you prefer cheddar or swiss cheese" to the meaning of life in five minutes.

Jennifer's a little plump blonde—you know, roly-poly, low center of gravity. Solid. I like that. And she's clever. And sweet. She's got these gray eyes, gray like a cloudy sunset over the ocean after a storm. Lovely woman. And she liked me right off too. I guess she goes for skinny gray-haired butches—though it's too soon to tell her patterns. She's 38, but she's only been out a year. That night I became her second woman lover—imagine. Thirty-eight, and she's only done two.

Anyway, there we were, in her bed. It was afterward, y'know? And I was holding her close, and I wanted to say something nice. I wanted to call her something sweet, and personal.

And that's when the trouble started.

I couldn't use *babe* 'cause Chris and I used *babe*. It was years ago, 1957, when I was 18, but in my mind—and heart—it's still Chris's word. I mean, Chris brought me out, you know? There I was, cute, boyish, with short brown hair—already a little butch. I wore dresses because I was supposed to, but they always looked weird on me. The waists would ride up and the skirts would get tangled. And my nylons *always* had runs in them.

I had no idea I was queer. But I was, and Chris knew it. She knew as soon as she saw me. Chris lived next door to my grandmother—she was the "single neighbor lady." She invited me over for coffee...sometime.

I went the very next day. I didn't know why—I just felt like talking to this woman some more. I had never known anyone like her—not any *woman* like her, anyway. She swaggered. She rolled her own cigarettes. She wore pants—trousers, like Marlene Dietrich wore—with men's shirts with the sleeves rolled up just below her elbows. She had this deep sexy voice. And she was funny.

I sat down on her couch—real nervous, with one foot swinging back and forth. And she grinned at me and said, "So, what can I serve you?" Only it wasn't food she was talking about—even at 18 I understood *that*.

We made love for the first time a week later. I had no idea what I was doing, but I knew I liked it *a lot*. At one point, I was...down there, and Chris's body got all tight and heaved in the air. I started apologizing like mad, but she laughed and said, "Oh, babe, you've got nothin' to be sorry for."

So, I couldn't call Jennifer *babe,* you know?

Then I thought of *honey*. But *honey* was Betty, my lover in the army. *Sweetheart* was Ginger—and was she ever sweet. Lila was *darling*. Judy was *honeybunch*.

Dear was what Leslie, the English teacher, called me. Whenever anyone else said *dear* it sounded funny, but when Leslie said it, it was sexy—and elegant. It was like making love and then drinking wine with your pinky in the air, you know?

Sugar was Stephanie. I called Susan *girlfriend*. I called Joni *wife,* but that was a mistake.

So, anyway, I'm going through all of this in my head with Jennifer in my arms, and she starts humming this little tune, and then she starts putting words to it. And it's that song from *Guys and Dolls*—you know, "Bushel and a Peck?" And she's so sweet and cuddly and she looks up at me with those gray eyes. But meanwhile, I'm freaking out. "Bushel and a Peck!" And I'm thinking of Leslie again!

Leslie tried to educate me. I had dropped out of school after I got involved with Chris, 'cause my parents disowned me—wouldn't have no queers in the family. And I'd never read much—mostly played softball and shot pool. But Leslie thought I'd like books and plays, and you know what? She was right!

Guys and Dolls was the first play we ever went to. I loved it. I had thought all plays were Shakespeare or something, but *Guys and Dolls* was funny and friendly—and sexy. And the actress who sang "Bushel and a Peck" sang it in this sweet little voice—she was so cute. Later that night, Leslie sang "Bushel and a Peck" for me in private, doing this sort of lady-like striptease, you know? Then she started singing "I love you, a peckel and a bush, a peckel and a bush and a kiss upon the tush." I laughed right up until we started making love—maybe a little bit during, too. So how could I listen to Jennifer sing that song now? It would be—disloyal. But I didn't know what to say.

I got real panicky, and my head starting swirling, so I told Jennifer I had a headache. She got all worried, with these little lines between her eyebrows—just like Lila used to get. Then her chin quivered—like Susan's. And all of a sudden it felt like the bed was real crowded, with all these women from my past watching and talking and laughing. Meanwhile, Jennifer's getting me aspirin and a cold compress and taking care of me. But *I'm* the one who takes care! I put Ginger and Joni through school and I took care of Susan when she had her operation. I can fix any car on earth! I don't need to be taken care of!

Anyway, there I am, feeling like an imposter. Jennifer thinks I'm just sick, that I just need a little attention or maybe some aspirin. Instead, I've got this whole circus of ex-lovers with me.

So I told Jennifer that I was getting a migraine and that I needed to be alone. And I went home and went to sleep. By myself. And that's how I decided *always* to sleep. By myself.

Though Jennifer really is nice...

I don't know how I ended up with so many lovers. I had always planned to marry and have some kids—anyway, that was the plan my mother taught me to have. Then Chris said *babe,* and my whole life changed. But none of it lasted. None of it.

Chris got bored with me, said I was just too young. God, it hurt when she left me. I met Betty in the army, but she was transferred to Guam and I was sent to Texas. Ginger and I worked together in a mayonnaise factory. She was the first official femme I ever dated:

make-up, skirt, jewelry—she looked like a movie star. We lived together for a year. I supported her while she went to night school to be a secretary. But as sweet as she was, it wasn't enough. We just didn't have that much in common. She'd come home from school and ask "Did you have a nice day?" I'd say "Yes," or "No," and ask her if she had a nice day. She'd say "Yes," or "No"—and then she'd study and I'd watch TV. Later we'd cuddle, and that was nice, but that's all there was. She got involved with another secretary.

Soon I met Lila. We had one thing in common: SEX. What I had been doing with the others was nice, don't get me wrong. But what I did with them was lighting a match, and what I did with Lila was burning down a house!

Anyway, Lila liked to fix cars, and I helped her. At first I would just hand her tools, but then I learned about oil changes and minor repairs. Before long I could do a complete overhaul. Lila and I would buy cheap old wrecks and make them run like new. Then we'd sell them. It was fun and I made some money.

Lila and I fizzled out when the passion did.

My next lover, Judy, was the pitcher on my softball team. She came on hot, but...well...it turned out she was a "no-touch butch." I had never heard of such a thing! Who wouldn't want to be made love to? Anyway, I got frustrated, then bored, so we just stopped seeing each other. After me, she got involved with a woman with all this make-up and a beehive hairdo—a real femme. I guess that's what she was really looking for.

I was single for a while, but then I met Leslie. She was wonderful, and I loved the plays and reading and all, but she wanted me to be more, well, prim and proper. I was almost what she wanted, but not quite. When I finally left her I was surprised at how upset she got. It had never seemed that she *really* wanted me, who I really was.

Then, in the late sixties, I got on a new softball team, the GH's. We told people it stood for Great Hitters, but it really stood for Girl Homos. One afternoon, after practice, we went on a picnic and I sat in poison ivy. It was horrible. I couldn't stop itching. Then one of the girls on the team told me about this remedy you could get at health food stores. So I went into my very first health food store— and there I met Stephanie. Funny-face Stephanie, with one blue eye and one green eye.

Sure enough, she cured my poison ivy. And she got me to stop smoking. But I got addicted to her.

I called her *Sugar* for fun, since she only ate health food. She didn't even eat chocolate!

Anyway, *that* was the marriage of a lifetime. I liked everything about Steph. I liked her crackly voice, her round face, her lopsided smile. Life was magic with her. She put something extra into everything she did. Like, if she had to leave me a note, she would draw flowers all over it, or naked women. If we went to the park, she'd decide we were 18th-century lesbians running away from their husbands together. And every time we made love, she found a new way to do it. She could make toes exciting, and elbows, and eyebrows. *Everything* was fun with her. The sky was bluer, sex was sexier. I could have stayed with her forever.

No, she didn't leave me—I wish she had.

She was in a car accident. Killed instantly. At least it was instant.

Well... Well... Anyway, by this time, I had gotten a job working in a garage. It was tough to deal with the men, but I liked the work. So I drowned myself in it: worked and slept, slept and worked. Didn't even go on a date for *eight years*. Then I met Susan, but I just...couldn't... We ended up staying together for a couple of years, but I was never really there for her. I mean, I took care of her after her hysterectomy and all, and we were friendly, but...finally we just drifted apart. And I went back to working and sleeping, with a little softball thrown in.

A while later, I met Joni at a party after a game. I was 42 already, and she was only 25, but she latched on to me, and I started caring about her. Intensely. It had been so long since I cared *intensely*.

I was stupid. I thought, "This is true love." She moved in. I supported her and paid her college tuition. I called her *wife*. The day after she graduated, she left me. The very next day. She had a 26-year-old waiting for her—a 26-year-old male!

I guess I should have known better.

All those lovers. All those...messes. I loved them all though—every last one. Even Joni, God help me. The movies teach you that there's only one love for a lifetime, but it's not true. Not in *my* life.

I'm 51 years old, and there's been enough time for babe, honey, sweetheart, darling, dear, sugar, girlfriend, and wife. But that night with Jennifer, I figured that maybe I had just run out of words. It was easier to stay single.

The thing is, a few days later, Jennifer called me. Wanted to know what was wrong. Said the love making was the best she'd ever had and wasn't it good for me? "Yes," I told her. "Of course. It was wonderful. Sweet. Special."

"And I like you a lot," she told me. "Don't you like me?"

How could I answer? How could I tell her I was too filled with the past to have room for the present? How could I tell her about Chris, about Leslie, about Joni—about Steph?

But while I was thinking of all my past lovers, Jennifer misunderstood my silence. "I'm sorry," she told me. "I'll just leave you alone."

And she hung up.

I was relieved! I didn't have to learn how Jennifer liked her coffee, what foods she hated. Chris hated seafood; Betty hated ketchup; Ginger hated onions; Lila—well... Enough! I wouldn't have to hold Jennifer in the night when she was scared, or rub her back when she was tired, or let her talk to me when I wanted to be alone, or let her watch *Thirtysomething* when I wanted to watch *Knot's Landing*. Leslie always wanted to watch PBS specials and Chris couldn't miss a football game—never mind!

But why didn't I feel happy? Why did I feel sort of...sad? I sat there and thought about it. No jealousies, no silly teasing. No one to worry about if I had to work late. No one to need me or want things from me. No one to disappoint. No one to yell at me. No one to look at me like I was suddenly a stranger. No one to leave me.

Oh.

And then I saw my heart, all chipped and cracked. There was the part that crumbled when Chris outgrew me—the parts I built over so I wouldn't care when the relationships with Betty and Ginger and Lila ended. There was the part that got fractured when Leslie screamed "I hate you!" when I left her—the part that got pulverized when Joni danced out the door to join the blond boy in the red convertible.

The part that died when Steph died.

Jennifer

I stopped believing in forever years and years ago—but every breakup hurt me anyway. Every woman who left took part of me with her. Maybe I wasn't too full with the past—maybe I was just too empty. I just didn't know if I had anything left.

Then the phone rang again. It was Jennifer. "I just wanted to talk to you a little bit more," she said. "I just wanted you to know I'm glad it happened anyway. I'll leave you alone if you want, but—"

"No!" I said. "Don't hang up. It was wonderful. I just got scared, you see. I just got...scared."

And that was something I'd never done before. Not with Chris, Betty, Ginger, Leslie, Lila, Susan, or even Steph. Admitted I was scared.

Jennifer sounded real worried: "Scared of what?"

"Scared of you," I answered. And I laughed. After 51 years of life on this earth, the first thing I've ever admitted I'm scared of is the gentlest, sweetest, littlest woman. She couldn't hurt...well...she couldn't hurt my body, anyway. But she sure could hurt my heart—my patched up, banged up heart. And I told her that I was scared of us breaking up.

She didn't laugh at me.

I told her that I saw my whole past in her. That I saw endings in beginnings, death in life, heartbreak in happiness. She said, "Can I come over and hold you? It sounds like you need to be held."

It sounded like *I* needed to be held? If that doesn't beat all.

But I do need to be held. I surely do.

And she's on her way over.

So I am giving up women—all the women in my past. I'm giving up the ghosts and the lists and the habits and the ruts. I'm focusing on today—and on one woman today. And I know what I'll call her.

Jennifer.

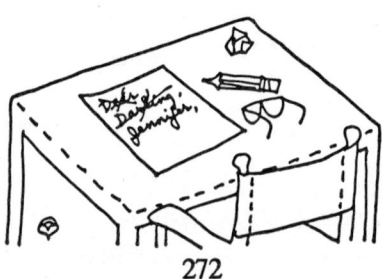